VALLEY
IN BLOOM

Grace Thompson

This first world edition published in Great Britain 1993 by
SEVERN HOUSE PUBLISHERS LTD of
9–15 High Street, Sutton, Surrey SM1 1DF.
First published in the USA 1993 by
SEVERN HOUSE PUBLISHERS INC of
475 Fifth Avenue, New York, NY 10017.

British Library Cataloguing in Publication Data
Thompson, Grace
  Valley in Bloom
  I. Title
  823.914 [F]

  ISBN 0-7278-4499-7

Typeset by Hewer Text Composition Services, Edinburgh.
Printed and bound in Great Britain by
Redwood Books, Trowbridge, Wiltshire.

CHAPTER ONE

The lane was icy as Nelly walked up on her way home. The dogs bounded about her and even they occasionally slipped on the treacherous surface. She stopped to catch her breath, aware that she had been hurrying, and stood for a moment, watching them as they examined every fallen leaf on that cold November day.

She had been hurrying as she planned to have a casserole ready for when George finished work that evening, knowing he would be both cold and hungry after his day working for Farmer Leighton. The parcel of meat and vegetables under her arm slipped a little and she tried to rewrap it. The newspaper covering her purchases was damp and, as she struggled with it, carrots, onions and potatoes slipped and began to roll away from her.

The dogs, sensing a game, ran off with a couple of potatoes and she leant against the wintery hedge and laughed.

"Worse than a couple of kids you two are, Bobby an' Spotty," she shouted. "Thank Gawd it wasn't me meat I dropped!" She eventually managed to store the vegetables in the large pockets of her over-sized coat and they went on up the lane.

Nelly was a plump, rather untidy figure in the flapping coat that almost reached her ankles and the wide-brimmed hat from under which hair escaped like fronds of seaweed waving in the tide.

She went through the gate and while the dogs went down to wait for her at the back door, she crossed the lawn, ducked under the spreading branches of the old apple tree

1

and opened the door of the hen-run to let the chickens out to scratch for what they could find. There were five hens and she greeted them all by name.

The path of her cottage was made of cinders, built up from the ashes of her fire over many years and, with it being safe under foot, she hurried determinedly down it, and charged against her door. It gave easily and she staggered, half falling, into her living room.

"Dammit!" she told the dogs, "I keep fergettin' that George 'as fixed it." The door had been ill-fitting for many years and had rarely been closed even at night, as the effort was too much for her. Since George had arrived in the village as a tramp and stayed to marry her the cottage had become almost trouble-free. But she still forgot the ease with which the door now opened.

Nelly had lived in Hen Carw Parc since the beginning of the war when her snobbish daughter Evie had been evacuated here and Nelly had followed. Her daughter was unhappy at living near her amiable, good-natured and very untidy mother, whom many of the villagers still called Dirty Nelly. Evie and her head-teacher husband, Timothy, had once tried to remove her by placing her in a home for the elderly, but marriage to George – another of Evie's embarrassments – had dismissed the threat for good.

Nelly unloaded her pockets and put her shopping on the table. As soon as her hands were free she leaned over to turn on her radio. Then she started with fright as, before her fingers touched the switch, a voice said: "Nelly, my dear. I hope you didn't mind me walking in?"

"Blimey, Mrs Bennet-'Ughes! You frit me nearly to death!"

"Now that must be one of your London expressions," Mrs Norwood Bennet-Hughes laughed. "All these years here in Wales and you still talk like a Londoner! I'm sorry if I frightened you, but I did speak as you came in and look, the dogs saw me at once."

Bobby and Spotty were large ungainly dogs and it was

2

an amusing sight to see them both trying to sit on the lap of their visitor.

"Get down you stupid animals," Nelly shouted, her raucous laughter filling the room. "'Ere, keep an eye on me meat will yer, while I give 'em some biscuits to shut 'em up."

Pausing only to turn the swivel over the fire in the oven range to allow the kettle to heat, Nelly went to a small cupboard and took out some dog biscuits which she threw onto the frost-tipped grass in the garden. "That'll keep 'em quiet for a minute. Nice to see yer," she said, puffing as if she had run a fast mile. "Not the most peaceful of 'ouses ter visit, is it?" She laughed again, her missing teeth creating almost a snarl which was belied by the twinkling merriment in her dark eyes.

Nelly took off her hat and coat, wrapped an apron around her plump middle and busied herself preparing tea for her visitor. She seemed calm and at ease but, as always with unexpected visits from what she considered "authorities", she was half afraid of trouble. She glanced at Mrs Norwood Bennet-Hughes as the woman preferred to be called, using her husband's Christian name as well as their hyphenated surnames. She smiled as she caught the woman's eye before turning back to her large fire-blackened kettle and the brown china teapot which she warmed with the near-boiling water.

Mrs Norwood Bennet-Hughes wore her generously cut fur coat and brown leather fur-lined boots. What could be seen of her legs were covered in hand-knitted, patterned stockings in brown wool. Her handbag, large and also of good quality leather, was near her feet. Nelly wondered curiously what she could find to fill it, she managed with just her pockets most of the time. And why would she want to carry such a heavy thing? Not for the first time Nelly decided that the richer you were, the more problems you made for yourself.

Like her own daughter, Evie. There was a one for making work for herself. So vain, she was afraid to go out without adding to her makeup, polishing her shoes, brushing her coat in case a particle of dust had the audacity to land on her shoulders, and conducting long searches in the mirror for signs of imperfections. The saddest thing, in Nelly's opinion, was that she treated her son Oliver in the same way. A ten-year-old boy wasn't meant to be neat and clean all the time! And Evie's home was bereft of anything that wasn't absolutely necessary. *Evie* carried a big handbag, too. Not as big as Mrs Norwood Bennet-Hughes's though. Perhaps, to Evie's constant regret, she wasn't as important.

"Why I have called," her visitor said when they were both seated comfortably with cups of tea beside them, "is to ask for your advice."

"Me? Blimey you must be 'ard up!" Nelly laughed.

"It's about money for the Community Hall."

"You come to the wrong 'ouse. I ain't got none of that!" Mrs Norwood Bennet-Hughes smiled and waited. "Yes, I know we needs more money to finish the building," Nelly went on, "want a donation, do yer?"

"I want your opinion on something we haven't tried before. Do you think the villagers would be willing to enter the Best Kept Village competition next year?"

"Can I see to my George's dinner while we talk?" Nelly stood up and began chopping meat and vegetables, which she placed in a casserole and put in the oven at the side of the now roaring fire. She frowned as she thought before replying to the question, chewing on a carrot which she had absent-mindedly popped into her mouth.

"Seems to me that you'll 'ave to talk to them on the main road. It's only fer the likes of them, especially them with plenty of money to spare for flowers, to decide yes or no. Fer meself, yes, I'd love ter see the place all colourful and lookin' good. Mind you, you can't ignore half the population – you'll 'ave to 'ave another Bring-an'-Buy sale, especially now Prue Beynon's back to bully them into working. All them knitters and sewers would 'ate to be left

4

out. But to fill the gardens and windersills with flowers," she sighed, imagining the spectacle, "lovely that would be. Yes, I bet there'll be plenty willin' to 'elp with that."

"We've just had a Bring-and-Buy, but I'm sure you're right and the ladies of the sewing bee will soon have enough work finished to arrange another one. She took out her notebook and made a few entries, while Nelly stirred the fire to encourage the heat to increase and start the casserole cooking.

"I'm a bit out of the way up 'ere," Nelly went on, "but I'll do something. My George is real good at growin' things and," her eyes lit up and she brandished the poker like a foil as she added, "we could make our garden into one of them where you pays to come in!"

"Nelly Luke – I mean Masters! You never cease to amaze me. An 'At Home' with Nelly and George!" She laughed good naturedly as she scribbled into her book, while Nelly poured them another cup of tea.

When it was time for Mrs Norwood Bennet-Hughes to walk down to the main road where her car was parked, it was with regret that she said goodbye. She always found pleasure in talking to the woman some still referred to as Dirty Nelly. The casserole simmering in the oven heated by the coal and wood fire was sending out delicious smells. The room was warm, cluttered and over-full, its furniture large, old and comfortable, and it was without haste that she collected her discarded boots and her fur coat and her handbag, which the dogs were using as a pillow, and promised they would meet soon.

"I'll walk down with yer," Nelly said.

Taking much less time to dress, she slipped on the coat which she had thrown onto the couch and pulled on socks and wellingtons. Reaching for the dogs' leads, she paused to give the fire a stir to lift a few lumps of coal, and gave the underside of the fire a fierce poke to loosen the ash and send it showering, spark-filled, to the ash-pan below. Then, giving one slow appreciative sniff, she announced herself ready.

5

Although it was only half-past three, it was already quite dark. The day had been dull with low clouds covering the surrounding hills, wrapping the village in an icy grip. The roads were wet but Nelly knew that the lower temperature of the evening would harden the moisture into ice again and make a slippery and dangerous surface. Below them, as they walked down towards the main road of Hen Carw Parc, lights showed along the street and reflected through the water sprayed up by the occasional passing vehicle. They turned left and soon saw the brighter light of Amy's shop throwing a wet gleam across the surface of the road.

Nelly smiled as she thought of Amy Prichard serving in the shop, her makeup as immaculate at this time of day as it was in the morning, her fair hair attractively styled. Pretty as a film-star, was Amy, Nelly thought. While she was serving her customers efficiently and with a smile her mind was probably wondering which of her two boy-friends she would marry. Amy had two children but no husband and now there were two men anxious to make her their wife.

There were no lights on in the flat above the shop, and Nelly guessed that the Powells who lived there were still out at work; Ralph at his office in town and Mavis working beside Amy in the post-office-cum-general stores. The Powell's daughter, Sheila, still lived with her grandmother up in the council houses. Sheila who, although still very young, had caused so much trouble.

Outside the shop a tractor was parked. "That Billie Brown, 'e don't give up," Nelly said, and when her companion looked puzzled she went on, "'e wants to marry Amy but she's stuck on that Victor Honeyman, him whose wife died after my Evie crashed into the ambulance she was in."

"That was very sad. And so upsetting for your daughter, even though she was hardly to blame for the woman's death."

"Shouldn't never 'ave been drivin'. Some things is best left to men and where my daughter Evie's concerned, that includes drivin'. Now Amy, I reckon she'd drive well enough, but not my Evie."

"Will they marry do you think? Amy and Victor Honeyman? Now he's a widower there's nothing to stop them, is there?"

"Can't say. I think the sudden death of Victor's wife, leavin' 'im so conveniently free, well, it's made it more difficult for Amy than if they'd separated, legal and above board."

"And Billie Brown the farmer hasn't given up then?"

"No, 'e ain't given up. But can you see Amy as a farmer's wife? No, neither can I, more's the pity," she added as her companion shook her head.

Amy re-filled the shelf with bars of chocolate as she talked to Billie Brown. Never one to be idle, she allowed customers to stay and talk occasionally, but always used the time dusting or re-arranging the displays. Billie was used to it but today he was slightly put out.

Since the death of Victor's wife Billie had guessed, with the extra sensitivity he had developed where Amy was concerned, that she was far from content to step into the dead woman's shoes. While Victor's wife Imogine had been alive she had seemed an insuperable barrier, but now she was dead the barrier had become more dense, and Billie was glad of it.

"I'm going up on the hills to look at the sheep tomorrow," he said. "I wondered if your Margaret would like to come. Young Oliver as well, I know how they like to be together."

"Thank you, Billie. I'll ask her when she comes in from school. Will you need food to take?" She didn't look at him, concentrating unnecessarily on the sliding bars of milk chocolate as she put them in orderly piles.

"My sister will see to that. Mary loves to feed people." He stood back from the counter while Amy served a customer with a packet of tea. He was ill at ease, knowing she wanted him gone but unwilling to leave. When he stepped forward again, his wellington boot caught against a biscuit tin and he lurched against the counter, their faces

7

hardly six inches apart. She smiled then, and his heart lightened.

"Clumsy I am," he smiled.

"Big, that's your trouble Billie Brown, you're too big for my little shop and that's a fact."

"I can't deny that," he laughed, his tawny-brown eyes shining as he looked admiringly at her. He was large. His presence filled the shop so people hesitated to push their way in while he was near the door; head not far from the ceiling, size thirteen wellingtons taking up so much of the floor. He rarely wore anything other than the brown dungarees and cowboy shirt he was presently dressed in. It was only in the coldest of winter weather that he added a coat, although she saw that he carried one draped around the back of the tractor seat.

Amy moved away and went back to stacking the chocolate bars. She knew she shouldn't tease him. It only took a warm smile to bolster his hopes that they would one day be together. And warm smiles were Amy's speciality. Kind-hearted and friendly, she gave them without thinking. She shook her blonde head and glanced at her reflection in the small mirror behind the display cabinet. Blue eyes smiled back at her in the pretty face. The earrings which she always wore, dangled and sparkled in the artificial light from the bulb above her, partnering the necklace around her throat. She fluffed out her hair and handed him a bar of Cadbury's milk chocolate with another generous smile.

"Take this, love, keep you going 'til you get home to one of Mary-Dairy's fine dinners." She watched him go, returning his blown kisses, and felt a melancholy guilt, knowing that she ought to discourage him, treat him less than kindly for his own good.

Billie Brown was a gentle, caring man. He loved her and she knew that as his wife she would want for very little, but there was a lack of that special spark, that inexplicable magic that made someone special. Only Victor Honeyman had that.

She and Victor had gradually drifted into an affair and

8

she knew he loved her, but with a wife and a grown up family it seemed impossible that there would ever be a happy ending to their story. Now, with his wife dead, having suffered a heart-attack after a slight road accident, her ghost was more real than her living presence. She was standing beside them whenever they met, forbidding them to be content. Amy had tried to relax, to be happy and pretend that they were now free to love each other openly, but she sometimes doubted if she and Victor ever would be able to convince themselves that their love was right.

When Nelly came into the small shop, her face red with the coldness of the late afternoon, Amy gave her a dazzling smile, genuinely pleased to see her, glad of the distraction from her thoughts in which a lonely future beckoned.

"Nelly, love. What can I do for you?"

"I just had a visitor," Nelly reported. "Mrs Hyphen-Hyphen no less! She came to ask my advice would you believe."

"Yes, I would believe. You've a great deal of common-sense, Nelly Luke - er - Masters."

Nelly explained about the idea for Hen Carw Parc to enter the Best Kept Village Competition and, as she had guessed, Amy was delighted with the idea.

"With Victor and Billie competing to make my garden the best kept garden, I'm sure to be popular!" she laughed. "There isn't a chance of survival for any weed that dares to pop out a leaf. And as for flowers, good heavens, sometimes there isn't a thing for my young Freddie to do when he comes home on leave."

"The shop, too, Amy. You could 'ang out them winder boxes and things. Pop a few flower pots among the sacks of vegetables outside."

"I can just see Constable Harris' face if he comes along and sees the sacks and crates he's always asking me to move decorated with flowers!"

"But wouldn't it be lovely, Amy."

For a while the two women discussed the idea and Amy agreed to place a notice in her shop window asking people to consider the idea before the meeting which Mrs Norwood Bennet-Hughes planned to set up.

"Well, I'd better get off back 'ome to see to George's casserole. I likes to 'ave 'is dinner ready for 'im this cold weather."

Amy watched Nelly wander across the road and through the main road towards the lane, coat reaching her ankles, the large long-legged dogs at the full extent of their leads so it looked as if they were towing her. "There are times when I envy you, Nelly Luke – I mean Masters," Amy whispered. Nelly had been Nelly Luke for so long everyone forgot that since she had married George, who had once travelled the roads as a tramp, she was now Mrs Masters. Nelly had seemed not to mind about people using the wrong name, but lately she had taken to reminding everyone of her proper title. Proud, she is, to be George's wife. And why not? Amy thought. Everyone needs to be important to someone, even the independant Nelly.

Opposite the school in a building similar to Amy's shop-cum-post-office was the village fish and chip shop. It was run by Bethan Toogood. Bethan was the shy unmarried daughter of Milly and Tommy Toogood who lived in the flat above the shop with Bethan's son, Arthur Toogood. Bethan was a very retiring young woman who seemed to have little or no social life, hardly ever leaving the shop and the bed-sit behind it, apart from necessary shopping trips into Llan-Gwyn, the nearest town. She had a habit of walking with her eyes studying the ground when she did venture outside her home and rarely, if ever, instigated a conversation, restricting her speech to the briefest of replies to any remarks she received.

On the morning following Nelly's discussion with Mrs Norwood Bennet-Hughes, Bethan was in the fish and chip shop washing down the surfaces and polishing the chrome covers of the fish fryer. Behind the shop she could hear water running and the occasional clanking of buckets. Hilda Evans was preparing the potatoes ready for the lunchtime trade. Bethan hadn't greeted Hilda when she arrived for work, but that was not unusual. Hilda Evans, who lived a few doors away, came in through the back gate and began her chores without the need for any instruction. Hilda had been doing the job for years, unaware that while she stood in running water and handled the cold potatoes and heaved about the heavy sacks, Bethan was entertaining Griff, her wayward husband.

Now Griff was in prison Bethan felt uneasy, unable to face Griff's wife, afraid that the secret that had been kept from Hilda for years, would somehow be broken now the man was in the hands of the police. He's confessed, people were saying in hushed tones, and Bethan feared that the revelation that she and Griff were lovers was certain to be announced with the rest. What would she say once Hilda knew? How would the woman react? Bethan rubbed with extra energy on the chrome and saw her frightened face in the curved mirror-like surface and shivered. She wanted to run away and hide.

Outside the icy conditions seemed to worry Hilda less than usual. Her movements were more hurried and although her hands were blue with the cold, and the back of her legs above the turned down wellingtons were marked with chilblains, there was a glow to her face that revealed an inner fire. Her dark eyes sparked with anger, her dark hair, recently released from metal "Dinkie" curlers danced about her scowling face like puppets in the hands of a drunken puppet-master. The peeled potatoes were picked up and thrust into the chipping machine, the handle pulled in a rhythmical one-two-one-two movement and Hilda's lips chanted with it all the insults she could remember and invent. In his prison cell Griff's ears should have been burning to cinders.

"Cheating, lying, under-hand, pig-face; cheating, lying, under-hand, pig-face; cheating – " At last she stopped. She pushed the white enamel bucket, now full of chipped potatoes, to one side with her wellington and pulled another one into place below the chipping machine. She looked around her and her face relaxed from anger into sorrow. All the money Griff had cheated and stolen, yet this was what she would have to do until she was too old to lift the sacks, or too stiff to manage the cold water. If he'd only shared some of his thieving with her she might have felt at least some sympathy for him. But to allow her to work like this while all the time he was filling his pockets, it was too much for her to forgive that painfully cold morning. "Cheating, lying, under-hand pig-face. PIG FACE!" she shouted. And bending down she pulled off a wellington and sent it winging down the yard and over the wall into the lane. It was closely followed by the other and, wearing only socks on her feet, she stomped towards the gate.

"'Ere, what's going on, flyin' boots and at this time of a morning?" Nelly demanded as first one then the other sailed over the wall to land near her. Hands on hips, she waited as the gate opened and a scowling Hilda stormed out.

"I'm going to see that pig-face of a husband. I'll give him 'Forgive me, pet and we'll make a fresh start when I come out'! I'll never forgive him. Never."

"Come on, Hilda, you'll get over it. It's only yer pride what's hurt, and now you know, you can face it and start over again. I don't say you shouldn't make 'im suffer a bit first, mind. But you'll get over it."

It was several weeks since the police had called to talk to Griff, and Hilda had appeared to carry on in the same way as always. So Nelly guessed, wrongly, from the sudden outrage that Hilda had finally been told about Griff and Bethan.

"Forgive him? He's cheated on me all this time, he's cheated on me," Hilda said, referring to the money Griff had made and not shared.

"A bit on the side ain't that unusual, Hilda, and your Griff's still an attractive bloke even if 'is 'air is a bit on the greasy side and his moustache is sometimes a bit uneven because of the drink makin' 'is 'and shake!"

"A bit on the side?" Hilda stopped and glared at Nelly.

12

"Well, whatever you wants to call it. 'E's never left you, 'as 'e, and with your Pete sixteen and working he could 'ave. He loves yer really, don't doubt it."

"You think so?" Hilda continued to stare at Nelly, who failed to see the warning signs. "And what about her –?"

"Bethan ain't no catch, got no go in her. Griff ain't daft, Hilda, he knows you're the one 'e needs."

"Bethan? Bethan Toogood?" Hilda's jaw dropped and her ill-fitting teeth fell with it.

"Oh Gawd." Too late Nelly realised her surmising had been wrong. Hilda hadn't known about Griff and his lady love at all. She stared at the shocked expression on Hilda's unattractive face and wished the words could be brought back and swallowed. She didn't know what to say yet she couldn't stand there in the freeezing cold of the early morning and not at least try to offer some comfort. "Get yerself 'ome and find some slippers fer yer poor frozen feet, come on, we'll come with yer, me an' the dogs. Make us a cup of tea why don't yer?" Slowly, still dazed, Hilda allowed herself to be led home and pushed into an armchair.

"How long, Nelly?" Hilda asked at last. "How long have they been carrying on?"

"Couldn't say, and anyway, who's to say they were . . . 'carrying on'? Gossip that's what it is and no evidence of anything other than a bit of kindly 'elp from a neighbour. Just helping Bethan, that's probably what your Griff was doin', her not 'avin' a man to 'elp except her dad and 'im about as much use as a swarm of wasps on a summer picnic!"

Nelly poured tea and gave Hilda a cup. Hilda sipped it, saying little as Nelly chattered on, first about Griff and his innocent kindnesses to Bethan, then about anything else that came into her mind. When Hilda spoke, Nelly thought she had heard none of it.

"I'm going to see Griff, Nelly. But I don't want him to know that I've been told about him and Bethan."

"Him and Bethan!" Nelly said derisively. "I've probably got it all wrong." Again, Hilda wasn't listening.

13

"I don't want him to know. Promise you won't let on you've told me?"

"There's probably nothing to be told, nothing more than malicious rumours."

"Promise?"

Nelly knew when she was beaten. She nodded and poured them another cup of tea.

After Nelly had gone Hilda sat for the rest of the day thinking of what she should do and the best way of setting about it. There were several knocks on her door but she didn't answer them, she hardly reacted to the sometimes loud and impatient demands, she just sat and slowly incubated her plan.

When her son, Pete, came home for his tea she was still sitting there, but the scowl and the shock had lifted. She was smiling and in a good humour. Later she went up the dark slippery lane to see Nelly. She found her sitting in the armchair listening to the radio, with George opposite her on the couch, and the sight made her feel deprived, lonely and even more determined.

"I'm going in to see Griff, will you come with me, not to visit, just for company on the ride? It's Swansea, and we could perhaps go to the pictures after? Doris Day's at the Albert Hall. *Lucky Me*, with Phil Silvers – he's a laugh."

Nelly would have preferred to go with George or Amy, but she agreed, still feeling ashamed of the way she had let out the long-standing secret.

"Yes, why not. Perhaps we can look in the market for some Christmas presents, eh? And," she said excitedly, "p'raps, while I'm waitin' for yer, I'll 'ave a ride on the Mumbles train. Perishin' cold it'll be, that close to the the sea, but fun all the same, eh?"

"Everything is fun where you're involved, Nelly Luke," Hilda sighed. "Got a gift for it you have and no mistake."

"Masters, me name is Masters," Nelly corrected, but she sighed as once again Hilda wasn't listening.

CHAPTER TWO

The term approaching Christmas was always a busy one for Delina Honeyman. Besides the normal school work that had to go on whatever the extra calls on her time, there were the decorations and cards the children made, and the carol concert for which she was responsible.

On Monday mornings of late she was disorientated after a weekend in which she had taken on her other role; that of temporary mother to her younger brothers, Daniel, eighteen, and David, thirteen, and housekeeper for her father, Victor. Since her mother's sudden and unexpected death, her life had become filled with confusing and unwanted demands and she was beginning to feel resentment.

She was normally a calm, capable twenty-two-year-old woman, but having to deal with the grief and the day to day needs of a family had jerked her out of her regulated life in a way she disliked. Her father and her brothers were already beginning to accept her as a substitute for her mother. It wouldn't do. It really wouldn't do.

She walked down Hywel Rise, a smartly dressed young woman, blonde hair in a page-boy style with not a hair out of place, neat shoes and a slim-fitting suit over which hung a mauve plastic mac in case the cold mist precipitated into rain. She glanced up and saw Dawn Simmons waiting for her. Dawn had also lost her mother and was being cared for by her father who, Delina thought with an uneasy feeling of shared guilt, also found it hard to cope – not with resentment but with an inability to understand and deal with a rather wayward ten year old.

Tad Simmons, she had to admit, showed no sign of

15

resentment towards his small daughter while in her heart she, Delina Honeyman, wanted to refuse the position of *loco parentis*. Why, she sighed, did it spring automatically to people's minds that the daughter should accept responsibility when the mother was lost? For Tad, she thought, defiance showing in her remarkably blue eyes, it was different. It was a wife he had lost and a daughter he was caring for. But still the guilt remained. She ought not to mind, but she did.

"Mor-ning-Miss-Hon-ey-man," Dawn chanted in the way all her pupils said her name, whether in chorus or alone. Delina was so prickly she almost chanted back, but didn't,

"Good morning, Dawn. Have you got your homework?" she asked briskly, increasing her pace and making the girl hurry. She was leaving behind Delina Honeyman, aggrieved daughter of Victor and older sister of David and Daniel, and becoming Miss Honeyman, teacher of small children.

During the previous summer Dawn Simmons had become a problem to the neighbourhood by stealing small items, mostly to throw away, and it was thanks to the kindly villagers that she had not ended up in the hands of the police or been taken into care. Delina had offered to take responsibility for the child and watch her after school hours so Tad could recommence the studies he had been forced to abandon during the war. He was an engineer and because of the death of his wife he had found part-time work in a factory, sweeping up, so he could look after Dawn. His efforts had not been a great success and although he was a prickly and ill-tempered man, Delina had persuaded him to allow her to help.

At the bottom of Sheepy Lane they waited on the main road for the bus, Dawn holding Delina's hand and chatting cheerfully about the doll her father was going to buy her for Christmas. Delina remained silent, still wondering how she could either cope with the situation that had befallen her or escape from it without burdening herself with equally destructive guilt.

16

Almost opposite the bus stop was Amy's shop. Delina looked across and saw the curtains in the flat above move. Idly she wondered if it was Mavis Powell preparing to leave the flat and go down to help Amy in the shop. She saw a hand wave, but she didn't respond. The Powells weren't her favourite people, particularly their daughter, Sheila.

After the day's activities had ended, Delina returned home, but Dawn didn't go to the house on Hywel Rise where she lived with her father, but continued on to Delina's home. Tad wouldn't be home until after nine o'clock when his evening class finished, and until then Dawn was the responsibility of Delina. As she opened the front door Delina gave a sigh. There were football boots still caked with mud on the stairs and an equally dirty shirt hung carelessly over the banisters where it had been thrown by David. With an even louder sigh, Delina put down her brief-case overflowing with books for marking, and picked up the abandoned clothing.

"David," she called softly, her voice revealing none of her irritation. "I'd like you to take these outside and scrape off the worst of the mud, then wash them. You can deal with the dubbing tomorrow."

"I'm tired, Del. I'll do it in the morning."

"Now, David. Or, if you prefer, I'll do them while you see to the vegetables and start cooking the meal."

David came out of the living room, a dark and sombre room where heavy maroon curtains were drawn against the chill of the evening and only a small lamp glowed. He looked sulky and he didn't speak to Dawn as he slouched past them heading for the kitchen.

"David," Delina said again, softly and without anger. She handed him the boots which he took from her with a scowl.

"Hello, David," Dawn said. "Shall I help?"

"No, I'll do it or Del will find me something else to do."

Delina watched as David's fair head bent about his task

17

just outsided the back door in the light from the porch. He had always been so polite, mannerly and pleasant, but now he seemed to be in a constant bad mood. The inhibiting guilt again swept over her as she realised that for him more than herself the loss of a mother was devastating. She turned away and determinedly smiled at her young charge.

"Now, Dawn, would you like to help me? What about setting the table. You know where everything is."

"Am I having tea with you tonight?" Dawn asked.

"Of course. It's one of the nights for your father's class. I'll take you home about eight and wait 'til he comes in, as always."

"Thank you, Miss."

Something will have to be done Delina thought sadly. As things were at present no one in the house was happy. If her father were to marry Amy at least there would be some improvement although, she decided, looking at the defiance in the tilt of David's chin, Amy wouldn't have it easy!

At seven-thirty, having washed up after a silent meal and helped Dawn with her homework, she walked the little girl home. Even Dawn had become subdued by the atmosphere in the house she realised, remembering the lively, naughty and difficult child she had promised to help control. Perhaps it comes from me she thought with a stab of alarm. Perhaps my discontent is reflecting on everyone else. In a vain attempt to change things she took hold of Dawn's hand and ran with her the last few yards to arrive breathless at her front door.

"In you go, Dawn, you have your key," she said, then followed her into the plain hallway and towards the kitchen, where she prepared a tray of tea and a slice of cake ready for Tad's return.

"Shall we listen to the radio, Miss?" Dawn asked.

"If you wish, just for a little while, but I'll have to get on with this." Delina patted the bag of books she had brought to mark. Dawn turned on the radio and sat silently listening to the last few minutes of Wilfred Pickles' programme *Have*

A Go. But she wasn't concentrating, she was watching Delina and shifting and squirming in her chair.

Though her attention was on the book she was marking Delina sensed Dawn's need to speak to her and, putting the book aside, she looked at the girl and smiled encouragingly. "What is it?" she asked in her gentle way.

"How did you know there was something?" Dawn demanded. "How do you know what's happening without looking up?"

Delina laughed and shook her head, her hair swaying then falling back into its neat style.

"It's about Christmas, Miss," Dawn said when it was clear Delina wasn't going to explain. "What will we do? I mean, will Dad cook our dinner? And can I have a tree? And will you help me put up some chains to decorate the room?"

"If I can answer the last first," Delina said, smiling wider at the anxiety shown in the rapidly fired questions. "Yes, I think I would enjoy helping you make some paper chains and perhaps we'll come home early one day in a few weeks and make a start so they're ready to hang a week or so before Christmas."

"Thank you Miss."

"As for what will be happening at Chrismas, well, that isn't up to me. Your father will decide what you and he will be doing. But I'm sure he'll make Christmas Day very special."

"Couldn't we . . . I mean, perhaps he'd like to come and share Christmas Day with you, Miss."

"Perhaps." Delina went back to her marking as applause ended the radio programme. It was something she had herself considered, but it was too soon to suggest it yet. Christmas was still seven weeks away.

On the radio *The Adventures of Sherlock Holmes* began and Delina put the marking aside and said, "Eight o'clock, Dawn. Time for bath and bed."

Dawn began to protest but thought better of it. If she was quick Delina might read her a story. She loved being read to, both by her father and by Delina. Sometimes it was worth swallowing a protest she decided.

It was just before nine-thirty when Tad came in. Delina went to light the gas under the kettle as he greeted her and went upstairs to look at his daughter. She brought the tray in and sat waiting for him beside the electric fire, her books in two piles at her feet. The unmarked pile she saw with dismay was still higher than the marked one.

"She's asleep," he said as he slid into the chair opposite her. "Thank you for your care."

"It's a pleasure, Tad. But I hope I'm handling her right," she added doubtfully.

"Handling her right? But she's a different child since you began to help with her!"

"When my mother died so many things changed and now – "

"You can't do it any more. I understand." Tad's head dropped and he stared into the glow of the electric fire, his jaw tightened and his small neat hands gripped his cup like a lifeline.

"I'm happy to continue looking after Dawn. I just think that with the atmosphere in my home so charged with unhappiness she is becoming too subdued. I just hope she isn't being badly affected by it. That's all I was going to say."

He looked at her then, the small, rather aggressive, eyes almost disbelieving. "You only have to say if you want to give up looking after her. For what you've done so far I will always be grateful."

"Tad, I want to continue to care for her, it isn't Dawn that's the problem, it's – "

"The role that has been alloted to you and for which you've no liking? I felt that, believe it or not, when I lost my wife. There was anger in my grief, anger that she could die and let me down so badly. It's normal, Delina, don't distort it into guilt."

She was surprised by his understanding. Heartened by it she went on and explained about her father and her brothers wanting things to go on as they had before but with her carrying the burden of a job and the household duties.

"Shall I talk to Victor, your father I mean?" asked Tad.

"No, I think it's something I must sort out myself." She smiled then and Tad felt his heart lift with pleasure at the sight. "He'll be uneasy if you try to discuss something with him, remembering how you made his nose bleed on a previous occasion!"

"I wouldn't hit out now, that stupid aggression's all gone from me. Well," he grinned, a boyish grin that eased away the almost constant frown he wore, "almost gone. I wouldn't be able to hold back if someone hurt Dawn. Or you." Their eyes met and there was a spark of a growing awareness.

On the radio, *Hancock's Half Hour* finished and Delina stood to leave.

"I hate not being able to walk you back home," Tad said, holding her coat for her. "One day I'm going to make it up to you."

"I'll see you tomorrow," Delina said as she slipped out of the front door into the dark chill of the night.

"Talk to Amy," Tad called as she ran to the gate. "She might have some ideas on the future, her and your dad."

"I might do that," Delina called back, but the reply hardly connected in Tad's brain, he was thinking of how beautiful she was and imagining how he might help solve her difficulties if only he weren't broke and without a decent job.

"Delina wants to see me," Amy reported when Nelly came into the shop a few days later.

"So what? You and Victor are – well, you know – and she must want to talk to another woman about how she's coping."

"I hope she doesn't want me to take over and manage the family for her!" Amy snapped, earrings sparkling and her blue eyes flashing with the emphatic shaking of her fair head. "Heaven's above, Nelly, I manage a shop and run a home for Margaret and Freddie when he's home on leave. I can't take on Victor's family as well."

"I suspect Delina's feeling much the same. She ain't 'ad much luck lately 'as she? First Maurice Davies ditching 'er for that Sheila Powell, then 'er mother dyin' and leavin' 'er with two brothers to look after. Gawd 'elp her, she's only twenty-two. I bet she's 'opin' you an' Victor'll marry and take it all off of 'er 'ands, Amy."

"She's got another think coming!"

Nelly began the Sunday morning chores by putting the kettle on. While the tea settled she began to open out pages of the local paper to spread on the floor when it had been scrubbed and soon she was kneeling on the floor with a paper spread over the first of the stairs leading up the the flat, studying the items of news she had missed.

Amy handed her a cup of tea, complaining, "Come on, Nelly love, I don't pay you for doing this!"

"Ere, Amy, it's Prince Charles's sixth birthday on the fourteenth an' 'is gran, the Queen Mum, won't be 'ome. It says 'ere the Queen Mother is in America and will miss the party. Shame, ain't it. You going to 'ang out a flag or two?"

"If you like, but let's get on, I have to make tea for Delina and I don't want her to arrive while I'm washing the after dinner dishes!"

"Coming today, is she?"

"Yes. And as Margaret is going to Billie's farm with Oliver I'll be on my own. I confess I'm not looking forward to it, Nelly. What does she want to say to me?"

"What d'you want to say to *her* is more important! If you ain't goin' to marry Victor then tell 'er. I always said Billie Brown the farmer is a better bet fer you. Filthy rich 'e 'is."

"Filthy clothes, too! And sheep to be shorn and chickens to be fed and killed. Ugh! *And* a sister who'd expect to be the boss of my home. Mary-Dairy wouldn't take kindly to my intrusion. No thanks, Nelly. If I marry anyone, it won't be Billie, nice as he is."

"Shame. But then you never did 'ave any sense where men was concerned." Nelly pursed her lips, unrepentant.

Delina and Amy sat uneasily in front of Amy's log fire and made small talk. Each waited for the other to begin the discussion they both wanted. Both blonde and with sixteen years between them, they were superficially alike, but the way they dressed showed very different personalities. Amy wore an angora jumper in pale pink and had added a crystal necklace with matching earrings that dangled and swung below her ears, catching the light from the fire. Her blonde hair was fluffed out and she looked boldly attractive. Delina was beautiful. She wore clothes that were formal and with little ornamentation. Her slim fitting navy skirt and the neat Peter-Pan collared blouse in pale blue with a cardigan that matched spoke of quiet confidence. The way she sat reinforced the impression. Neat court shoes placed precisely together below straight legs, hands curled and resting on knees that touched, the straight back that refused to relax into the comfort of the armchair all told of a formality both in fashion sense and character.

Amy thought her dull. Beautiful, with her naturally blonde hair, translucent skin and those lovely blue eyes, but dull.

"I shouldn't have come," Delina said, staring out through the window at the dark November sky. "I'm sorry, I'd better go."

At once Amy was swamped with remorse. Delina was Victor's daughter and she had been made to feel unwelcome. She stretched out a hand and touched the girl's shoulder. "Please, Delina, let's talk. You know I love your father. You know he and I were meeting before your mother died. Let's get it over with. I suppose you're going to tell me how much you disapprove."

"No. Strange to relate, I don't think badly of you and I don't blame Dad for finding someone who cared. My mother didn't care for him you see, and he's been very unhappy. I just wondered if you and he . . . I wondered what plans you and Dad have made."

"None," Amy answered in her forthright way. "Your mother dying like that was a shock that pushed us apart somehow. It was what we'd wanted, for Victor to be free of her, but coming the way it did made us feel ashamed, as them agreeing to separate would never have done." She looked at Delina and her heart softened towards her. "Fed up, are you, love? It's quite a burden you've been left with for sure."

"I shouldn't mind, but I do. I'm selfish. I want to feel able to plan my own life and now, with David thirteen and Daniel eighteen and planning to go to university, I'm trapped into caring for them for years."

"So you hope I'll take them off your hands?" Amy's voice was sharp and Delina looked up and saw to her relief that she was smiling.

"I don't know what to do."

"Neither do I, love. Neither do I."

"Then you and Dad won't marry?"

"Not for a while, out of respect for your mother we have to wait a few months at least, but I love him and I know we'd be happy together. But whether a new marriage would stand the strain of David, Daniel and you, plus my Margaret and my Freddie, well, I go cold at the thought of it to be honest."

"David would be difficult," Delina admitted sadly. "Daniel will be away. I – I'd do all I could to help."

"Thank you, love." Amy patted the stiffly held shoulder. "My Freddie is a boy soldier and he doesn't get home much, so I suppose there'd be you and David and my Margaret. It doesn't sound so bad said quick, does it?" She laughed and to her relief she saw Delina relax slightly and smile with her. "Sort it out together, we will."

When a more cheerful Delina had left, Amy sat for a long time considering what had been discussed. Her life had been filled with dilemma's she thought. Two pregnancies and in both cases, no husband. An affair with Victor, who

24

was married. Now there was the chance of marrying him and she still considered it a dilemma.

Victor's wife was a disapproving spirit hovering around her and preventing her from feeling joy in the chance she had of marriage to the man she loved. Victor was the second great love of her life; the first had been Harry, her sister, Prue's, husband, now dead. There had been lovers, but only two loves. She would be a fool to risk losing Victor by refusing the challenge of taking on his sons.

Victor arrived an hour later having seen Delina and been given a blow-by-blow account of her meeting with Amy. He knocked on the door and walked in.

"Amy, love? You there?"

"Oh, Victor, I wish it was six months hence and we were together," she said as she ran into his arms.

"Six months? You mean you'll marry me in six months time?"

"I give myself six months to talk your stiff and stilted sons around!"

"And then?"

"And then, whether they like it or not, I'll become the dreaded step-mother. I might even borrow a broomstick to frighten them into behaving like reasonable people!"

"Oh, Amy. We'll be so happy."

"And they'll come and live here," she said dodging away from his kiss. "I can't face that dark, gloomy morgue you've called home all these years."

"Right then." It was Victor's turn to avoid a kiss. "Now can I tell that Billie Brown to stay away from your garden?"

"*Our* garden, love," she said as their lips touched. "From now on it's all ours; our Margaret, our Freddie, our David and Daniel and our Delina."

When Hilda Evans went to see her husband, Griff, in prison, she was shocked at the change in him. He seemed to have faded. His rather florid face was paler, especially around the eyes. His hair, while still black, was showing traces of the grey she had not noticed before. Perhaps, she thought with a frown, she had been so used to his comings and goings she hadn't really looked at him for years.

He was forty-three, they were both in their forties and there was she being surprised to see grey hair. His body was badly run to fat, too, she noticed for the first time. His belt worn under his bulging stomach had been tightened a notch or two since his arrest, but the paunch still hung like an over-ripe fruit, the top button of his trousers failing to fasten.

She smiled at him, her false teeth revealed in an over-sized double row, and he smiled back, his teeth identically artificial, large and ill-fitting.

"There's glad I am to see you," he said.

"I'm your wife, it's my duty to come," she said, the smile widening. "I came to see if you wanted anything and to tell you the police are still searching everywhere for some of the stuff you stole, or the proceeds!" She whispered the last words, in a hiss that could be heard in the next building.

"Hush, you old fool!" Griff growled. "Want to get me put away for ever, do you?"

"You'll only get a few months, the money will be handy for when you get out, you with no job to come back to. Yes, I doubt the forestry will have you back, not with a record for thieving. Best I put the money somewhere safe, Griff. I'll make sure it's there for when you get out."

Griff's eyes rolled around the bare room, seeking some answer to his unspoken question in the green walls and small, barred windows. He had to trust her. At least she wasn't a fly-by-night tart who'd cheat on him. He looked at her, dressed in a black dress that had once been smart but now looked as if it had been slept in for months, hem dropping and a button missing from the bodice. Yes, Hilda would keep her word. Thank God she hadn't found out about him and Bethan, then it would be a different story. He looked at her inane, smiling face and decided that even if she had found out, she would still be loyal, she didn't have the gumption to be otherwise.

He had spent a lot of time thinking about the future during his brief confinement, and as Hilda talked about the small happenings in Hen Carw Parc, his mind drifted back to his conclusions. Perhaps he could leave Hilda and set up a home with Bethan. She was much more to his taste and, although shy, was a passionate woman who would treat him well in all aspects of life. The thought gave him a warm feeling towards Hilda, simple Hilda, who had no idea of his second life and would still love him if she had. In the lowest whispers, interspersed with louder, more general chatter for the benefit of the guard, he told her where he had hidden the money.

Coming out of the tall prison gates and crossing the busy Mumbles Road, Hilda felt an urge to run and whoop in excitement, like a child. Instead she stood and waited for Nelly, whom she saw hurrying towards her from the direction of the town. Behind them was the beach and impulsively, Hilda led Nelly towards it. Along past rows of identical terraced houses and down over the dunes to the wide expanse of Swansea Bay they went, Nelly carrying a wicker shopping basket filled with produce from the market close by, Hilda carrying a secret that she hugged to herself like a warm coat.

The beach was grey and empty, the cold sands stretching in a curve to the distant Mumbles pier, barely visible in the mist. There was no one to be seen apart from a solitary dog who was sniffing along the tide line in the hope of a snack. The sea was reflecting the grey sky above, the scene was sombre, the day almost spent, but to Hilda it was beautiful. Today, everything she saw was full of wonderment and joy. Today she had become a woman of means.

"Is Griff all right then?" Nelly asked, when Hilda seemed unlikely to tell her anything.

"Oh, him! He's all right, but he won't be when he gets out. I'm not having him back you know, Nelly. Not him being a confessed thief. He doesn't know it yet but today's the last he'll see of me!" She took the arm of a surprised Nelly and led her back towards the road. "Come on, let's have a cup of tea to celebrate. Pity the pubs aren't open or we could do it proper."

Nelly stared at Hilda, a woman who had never been inside a pub in her life so far as she knew. What had happened inside the prison to change her so much? Almost bursting with the need to know, Nelly allowed herself to be led to Eynon's cafe on Bryn Y Mor Road, where they ate one of the popular pies and drank a welcome cup of tea.

Hilda said very little on the bus journey home, but Hilda's excitement was clearly written on her wrinkled face. Nelly was aching with curiosity but when Hilda and she alighted she had learned nothing of what had been said inside the prison visitors' room. She consoled herself with the thought that nothing stayed secret for long, not in Hen Carw Parc.

CHAPTER THREE

Before Amy had opened the shop, there were three people waiting to be served. One was Nelly who, always willing to wait, went straight through to the small kitchen behind the shop and put the kettle on for a cup of tea. Amy looked at the second person to enter and said sharply:

"Well, Milly Toogood, what you run out of this morning then?"

"I want some Trex cooking fat. I'm making some pastry for the supper after tomorrow's meeting."

"What meeting is that?" Amy asked reaching for the blue and white packet. "That'll be two shillings and threepence."

"This idea for the best kept village. There's a meeting to discuss it and the vicar asked specially for some of my apple pies."

"'Andy if we run out of bricks to build the 'all," Nelly muttered near Amy's ear. "Kettle's on, Amy," she said more loudly.

"My Bethan wants to see you, Nelly," Milly said as she took her change. "That Hilda Evans hasn't come to work and she won't answer the door when my grandson calls to ask why."

"Upset she is, her husband being in prison, poor dab. Besides, I don't think I'd want to go to that cold storeroom behind the fish and chip shop and spend ages chopping up potatoes, not in this weather."

"Hilda doesn't mind, she's done it for years."

"What does Bethan want to see me about then?" Nelly demanded, coming from the kitchen with a cup of steaming tea for Amy. "I hopes she doesn't expect me to do the job. I got all the work I can manage, thanks."

"Oh well," Milly replied, a disappointed look on her face. "I think it might have been that. Shall I tell her you'll call in and see her?"

"What for? I ain't goin' to do no sacks of potatoes, you can tell 'er that."

"The poor girl, she has to have help, Bethan can't run the business on her own."

The third customer stood quietly listening to the discussion and when Milly Toogood had gone, he stepped forward.

"Hello, Victor love," Amy said, leaning across the counter for his kiss. Nelly glowered slightly and muttered that she would be off.

"What did you come in for, Nelly," Amy asked, "anything special?"

"Oh yes. There's a piece about Winston Churchill in this week's *Illustrated*, to celebrate 'is eightieth birthday. Me and George'll enjoy that." She paid the fourpence and went out.

"She still doesn't approve of me, does she?" Victor laughed. "She doesn't even wish me a good morning."

"Nelly appointed herself my protector years ago and knowing of my propensity for falling in love with married men she watches me and scowls her fiercest frown when I'm in danger of repeating the disaster."

"But I'm not married, not any more."

"Farmer Billie Brown is richer!"

"Oh, I'll have to increase my investment in the weekly football pools, won't I! That's the only way I'll ever be rich."

Victor left as Mavis Powell, who lived in the flat above, arrived to help. The shop began to fill up with impatient early morning customers and he paused for a while to watch through the steamy windows as Amy dealt with the small purchases swiftly and with a smile for each. Then he drove off in the delivery van to the next village.

He had lost the happy mood that sight of Amy had given him. Every time his thoughts were thrust back to the death of his wife he swooped into the depths of dismay, the loss of her was too convenient. What could they do to escape from her?

He wondered if Amy would consider moving away, beginning again in another town, not far away, but far enough to avoid seeing the well known things, things that were a part of his life with Imogine. He knew before he asked himself the question that Amy would refuse. Her life was here, her children were a part of the village. Margaret settled in school, her music lessons, even Freddie, who was a boy soldier, still belonged here. No, the answer lay in facing it, being bold and facing it. People would show their disapproval but it would all die away. A few months and they would be just another married couple.

His shoulders sagged slightly as he sat at the wheel of his van waiting for a herd of cows to pass across the road and into a field. How, with two sons and a daughter still grieving for their mother, how could he and Amy celebrate their love for each other? When they were together it was easy to pretend all would be well. Amy's brave words of them marrying in six months' time heartened him, but the glow faded as soon as he left her, leaving him with a dragging realisation that with the loss of his wife and the freedom it brought, nothing had really changed.

He stopped at a phone box and dialled the number of the shop.

"Amy, come to the pictures tonight?"

"I don't know. Where will I find a baby sitter with such short notice?"

"Ask Nelly. Tell her you've got a date with a handsome man. If she thinks you're going with Billie Brown she'll come like a shot," he joked. She agreed to try and he climbed back into the van with a feeling of excitement. At least they would be together, touching, alone in the darkness of the cinema for a few hours. It wasn't much, but better than the loneliness in which thought chased thought and got him nowhere. He began to whistle cheerfully as he approached his next call.

When Nelly finished her work for the day she didn't go home. With the large dogs pulling her along like some parody of a Art Nouveau statuette, she headed past Amy's shop and on to where Hilda Evans lived. She had been uneasy ever since she had let slip that Griff and Bethan Toogood were having an affair, specially since no one had seen Hilda since the visit to Swansea Prison.

There was no reply to her knock on the front door but not one to give up easily, she went around to the lane and walked through the garage that smelled of oil and grease, and in which the remnants of several motor-bikes were spread. Another door led her into the garden and she saw at once that the back door was open.

She tied the dogs to a convenient tree and called:

"Hilda? You all right?" There was no reply, but sounds from within suggested that Hilda might be on her way to the door. "You all right, Hilda?" she called again.

Hilda appeared in the kitchen, her usual, large toothed smile on her wrinkled face. "Come in, Nelly. If you promise to keep a secret, I'll show you something."

"Cut me throat and 'ope to die," Nelly said, drawing a finger across her neck with enthusiasm.

Hilda led her into the small front room of the house and there, half in and half out of a shoe-box, were more pound notes than Nelly had ever seen. More, many more than when Amy counted up her day's takings.

"Blimey, 'Ilda! Where did that come from?"

"My Griff's little nest egg. He hopes to give himself a good start when he comes out of prison. Poor dab. He's going to have one hell of a disappointment!"

"What d'you mean? You're going to 'and it to the police ain't yer? It is stolen, ain't it? Money pinched from the likes of Archie Pierce?

"Yes, but I'm afraid the police won't see any of it. I might slip a few pounds under Archie's door, mind, but as for the rest, well, people have recovered from the loss now and . . . Nelly, I've never had any luck, not in all my forty-three years. I can't hand it back."

"But what will you do with it?"

"I don't know yet, but I do know I'm going to have some fun with it. Fun, Nelly. Fun has always been what other people have. This is a chance for me to find out, first hand, what it feels like to have fun."

"This is all my fault," Nelly sighed. "If I 'adn't believed you knew, and let it out about your Griff and that stupid Bethan Toogood, you'd never have considered doing this."

"I went into that prison and acted the devoted, forgiving wife, stupid and trusting and honest. I came out and threw off the act like a coat that no longer fitted. I'm glad you told me, Nelly. I might have gone on the way I am for the rest of my life. D'you know," she went on, her dark eyes shining in the animated face, "I look in every mirror I pass and each time I see my reflection I like it less. Tomorrow all that will change."

"Blimey, what you goin' to do, for Gawd's sake?"

"A proper hair-do for a start." She pulled down one of the curls which had just been released from a curler. Black, but with a touch of redness that makes it look like rust has set in, Nelly thought. "And I'm going to Boots and ask the girl there about makeup. Yes, don't look so shocked, Nelly. And," she leaned towards Nelly and widened her smile so that her teeth threatened to engulf her, "next week, I'm going to order a new set of teeth.

"Thank Gawd fer that!" Nelly said. "Those look like they was made for a pantomime horse!"

"Being a mistress isn't fair on wives you know," Hilda went on, her fingers tucking the piles of notes back into the box. "She gets the best of a man while the wife is left with the worst. She only has to be attentive for a little while now and then, so she can be glamorous and can pretend to be interested in his every word. She has to be fun for the short while they're together. Not for her the washing boiling over or the grease on the carpet from the motor-bikes, the hurry to iron a favourite shirt, the irritations and the anger. She will listen sympathetically as he tells her of his wife's nagging, her untidiness and extravagence. Married women stop seeing their husband as the man they'd once found attractive and irresistible. They become wrapped up in the day to day routine worries and the boredom. The 'other woman' doesn't."

It was the longest speech Hilda had ever made. Nelly wanted to spring up in defence of the "other woman", knowing Amy had been in that situation three times, but this wasn't the time or the place.

"So you're going to spend his money while he's in prison then."

"Can you give me one good reason why I shouldn't? He's been giving 'her' the money that I had to work in that fish and shop shop yard to earn! She was paying me and he was giving it back to her and Arthur, that son of hers! Don't you find that ironic, Nelly?"

"Don't you think you ought to return it to the police?"

"Would it go back to Archie?"

"I don't know."

"Here." Hilda handed four pound notes to Nelly. "Take this and stuff it through Archie's door. He's the only one I feel any regret for. Hasn't got much and him old and on his own." Nelly put her hands behind her back.

"I wouldn't touch it. You do what you think is right."

"You won't tell, Nelly?"

"You can be sure of that. I'll try and ferget I've seen or 'eard any of it."

"D'you know, that brazen Bethan has sent her son up here to ask me when I am going back to work? The cheek of it! I didn't let on that I knew about her and Griff, mind. I just said I didn't think I would be well enough to work in the cold yard for a few weeks. I don't want her going to Griff and letting on that I know. I want it to be a wonderful surprise when he comes out and finds there isn't a home for him here any more!" Hilda's face glowed and, for a brief moment, Nelly glimpsed beneath the wrinkled skin, the ill-kempt hair and the over-large teeth, a new personality emerging.

Mavis Powell lived in the flat above Amy's shop with her husband, Ralph. Their daughter, Sheila, the wife of the absent Maurice Davies, lived with her grandmother up in the council houses. Although Sheila was married, Mavis felt no release from the torment of having a rather wayward daughter. Married she might be, but she was still a constant worry and, although Mavis hated admitting it, an embarrassment, too.

The post had arrived as she had stepped out of the side door and walked into the shop. Phil the post handed her an envelope which she recognised as an airmail letter. It had to be from Sheila's husband. Maurice had admitted being responsible for Sheila's pregnancy, called off his wedding to Delina Honeyman and married Sheila.

Unwillingly forced into the change of plan by herself and his own family, Maurice had made plans to compensate for their persuasions and the ruination of his life. The day following the wedding to Sheila he had disappeared, leaving a note to say he had emigrated to Australia.

There had been talk of him returning, Sheila had told them he was grief-stricken over the way he had treated her and was coming home to her. But that, Mavis thought with a frown, was as likely as having snow on mid-summer's day! Any remorse shown by Maurice Davies would be a ploy to get something he wanted and nothing to do with his responsibilities to Sheila!

The letter remained unopened in her apron pocket until there was a lull in the flow of customers and Amy had made them a cup of coffee. She fingered the flimsy paper and wondered if she dare open it. Whatever news it contained it almost certainly mean trouble. When had Sheila ever been anything else?

"I've had a letter from Australia, Amy," she said, taking it out and fingering it.

"Oh? From Maurice I suppose. Does he say when he's coming home?"

"I haven't opened it."

"Why? It's the first communication you've ever received from your son-in-law, that must be exciting."

"Why do I expect trouble every time I hear about him? Him and that daughter of mine, they're a right pair!"

"Good might come of it all now he's decided to come home."

"If Sheila's baby had lived I'd have thought it worth while, but all he did was mess her up even more than getting her in the family way. Best he'd married that Delina Honeyman and left us to sort out the rest."

"Open it for goodness sake!" Amy took the envelope and slit the top and handed it back to Mavis.

"He didn't spend long on it, did he?" Mavis said, holding up the single page of writing. She began to read and when she had done so, she handed the letter to Amy. "Go on, read it and tell me what I should do."

Maurice had begun the letter, "Dear Mr and Mrs Powell", not mother-in-law and father-in-law. He said he wanted to come home to Sheila but had the chance of a job which, if kept for a year or so, would help clear his debts and return the money his family had sent out for his fare home. He asked that Mrs Powell look after Sheila for him and asked her to understand that this was for the best.

Amy handed the letter back to Mavis and shrugged. "Knowing Maurice Davies, I suspect that he's found himself a girl and is enjoying himself too much to leave Australia at present!"

"And how am I going to comfort Sheila with that bit of news!"

"Sheila already knows."

Both women jumped and stared at the doorway where Sheila stood, haloed in the light of a weak sun. She stayed there, a slim and very attractive young woman, dressed in a tight-fitting blouse and a straight skirt that enhanced her generous bust and her small waist. The three-quarter coat she wore was open. Sheila always refused to put comfort before appearance. She tried never to hide her figure. Even in the coldest weather she would defy the chill wind and allow her coat to be blown wide to show the way her full breasts stretched the cloth of her blouse.

There was something in her expression, too, that made men stare and her mother feel fear. She was so brazen. Where did she get such boldness, Mavis constantly asked herself, and why did she court trouble by showing it?

Sheila stayed in the doorway and, opening her shoulder bag, took out a letter identical to the one her mother still held. "I see you've had a letter, too. From my loving husband telling me he can't come home to me and how devastated it makes him? He must think I'm *twp*! Found a girl he has and he thinks you can keep me sweet until he's bored with her. Well, two can play that game!"

"Sheila!" Mavis ran to the door and scuttled after the hip-swinging figure of her daughter. A blue letter fluttered from the girl's hands and fell to the road way. Mavis stopped following her daughter to capture it. Best that no one else read it, her anxious mind warned. She walked slowly back to the shop.

Sheila caught the bus into town. She was late for work but that didn't matter. The way she felt at the moment she would resign if the manageress even began to complain. She stopped in the post office in Llan Gwyn and wrote a letter to Amy's soldier son, Freddie. At least she had the sense to keep him hanging on. He'd console her for her disappointment. "Freddie Prichard," she whispered, "you are too young, too dull, but at least you're available and relatively harmless."

On Freddie's next leave he didn't write to tell his mother he would be home. Amy would be pleased to see him whether or not he had told her he was coming. Best wait to see what Sheila had in mind. From her letter and a subsequent phone call, she was beginning to feel more affection for him. Hope, which had been dashed more often than he cared to remember, was rising once again.

He arrived at Swansea station and stepped out into the dull winter day and looked around. Tall and strongly built, he looked older than his sixteen years. He wasn't a vain boy but he stopped and put his rimless glasses back on his nose, the ones he used when in uniform happily abandoned for a few days.

He didn't expect anyone to meet him but paused just to take in the sounds and scents of his home town. To his surprise and proud pleasure, Sheila hailed him from the doorway of the Grand Hotel opposite the station entrance and ran into his arms.

She kissed him, lightly he had to admit, but nevertheless with obvious delight. Then, with her arm around his waist he tucked her into his shoulder and they walked down the High Street to catch the bus for Hen Carw Parc.

Johnny Cartwright was driving the bus. Just his luck. Now he'd tell everyone and his mother would know he was home.

"Don't tell Mam I'm home," he pleaded, "I want to give her a surprise."

Johnny winked and touched his nose. "Not a word, boy," he said, then he jerked his head back towards the women who were getting on in front of them. "Can't say you've much chance with them, mind. Nosy-bugger Beynon and her friend."

"We'd better go straight to Mam, I think," Freddie sighed, recognising the prim and disapproving face of his Auntie Prue.

"Do we have to?" Sheila pleaded, widening her eyes in a way she knew he liked.

"To be honest, I'm broke. I'll have to go and ask Mam for a sub."

"All right, we'll go to your Mam's then we'll go up to Gran's, all right? It's quiet there, we can . . . talk." She said "talk" as if she meant a great deal more.

Waving goodbye to Johnny, they crossed the road from

the bus stop and walked towards Amy's house. The sound of a piano met them as they touched the gate and Freddie stopped.

"Good, isn't she? Little Margaret passing exams and playing on a stage. Who'd have believed it?"

"Come on, Freddie, I want us to get home."

Amy was in the kitchen and when she opened the door she expected to see Victor. For a brief second she hesitated, confused seeing her son and Sheila Davies standing there smiling.

"Freddie, love! What a surprise! Why didn't you tell me you were coming? There's only a scrap meal and I'd have done something special. Sheila, come on in." She bustled them through the cold hallway to the living room where a fire burned brightly. They sat close together, holding hands on the big, comfortable couch. "How long have you got this time, love?" she asked, busying herself with the kettle. "I hope it's longer than a few hours." She wished she could stop talking full pelt. But Sheila always made her on edge. The girl was using Freddie and he was too stupid, or too infatuated, to see it. That he might be really in love with her she refused to consider.

"There's no need for you to bother with food, Mrs Prichard," Sheila said, "I've got something in the oven at home."

"Oh, you aren't staying then?" Amy looked at Freddie, his eyes so blue behind the shining lenses. So *much* like his father, whom Amy had loved so much. Harry Beynon, her sister's husband, would never be dead while Freddie lived.

"I'm going up to Sheila's for a while but I'll be back later. Tomorrow, while Sheila's at work I might be able to spend a few hours on the garden. What's this I hear about a competition for the best kept village then? I'll have to get something planned for you, Mam."

The music from the next room stopped and nine-year-old Margaret, having heard her brother's voice, burst through the door with a shriek of delight.

"Freddie! When did you come? When do you go back?" The lovely young face with its deep brown eyes and thick frame of rich red hair showed no kinship with Freddie, but affection was without doubt. Ignoring the presence of Sheila apart from a cursary polite "hello", she began chattering to Freddie, telling him all that had been happening in school and in the shop.

"Wait a minute, Margaret. There'll be nothing left for me to tell him if you don't stop for breath!"

Exchanging news, sharing reminiscences and making laughter out of the ordinary, made three hours fly past and it was ten o'clock when Sheila finally persuaded Freddie that she, at least, had to go.

"Sorry, Sheila. But it's so good to be back home and part of a family. I never realised how much I'd miss it when I signed on." He stood up and offered his hands for her to rise.

She stood beside him. The fact that she was put out by not being the centre of attention showed clearly in her face and in the way she snatched her coat from Freddie, refusing his help to put it on. Families! They were nothing but a drag. If she had her way Freddie would forget he ever had one.

They walked towards the village, Freddie guiding her up the hedge-lined lane which led past Nelly and George's cottage, past the wood and almost to the edge of the old castle ruin, before turning back down to the road leading into the council houses where she lived with her gran. Several times he tried to kiss her but she turned her face away. She was smarting with disappointment, having imagined an evening of Freddie's undivided attention.

Before they left the last of the trees that bordered the lane to her consternation she was beginning to want his kisses. More than his kisses her body was crying out for loving. It had been so long and, although she had never before felt an urgency so strongly as this with Freddie, there had been many moments when she would have given herself if only there had been someone with whom to share an escape from loneliness for a brief hour.

40

Gran was in bed and Sheila opened the door and let them inside. The house was dark and they walked in like guilty intruders until they were in the living room. Only then did Sheila's hand reach for a light-switch. Freddie's hand covered hers and stopped her.

"Don't put on the light, not for a while." Holding her hand he pulled the curtains apart and let in the weak light from the street lamp near by. "There's enough light. We'll have to pretend it's moonlight."

A ripple of excitement spread from the centre of Sheila's body as Freddie took her in his arms. She should stop this now. Somehow the warning that sprung to her mind only heightened her urgent need of him: "I mustn't", became, "I must". "This is wrong", became, "this is so right".

She hardly knew how she became naked. Freddie's kisses sent her into a dazed and wonderful world where she floated on the edge of an abyss that promised utter joy. His slightest touch sent her further into the realms of ecstasy as he eased the last thread of clothing from her. There was still time, her fevered brain told her, but then Freddie's body was on top of hers his hands gently caressing her and in moments desire reached its height and then there was the slow subsiding of passion and they lay, clinging to each other like victims of a fearful and wonderful storm that had them ship wrecked and then brought them safely to land.

They both slept. Unbelievably, in a house where Sheila's grandmother could walk in on them at any time, naked and as peaceful as children they slept. At four o'clock, frozen and stiff, Freddie woke and pulling on his trousers and shirt, he carried Sheila to her bed. She roused, clung to him and as the bed was icy cold, he went in with her and wrapped himself around her to warm her. Then she woke, felt him close to her, and the loving began again.

It was six o'clock when Freddie walked home. He let himself into the house warily, knowing his mother was likely to be up at any moment. Whether she heard him or not he didn't know. He put on the pyjamas his mother had put out for him and slid into the cold-sheeted bed and lay

41

for a while re-living the last few hours. After all this time, he and Sheila were together. Now nothing mattered. All the hurdles would be easily cleared. Her marriage to Maurice would take a while to dissolve but it would happen. He only had to be patient. The army service would come to an end and he could begin to make a career for himself, a career in which he could make a lot of money so Sheila wouldn't have to work. They'd be so happy.

He would have been devastated to know that up in her grandmother's house Sheila was crying, knowing that once more the dictates of her demanding body had let her down. She had messed up her life even further and set off a trail of events that she did not want, yet probably could not stop.

CHAPTER FOUR

The evening of the meeting to discuss the entry for the Best Kept Village was bitterly cold. A damp mist had fallen on the valley and wrapped everything in a blanket that chilled, not warmed. Skeletal trees loomed out of the mist, wintery and stark. The stage was set for winter.

Nelly and George went down the dark lane wrapped in as many layers as they could comfortably wear and they were not surprised to find seats half empty when they arrived a few minutes before the meeting was due to begin. They found a seat near the back of the hall. Nelly preferred to be able to watch the people in front of her and prepare a laughter filled version of the event for telling to her friend, Netta Cartwright, later on.

"Not as many as I'd hoped," the Reverend Barclay Bevan said to Mrs Norwood Bennet-Hughes.

"Blame the television," Nelly shouted, her sharp ears having caught the remark with ease. "These days you 'ave to look at what's on before arrangin' a meetin'."

"Hush, Mother," her disapproving daughter Evie hissed from the front row.

"Thank you, Nelly, I think that's something we ought to keep in mind for the future," Mrs Norwood Bennet-Hughes chuckled, and Nelly watched with amusement as Evie sank lower in her seat.

"My Evie's what some calls a social climber and having me for a mother cuts the growth off at the roots!" Nelly hissed to George.

"It's a pity she doesn't follow you more," George whispered back. "She'd have a greater capacity for laughter and that's a fact." They both looked across at the young woman who sat stiff-backed, her hands held neatly on her lap, her expression one of disapproval.

"An' young Ollie would be happier, too. She promised to take more heed of him after she'd almost killed 'im tryin' to learn to drive a car, but she 'asn't changed. Thunder, flood, world wars an' earthquake, my Evie would come out of it all with the same prim and disapproving look on her chops!" Nelly's rare anger showed whenever her grandson was mentioned in the same breath as his mother. "An' that father of 'is is no better. Look at him, Tedious Timothy, prancing about tryin' to look important while 'is only son is being minded by Gawd knows 'oo!"

Timothy Chartridge was the headmaster of the village school and very involved in local affairs. With Mrs Norwood Bennet-Hughes and the Reverend Barclay Bevan, he was already planning the competition arrangements. Knowing nothing about gardening didn't stop him, he didn't intend to get that close to the action, only be in a position to take the glory should they win. As a prospective councillor the publicity would be very useful.

Nelly noticed that the village, even on this small occasion, was separated into several camps. The main separation was between those who lived in the older part of the village, mostly the ribbon of houses along the main road, and the newer council house estate further up the hill. Those from the council houses sat together and apart from the rest. Those from the village were separated less obviously by which ever side of the road they lived. There was one exception she noticed with disapproval. Sheila Davies from the council houses was sitting next to Freddie and sharing glances that showed a lot more than friendship. Amy wouldn't like that.

Mrs Norwood Bennet-Hughes stood up to begin the meeting and asked them to move and fill the vacant seats in the middle of the rows. "Come forward will you?" She waved her fur-clad arms. "It looks much more friendly and that's what we are, friends. We are gathered here on this

44

cold evening to discuss stretching friendship to sharing our skills and facilities to the benefit of us all. I presume we are all in agreement on the plan to compete?"

There was a murmur of approval with the exception of Bert Roberts, who shook his head as if convinced already of the hopelessness of their attempt. His wife, Brenda, dug him in the ribs so he didn't say anything but continued to shake his head.

Billie Brown and his sister, Mary-Dairy, were there and they offered the use of an old greenhouse to bring on annuals, should anyone need it. Victor at once stood up and made the suggestion that they should start a village gardening club:

"That way, even those who know nothing about growing flowers would have help and encouragement. If we all contributed the plants we have left from our own gardens, there would be plenty for all," he said. "And what if we encouraged the children to assist the old folks by planting their gardens for them? Old and young getting together would be a benefit for both."

The suggestion was received with delight and the murmur of voices swelled as, ignoring the calls for order from Timothy, they each voiced their opinions on how and where it should be arranged.

"If you will all give your suggestions through me," Mrs Norwood Bennet-Hughes pleaded, "we would soon have something planned." She pointed at Bert who had raised his hand to speak.

"I think we should start straight after Christmas and make a plan so everyone knows what he's doing. We don't want everyone growing the same things, now do we?"

"An excellent idea," Timothy agreed. "We'll get some letters out with the date of the meeting and a few preliminary suggestions as soon as we can."

Mrs Bennet-Hughes nodded to Phil-the-post next, but Bert didn't sit down. Given the floor he wasn't going to yield it up easily. "And I suggest we meet here, in the hall, at the end of January." Bert sat down, lips pursed as if already thinking profoundly about how he would deal with it all.

"Gawd 'elp us if Bert's in charge," Nelly muttered.

"Someone with plenty of time is needed. He does work hard at anything he does," George whispered back.

"'E works 'ard? He's hard work more like!"

George began to laugh and the laughter changed to coughing which to Nelly's surprise and alarm soon became uncontrollable. Red in the face, his beard white against the hot skin, his blue eyes wide and spilling tears, he tried in vain to control it.

"Stop making me laugh," he growled between bouts of coughing.

On the platform the three V.I.P.'s called the meeting to an end and, with a pile of notes shuffled together importantly, Timothy jumped down and came to see what could be done to help his father-in-law. Brenda Roberts brought George a cup of tea as his coughing subsided. Others left their seats and made their way to where Milly Toogood, her constant companion, Sybil Tremain, and Amy's sister, Prue Beynon, were handing out teas and cakes and sandwiches.

There was a air of excitement in the room as everyone began to share ideas with their neighbour. Nelly had wanted to ask a few questions but the coughing had put them out of her mind. Now, as George sat gradually recovering, she made her way through the small gathering to where Timothy and Mrs Norwood Bennet-Hughes were talking to the vicar.

"Where will the judges go, Tim?" she asked of her son-in-law. "I live right out at the edge of the wood but I don't want to be missed out. Me an' George'll do our bit. Good at flowers my George is."

"I don't know yet, dear," Mrs Norwood Bennet-Hughes answered for a hesitant Timothy. "But if I have any say, I'll make sure the tour of judges passes your gate."

The buzz of a dozen conversations was halted by the loud voice of P.C. Harris asking for a word.

"I know this isn't the correct time, but I have a suggestion that I thought you might like to consider." There was the chink of cups being replaced on saucers, then he went on. "It's many years since I played, but once we had regular cricket matches in the village. What about organising one between those of us who live in the council houses and the rest of you who live in the older part of the village? It seems to me that Nelly is right and we have to consider what's on the box these days before arranging anything. A challenge match would bring back a bit of the community spirit that we are beginning to lose."

"The village versus the council 'ouses? It'll be a blood-bath," Nelly joked. "Look at 'em. They can't even sit together in this 'all!"

But the idea was met with obvious approval as men smiled over memories of their successes and women thought of the teas they used to supply so generously.

"Can we leave you to make enquiries and perhaps sort out a team, Constable?" Barclay Bevan was at his most animated, his round, plump face beaming at the thought, his imagination already showing him taking a century to loud applause. "And for the village, perhaps I can be the one to select a team?"

"Select!" Nelly muttered. "Finding twelve men that can manage to hit a ball would be an achievement!"

"Nelly, love, don't start me coughing again," George chuckled.

"And who," Nelly added thoughtfully, watching the young couple in the corner, "who would young Freddie play for supposin' 'e's home? The village for 'is mum, or the council 'ouses for that Sheila Davies? 'Er that's married an' carryin' on as if she wasn't!"

It was only nine-thirty when the meeting broke up and people began to scurry out hurrying through the bleak cold night to their homes. Nelly and George waited until Freddie and Sheila came out.

"Going to your mother's are yer, young Freddie?"

"Yes, for an hour, then I'll have to take Sheila home,"

47

Freddie smiled and hugged Sheila close. "She has to get home and to bed early with having to get to work by nine in the morning."

"We'll walk down with yer as far as the lane." She grinned as she imagined the look of disappointment on their faces. They looked as if they wanted to be alone to drool over each other and tell each other how wonderful they were. "All right, we'll let you off. I want to call in to Netta Cartwright's anyway and tell 'er what's been said. I bet her Johnny'll want to be in the cricket team."

Sheila and Freddie walked a little way towards the end of the village where Amy lived, but when they reached Nelly's lane they changed their minds without discussion and turned right and strolled through the dark lane, stopping at intervals to kiss and hold each other tight. They were oblivious to the chill air coming from the trees, touching their faces with still, glacial air and making their faces turn to marble; the dampness underfoot that rose and stiffened their muscles. Though Sheila was less happy than Freddie.

She wanted him so much, felt the urgent need of his loving draining her of self-control, and she knew that as soon as her gran was safely asleep she would again allow him to share her bed. But deep inside was the knowledge that it was a mistake, that her over-powering need of a man's body had destroyed her common sense and she was going to regret the weakness. All these months she had held Freddie off and now, when she thought she was safe from such urgent longings that sent level-headedness winging out of the window, she had given in to his pleading and her own frailty.

It was the letter that had caused it; Maurice writing to say that he was delaying his home-coming on some pretence about a job. She knew that with him there was almost certainly a girl involved. She hadn't been the first girl and she held no innocent views on how he felt about the sanctity of their farcical marriage. He had left her with a marriage

48

unconsumated, yet she had been pregnant by him. The irony of it was almost funny. Getting her pregnant while in love with Delina, then leaving her immediately after the ceremony that made them man and wife.

The plea to her and his family to send money so he could come home had been a moment of excitement and hope but that had soon been dashed. She knew he didn't love her, and whatever happened in the future she would never be conned into believing he did. The need for Freddie's love became more important and she increased her pace, anxious to be in his arms, to blot out all thoughts of Maurice, knowing that for Freddie Prichard, at least, her happiness was paramount.

Hilda was momentarily anxious. She looked at the money in her purse and realised she had spent almost forty pounds of Griff's money. The foundation garments the woman in the dress shop said she needed had cost more than she had expected, and there was the new hair-do and the three dresses. And the winter coat from C & A had cost five pounds nineteen shillings and sixpence. Her new shoes, too, had been far more than she normally spent. She looked in the window of the shop she had just left. Nearly three pounds on makeup and she had paid the bill without turning a hair, pretending she spent that amount all the time. It was unbelievable. She went into a nearby cafe to sit and recover. It was making her feel quite breathless but she had never enjoyed herself as much in all her life.

Police Constable Harris was sitting at one of the tables and, although he had glanced at her, he had not recognised in the smartly-dressed lady with the expensively cut hair, the drab, untidy woman he knew as Hilda Evans. Her dark eyes stared at him and for a moment or two made him squirm uneasily. She chuckled as she called his name and watched the sudden realisation dawn in his eyes.

"Surprising what a bit of a trim will do, isn't it?" she laughed, patting her short, dark hair with a coyness that, days ago, would have made her look ridiculous.

49

"Mrs Evans. I – well you do look nice. Getting ready to visit Griff?" he asked in a hoarse whisper.

"No, I'm off to the pictures. Pity to waste all this on Griff, isn't it?"

Constable Harris began to squirm again. For a moment he thought she was going to ask him to go with her! There was a look in her eye that made him wish he'd gone to the pub instead of coming for a quiet cup of tea. He stood up, leaving his unfinished cake and half of his tea.

"Got to be off, Mrs Evans, I'm meeting someone. Got to go." He sidled out from behind his table, paid for his snack, and left.

Hilda laughed. This was fun. You could almost see the release of steam as he sighed with relief to be away from her. Hilda Evans, *femme fatale*! The power of it made her laugh out loud and a waitress came across to see if everything was all right."

"The tea could be hotter," said the new Hilda. She was gratified with the speed at which her complaint was rectified.

The bus slowed as it reached the beginning of the village and Johnny Cartwright swung from the platform and ran alongside the vehicle for a few paces to keep his balance. He called "*Da bo*," and waved goodbye to the conductor and turned to cross the road. Walking towards Sheepy Lane he hesitated and looked left, wondering whether to call on his mother who lived in the row of cottages past the school, but decided against. He wanted to be home before Fay, to have a meal ready so she could eat and then rest. Her pregnancy hadn't reduced her capacity for work and he worried about her.

Fay sold hats to shops over a large area of South Wales and was often out of the house for twelve-hour stretches, when her visits took her to Breconshire or down to Pembrokeshire. Today she was working closer to home and he thought she would be home about six o'clock. Time, he thought, to get a couple of pork chops in the oven with a bit of stuffing and a few roast potatoes.

He hurried up the hill, his movements quick, his face holding the usual excitement at seeing her. She was so lovely that every day he blessed his luck in winning her. He was never completely sure that Fay was his. His love for her was still an unbelievable dream come true. At the slightest hint that she was less than content he felt the beginning of a cold, creeping fear. Now there was a baby on the way he thought he would never ask for anything more. The baby would mean she would be there every time he entered the house, a luxury he had dreamed of but never really thought would come true.

Johnny was a small man with dark straight hair and smiling brown eyes and there was about him the bounce of youth. There was also an air of strength and power; a hint that the aura of amiability he habitually he wore could be quickly dispersed if the need arose. He liked everyone, except Prue Beynon whom he had christened "Nosy-Bugger Beynon". His face was that of a boy and even the moustache he grew in the hope of adding a few years didn't hide his youthfulness. To his chagrin at twenty-five he looked little more than eighteen.

He walked up the hill, an overcoat and a thick woollen scarf hiding the uniform that showed his job to be a bus driver, and almost ran the last few yards, so anxious was he to look down the close to see if by any good fortune Fay was home before him. The car wasn't there and, with his initial disappointment smothered, he hurried on and let himself into the neat, rather sparsely furnished house and began to prepare the meal.

At six o'clock he heard the car and opened the door to great her. She smiled and his heart turned over.

"Hello, Johnny, what's that I smell cooking?"

"Enough to feed the pair of you my lovely. *Duw Annwyl*, you're cold," he gasped as he kissed her. "Come on in by the fire. It's been on for a while so the room's warm."

51

Fay allowed him to fuss over her and she ate the meal he had prepared with real appreciation. It was after they had washed the dishes and were sitting sipping the cup of coffee that Johnny insisted he made with milk, that she brought the conversation around to the one flaw in Johnny's happiness.

"Darling, I've been talking to my manager, about my plans for when the baby arrives."

"You're leaving work! There's glad I am. It's too much, all this driving around and carrying boxes in and out of shops, and the evenings filling in your books. Next week, is it?"

"Johnny, I want to go back to work as soon as I've had the baby."

"Fay, you can't mean it. We've discussed it and you agreed."

"I love my job and I can't see me sitting around making goo-goo noises day after day. It really isn't me."

"Fay, don't you think – "

"Let me finish, Johnny. You never let me finish. I didn't want this baby and for a while I was sorry it had happened, but not because I don't want to have your child, at thought of giving up work. We need the money apart from everything else. I'd hate to have to 'manage' as your mam's done for years. I'm not the sort to 'manage' and to 'make do'. I need to be able to buy what we need when we need it, not put money into a jam-jar until there's enough for a pair of shoes or whatever. I'd be unhappy and because I was unhappy, you would, too."

"I'd never be unhappy with you to come home to, my lovely."

"Johnny," Fay said in exasperation, "you aren't listening!"

"You can't really expect me to take you seriously when you suggest leaving our baby with someone else to bring up?"

"I am serious. And she won't be brought up by someone else, only minded for a few hours each day while I work. I'd

be better at selling hats than bringing up a child anyway."
To her irritation, Johnny grinned widely.

"She? D'you think it'll be a she?"

"Johnny!"

"Talk about it later, shall we? When she's arrived.
There'll be time enough then."

"I want to start looking for someone now. I know
April's a long way off but I want to be sure I find the
right person."

"More coffee, lovely?"

She gave up trying to discuss what was for her a very
important issue and accepted the refill of her cup with a
controlled smile. Tomorrow she would call in and talk to
his mother. There she might have a better response, only
might, she thought with a long sigh. It was so difficult to
make other people realise that for her having a baby wasn't
the end of a career.

Netta Cartwright heard the front gate opened and looked
through the window to see her daughter-in-law coming
towards the front door.

"It's Fay, Nelly," she said to her first visitor of the
morning. "I wonder what she wants calling so early? I
hope nothing's wrong."

"That ain't the way to greet 'er, Netta," Nelly laughed.

"It isn't often that she calls, and she usually comes with
Johnny."

She went to the door and opened it wide, "Fay, love,
there's a nice surprise on a dark morning. Not working
today, then?"

"I'm sneaking an hour off to talk to you, mother-in-law,"
Fay smiled as she entered. Then she saw Nelly's two dogs
sprawled across the hearth rug and she hesitated. "If you've
got Nelly here it doesn't really matter," she said. "I'll just
have a cup of tea and then go."

"I'm just off," Nelly said, pulling herself up out of Netta's
deep armchair with a groan and a showing off her gappy
teeth. "Blimey, I'm gettin' that stiff I'll need an oil can

to get me going in the mornin's soon!"

On impulse Fay gestured for her to sit back down. "No, don't go, Nelly, I'd like to hear your opinion on what I have to say."

Nelly sank back with obvious relief, her bright eyes polished with curiosity.

Netta went into the tiny kitchen which housed a bath as well as a cooker and a sink and a washing boiler, and emerged with a tray of fresh tea. Netta Cartwright was a small dumpling of a woman, spotlessly clean, with rosy cheeks, dark brown eyes like her son, and her beautiful hair, once black but now perfectly white and full around her head, like a shining halo. The tray was set with an embroidered tray-cloth and her best china cups. A plateful of welsh-cakes was set on a crotcheted doily. She knew how much Fay appreciated nice things and always made a special effort when she called.

"That looks lovely, Mother," Fay smiled. "You shame me, always having home-made cakes whenever I call."

"We all do what we do best, Fay," Netta said in her quiet, gentle voice. "Can you imagine me trying to do what you do?"

"That was what I wanted to talk to you about." Fay put down her cup and saucer and smiled at Netta and Nelly. "What I do best is sell hats and when the baby is born, that's what I want to continue to do." She watched the faces of the two women for the disapproval she knew would come, but to her surprise Nelly nodded and said:

"If you ain't 'appy bein' 'ome all day, then neither you, nor Johnny nor the baby will be content, don't you think so, Netta?"

Netta thought carefully before replying. She didn't want to outwardly disagree but neither did she want to agree so promptly that Fay would guess at her insincerity.

"I don't think it's for me to say, my dear. I want you to do what's best for you. So long as you get someone utterly reliable to look after the baby then I don't think you should worry about what I or anyone else thinks. I do know this,

54

it isn't the time you spend with the baby that's important, but how you are with him when he is with you. A loving relationship is what you and he will want, not a resentful mother who wishes she was somewhere else."

"Take my Evie, now she's a resentful mother an' no mistake," Nelly added. "I 'ates to say it but it's true. She loves Ollie, I'll give 'er that, but she'd be 'appier an' so would 'e, if she'd been honest enough to face facts and let someone else take the burden off of 'er 'ands."

"Then you don't think it's wrong for me to find someone to mind the baby?"

"Lots of people did it during the war and I think more and more women are considering it. I think the days when children did the same as their mothers and fathers is disappearing fast." Netta smiled and added softly, "Not that I regretted staying at home, mind. I wouldn't have missed a minute of it. But there, I wasn't a career woman and you are. You do what you think best. You and Johnny are a partnership, work it out between you."

"With his shifts there'll be some days when we won't need anyone," Fay's face was smiling and she slipped back in the deep armchair more relaxed that Netta had ever seen her.

"There you are then, it isn't even every day. And, although I wouldn't take on the job full time even if you wanted me to, I'm too old to chase after babies, I can help in and out, if necessary."

"Thank you mother-in-law. You don't know what a relief it is for you to take the news like this."

"How d'you really feel?" Nelly asked her friend when Fay had driven off to her first appointment. "You don't agree, deep down, do you?"

"I only know that I think I passed some kind of test this morning. I could have reacted like the typical mother-in-law, interfering and trying to persuade someone to do what they didn't want to do. No, I don't like the idea of someone else bringing up Johnny's child, but if it keeps Fay happy

55

that, in the long run, is what's best for them all. Fay isn't like us, Nelly, she thinks in a completely different way and I don't want that to make a barrier between us. I need her to treat me like a friend. And – " her dark eyes twinkled in the calm face, " – there's months yet for her to change her mind?" She picked up the tray and carried it into the kitchen. "Now, Nelly, tell me more of what happened at the meeting."

CHAPTER FIVE

While Sheila was reading his letter saying he wouldn't be coming home, Maurice Davies was already setting off on his journey back to Wales. On accepting the ten-pound-passage to Australia to escape from his marriage to Sheila Powell, he had also accepted staying in Australia for at least two years. Having decided that he didn't want to stay, he was only allowed to return when the full fare had been repaid.

The money had been sent to him after being raised by a collection among members of his family. His mother, Ethel Davies, and his brothers Phil-the-post, Sidney, who worked with George on Leighton's farm and Teddy, who worked in a factory in Swansea, had all given a contribution. Even his parents-in-law, Mavis and Ralph Powell, had given something in the vain hope that with her husband home Sheila would cease to worry them.

The letters Maurice had written to Sheila and his mother had been written after a brief but exciting affair with the wife of another immigrant. Now that was over and he again felt the need to be on home ground.

Sheila would have been surprised to know that in his pocket Maurice carried a picture of her. In it she was wearing her favourite dress which was tight-waisted and low-necked and with a skirt that was very full and unfashionably short. She was on the grass in front of the woods above Nelly's cottage, half sitting half lying, her head propped up on her arm and showing her tantalising figure to perfection. He often looked at it and dreamed of her passionate loving and wondered if, now time and travel had separated him from the disappointment of losing Delina, he could ever settle and build a marriage with her. She was certainly exciting but they had little in common except desire for each other and, wild and restless as he was, he knew it wasn't enough.

In another pocket, less often studied, was a photograph of Delina. This one was taken with her school class and she stood straight at the side of three rows of children with no attempt to look attractive let alone provocative. Without trying Delina was beautiful. Just standing there with a bunch of seven-year olds, she made his heart beat faster. He pushed it away and stared into space, seeing what might have been, and his eyes were sad.

Sheila had had several "pin-ups" on her bedroom wall. The latest had been Nigel Knighton, with whom she had begun a friendship that she had hoped would lead to better things. He was an accountant and very much a gentleman. She had begun to imagine a role for herself in which she lived in a large house wearing expensive clothes, playing the role of a successful man's adored wife. Nigel said goodbye when he discovered that she was married. His picture had replaced one of Cornel Wilde and it had followed it to the dustbin.

When the letter from Maurice came, telling her of his wish to come home, she had filled the place on the wall beside her bed with a picture of them both on their wedding day. Now she tore it down and glared at it. Wanting to come home! Only for as long as it took him to find another woman! she thought angrily. She threw the black and white picture into the corner of the room but later retrieved it and put it in a drawer. They *were* married and he still *might* come back to her.

It was a Sunday and having finished the usual weekend tasks that took up most of her Sunday she felt restless. It was almost four o'clock and dark outside, but she put on a thick cardigan and a shining plastic mac which she tied tightly around her waist and set off for a walk. Down Hywel Rise and into Sheepy Lane to the main road she went not really thinking about where she was going, just enjoying the chill air on her face and the exercise.

She looked across the road and to her right and saw that there were lights on in the flat above Amy's shop. She thought of her parents sitting there, listening to the wireless and occasionally discussing what they heard. Dull people, nervous, anxious people and a world apart from herself. She walked past Evie and Timothy's house on the corner of Sheepy Lane and then past the church and the school. She crossed over the road then and saw Nelly and George with their two dogs approaching. More dull and boring people. She didn't want to talk to them so she went down the lane at the side of the fish and chip shop to the lane behind.

It was like the inside of a deep cave, she thought, the blackness was complete, almost like a wall in front of her, tangible and solid, and very unnerving. She paused, afraid to go further, imagining a thousand terrors awaiting her, close but beyond her vision. Best to wait until Nelly had passed then go back on to the road where there were lights and the possibility of people. She turned to face the glow from the main road, pressed her back against the wall of chip-shop yard and immediately felt safer.

There were lamp posts in the lane but they weren't lit, and beside the darkness the place was almost silent. Almost, but there was a sound, unrecognisable at first. Then she realised with rising curiosity that the faint hissing and sniffing was the muffled sound of someone crying.

The darkness held less threat as she recognised the nearness of another person. It must be Bethan, she decided. Making her way down the wall she called when she reached the gate,

"Hello, anyone there? Bethan, it's me, Mrs Davies, Sheila Powell as was. Are you all right?"

A light was switched on in the yard and she heard footsteps coming down the path to open the gate. A latch lifted. The gate opened and Bethan peered around its edge,

59

the light behind her throwing her face in shadow but her voice revealing her recent crying.

"What d'you want?" Bethan asked.

"Nothing, I heard you crying and I wondered if you were all right. Can I do anything?"

"Not unless you can chip half a hundredweight of potatoes for me." Bethan opened the gate wider. "Best you come in, it's cold standing out here."

"Surely you aren't peeling potatoes in this weather?" Sheila went into the cemented yard. The ground was wet, wetter than outside the yard and Bethan pointed to the buckets of chips soaking in water.

"I won't have time in the morning, what with everything else I have to do, I thought I'd get ahead of myself."

Sheila looked with disapproval at the sacks of potatoes, the pans in which batter was mixed and at the cold water that spilled into the buckets and over-flowed down the yard to the drain. How could anyone do this work day after day?

"You don't do all of this yourself?" she asked.

"Now I do. Since Griff has been arrested and Hilda has felt too distressed to come to work." She touched her eyes with a knot of a handkerchief and asked, "Are you going anywhere special? Fancy a cup of tea?"

"Make it coffee and it's Yes," Sheila said, "tea is so unsophisticated, don't you think?"

Bethan lead the way past the shed-cum-workroom and into a small snug living room where a fire glowed and music played. The *Sunday Dispatch* was spread across a low table, open at the serialisation of Winston Churchill's novel, *Savrola*. Sheila picked it up as if idly reading it while Bethan went to a corner and set the kettle to boil on the single burner gas jet. She wasn't reading but using the newspaper as a shield to look around the room, taking in the pleasant and comfortable chairs and the couch, the small table and two chairs in one corner, and the geometric design curtains in blue, red and brown that separated off a bed and a small cupboard. She realised that Bethan lived

60

here in a bed-sit while her son, Arthur, lived in the flat similar to her own parents' above the shop.

What luck, she thought, privacy and independance. But not worth ruining your hands washing potatoes for, she added with a disapproving curl of her lips. She looked at her own hands, already marked with cleaning out the ashes of her grandmother's fire every day, scrubbing the kitchen floor and front door-step and soaking for several hours each week while she did the weekly washing. Those things were necessary and quite enough without adding a daily dose of cold water and filthy potatoes! She shuddered at the thought.

Bethan put a saucepan of milk to boil and juggled with kettle and milk on the single jet until satisfied they were both hot enough. She poured milk and water into the cups on top of the coffee powder and finally handed a cup to Sheila.

"Where were you going?" Bethan asked.

"Nowhere in particular. I was a bit bored, fed up with my own company, so I came out for a walk. I ducked down the lane to avoid that old Nelly Luke and the tramp," she said unkindly. "Proper gossip she is and wants to know everything I do."

"I wish she'd come and help with the yard work," Bethan sighed. "I don't know how I'll manage now Griff doesn't come and Hilda is ill."

"Ill?" Sheila laughed. She showed her teeth in a smile brightened by special toothpaste which reddened the gums as she added, "I'll you say? Not when I last saw her! Off on the town she is and her dressed up like a twenty-year-old what's more! Spending money like she's won the pools, according to my mother. New clothes, new hair-do, lipstick so bright you'd want to post letters in her mouth."

Bethan looked puzzled. She frowned and stared at her visitor. "Sorry, I think we're talking on crossed lines. I'm talking about Hilda Evans, Griff's wife."

"And so," Sheila said with emphasis, "am I." She put down the cup of coffee on which a skin had formed and said sweetly, "Think she's found out about you and Griff then, do you?"

"What d'you mean?" For a moment Bethan straightened her back and began to protest, but then she drooped again, took out her sodden handkerchief and nodded. "I suppose it's common knowledge?"

"I wouldn't know about that, but my mother works in Amy's shop and what they don't know between them isn't worth bothering your head about!"

"What am I going to do?"

"Advertise. There must be plenty of people willing to work for a few hours each morning, that's all you need, isn't it? Pity that Arthur of yours isn't a bit older, or your dad a bit younger."

"Dad would help but Mam won't let him. She says it's bad enough having a daughter in the fish trade without dragging Dad in, too."

"Something special was he, your dad?"

"He worked in an office and to Mam that's second only to a profession like doctor or school teacher!" She sipped her coffee again then added in a low, disheartened voice, "What will I do?"

"Get a couple of postcards. I'll get one put in Amy's window and another one on the notice board in the church hall. Plenty of people will see them and I bet you'll have a job chosing from all the applicants!"

"Thanks, Sheila, I feel better already."

"Another thing. On your day off we'll go to the pictures and have a cup of coffee and a Kunzel cake."

"I don't open on Tuesday."

"Meet me from work then. Now, I have to go, must get my beauty sleep."

Sheila walked home and began to regret the impulse that had made her invite Bethan out for an evening. Bethan was years older, with a nine-year-old son and a lover who was at least forty-five. Bethan herself had to be thirty, almost the next generation! But still, she consoled herself, the pictures meant little time to chat and she could always make an excuse if another meeting was suggested.

In fact, she enjoyed the evening out more than she had imagined. Bethan, once out of the white overall in which she seemed to live most of her life, was a light-hearted companion and more daring when it came to smiling at young men than Sheila herself.

The difference between the two young women was in their experiences and up-bringing, not their ages. Bethan, she discovered, was only twenty-six, just four years her senior, but her manner and attitudes were much older. Sheila's influence would soon change those things and persuade Bethan that there was fun to be had in the wider world, outside Hen Carw Parc and its boring, dull inhabitants.

Between flirting with people in the cinema queue and in the pub where they boldly went for a shandy, and sharing their previous experiences and disappointments, they came to the conclusion that men were best taken in large numbers, not as solitary, inhibiting custodians.

After having their drinks and crisps paid for by two boys from the forestry that they had seen once or twice with Griff they caught the bus laughing and recounting the evening's adventures like school children after a party.

Bethan said goodbye and with a last giggling reminiscence went down the dark lane to her single room. Sheila walked up Sheepy Lane and on the way up Hywel Rise heading for St Illtyd's Road saw Delina stepping out of Tad Simmons's doorway. She hurried a moment, unable to resist an unkind remark to the girl who she thought had stolen Maurice from her.

"Courting again, are you?" she called, and smiled as Delina turned away and hurried back up the hill without replying.

Delina felt annoyed with Sheila for seeing her and for making a remark that touched a weak spot in her armour.

Since her cancelled wedding to Maurice Davies she had determined to avoid any involvement, but lately she had found excuses to visit Tad under the pretence that Dawn was the reason. She was having to admit to herself that although she had taken part responsibility for the daughter, she felt a growing interest in the father. What a pity that when Maurice emigrated he hadn't take Sheila with him.

Tonight she had called with a book which she had found while sorting out some of the cupboards that her mother had filled with memorabilia, and which Delina was gradually discarding. She had stayed to read a story to Dawn after the little girl had been put to bed by Tad, and when she had come down Tad had made coffee and a sandwich. On the previous Sunday, she remembered with some embarrassment, it had been a book on photography and a film for Dawn's camera. The Sunday before that a trifle for Dawn's supper. She had made one each for her brothers and her father, and when Victor failed to come in for tea she had carried the trifle in the glass dish down the road for Dawn.

On the Sunday before that, Tad and Dawn had called and invited her to go with them for a walk across the fields towards Billie Brown's farm. Sundays had become a special day, one to which she looked forward with growing pleasure. Now, Sheila shouting about her courting had spoilt it. She hurried up the hill and into her house wearing a frown that sat on her face like a beacon to warn her brothers not to argue.

Of her brothers Daniel was the least difficult, facing his mother's death with quiet acceptance. Almost eighteen, he knew where he was going in the world, his plans mapped out in front of him although he kept most of them to himself. He was tall and fair like his sister and had her serenity, and like her he kept his emotions in check and hadn't shed a tear over the loss of his mother.

David was far more of a problem and neither Delina nor her father could persuade him to talk about how he

64

felt. Whatever was suggested to him he disagreed. Pain or pleasures, he turned them all down and refused to co-operate. Now, Delina saw with a sigh, his shoes were uncleaned, and she could see one of his football boots still lying near the back door having been half washed, then left for her to see to.

Today, she thought with rising irritation, today I won't. He will have to wear them as they are and face his teacher's disapproval. Then she sighed. It was only a month since the funeral. The teacher would only hear him complain that his sister forgot. Sympathy for a boy who had lost his mother was something David was enjoying and something he would feed on for a long time.

The other boot was missing and when David came in she asked where it was.

"In the shed," the boy said in his surly way.

"What's it doing there?"

"I threw it there."

"Why?"

David left the room, slaming the door behind him and Delina picked up the torch and went to find the boots and clean them.

Perhaps that was why she was glad to visit Tad? Because it meant getting away from the situation of being unwilling mother to her brothers. In the sparsely furnished, uncomfortable house on Hywel Rise, she could pretend for a while that she wasn't becoming a drudge to her family. As soon as she stepped once more into her own home she felt the jaws of the trap closing.

The boot was in the shed. It had been thrown through a window to get there. She snapped off the torch and left the boot where it lay, among the shattered glass. She would leave a note for her father. This was something he must deal with, whatever time he came back from Amy's. Taking the daily papers with her, she went to bed.

Saturday morning was one of the times Nelly worked for Mrs French. She usually took the dogs with her and tied them up in the yard until she had finished, knowing they were much happier being with her than shut in on their own at home. November was on the way out and Mrs French had gone into Llan Gwyn to do some of the extra shopping that the approach of Christmas always entailed.

Nelly locked the door and pocketed the key as Mrs French had asked. Nelly and George would bring it down later when Mrs French returned. Since the burglaries of the previous summer people were more careful about locking doors and no longer hid keys under stones or behind the door on a string. Constable Harris's warnings on keeping keys safe from watching eyes had been heeded. Even though Griff Evans had confessed to the burglaries and house-breaking, the fear had remained.

The dogs began to bark before she had made sure the door was safe and she called to them to hush their row.

"It's me, Nelly," a young voice called and she opened the gate to see Dawn waiting for her.

"'Ello, young Dawn. What you doin' 'angin' about down 'ere?"

"I've been waiting for you," Dawn replied. She held up her camera given to her by Nelly and with which she had won a few small prizes. "Will you take me to see the gypsies? I want to take some photographs if they'll let me. D'you think they will?"

"O'course they will, friends of mine they are. But I ain't goin' wanderin' up the lane now. I got to get 'ome to get me dinner cookin'. Come an' 'elp why don't yer?" Nelly looked suspiciously at the camera, wondering where the girl had found the money for the film. As if reading her thoughts, Dawn said brightly:

"Delina gave me the film. She brought it down a couple of Sundays ago, with a book of photography."

"She's very kind to you, better'n you deserve some-times," Nelly chuckled.

"Oh, I know why she's nice to me. It's because she soft on my Dad," Dawn replied airily. "I've talked it over with the girls in school."

"Then you shouldn't. 'Er bein' a teacher she mustn't be made to look silly, or you and yer Dad'll be without 'er friendship, an' you'd miss 'er, wouldn't you?"

"Yes, Nelly, I won't talk about her and Dad again," Dawn said in the submissive way that didn't fool Nelly for a moment.

When they reached the cottage gate Nelly looked in surprise at the open back door. Although she had never succumbed to the anxiety that made everyone lock their doors, she usually pulled it shut and now it was standing wide and the chickens, freed from the run, were wandering in and out of the door.

"Someone's been here," she said to Dawn. "If that Phil's been in to make a cup of tea and forgotten to shut the door I'll – Oliver!" Her face creased into a welcoming smile as she recognised her grandson. "Let the chickens out for me I see!"

"Yes, Gran, and I've pushed the kettle a bit closer to the fire for your cuppa."

"Blimey, don't let your mother 'ear you sayin' cuppa or she'll stop you comin' again!"

"Mum and Dad have gone shopping and I'm here for you to look after me. I said you wouldn't mind."

He spoke in a formal way that seemed odd on such a small boy. He was very small for his age and thin. His hair was thin too; fair and straight and inclined to stick up. He patted the dogs that bounded to greet him as he walked up the cinder path to meet them.

As soon as he had appeared in the doorway Dawn waved and clung on to Nelly's arm possessively.

"Me and Nelly's going out later, to see the gypsies," she said, hoping it would be after his parents had come to claim him back.

"Good, I'll be able to come too," he said, his face lighting up. "Mother isn't here so we can't ask and be refused, can we, Gran?"

"You're gettin' as devious as the rest of us, Ollie, in spite of all yer mum's efforts!" Nelly laughed. "Come on, then,

let's get the dinner on it's way, an' 'ow about a cup of
cocoa and a sandwich then? Brawn suit yer?" Both children
pulled a face as Nelly knew they would. "All right, a bit
of cheese and a bag of crisps between us," she said with a
loud laugh.

It was raining as they set off an hour later and Dawn and
Oliver were sheltered under an old mac that belonged to
George. They each put an arm down a sleeve that was far
too long and laughed as they skipped along beside Nelly
and the two dogs. Down to the main road they went and
then right to where another lane led off towards Leighton's
farm. After a while the hedges became set further back from
the lane and a grass verge widened, and when they turned a
corner, they came upon the caravans and the paraphernalia
of the gypsies camp site.

There were three caravans settled for the winter, each
with its small collection of belongings gathered around
the steps. They were all painted green but each had been
decorated with beautiful designs so they were all different.
The flowers and scrolls touched with edgings of gold seemed
as if they had grown there, climbing around the immaculate
woodwork that had been carved by hand. The wheels and
the framework of the caravans and the intricately etched
glass inside the small orderly homes were a constant source
of fascination to Nelly.

There was a large iron pot on the grass nearby, out of
which Nelly had eaten many a savoury meal, and there was
a pile of wood covered with a tarpaulin besides which stood
a large, shining axe and a bow saw. Nearer the steps of the
first caravan was a kennel, a large dog tied to its entrance.
He was a lurcher, a breed that was popular with gypsies,
and poachers too. It stood at the furthest stretch of its lead
and growled disapproval of the intruders.

"Seems like Clara and the others are out," Nelly said.
"Still, this ain't the weather fer taking photographs, is it?"

"It'll be dry by evening," a voice said and Clara stepped
out on to the veranda at the top of her steps. She leaned
over the sill and smiled a greeting to them all. "Come in

68

and welcome, dogs and all," she said, and she kissed Nelly as they all climbed up the gaily painted steps and went inside the neat caravan.

Dawn and Oliver had seen Clara before. The gypsy woman was a regular winter visitor to the village, her people having camped in Gypsy Lane for longer than even Grandad Owen could remember, and he was over ninety. But the children were still nervous of the unusual woman, who wore black skirts and tops covered with beautifully embroidered shawls and scarves, and wore gold on her fingers and gold in her teeth, and whose hair was as black as night, coiled in intricate plaits around her small, slightly wizened face. They each fought to sit beside Nelly and away from their hostess. Clara saw and shared a look of amusement with Nelly.

"So this is your scholar of a grandson, grown hasn't he?"

"I'm no scholar," Oliver said, gradually beginning to feel at ease in the fascinating home. "I don't do well in school and that's being a scholar, isn't it?"

"Not yet, but as sure as the rain will stop before evening, you'll be a man people will look up to one day." Oliver looked at Nelly who winked and nodded her head.

They drank tea which tasted strange at first but which neither Dawn nor Oliver refused to drink for fear of teasing by the other. Then, while the two women talked, Dawn and Oliver studied the caravan and its foreign-looking contents; the china and brass that seemed only for show; the decorated doors which hid the necessities of life for people always on the move.

The day grew darker and the rain continued. When it was time to go, the evening had closed in around them. The fields were hidden by the falling rain and the sky seemed to have fallen around them like grey snow. Oliver didn't say anything about the darkness of the late afternoon, but he constantly looked up at the sky as they began to wave goodbye to Clara, his serious face anxiously watching for a break in the clouds. If the clouds lifted and the rain stopped

69

before dark, Clara said he would be a scholar. Of all the things he could wish for, he wished to be a scholar. It was what would please his parents most.

Nelly decided to walk both children home although it wasn't late. The dogs wouldn't mind the extra exercise and the pigs trotters she had simmering for dinner wouldn't harm for an extra few minutes. They went down to the main road again and walked slowly through the village, ignoring the rain that continued to fall.

In the fish and chip shop they could see Bethan preparing for opening. The door was open and they could see the gleam of the silver and glass counter. Bethan was in her white coat and busily cutting up reams of paper with a long knife. Nelly felt a brief sympathy for the young woman managing alone, but knew that she couldn't help. Doing for Mrs French and Mrs Williams and helping Amy was as much as she could comfortably manage.

She wondered about the unlikely friendship that had grown up between Bethan and Sheila Davies. She smiled as she imagined Sheila's reaction to being offered the job of cleaning potatoes. What those two had in common she couldn't think. Sheila bold and vain, Bethan shy and unsure of herself. Both had suffered from over-anxious parents though and perhaps that was enough of a bond upon which to build a friendship.

Although her son was now nine years old Bethan was still suffering from the shame of becoming pregnant and having to make up a story about a handsome American-soldier husband. Sheila's pregnancy had caused her very little embarrassment, in fact the young girl had gloried in the furore it had created. She had announced it just before Maurice and Delina Honeyman were to be married. One of the two young women would change, that much was certain, and somehow she doubted that it would be Sheila.

Amy's shop was still busy, she could see Amy and Mrs Powell serving inside through the mist-covered windows that had been wiped in wide sweeps to clear them.

A customer came out of the doorway and Nelly recognised her daughter.

"Evie!" she called, her raucous voice clearly heard by the well-dressed woman with the umbrella held above her curly hair. But Evie didn't look across the road, she hurried on. She reached her house on the corner of Sheepy Lane and by the time Nelly and the children had reached it she was standing in her door waiting for them.

Oliver stood at the gate for a final word with Nelly and Dawn. Evie called: "Come on, Oliver, I haven't got all day."

"'Ere, young Ollie," Nelly said as he closed the gate behind him. "'Ave you noticed anything?"

Oliver looked up and spread his hands as if to catch raindrops. Then his thin face lit up and he shouted, "It's stopped raining. Clara was right!"

"And if she's right about that then she's right about other things as well, like you being a scholar."

Nelly waved as he ran down the path excitedly shouting, "Fine before evening, fine before evening! Good old Clara!"

"Clara?" she heard her daughter say in tones of accusation. "Clara? You haven't been to see those dreadful gypsies again have you?"

The door closed and Nelly sighed and looked down at Dawn "One day I'll persuade my Evie to come with me and see fer 'erself just how well Clara lives."

"She won't go, she's the sort that prefers not to know so she can grumble."

Nelly looked at the ten-year-old in surprise. Dawn was maturing, fast!

CHAPTER SIX

One evening after school, while Delina was preparing to cook the evening meal and David was attempting to deal with his homework, Dawn had nothing to do. A few months before she would have been looking for some mischief to involve herself in, but now, with the steadying influence of Delina to help, she was less inclined to create trouble for herself and others. She daren't talk to David who, although obviously lacking concentration on what he was supposed to be studying, was likely to complain to Delina that Dawn was disturbing him.

She quietly opened the back door and looked out at the star-beaded sky and shivered. It was too cold to even consider standing out there until Delina was free to talk to her. But then she remembered the first words Delina had spoken when they had entered the front door. She had asked David if he had cleaned out the rabbit hutches as he had promised. David had bent his head and shrugged. Dawn, with the remnants of rebellion still about her, had recognised the defiance and hurt in the drooped shoulders and the sulky response.

Closing the door behind her she hurried across to the shed where the rabbits lived during the dark hours and began to clean them out. When Delina called her for dinner she ran in and straight up to the bathroom to clean herself. She said nothing of what she had been doing to either Delina or David. Tomorrow morning, when David carried them to the large run where they spent their day, he would know and might even be pleased.

"Can I ask you a favour, Delina?" Dawn asked as she and Delina prepared to leave for her own house.

"Of course. What is it?"

"Can we go and see Nelly and George before you take me home?"

"It's rather late, can't it wait until the weekend?"

"Well, it could, but it might be too late."

"All right," Delina smiled. "But we can't stay long, mind. Your father will wonder where we are if you aren't in bed when he gets home from night-school."

The back door of Nelly's cottage was open and from it the sounds of laughter came to greet them. Dawn pulled Delina to a stop.

"They've got visitors."

"Perhaps. Or it might be the radio. Come on, we can always make our excuses if you don't want to stay. We'll say we were out for a walk and called in to say hello. All right?"

As they touched the gate the dogs pushed the door open wider with their noses and ran up the path to meet them, their muffled barks of pleasure heard by the sharp-eared Nelly.

The door spilled out a wedge of lamp-light and Nelly's plump figure was silhouetted in the doorway.

"Come on in out of the cold," she called, "'oo ever you are."

"It's me," Dawn answered. "Me and Delina, come to say hello."

They hurried in and pushed the door to behind them. To Dawn's relief only George sat beside the roaring fire. He was asleep, his rosy skin reddened by the fire's glow, the beard white and silky, the gentle blue eyes closed. He looked larger than usual, slumped across the couch, his long legs across the hand-made rag rug, his feet touching the brass fender.

Nelly turned off the radio and he woke, opened his eyes and stiffly rose to greet them.

"I must have dropped off for a moment," he said, smiling and rubbing his face with his hands. Nelly pushed the kettle nearer to the heat.

"Stay for a cuppa why don't yer," she smiled, pushing the dogs out of the way so Delina could get to the couch. Dawn found her usual place on the floor and at once the dogs went to lean on her, their long tongues washing her bare knees.

"Silly things." Dawn smiled up at Nelly. "If I move, they'll fall over!"

"They does it all the time, they never learn," Nelly laughed.

"George, remember us saying your garden needs a pond?" Dawn said when they were all seated and comfortable. "A few weeks ago it was, when you finished digging up your garden for the pipes to be laid for your bathroom."

"Yes, I remember," George replied. "When the weather is warmer we'll make a start on it."

"D'you think we could start now?"

"There isn't much daylight at this time of the year, and it's a bit cold for you to be out of doors."

"There's Saturday afternoon and Dad wants me to go into town to help him with some shopping. I thought –"

"You thought you don't want to go, young Dawn," Nelly grinned.

"Well, Delina is going too and they won't need me to help carry things, will they?"

"We were intending to buy you a new jumper for school," Delina laughed. "How can we choose it without you with us? We might buy something you don't like."

"I'll like it, I promise I'll like it!" Dawn said earnestly.

"Dawn," George said hesitatingly. "I don't think I feel like starting yet. By the time I've finished at Leighton's farm at twelve and come home and had a bite to eat well, the day is almost gone."

"Sunday then?"

"All right," George agreed, "we'll make a start but just an hour or so."

"Thanks, George."

*　　*　　*

74

Nelly was surprised by the lack of enthusiasm on George's part. He usually loved the company of the children and welcomed any excuse to invite them down during his spare hours. After Delina and Dawn had gone she asked him if he would rather abandon his promise.

"You don't have to start the pond yet, George, not if you don't want to. Dawn won't be upset if you leave it 'til the spring. The ground'll be hard with this frost."

"We'll make a start and if I feel too tired we'll leave it for later."

Her stomach churned in alarm. It was the first time George had admitted to being tired, yet over the last few days he had slept on the couch almost as soon as he had eaten his meal. Surely he wasn't ill? The thought frightened her. They had been married such a short time and he had lived with her in the cottage on the edge of the village only months. Surely he wasn't going to die and leave her.

"Come on, dearie, I think I need an early night, don't you?" She was even more alarmed when he willingly agreed.

Bert Roberts tried, in his rigidly official way, to arrange a meeting to begin a village gardening club. He made a list of those he thought should be present and tried time and again to chose an evening on which they were all available. Timothy and Evie Chartridge weren't interested in gardening but insisted they were included for the prestige it might bring to the village. That was something they wanted to share. Johnny Cartwright, working shifts, was difficult to pin down but he, too, demanded that he be included. Phil Davies and his brother Sidney also warned Bert not to start without them.

He repeatedly planned a meeting then had to cancel it because one or other of the main enthusiasts were unable to attend.

"And," as he explained to his critics, "we have to have the main participants. Without the main participants we can't get started!"

The meeting eventually took place, impromptu, in the living room of Ethel Davies, who lived in a small cottage off Sheepy Lane. The house was almost hidden from passers-by, tucked in among the trees and backing onto a field, yet half the village turned up there some time during each week and sat to share a pot of tea and some of Ethel's baking.

If they missed a bus and had half an hour to wait, it was at Ethel's they waited. If there was some gossip to share or to which they wanted some fresh additions, Ethel Davies' was the place to go. All through the long years of food rationing, when cake making was almost impossible, Ethel managed to find something for callers to eat with their cup of tea. It was partly due to the generosity of her friends, who often found an extra ounce of fat or some unneeded sugar to give her, and partly due to the illegal generosity of the local farmers who also found a welcome break from the rigors of winter work in her cosy room.

Ethel Davies had four sons. Phil-the-post was a regular caller as was Sidney. Teddy lived in Swansea and worked in a factory and her youngest and best-loved was Maurice who had married Sheila Powell before going to Australia.

On this Saturday afternoon the room was already full by twelve o'clock, with Phil-the-post visiting his mother and bringing her messages from the people he met on his rounds, and her son Sidney, sitting with George and Leighton, having just finished lifting the last of the sugar-beet in the field behind her house. Nelly was there, too, with her dogs looking longingly at the plate of sandwiches Ethel had produced.

It was Johnny and Fay arriving and close behind them Billie Brown and his sister Mary-Dairy – who had just finished her milk-round – that gave Phil the idea.

"We're most of us here, so why don't we make this the official first meeting of the Hen Carw Parc Gardening Club!" he suggested. The roar of approval was filled with laughter at the chance of outwitting Bert Roberts.

76

It was quickly arranged that Johnny should make enquiries about the bulk purchase of hanging baskets and tubs, and Billie offered the use of his large greenhouse that had once been used to grow tomatoes but which had fallen into disrepair. Ethel sat at the table, her deep eyes watching with amusement, as they argued about who should grow what. She wrote down all the relevant details and, with Fay helping, made a copy of the list for each person present, with a special copy embellished with drawings for Bert.

With the inexplicable telepathy that spread through the village, Bert and his quiet wife, Brenda, arrived as they were preparing to depart. Nelly and George were at the door and Fay was helping Johnny to clear the dishes and wash them for Ethel.

"Just in time, boy," Phil called. "We've got news for you.

Ethel took Brenda on one side and plied her with tea and cake while the others explained to Bert how far the arrangements had gone. Bert nodded approval as he noted the items on the list.

"Not bad for a start off," Bert said. He took out a pencil and ticked each item as it was explained to him. "Now we have to get down to the real work, persuading some of you lazy sods to get digging."

"I think we all ought to think what we're going to do and then bring the plans here, to Ethel. We can all look them over and share any ideas for improving them."

"We can use my garage for storage," Bert offered. "And you can all start off by handing me ten shillings towards the first order, right?"

And so it was decided. Ethel's cottage on Sheepy Lane was HQ and Bert Roberts was the quarter master. Fay, to Johnny's surprise and delight, offered to be secretary and decided to begin by writing to various firms for offers of help. Mrs Norwood Bennet-Hughes's idea was underway. Hen Carw Parc was set to win the competition for the Best Kept Village.

*   *   *

The pond in Nelly and George's garden was intended to be a part of the grand plan but when George and Dawn began to dig it out Nelly saw at once that George was finding it hard. She went out with a large fork and began to loosen the soil for them to lift out. After an hour, during which time the pond hardly looked more than an untidy patch of amateur digging, George admitted he had had enough.

Disconsolately, Dawn went home.

"I was hoping there'd be some frogs in there by the spring, Dad," she complained to Tad. "And there's all the concreting to do yet. It won't be finished in time for next year!"

Tad discussed it with Delina when Dawn was in bed. He would like to help but was never sure how well his offers to join in the village activities would be received. Tad had arrived in the village with a very defiant and difficult daughter in tow. The ten-year-old Dawn had been a source of trouble from the moment they arrived, wandering about at night and stealing from those who tried to help her and, if it had not been for the generosity of the villagers, Dawn would almost certainly have been taken from him.

He was grateful but still found it difficult to show his appreciation. His quick temper and his habit of hitting out at those who angered him had hardly endeared him to his neighbours and although they appeared to have forgiven if not forgotten his attacks, he was unable to relax and become one of them.

Even his relationship with Delina was still fraught with anxiety. He was more and more attracted to the quiet, gentle, and very beautiful, young woman, but feared losing her if he showed his regard for her. He was bitterly aware of how little he could offer her.

"D'you think George would be cross with me if I asked Billie to help us?" Dawn broke into his thoughts to ask.

"I think he might," Tad said. "It's his garden and if it were me I wouldn't take kindly to someone coming in and telling me what to do."

"But George wants it done, he's just tired after working all day for Farmer Leighton, Dad."

"I'll come down with you and ask if I can help. How will that be?"

"Thanks, Dad!"

"But if he is even slightly hesitant, then we won't say any more, right young lady?"

"Promise, Dad," she said, but her eyes were shining. George wouldn't refuse help, she was sure of it.

She went upstairs to look through her growing collection of photographs and began to plan how she would show, with the aid of her camera, the developement of the wild-life pond. She had already taken several snaps, the first showing George standing with the spade in his hands ready to take out the first sod. She thought of the word "sod", and wondered with a grin if she dare use it to describe the first photograph. It would be fun to see the Mr Chartridge's face when he saw it.

George agreed happily to Tad's offer of help with the pond, mainly because he knew how difficult it was for the young man to make friends. He and Nelly had seen Dawn through some of her most difficult times and the reward had been a punch in the nose from her irate father. George smiled as he remembered the dull ache that had lasted for days, as he watched the small man efficiently removing the soil from the marked out area that was to be the pond. Better way to deal with frustration, he thought, and wondered if the tension in Tad had lessened or whether he was simply better at concealing it.

Delina called at the cottage after morning church and when he saw the way Tad greeted her George knew that Victor's beautiful daughter was the reason for Tad's growing sociability.

"Come on, Dawn, we'll go and help Nelly with the cups of tea, shall we?" he suggested, leading Dawn away from the couple near the gradually enlarging hole.

79

"Dawn told me you were helping with the pond," Delina smiled. "That's very kind of you."

"I have more than a suspicion that it's Dawn's pestering that made George want to start it now instead of the spring," Tad smiled. "Insistent my daughter, as well you know."

"I think this will be a fascination for many of the children, and if I know Nelly and George they'll love the extra visitors it will bring."

It wasn't only children who were interested in the progress of the pond. On Monday morning Phil-the-post called. He had no letters for Nelly but stayed for a cup of tea and a look at the work in progress.

"Tad did most of it," Nelly told him as they looked at the neat hole ready for the concrete. "I don't think George is all that well, and although he don't complain, that not bein' 'is way, I'm worried that he'll try and do too much."

"I'll have a word with Johnny and Sidney," Phil promised. "They'll make an excuse to come and give a hand."

"I'd better make some more cakes," Nelly said as Phil finished his fourth.

On a Saturday in early December George arrived home from the farm with Sidney Davies to begin the mixing of the concrete. George was at once given the position of foreman while Johnny, Sidney and Victor Honeyman set about the work. Phil was there too but, Nelly noticed with a chuckle, he avoided the heavy work with practised ease. Dawn came with Tad and Delina called in on her way from town with her brother David. Oliver and Margaret were there and Nelly's face was a constant smile as her garden and kitchen were filled with the noisy, good-natured crowd. The only worry was George, although he seemed less weary and he too was smiling happily amid the friendly jeering and the insults flying between the helpers.

It was dark before they had finished and boards and sacks had been placed over the pond to protect its new surface. Nelly held her tilley lamp for them to see by

80

for the last few minutes, its gentle hissing and circle of soft light adding a magic touch to the evening. With the close of day the voices of the men were lowered and their figures, moving in and out of the light as they cleaned their tools and made everything tidy, tempted Dawn to try her luck with some extra photographs. She took several of her father and Delina.

Amy closed the shop and walked up, laden with some left-over food, to collect Margaret. The cottage was still full, with Nelly and George handing out beer, home-made lemonade and meat-paste sandwiches. Nelly was red-faced in the heat of the small room, laughing at the remarks of the men.

"I don't know what it is about you, Nelly," Amy laughed, "but everything you plan ends up as a party!"

"Stay why don't yer? There ain't much beer left, but I 'spect Victor'll give you a sip of 'is," Nelly laughed.

Dawn was in her usual place with the dogs sitting beside her, their long legs a constant hazard to anyone foolish enough to try and move. She looked up and watched her father talking to Delina and her heart felt sad. The way they looked at each other excluded her. She knew that for her, life was going to take yet another change of direction. She frowned as she wondered how she would cope with having Delina for a mother. No, she realised with alarm, her *step*-mother. The connotations of the title deepened her frown.

"What's the matter, young Dawn?" Nelly asked, and voices stopped and looked at the glum-faced girl.

"I've finished the roll of film and I haven't enough pocket money to have it developed," she extemporised. "I'll be ever so glad when I'm grown up," she added with a deep sigh.

Delina walked back with Dawn and Tad in the deepening darkness, and she found it difficult to see her way clearly with the torch beam giving its slender thread of light. It was Tad who held her arm to guide her. She felt herself stiffen at his touch, the shock making her want to move away from his protection, but she didn't. With Dawn and David following behind and Tad gripping her arm and forcing her to feel his warmth, she walked slowly to Tad's gate where they would part. But Tad walked on.

"We'll see you safely home tonight," he said. "It isn't often that I can."

At the house where Delina lived Tad hesitated. "Will you come in?" Delina asked. Silently Tad agreed. Behind them Dawn and David followed.

Delina was at a loss. She wasn't sure why Tad had come. Should she offer some supper? In her mind she rummaged through what she had in the house that would produce a meal for them all.

"I just wanted to see you home," Tad smiled. "I'll go now. I need a walk and to freshen up after all that messing about with cement."

"I'll see you on Monday, then?" Delina said to Dawn. "Oh, and this is for you, for helping David with his chores." She handed the girl a shilling. "Perhaps it will help to pay for your film to be developed. She turned to her brother. "David, haven't you got something to say to Dawn?"

"Thank you for cleaning out the rabbits."

The words came out in a surly staccato and Delina began to protest, but she changed her mind. Best not start an argument now, she would talk to him later.

Dawn sensed the change in her father the moment Delina had closed the door. She had no idea what had caused his temper to return, but from the way he walked and the tightness of his lips as he hurried her back down the hill something had changed his mood from a happy one to the approach of ill-temper. She wanted to chatter, talk about the beginnings of the pond and how she had planned her series of pictures, but she held her tongue. Now wasn't the time. She would tell Delina on the way to school on Monday.

Tad's anger had been caused by Delina giving Dawn a shilling. He was so short of money that although he longed to help Dawn with her hobby, he couldn't. Seeing Delina rewarding his daughter for some imagined favour tightened the rage, frustration and dismay around his heart. When would he ever escape from the mess he was in? The fact that the mess was not of his making only made him feel worse. If there had been something in himself that needed changing he would do it. But caught as he had been by a war, losing his opportunity for a university place, and then losing his wife while Dawn was a baby, it seemed that the gods were heaping disaster after disaster on top of him. Now, with Delina coming into his life at a time when he had less than nothing to offer, it seemed that the fates were even more determined to torment him. Paying the rent and buying food and the occasional item of clothing was all he could manage.

Why did he have to fall in love with Delina? If he had been able to remain detached and simply grateful for her help with Dawn things would have improved. He would have been free to study knowing Dawn was safely cared for and life would have become more tolerable. Delina had handled Dawn firmly yet with a genuine affection and the child had responded to her in a way that was quite amazing. His own response to Delina's friendship was the problem now and there was nothing he could do about it.

"Here you are, Dawn." He handed her half a crown. He would have to manage without a canteen meal for a day or two but that wouldn't kill him. "Put it towards your photographs."

Ethel's house was flooded with drawings and plans for gardens and displays over the next few days as more and more people heard of the village gardening club and added their contributions. Her table was covered with lists of plants and orders for seeds and Fay called in often on her way home to add to it, showing copies of letters she had written and the replies. There was an air of excitement throughout the village that seemed to threaten the celebration of Christmas. Everyone was looking further ahead to the day when the judges would travel along the roads and lanes to see the results of their efforts.

Nelly's pond was laboriously emptied and refilled twice to get rid of the lime making it safe for any creature that decided to make it's home there. Bert Roberts excelled himself.

"Leave the emptying of the pond to me, George, he announced one day as he hurried down the cinder path and into the living room. "Look what I found up in the loft!" It was a stirrup pump. "Left over from the war. Miracle it was still there. I'll get it done in no time with this. The pump was a remnant of the time when every fire-watcher had one on hand in case of incendiary bombs. With one end in a bucket of water, the handle had to be pumped up and down to spray the fire.

With great enthusiasm Bert lowered the end of the hose into the water and pumped the handle up and down, while the water flowed away down the garden.

"I'd better 'elp with me bucket or we'll be all day squirtin'," Nelly said, bending to fill the bucket she had once used to carry her water down from the tap in the lane.

Panting with the effort but smiling in delight at being able to use the forgotten tool, Bert admired the emptied pool, then set to help re-fill it. He left the pump at the side of the house for the final emptying a week or so later.

"I want it back, mind, there's no telling how valuable it'll be with this garden competition coming off."

Nelly was tired with the bending and lifting and when she went inside she lay back in her chair and dosed. George came in from the farm an hour later and, without disturbing her, settled opposite her on the couch. Within minutes he, too, was sleeping and darkness crept into the corners of the room and the kettle sang on the side of the fire and it was the sighing of the hungry dogs that eventually woke them.

Delina went with Dawn to collect her photographs from the camera shop in town, but Dawn wouldn't let her see them.

"I want to show Dad first," she said, although she was dying to look at them herself.

It was one of the evenings Tad went to school so Delina was there when he came home. Delina had allowed Dawn to wait up to show him the photographs when he came in. She watched him as he smiled over the ones taken around the pond, many of the characters revealing themselves to the sharp observations of his talented ten-year-old. The good humour of Johnny and Phil, Nelly leaning back and laughing over some stupid joke, then, his face changed and he hurriedly tucked one of the photographs under the pile. Curious, Delina asked to see it. It showed herself and Tad, and the way they were looking at each other left no doubt as to their feelings for each other.

"She's very clever, your Dawn," Delina said when Dawn had been settled into bed. "She has a rare ability to show what people are thinking."

"She's just a child."

"We aren't, Tad."

He looked at her then. She remained still, her lovely blue eyes looking into his own as he fought with his emotions. He turned away but she rose and came to stand beside him.

Above them, Dawn had crept from her bed and sat listening, watching, from the landing.

"It's no use," Tad said. "What have I got to offer?" His voice was barely heard.

"Your love?"

"It isn't enough."

"How d'you know if you don't ask?"

He still stood a little apart from her and she knew she dare not say any more. Perhaps she was wrong and his attraction to her was less than she believed. She had already said more than she intended. Tad was not a man to take kindly to pressure. Hardly daring to breathe she waited for him to say something or to move, either towards or away from her.

He turned slowly and she was unable to read the expression on his face. Was it tight with anger? embarrassment? regret?

"You know I love you, don't you?" he said and the solemn expression was one of confusion and indecision.

"You know I love you. It must be clear if Dawn can see it."

"What should we do?"

"Tad," she asked softly, "what d'you want to do?"

"This." His arms were around her and he pressed her against him with a groan. Their lips met in a kiss so sweet that for them both it was as if they had been lost in a bewildering landscape and were at last safely home.

Dawn watched them with a mixture of excitement, guilt and fear. What would happen to her now?

CHAPTER SEVEN

Delina walked home after a brief and hesitant talk with Tad. They loved each other but that wasn't the end of anything. It was a beginning; a beginning of problems that seemed insuperable. She was responsible, whether she wanted it or not, for the day to day running of her father's home and the care and support of her brothers. Tad had no money to support a wife and needed to study for his place in the world. And there was Dawn. Where, in all that, could they find level ground on which to build a marriage? Because marriage was what they both wanted. The first thing, she decided, was to talk to her father.

She began to think about how she would broach the subject but when she got home and opened the door and saw Victor sitting beside the fire, she couldn't discuss it. This revelation between herself and Tad was new and very fragile and for tonight, at least, she wanted to keep it safe and private, to hug it and allow it to simmer in her heart. It was something wonderful, this thing that was newly burst upon her, yet, she remembered with a stab of unease, not so many months ago she had been planning to marry Ethel Davies' son, Maurice. Thinking of Maurice now gave her a strong feeling of relief that the wedding hadn't happened. This love she had for Tad was different and so absolutely right. Maurice was handsome and had awoken her to womanhood, but it was Tad who had really made her realise the meaning of true love.

"All right, Delina?" Victor called as she closed the door. "A bit late aren't you?"

"Yes. Tad and I had something to discuss."

"Have you got time to discuss something with me?" Victor asked.

"Of course," she replied, her spirits dropping. She wanted the privacy of her own room and her own thoughts tonight. "But I still have some preparation to do for school."

"I won't keep you, it's just that, well, how d'you think the boys would take it if Amy and I were to marry?"

She wanted to reply: How would you all take it if I married? but she didn't. She said, "I think that if it's what you want, and if you know it's really right for you, then you and Amy will work out any problems that crop up. Why, have you asked her?"

"Many times, love, but sometimes it's yes and other times it's no. We're convinced about wanting to be married, but afraid of what it will mean to the others involved. There's you and David and Daniel, and Margaret and Freddie. There are so many reasons not to that I sometimes despair."

"It's more likely to be because Mam had to die to make it possible," Delina spoke firmly and saw her father's head jerk around, his eyes staring at her.

"Don't say that! I didn't want you mother to leave me in that way."

"Of course you didn't. That's what I'm saying. You and Amy must remind yourselves that what happened wasn't what either of you wanted. You aren't to blame. Wishing someone isn't there won't kill them. That's a foolish superstition and needs weeding out by the roots."

"And what about you, Delina love? How do you feel about having Amy for a step-mother?"

"I – I might have plans of my own before long, but whatever happens, I'd welcome her if she makes you happy."

"Thanks, love." Victor was so deeply immersed in thoughts of his own future he didn't think of the implication of Delina's words until much later.

"Dad, d'you think it might be a good idea for us all to

get together, you and Amy and Margaret, me and the boys?"

Victor smiled and shook his head. "I don't think I could face it, love. Not yet. I think Daniel will be amenable to anything we decide, but I think I'd better wait until David is less of a handful, don't you?"

"No," Delina said in her quiet yet firm way. "I think we ought to clear the air a little and the sooner the better."

Hilda Evans had startled her son, Pete, by coming home with a new hair-style and some smart clothes, but that was nothing to the surprise he had when, while he was queueing for the pictures one evening, he saw her arm in arm with a strange man. He left his pale lanky friend, Gerry Williams, and ran after the couple, hoping against hope that he had been mistaken and that the heavily made up woman was not his mam. It was.

"Ma," he said, "where you going?"

"Just for a drink with my friend, Pete." She turned a smiling face to her companion and said, "This is Pete, my son. Pete, this is – "

"I don't want to know who he is. I think you ought to remember where our Dad is!"

He ran off and Gerry called after him as he ran past the waiting queue but he didn't hear. He ran on, through the town to the lane where they had left the motor-cycles. He kicked-started his angrily. What a mess. Dad in prison waiting trial and Mam carrying on with God knows who, dressed like a tart.

He rode around the town for more than an hour, then went back to the cinema queue. Gerry wasn't there and when he went back to the place where they had left the motor-cycles Gerry's vehicle had gone. He rode off back to Hen Carw Parc, not to go home, but to ask Gerry's mother if he could stay there. How could he go home and face his mother knowing she was "carrying on"? He returned to the house near the fish and chip shop briefly and left a note to tell his mother where he was then went to the council house where Gerry and his brothers lived with their parents.

When he returned home after three days, fed up with the noisy household and the lack of decent food, he had another surprise. All the furniture had been changed. Hilda had spent most of the remainder of Griff's money and had completely re-furnished her home.

She smiled a welcome with her new and better fitting false teeth, didn't bother to ask where he had been, and said cheerfully, "Tomorrow I'm having the locks changed. Your father isn't coming back here again."

"Who was he, Ma?"

"You mean the man with me in town? No one important, just someone I met in a pub. He was walking me back to the bus stop, that's all. It's nice to make a few friends after all the years I've had to put up with only your Dad for company."

Pete stared at his mother in disbelief. *She* was the stranger! He hadn't been told, but he guessed she had found out about his dad and that Bethan in the fish and chip shop. He wondered if she had also worked out that Griff was the father of Arthur Toogood, Bethan's illegitimate son.

Bethan Toogood and Sheila Davies quickly became friends. Sheila's boldness appealed to the shy young woman who had rarely travelled further than Llan Gwyn. Now, under Sheila's tutelage, Bethan began to discover the delights of café's, public houses and dance-halls. She didn't have very much money: her mother, Milly Toogood, demanded a large sum each week for taking care of Arthur.

Now, with Sheila reminding her that life was short and meant for fun, she gradually increased the amount she kept for herself and soon the ubiqitous white overall was a thing of the past. Only when she was serving in the shop was it seen. At other times Bethan showed her trim figure in angora jumpers and slim fitting skirts that were shorter than the approved length by several inches. A pair of high-heeled shoes and a saucy hat made her feel different and, over a period of only a few weeks, act differently, too.

She still needed Sheila's company to support her new image, and when Freddie was home and Sheila not available she sank back into her previous existence and hid herself away in her solitary room behind the shop.

The day that Freddie came home for his pre-Christmas visit he didn't tell anyone he was coming. He had parcels for his mother and Margaret, and one for Sheila and he intended to surprise them all by arriving without warning. He was late getting into Swansea. His train reached the town at ten o'clock at night and he managed to get a bus to Llan Gwyn, knowing he was likely to have to walk the last lap of his journey.

He was quite cheerful as he walked through the town where late-night drinkers were gradually leaving the public houses and the crowds on the pavements were thinning as buses took them back to their homes. He was half running, hoping to get to the bus stop in time for the last bus to Hen Carw Parc when he saw them, Sheila and Bethan wandering towards the bus stop as if there was plenty of time. From the way they were laughing, he suspected they were drunk.

"Sheila? Where are you going at this time of night?"

"Freddie, darling!" She hugged him, her welcome leaving him in no doubt as to her genuine delight at the unexpected encounter. "Home, that's where we're going, if we haven't missed the bus." She smiled at him, widened her eyes in a way that made his heart flip and then hugged him again, while Bethan stepped back wondering whether to go or stay. "Freddie Prichard, where have you sprung from? I've missed you. Are you coming home with me?"

"I ought to go to Mam's but – "

"But you won't," she whispered, touching her tongue against his lips and then smiling provocatively. A chorus of "oohs" and "aahs" came from a group of boys passing by and she smiled at them, too, her head tilted, her lips parted. Then she turned to Bethan. "Bethan and I were

91

going for a taxi, now we can all go together. Oh, Freddie, it's *won*-derful to have you back." She pressed herself against his rough uniform and for the moment she almost meant it.

Freddie had forgotten Sheila's companion and the fact that he had suspected them of being drunk. They had just been fooling around, laughing because they might have missed the bus. She was five years older than himself but she was so young and helpless that she made him feel mature beyond his years. He asked nothing from life other than looking after her and protecting her from all life's dangers. He loved her for her helplessness as well as her sexual attractiveness.

He smiled at Bethan, the street lamp shining on his glasses and concealing the curious expression in his eyes. Bethan Toogood and Sheila? It wasn't a combination he could ever have imagined.

"Come on then, let's find ourselves a taxi." He shepherded his charges to the taxi rank, felt in his pocket for some money and thought that once again he would arrive home and almost immediately have to ask his mother for a loan that neither expected to see repaid.

Freddie's leave was short and having spent the first night of it with Sheila he felt tempted to return to his camp without letting his mother know had had been home. Smiling at Sheila he said:

"But that's impossible. Can you imagine doing anything here in this village without half the population knowing within fifteen minutes and the rest being told before twenty four hours have passed? No, I'll have to go down and see them. I want to anyway. Mam's letters have been a bit edgy lately. I think she's worried about something."

"We'll go after lunch and be back for a few hours, alone, after tea." The way she said "alone" made Freddie's heart somersault in his chest. He had wondered during the long hours he spent thinking about her, whether his mind had flipped with his heart-beat and he had only dreamt of being in her bed. It was something he had wanted for so long that he was half afraid it had all been in his imagination. Her welcome on the night of his return had convinced him that, at last, Sheila loved him as much as he loved her. Once she was clear of the unfortunate marriage to Maurice, life would really begin for him. Sheila as his wife, and work in some garden, that was all he wanted.

Amy knew Freddie was home. Coming into the shop to start work she had been greeted by Milly Toogood.

"Your Freddie's on leave then?"

Recovering swiftly, she had said airily "yes", pretending she had known. Then she spent the rest of that Saturday morning wondering if she would see him or whether he was going to spend the whole of his leave with that Sheila Davies. Mavis Powell would mind the shop while she went up to the council houses, and for a while she was tempted, but she decided it best to wait and see if he came. Once she began a confrontation, even hinted at resentment towards Sheila, it could easily accelerate, and the last thing she wanted was to have a less than easy relationship with her son. Not now, when there were so many problems to face.

At lunchtime he came into the shop with Sheila on his arm. He carried his kit-bag across his shoulder and when she saw them crossing the road she felt the usual stab of pain. He was so like Harry Beynon. He was a strongly built young man, looking more than his age, with a maturity about him in the serious expression in the blue eyes behind the rimless glasses, glasses like Harry had worn. And his eyes, like Harry's, they could suddenly show mirth or wickedness and, she thought with a momentary sadness, compassion and deep love.

"Freddie, love. I heard you were home. Milly Toogood took pleasure in telling me."

"Sorry I didn't let you know, Mam, I thought I'd surprise you." He kissed her and she gave him a hug, surprised at how he had filled out. Rather plump he had been as a child, the softness had hardened into muscle.

"Come and have some food," she invited, but Sheila smiled and said:

"It's all right, Mrs Prichard, we've eaten. Freddie was too hungry to wait, you know what his appetite is like." She glanced at Freddie, her eyes widening, and Amy felt a wave of embarrassment, guessing what appetite the girl was hinting at, hoping she was wrong. Freddie was too young, Sheila was married. Yet the looks that were passing between them told her clearly the unacceptable story.

When Amy put the key in her front door after the shop had closed, voices were coming from the living room. She heard Margaret and Oliver, and then the rather strident voice of her sister, Prue. She groaned. So much for a pleasant talk with her son. First Sheila in tow and now a visit from Prue!

Even before she called a greeting she began the automatic process of thinking out what they could eat. Margaret and Oliver would be sure to be hungry and Prue might want a sandwich. As for herself, all she could expect to do was drink a cup of tea, feed the rest, and get back to the shop. What a disappointment. Freddie on leave, a dozen things to discuss with him and it all dissolving into a few hurried moments surrounded by others.

Prue stood up and pulled on her coat the moment she saw them walk in. Wondering what had caused the sudden departure she glanced at her sister, about to ask if she wouldn't stay for a moment longer, then saw the venomous glance Prue was giving Freddie. Freddie, too, looked ill at ease. He must be a constant reminder to Prue of her husband's infidelity. I can hardly blame her for feeling angry with Freddie, Amy sighed, even though he could hardly be blamed for being born. She helped her sister out and declined to issue an invitation for her to stay.

On Tuesday mornings Nelly cleaned for Mrs Williams who lived at the end of the village near *The Drovers*. Today she was late finishing her work. She had intended to be home in time to have some food ready for George, but

94

with the extra Christmas cleaning it would have to be fish and chips.

When she went into the gleaming, glass- and chrome-fitted shop it was empty. The lunchtime rush hadn't yet begun. Hoping Bethan wouldn't notice, she hauled the dogs in behind her and pushed them to sit against the counter.

"Fish an' chips twice an' two meat pies fer the dogs," she instructed Bethan. "An' what's this about you an' that Sheila Davies out on the town then? Gettin' lively all of a sudden, ain't yer?"

"Fish and chips twice, and as the pies are a bit small I'll let you have three for the price of two," Bethan said, reddening under her newly applied makeup.

Nelly wondered how her words could have caused the young woman to feel uncomfortable. Surely her friendship with the flighty Sheila wasn't a secret? Then she turned and saw the real reason for Bethan's discomfort. Hilda Evans had walked in behind her.

"'Ello, Hilda," Nelly smiled. "Perishin' cold, ain't it?"

"My new coat keeps me nice and warm, thanks, Nelly." Hilda smiled with her new teeth and stroked the fur collar of her grey coat. "My Griff has bought me lots of new clothes to keep me warm and comfortable. Kind of him, isn't it?"

Nelly handed over the money, grabbed the newspaper-wrapped package and, nodding silently to both women, hurried out. She remembered the money Hilda had found and guessed that Griff wasn't aware of his generosity to his wife. What would happen when he found out was something she didn't care to think about. She sorted out the tangled leads, pushed and pulled the dogs into order and crossed the road.

Inside the shop Hilda stared at Bethan until Bethan was forced to ask,

"What would you like, Hilda?"

"Nothing from you."

"Oh, about your job is it? I'll be glad if you're ready to come back. It's difficult for me to see to it all. I'll have to

95

find someone else mind, if you're going to be on the sick for much longer."

"Stick your job, and as for managing you'll have Griff when he's out of prison and you're welcome to him."

"Griff? I'd be glad of his help, of course, shifting the sacks and heavy jobs like that, but it's the other things I need help with, the work you did." Bluffing her way through the conversation was making Bethan's chest painfully tight. Hilda knew about them. Why play cat and mouse with her like this? It wasn't fair. Best have a good row and see it finished. But she daren't say the first word.

"I've changed the locks on the doors and he isn't coming back, you know," Hilda went on. "Got plenty of room for him in your bed though, haven't you?"

"No! I – I don't know what you mean." The chance to bring it all out was there but she hadn't the nerve.

"You'll soon find out what I mean. He'll be back and when he is, it's to your address he'll be heading."

"No, I can't take a lodger. I've only a small bed-sit and – " but the door opened and Johnny Cartwright came in. Hilda greeted him and walked out.

"What's happened to her, won the pools has she?" Johnny asked. "Talk about glamorous. It's like she's been visited by a fairy godmother!

"I wouldn't know," Bethan replied.

"Got rid of that Griff and enjoying her freedom by all accounts."

"Lucky her!" Bethan retorted, Sheila's friendship having increased her courage. "Who'd want a man with a prison record?"

Johnny didn't go straight home, but stopped at the cottage on the main road next door to Phil-the-post where his mother lived.

"Mam," he called, pushing open the front door, "what about a cup of tea to go with these chips?"

"Fay not home, Johnny?" Netta asked as she went to fill

96

the kettle. "On a Saturday? I thought shops didn't want to bother with reps on Saturdays?"

"She was doing some written work this morning then going into town to do some shopping. Things for the baby, Mam. Isn't it great? It won't be much longer. *Duw annwyl*, I can't wait for this baby to arrive."

Netta chuckled. It was four months away and Johnny talking about it as if it were only hours.

To Johnny's delight Fay arrived an hour later with lots of shopping to show his mother. He sat happily while the two women drooled over the small garments and the items of equipment that were needed in readiness for the new baby. The only jarring point to the visit was when his mother asked why there were so many of each garment.

"Not expecting twins, are you, Fay?" Netta teased.

"I'll need plenty if I'm to expect a child-minder to keep her looking nice, Mam," Fay replied. "I can't expect her to be washing and ironing all day, now can I?"

Netta nodded agreement. She couldn't understand the need for Fay to continue with her job when she had a child to care for but she didn't show by the slightest change of expression that she was in any way disapproving. She had always known that Fay was different from herself and her family, and that included Johnny, she thought with momentary regret. Fay had need of things Netta hardly thought about, considering them unnecessary or so far removed from possibility as to be not worth dreaming about.

She looked about her at her living room, cluttered with the memorabilia of her family: ornaments that were of no monetary value but precious because they were presents from the boys; curtains that had begun life in a bedroom and been brought into service in the living room during the war when rationing made it impossible to replace things. Too many chairs, for visitors who came less and less frequently.

She remembered with a wry chuckle how Fay had once asked her why she had flowered curtains, a check-patterned wallpaper, and a different coloured flower design on the linoleum that covered the floor and another on the thread-bare rug in front of the fire, and why there were three odd armchairs. She had looked about her as if seeing the hotch-potch room for the first time and replied with wonder on her face, "I don't know, Fay. It just happened."

Fay's house was sparse and neat, with electric fires instead of coal, few ornaments, those she had been given were tucked away in drawers. Everything that was needed was there and of the best quality, but there was no surplus, and in Netta's opinion, little comfort. Although Netta visited often she was always glad to return to her incovenient little house and its over-filled room with the over-stuffed chairs and the fire that burned a bright welcome.

She went to a cupboard and took out a tissue-wrapped parcel. She handed it to Fay who unwrapped yet more baby clothes.

"Thank you, Mam. They're beautiful. You made them?"

"Yes, love in every stitch. You're right, Fay, you can't have too many, not if the child-minder is to give her time to the baby and not seeing to laundry. And as to that, I'll help with the washing, just bring it down, Johnny, it will be a pleasure to help. Plenty of help you'll need, with the baby and work as well, but you'll manage wonderfully, I don't doubt it. There's a lucky baby she'll be. Best of everything, lots of love, with you for parents."

Johnny frowned at his mother. How could he persuade Fay that her duty was to stay home with their child if Mam encouraged her to continue with her job!

Amy did find time to discuss her future with Freddie and Margaret after all. She invited Sheila and Freddie for Sunday lunch and when they had eaten, sat on the couch with her children beside her and asked:

"Freddie, Margaret, what would you think if I told you I was going to marry Victor?"

"Would it mean David and Daniel would be my brothers? I'd have three of them?" Margaret asked. "I think that would be nice, if only David would begin to talk to me

98

without a pout on his lips like one of Uncle Billie's big milk jugs!"

"Freddie?" Amy coaxed.

"I don't think it concerns Freddie, Mrs Prichard," Sheila said, idly playing with the switch of the radio. "Out in the world on his own he is, and with decisions of his own to make."

"This will still be his home," Amy said firmly, looking at her son.

"I wouldn't like you to move away from here," Freddie said at last. "The house where Victor lives is very dark and there's no garden. I've great plans for this one. You wait 'til you see what I've got planned for this competition next year."

Amy looked at Freddie seeing the serious look in the blue eyes and guessing he was uncomfortable talking about it. The garden was a neat way of changing the subject.

"You like Victor, don't you?"

"He's all right. He did a good job of clearing the old shrubs from the back of the garden. I'll be able to get that planted next time I have leave."

"He's good at playing games and he always asks me to play my new piano pieces," Margaret said. "We wouldn't have to move again, though, would we, Mam?" Her beautiful brown eyes grew wide with anxiety.

Unhappy at being ignored, Sheila turned on the radio and while the conversation continued sat, looking bored, occasionally increasing the volume. Regretfully Amy abandoned the attempt.

"Go on then, Margaret, love, play something for us now, will you? I'll make us a cup of tea and we'll sit and listen to you. That's my favourite way of spending my day off." She prepared a tray of tea and went back to sit on the couch. Freddie and Sheila stood up.

"I have to go, Mrs Prichard, sorry to miss Margaret's playing, but I have to see to food for Gran."

"Freddie, you'll listen, won't you? I've been practising this one for you," Margaret pleaded.

"Sorry, Margaret, but I'll be home again soon and we'll have a concert, me playing the mouth organ, badly, right? Here," from his pocket he took out three parcels. "Will you put them under the Christmas tree when Mam gets it? One for you, one for Mam, and one for Victor." He winked at his mother. "Oh, and there's a job for you, Margaret." He delved into his pocket. "Plant these seeds and look after them for me will you?" After hugging them both, he and Sheila left.

On Sunday afternoon Tad and Dawn were sitting listening for a knock at the door. Tad's anxiety showed in the way he sat, his back rigid and his face tense. What if Delina didn't come? What if the moment when they admitted their love for each other had been a mistake on her part? She would still look after Dawn, he was certain of that. She wasn't the sort to forget a promise, but Sundays was a separate thing, it had grown into a habit and now, watching the hands of the clock moving inexorably on, he began to feel more and more certain she wouldn't come.

"Will Delina come soon, Dad?" Dawn asked. "I want to show her this drawing I've done. It's the pond, or at least how it will look when it's finished."

"Can I see?" Tad avoided answering her question. He didn't know the answer.

Dawn had drawn the pond surrounded with wild grasses and plants, and he smiled and asked, "How soon will it look like this?"

"That's why I hope Delina will come soon. Billie Brown said we could go down and take a few plants from around his pond, there'll be grubs and small creartures hidden in the roots and the pond will soon come to life then. If she doesn't come soon it'll be dark."

The knock at the door made them both stand up, Dawn to run to open the door, Tad to stand and glance at his appearance in the mirror on the wall. He was nervous. It seemed that his future happiness depended on these next few moments.

Delina came in wearing a blue coat with a fur-lined hood, a warm blue and grey checked skirt, and boots that reached to her knees.

"Hello, Tad," she smiled. She hesitated as he made a slight move towards her then stopped. She stayed in the doorway, undecided whether to move closer or not. Both were smiling foolishly.

"Go on," Dawn said with an impatient sigh, deep and exaggerated as only a child can. "Kiss each other if you're going to!"

"Dawn?" Tad asked with a frown.

"I was sitting on the stairs when you did it before," she admitted with a cheeky grin. "Then can we go to see Billie Brown and get some plants for Nelly and George's pond, please?"

CHAPTER EIGHT

Delina was waiting for them when Tad and Dawn went up to talk to her father on the following day. Victor seemed startled by the announcement that they intended to marry.

"But when did all this happen?" he asked and the grin on his face puzzled Delina and Tad. Then he belatedly added, "Congratulations to you both, I hope it will be a good marriage, a happy one in which you can both be yourselves."

The bitterness about his own marriage was hidden by the smile, but Delina knew he was remembering the wasted years of her mother's silence and disapproval after Victor had been arrested for stealing. Her mother had not spoken to her father after the embarrassment of him being found guilty of stealing from Harry and Prue Beynon, for whom he then worked. She glanced at Tad and hoped she would be more sympathetic in his weaknesses, knowing that for them the path through life would not be easy. Tad was a complex man and would need all her understanding.

"It won't be for a long time, unfortunately," Tad said. "I have less than nothing and I won't accept a marriage in which I have to depend on my wife for money."

"Why not?" Victor asked. "It wouldn't be for ever and why not be together while you make your way? That way the success belongs to both of you. Not that I want you to go, Delina," he added, "but there's nothing you can't tell me about wasting time!"

Delina saw Tad's jaw tighten and knew he was not convinced.

"We'll think about it, Dad."

"Right then. And while you do, what about taking some of this furniture? There's too much, and if I have to see to the cleaning, I don't want more than half of it."

"I'll buy when we're ready," Tad said at once. "There's no need for charity."

"Charity? Be doing me a favour you will, boy. It'll have to go, so if there's anything you want, just take it."

"Thank you, Dad, we'll think about that, too," Delina said.

"By the way, I knew, about you and Tad," Victor said winking at Dawn who had stood silently watching them.

"How could you? We didn't know ourselves until last night."

"Milly Nogood and the Pup, saw you making a fond farewell outside your door, Tad."

"What a place this is for gossip!" Tad laughed when the nicknames of Milly Toogood and her friend Sybil had been explained.

"And what a place for friends, too. Pleased for you they'll be, in spite of you punching a few noses a while ago, including mine!" He rubbed his nose and shared another smile with Dawn.

Milly Toogood spent a lot of her time just walking around the village. She chattered as she strode along with her friend, Sybil Tremain, trotting in her wake and puffing with the effort of keeping up. It was this habit of walking a few yards behind the other that gave them the nick-names of Milly Nogood and the Pup, a description coined by Johnny.

"Are you going to announce your engagement or wait for Milly Nogood to do it for you?" Victor asked.

"We thought we'd make it public at Christmas," Tad smiled.

Victor called in to Amy's shop the following morning and told her of Delina's plans to marry Tad. She watched him drive off, wondering how the proposed marriage would

103

affect her own plans. It seemed from what Victor told her that the wedding would be a long way into the future, so should she agree to marry Victor and get the boys settled into a new routine and life-style before they had to face the loss of their sister? She sighed. It had all seemed so simple when Victor's wife was there to prevent their marrying. Since she had died everything was twisting into a tangle of if's and but's that threatened them with years of hanging on "until the time is right".

Mavis was looking after the shop and Amy was taking an afternoon off. There were extra orders to complete with the fast approach of Christmas and she decided that home was the easiest place to deal with the paperwork. At one o'clock she set off down the road on her bicycle, wondering, not for the first time, if she dare afford a small car.

She had begun to list the extra "fancies" for the following weeks – dates, figs, crackers, fancy biscuits, boxes of chocolates – when there was a knock at the door. Groaning her irritation, she was tempted not to answer it, but with the light on to dispel the gloom of the December afternoon, she knew that whoever it was would know she was at home.

It was Billie. She knew before she opened the door that it was Billie, no one else filled the opaque glass of the front door like Billie Brown.

"Come in but take your boots off," she said in greeting, not able to hide the sharpness caused by resentment at the interruption.

"I'll put the kettle on, shall I?" Billie didn't wait for assent but lumbered into the kitchen and filled the kettle.

"I saw the light when I was walking up the drive to put a note in," he explained as he waited for the kettle to boil. "Come to see if you want a few Christmas trees."

"I'd love some, but where will I display them? Constable Harris gets mad enough with the vegetables I put outside the shop, what would he say if he saw trees out there?"

"It's Christmas, he'll turn a blind eye."

"Worth a try I suppose. Thanks, Billie."

"What are you and Margaret doing at Christmas? Only

104

Mary wondered if you'd like to come to us. Children love a farmhouse dinner and, well, we'd like you to come."

"Thank you, Billie, but I like to do my own Christmas. I know Freddie won't be here, but Margaret and I will have a nice day. Thank Mary for me though, it was a kind thought."

"You'll be seeing Victor I suppose." It wasn't a question, more a thought spoken aloud.

"I don't know. There's likely to be an engagement announced and when that will be I'm not sure."

"An engagement?" Billie's brown eyes widened with shock. "Not you and – "

"Delina and Tad have decided to marry." She felt sadness at the look of relief that passed over his serious features. "It won't be for a while. Tad has to finish his studies, but they want to become engaged so Dawn can become accustomed to the idea of Delina as a mother."

"So he won't need you as a house-keeper just yet then?"

"If I marry Victor it won't be because he needs a house-keeper, Billie."

"But that's what you'd be doing, keeping house for him and his sons. Marry me and I'd employ a house-keeper to help you, and there'd only be Margaret to look after."

"Billie."

"I know. I'm sorry." He raised his arms in a "hands off" gesture and smiled. "I know we promised not to say another word about it, but you can't blame me for hoping, not while you're still free."

"When will you bring the trees?" she asked briskly, pouring them a second cup of tea.

"Next Monday? I thought I'd give one to Nelly and George. And there's one for you of course. Margaret can come and choose it on Saturday."

"Oliver can go with her and choose his, only we'll make sure Evie pays for it. Right?"

As she rose to encourage Billie to leave and allow her to get on with her work there was an explosive bang and the

105

sound of shattering glass. She clung to Billie and looked fearfully around. The window was smashed and a brick lay on the floor not far from where they stood.

"Stay inside and well away from the windows," Billie shouted and he ran from the house and down the drive to see who had been responsible. His footsteps fading in the aftermath of the shocking noise made Amy tremble. She clung to the edge of the table unable to move.

It seemed like hours before footsteps returned, slower this time, and Billie reappeared in the doorway.

"I couldn't catch him, but I saw him clearly enough. It was that David Honeyman, Victor's son."

"What shall we do?"

"Nothing. I'll go and talk to him, let him know I saw him, that should be enough to make sure it doesn't happen again."

"Victor will have to be told."

"That's up to you. Now, will you be all right if I go and get some glass and mend the window?"

"Yes, thank you, Billie, I'm so glad you were here."

"So am I. Now, some paper, a pencil and a tape measure, please, love."

Once more she listened to his footsteps fading as he walked down the the road. She heard the engine of the Range Rover open up and it too faded away. She shivered in the chill wind coming through the broken pane and wondered why David had behaved in such an unlikely way towards her. Was he telling her she shouldn't marry Victor? She went stiffly into the kitchen to make more tea.

When Margaret came home from school Billie was fixing the putty around the replaced window pane and she shouted with delight at seeing him there.

"Uncle Billie! Have you come for tea?"

"Not today, Margaret, but I've come to ask if you'd like to come to the farm on Saturday morning and choose a Christmas tree." He held up the tape measure. "See, we can measure how high the ceiling is and get one to fit perfectly, right?"

Amy smiled as they began to chatter about their plans and about the various things happening on the farm. She was still shaking but managed to make some sandwiches and take out a few cakes which she arranged for when Billie had finished the repair. They were still talking when everything was swept up and back to normal.

She wondered if Margaret would be happier if neither Billie nor Victor became her step-father. She enjoyed them both so much that to lose either one would be a great disapointment. Victor wouldn't welcome Billie as a regular visitor once Amy and he were married. But should duty to your children mean giving up a chance of happiness for yourself? Children were only with you for a short time, there had to be something left for when they moved away to begin a life of their own.

When Victor called that evening, she showed him the broken window and told him that his son had thrown the brick.

"David? But why? No, Amy, Billie must have been mistaken. Not David."

"Kids get frightened at the prospect of a change," Amy said. "He's still suffering from the death of his mother and with Delina talking about marrying I don't think he can face you bringing a wife home. It's too much too soon. He'll need to talk it all out."

"I'll talk to him when I get home. He'll understand that he can't get away with something like this!"

"No, Victor, I think it would be best if I talked to him. If he believes I haven't told you, well, it might be a small point in my favour. Billie thinks – "

"Billie. Why did you ask *him* to mend the window? I'd have done it if I'd known about it."

"He was here when the brick came through." She looked at the place where it had landed. "Frightening it was, almost like an explosion. I was glad he was here and could fix it straight away. I didn't want Margaret to see the damage. She's only a child, too, and I don't want her upset."

"Marrying me would upset her?"

"A bit," Amy said in her forthright way. "She's never had a father. And if you came here and tried to fill that role she'd be very pleased, but she'd miss Billie. She loves going to the farm and he's a special friend."

"Sorry, I was stupid to be jealous of him. But I still realise how much he has to offer."

"Victor, can you come shopping on Saturday afternoon? I thought we'd go into town and you can help me carry all my parcels home. Your David and my Margaret as well. We could end up at the pictures if you like. James Stewart and Grace Kelly are at the Plaza in *Rear Window*, that's supposed to be good."

"Sorry, love, I've promised to take the boys to the football."

"Shame. Never mind, I think I'll still go. Margaret has been asking me to take her for ages, she has a list of presents to buy and her money is burning a hole in her pocket."

"Don't forget I'm going to see Uncle Billie to choose a tree, Mam," a voice from upstairs called.

"I'd never dreamt how impossible it would be to get everyone together at one time!" Amy laughed. "I don't think there's any danger we wouldn't all get on. We'd never see each other long enough to quarrel!"

Several people planned to go shopping on that particular Saturday. Nelly had been saving up each week by putting a few shillings aside in a small jug on her mantel piece, as and when she could afford it. She opened it, counted it out and shared the money between the various people for whom she planned to buy.

Victor decided that after the football match had finished there would be time to go and get a tree and a few gifts.

Hilda had found herself a job in *The Plough*, locally called Tolly's after a previous landlord, near Llan Gwyn. With the confidence of regular money coming in she decided to go shopping with the remnants of Griff's money. She smiled at the prospect. After years of not spending an extra shilling without careful consideration, having a roll of notes in her purse was as addictive as gambling was to many of Griff's ex-clients. She was sorry it was almost gone.

When George and Nelly reached town the shops were heaving with people pushing and demanding to be served. Assistants were faced with a forest of hands waving tinsel and tree decorations, brightly wrapped gifts and occasionally a mundane item like a reel of cotton, a skein of wool, a packet of screws or a paint-brush. Children wore smiles on their rosy faces and mothers mostly managed to echo them although their patience and energy were weakening.

Inside the over-flowing shops they were easing woollen hoods from their heads, loosening collars and scarves, only to re-wrap themselves as the cold of the December day hit them when they pushed back outside. Nelly saw one little girl forced back inside by the enthusiasm of those entering and she and George went to rescue her.

"Give over!" she shouted to the unheeding customers. "This is supposed to be a time fer the kids, ain't it?" Leaving George to wait at the entrance she bent her head like a battling bull and charged in, unaware that she was as uncaring as the rest.

Having bought most of her gifts, she suggested that they stayed in town and went to the pictures. But George shook his head.

"I think I've had enough of town, dear. Give me your parcels and I'll take them home. You stay on for a while, I know how you love the bustle and insanity of Christmas shopping!" He smiled, his mouth pink and clean in the white beard, but his eyes showed how tired he was.

"Good idea, George. But I won't stay fer the pictures. I'll just go and look at a few more shops, I ain't got nothin' fer Amy an' I fancy buyin' a nice scarf."

They walked to the bus stop where crowds waited to be taken home. Everyone was laden with packages and on each face was the expectation of the happy time to come. Hilda Evans was near the end of the queue and, like the rest, her arms were filled with bags and boxes.

"Been getting your Christmas shopping I see," George said. "I think the shops will be empty before closing time!"

"This is for my Pete, good boy that he is," Hilda patted a large bag from the local motor-cycle shop. "This is a new cardigan, and this is a dress and some matching shoes." She touched each bag in turn. Apart from the parcel for her son, everything seemed to be for herself.

"Blimey, she ain't 'alf makin' up fer lost time!" Nelly said in her loud whisper. "I 'ope she's remembered to buy some food. An' what's she got fer that 'usband of 'ers, supposin' 'e deserves a present which 'e don't!"

"Move away," George said, laughing at her remarks. "I don't want you to start a riot. Go and have a cup of tea and a sandwich then finish your shopping. I'll be ages waiting here."

Rather unwillingly she went. She walked through the town searching for a place to sit and eat a sandwich but all the cafe's were full to over-flowing. So she bought an Eynon's pie and a custard slice and ate them walking along the High Street. She tried to go into the ladies toilets to wash the sticky remnants off her face but there were long queues there, too, so she lifted the hem of her coat and managed with that.

As darkness sidled over the town, and lights on the street stalls and the shop windows became more apparent, Nelly thought the Christmas spirit came with it. Buses sailed past and through steamy windows showed passengers sitting and standing, their odd shaped parcels crowded in with them. Nelly's smile widened with every minute.

Near the corner of a shop where the pavement widened there were stalls selling trees and doing a brisk trade. Next to them a man with rolls of Christmas wrapping paper. It was as she was buying some that Nelly saw Amy.

"Nelly, love, why do we put ourselves through this every year? I swear I'll start in July and have it all finished by September next year!" Amy laughed.

"It wouldn't be the same, dearie. Great this is, part of

110

Christmas. I couldn't imagine sittin' down to Christmas dinner without a few bruises!"

They tried again to find somewhere to sit down and this time they were lucky. Pushing her purchases under a table, Amy waved to the harassed waitress and ordered tea and cakes.

"Expensive, this'll be," Nelly said anxiously.

"But worth it for a sit down!"

They stayed for as long as they dared, with the waitress pointedly clearing their table and glancing to the doorway where people still waited to come in. Then, with a groan, they gathered the parcels between them and staggered out into the dark cold evening where a drizzle was beginning to fall.

The pavements were wet and dirty, the shops were almost ready to close, yet still the crowds hadn't thinned out.

"What on earth have you bought?" a voice asked and they turned to see Victor and his son David close behind them.

"More than I can carry!" Amy, said, her smile fading as she looked at the boy's sulky face.

"We're almost as bad, but we can help you." Victor stepped into the doorway of a shop that had closed its doors to customers and began to re-organise what he and David were carrying.

They had two trees, small ones but nevertheless long and awkward to manage. He gave these to David, tucking one under each of the boy's arms. He added one of Amy's carrier bags which he put into his hand. The bag was awkwardly filled, the contents widening the bag so David's fingers could barely reach around the string handles.

As they set off for the bus stop, David dropped first one handle then the other. The bag dropped on to the wet pavement and the contents spilled out. He picked it up again but not before abandoning the large package on the top, so allowing an easier grip. The crowds made it impossible to walk even in twos and as they pushed their way through the street to the bus stop, Nelly almost fell as her feet hit the abandoned package.

111

Amy tightened her lips as she retrieved it but said nothing. She stared at David until he lowered his gaze, resentment plainly seen in both pairs of eyes.

Two buses came in, filled and moved off before they managed to get on. They sat together in the side seats where they could watch over their parcels, pushed thankfully under the stairs of the bus. "Come back for a cup of tea, Nelly love, and I'll walk you home with your shopping?" Amy said as the bus started moving.

"Thanks, Amy, but I'll go back 'ome. My George ain't well, only a bit tired, but I'll go straight 'ome and get 'im something to eat. I bought a bit of Kiwi 'addock. Nice that'll be with a poached egg on the top an' a bit of veg."

"Kiwi Haddock?" Victor queried.

"Supposed to be smoked, but my George says it's only coloured with a bit of boot-polish!" Nelly laughed.

Struggling off the bus near the end of her lane, Nelly began to sing as she walked towards the cottage. Half way up the lane the street lights behind her making it very black, she was startled to see a figure standing near the hedge looking over into the fields where Farmer Leighton's retired horses spent their days.

"'Ello, what you standin' there for?" she demanded. Then she recognized the tall, slim figure with alarm. It was George.

"Hello, Nelly, love, I've been waiting for you."

"Out in this cold? Whatever for?"

"I couldn't quite manage the hill. It seems steeper all of a sudden."

She dropped her shopping bag carelessly and went to put an arm around his waist. Trying not to show her fear that he was ill she said with a laugh,

"That's easy remedied. 'Ere, push yer way through our 'edge. That way you won't need to climb no 'ill."

"No, it's a pity to spoil it; I'll take your arm and if we go slowly – "

"Rubbish, the 'edge 'll be recovered before the competition if that's what's worryin' yer." She took his arm and,

112

walking backwards, helped him up the bank and pushed a way through the hedge into their garden. "Now, stay there an' I'll run and open the back door for yer. There, dearie, we'll soon 'ave you 'ome and warm as toast."

She didn't try to put him to bed but made up a comfortable place for him to rest on the couch. Hot water bottles and a thick over-coat across the blankets made sure he would be warm, a hot drink helped the process. She sat with him as he slept through the night. He stirred occasionally, coughing and holding his chest against the pain he denied feeling.

The next morning she went down to see Evie and asked her to phone for the doctor.

"On a Sunday, Mother? Whatever is wrong with him can't be worth disturbing the doctor on a Sunday."

"My George is ill an' I wouldn't be askin' you no favour if it wasn't urgent." Nelly said. "Now will you phone 'im or do I 'ave to go an' ask Amy an' tell 'er you wouldn't 'elp me?"

Reluctantly, Evie spoke to the doctor.

Victor had bought two trees: one for his house and one for Dawn. While he was walking down Hywel Rise to deliver it he saw Billie delivering milk. On his van was a tree.

"Late this morning, aren't you?" Victor called.

"Milk round is finished long ago, I've just taken a tree to one of Mary's customers, and now I'm taking this one to Nelly and George."

When Billie went to the cottage and found George was sick, he stayed to help Nelly fix the tree in the corner of the room and then offered to tell Amy.

"Blimey, that Phil'll be mad not to be the first with the news!" Nelly said. She laughed as she repeated her remark to George when he woke a little while later, but her heart was heavy.

George stayed on the couch for three days, then he stood up and managed to eat some soup Nelly had made. Once it was known that he was on the mend, there were plenty of visitors to amuse him, although Nelly threw them out if there was a sign of him tiring.

She didn't work her usual hours for Mrs French and Mrs Williams, but while Amy or Phil or Netta stayed with George she managed to fit in a few visits to keep their houses clean. Spending her nights in the armchair watching over George she was exhausted and once, when she was sitting for a welcome cup of tea in Mrs French's kitchen, she fell asleep.

George walked down to the main road with her at the end of the week and insisted he would soon be well enough to return to work. Walking back up he agreed, without too much protest, when Nelly insisted they pushed their way through the hedge again, rather than climb the steep lane.

Nelly decided to go and see Clara. Gypsies knew more about healing than just charming warts. Leaving George sleeping, but covering him against the evening chill with blankets and coats, she left the dogs behind and went up Gypsy Lane to where her friend was camped for the winter.

In a cupboard in the neat caravan was a white sack. Inside it were bags of dried flowers and leaves, Clara's medicine cabinet. The stems of the contents were sticking out of the tied end of the bags, and each bag was neatly labelled.

"Elderflowers," Clara said. "Then when he's feeling better, some tansy for a tonic. I'll call and see him tomorrow and make sure there's nothing further he needs." She gave Nelly a reminder on preparing and giving the herbs and Nelly went back down the dark lane feeling more hopeful than before. The doctor had called twice but she wouldn't call him again unless George failed to improve. "He will," she promised herself. "He will."

When she went down to buy the paper that evening, she sat in the shop while Amy served and read out pieces of news to her. The best bit she left until last.

"There's funny people them Russians must be," she

114

remarked. "It says 'ere they've grafted a second head on a dog and both were lappin' at the same time. Now 'oo'd want to do that? I ask yer!"

"Don't, Nelly. It doesn't bear thinking about," Amy shuddered. "Can't you find something interesting?"

"What about this then. That Griff 'as got six months prison. Blimey, when you think what's 'apened to 'ilda in a few weeks, Gawd knows *what* she'll be doing after six ruddy months!"

"I don't feel sorry for him. Serve him right, it should have been five years! Breaking into people's houses and stealing. And the way he cheated on Hilda, daft as she is, she doesn't deserve that."

"Now 'ere's another funny thing, Amy. There's an 'orse runnin' on the ninth at Wincanton called Frolicsome Lover. Not quite as I picture Griff," she chuckled, "but how about it? Fancy a bob each way do yer?"

CHAPTER NINE

Margaret sang a solo in the annual Carol Concert given, this year, in aid of the new Village Hall. She also played piano for some of the pieces sung by the choir. Amy sat in the audience in the school building and marvelled at her daughter's talents. Margaret seemed to have it all. Musically gifted and very beautiful, yet with a calm and gentle personality that gained her friends wherever she went. Her hair was thick and a rich red, flowing over her shoulders in waves and her eyes were deep dark brown. Both of her children were copies of their fathers. Amy sighed, wonderful reminders of past loves.

Margaret's father was the result of a brief and beautiful affair with Richard French, the musical husband of Mrs Monica French, who had realised the likeness of Margaret to her now deceased husband only after Prue Beynon had maliciously given her a pointer.

Amy and Margaret had been invited back to Evie and Timothy's after the concert. Seeing Nelly a few rows behind her, Amy whispered, "Are you coming to your Evie's then?"

"I ain't bin invited," Nelly said. "Besides, I don't like leavin' my George fer long."

"Come on, just for half an hour, that's how long I'll be staying. I can't stand too much of your Evie, no more than you can! We'll come up the lane with you then, to say hello to George."

Nelly agreed and when the applause had died down she took Amy's arm while they waited for Margaret to appear.

Evie had hurried home before the final item to get the food out and fill the kettle for those who preferred not to drink alcohol. When she opened the door some twenty minutes later and saw her mother outside, smiling widely, she felt a strong urge to close it again.

"I ain't stoppin' long, Evie, just called in with Amy and Margaret to wish you 'appy Christmas."

"There'll be plenty of opportunity for us to exchange greetings, Mother," Evie said with a stiff smile.

"Don't she talk posh, you'd never know this one was mine, would yer?"

Stepping into the hallway Nelly hung her outsized coat on the end of the banister and Evie snatched it off and hurriedly hid it in the understairs cupboard.

"Come into the kitchen, Mother, and I'll find you a nice cup of tea."

"Tea! It's nearly Christmas and all you're offerin' yer friends is tea?" Nelly's loud voice carried to where Timothy was handing out drinks in what Nelly called the front room and Evie called the lounge.

"Here, mother-in-law, what about a gin and orange?"

"Timothy!" Evie's warning was ignored by her husband.

"That's more like it," Nelly shouted back. "Come on, Amy, we'll see Timmy and leave Evie to 'er tea." She pushed her way through the people standing quietly sipping at their drinks and went to find Timothy.

"Why did you have to bring her, Amy?" Evie hissed.

"Because it's Christmas and she's your mother," Amy hissed back.

Margaret found Oliver sitting in a corner of the kitchen surreptitiously reading a comic Nelly had bought him.

"Did you enjoy the concert, Oliver?" Margaret asked. Oliver shook his head. "You didn't?" Margaret was disappointed, she could usually rely on Oliver to assure her that she did well.

"Mother wouldn't let me go. I was bottom of the class again except for Arthur Toogood and she said I have to earn my rewards. I wish I was clever at something, Margaret."

117

"Mam says being clever isn't anything to boast about, it's something inside you when you're born. I could play a tune on the piano as soon as I saw one. There'll be something you're good at, you just haven't found it yet. Freddie isn't clever at sums and school work, but he's clever with gardens."

"Mother wouldn't like me to be clever at gardens."

"I think it's lovely to grow flowers."

"I just wish I could surprise them and do something really clever."

"Come tomorrow after school and I'll teach you a piece on the piano. You can do the left hand and I'll do the right."

When Amy and Margaret walked home with Nelly an hour later, they found George looking much better. He was, as always, pleased to see Margaret. He asked about the concert and sang "Silent Night" with her while Nelly and Amy sat and listened.

"You couldn't have done that a few days ago, George. That medicine of Clara's did the trick all right!"

"And that's the best Christmas present you could ask for," Amy smiled as she stood to leave.

The days leading up to Christmas were busy ones for Evie and Timothy. Every organisation to which they belonged had a party arranged or a meal at a local restaurant or a dance. Oliver was left with Amy, Netta Cartwright, even Dawn and Tad and, when there was absolutely no one else, with Nelly and George.

"I wake up in the morning and wonder which house I'm in," he joked to George one evening as they were preparing to go to bed. The evening had been spent decorating the Christmas tree given by Billie. Oliver was sticky with flour and water paste, which was highly coloured from making papier-mâché decorations which they had dipped in sparkling glitter-dust

George was laughing as the small boy climbed the stairs hoping no one would remind him to wash.

118

"What about hands, Ollie?" he reminded and Oliver, shamefacedly admitted:

"I hoped you wouldn't notice, Grandad."

"If your mother could see you now, splashed with red and yellow, blue and green, she'd be convinced you had a terrible disease, young man. Wash and perhaps Nelly will let you stay up a while longer and have a cup of cocoa with us as it's almost Christmas. Would you like a game of ludo?"

Oliver washed with great enthusiasm but little skill.

"I wants to give 'im a real good Christmas, George," Nelly said when Oliver was finally asleep. "But I don't know what."

"Take him to see the gypsies on Christmas morning, persuade Amy and Margaret to invite us for tea and make sure he goes to Ethel's in the evening."

"That ain't very excitin' fer a boy, George."

"No, but it will give Evie no time for nagging!" he chuckled.

"Evie won't let him visit Clara and the others."

"Don't ask her. That's part of the fun!"

Chrismas Day was rarely planned, yet the same routine was followed year after year. Whether they were formally invited or not, a crowd of neighbours made their way to Ethel's small house on Sheepy Lane in the evening, some taking food, others carrying a bottle, many taking nothing at all but just calling for a few minutes and staying for hours. Each knew that their welcome was assured.

In the early dawn Oliver opened his eyes and looked towards the bottom of his bed. There were raised shapes visible and he knew that after he had slept, it was his parents who had placed presents there, keeping up the pretence of Santa Claus to please them all. He switched on his bedside light and began to unwrap their gifts to him. A pair of socks were flung aside and a new shirt that he hardly examined followed them to the floor. Then, at last, something really interesting: a kit for making a model aeroplane. He tried reading the instructions, examining the contents of the box with care. His washed-out blue eyes were serious as he wondered who he would ask to help him. Not his father, he thought sadly.

For Dawn this Christmas was filled with excitement. She knew that at Auntie Ethel's that evening an announcement would be made. She fingered the new dress that Delina had bought for her and smiled. From her father there were two films and a postal order to pay for their developing. If she was lucky she might use one film up on Nelly's gypsy friends.

Margaret was given a doll and a small sewing machine plus a box of coloured cottons and a pair of scissors. Freddie's parcel contained an assortment of ribbons for her hair and a pretty glass dish for her dressing table.

"What did Freddie get for you, Mam?" she asked as she displayed her presents for Amy to see.

"It's just a note." Amy frowned as she opened the envelope and took out the single page of note-paper. She read it aloud.

Look in the shed. What can it mean?"

Still in their dressing gowns they went outside and in the corner of the shed, badly wrapped, was a brightly painted wheelbarrow containing soil and several packets of seeds.

"It's for the competition, Mam. Clever Freddie!"

"But how did it get there?" Amy frowned. Had Freddie been home again and not come to see them? Once before he had come home, spent his leave with Sheila, and failed to let them know he was in the village. The thought made the excitement of Christmas morning fade.

"It must have been there for weeks, since he was last home. How often do we go in there this time of the year?"

"Of course. Silly me." Amy hugged Margaret, trying to smile. Yet she remembered going into the shed recently to

120

find the heavy yard broom, and the wheelbarrow with its wrapping of gaily coloured paper wasn't there then.

In her grandmother's house on St Illtyd's Road, Sheila glanced at the clock and decided to award herself another hour in bed. She and Gran were going to her parents for dinner so there was no rush. A taxi was booked for twelve o'clock to take them down the hill to the flat above Amy's shop, Gran not being able to walk very far.

The parcel from Freddie was on her bedside table, left there by him when he had managed to come home for an unexpected twenty-four hours, arriving in the dark and leaving in the dark and hoping no one had seen him.

She smiled as she remembered how they had spent the day. Making love, sleeping, and hardly bothering with food. Gran had thought she was out, first at work in the small gift-shop where she had worked since giving her notice and leaving the gown shop in Llan Gwyn. Later, she told Gran, she would be out for the evening with some friends and home late. She had prepared breakfast and a cold lunch for her grandmother, pretended to leave for work, but had climbed the stairs again to where Freddie was waiting for her, his eyes showing desire, the secretiveness and the importance of silence adding spice to the occasion. It was just like one of the stories in the magazines she bought; romantic, daring and heavenly.

Sheila dosed, then woke and opened the parcel. It was a small, sparkling brooch with hearts entwined in a design picked out in red stones amid a diamante cluster. When she dressed she pinned it on a ribbon and wore it around her throat, opening the neck of her blouse as far as she dare, remembering that it was a visit to her parents she was dressing for and not a visit to town with Bethan.

Oliver arrived at the cottage before Nelly and George were dressed on Christmas morning, Evie having too much to do to cope with his chatter. He was excited as he opened and admired the small gifts George and Nelly had bought him. Dawn arrived and they all went for a walk through the crackling, denuded woodland, where the ground was scattered with fallen branches and last of the leaves were bedraggled and moist with the onset of decay.

"The woods smell like mushrooms, Gran," Oliver said.

"Fungus growin' and eatin' up the leftovers," she explained. "Takin' the leaves and tops off of the 'azel nuts so the squirrels can pack 'em away neat an' tidy."

The day was dull, the sky hidden by thick clouds as the four of them made their way to Gypsy Lane and Clara. It was very cold as they walked across Farmer Leighton's fields, the dampness seeping under their clothes and making their skin feel like marble.

They saw no one as they headed for the lane leading to Leighton's farmhouse. The village houses were all dark, shuttered in against the unpleasant weather, while inside, Nelly guessed, the occupants were sitting preparing for an excess of food, or to leave the comfort of their fires to visit friends.

As they reached the bend in the lane that would give them sight of the camp, they smelt smoke, then they saw it, rising and spreading wide on the moisture-laden air, falling about the fields, clinging to the hedges and adding to the dankness of the winter's chill.

In front of Clara's caravan a fire burned in a shallow hole in the ground. Over it, bubbling and sending out savoury smells, was a large cooking pot. Further away another fire burned less successfully and it was this one that was sending out the smoke. Several lanterns were hung from convenient places around the area near the cooking fire, giving the effect of a stage set for action to begin. There was no sign of the inhabitants. Nelly called, waited, her head on one side like a bird, then said:

"Gone orf somewhere but they won't be long, Clara knows we're comin'."

Dawn wandered around, looking with nervous interest at the ornate homes. Her camera clicked several times as she set it up on a firm base and attempted a time exposure, but

Nelly knew it was faces she liked photographing best. She stood up and leaned over a gate leading into a field beyond which lay Farmer Leighton's house. It was from there she guessed they would come.

"Look over 'ere," she called to Dawn. "It's like a procession. Dogs first, then the men, and Clara and the other women taggin' on be'ind." Over the hill they came, each with a lantern that made their silhouettes clearly visible, separating the long flowing skirts of the women and the trousered legs of the men. They were each carrying a parcel of food given by Mr Leighton: potatoes, carrots, onions and several loaves of bread. They were nine in all and, as they recognised Nelly, they called a greeting.

Introductions were a blurr but Dawn, having been given permission, snapped away with her camera as the strangely dressed wanderers added their lanterns to the rest and settled around them on the grass to discuss their news. Several of the group were new to Oliver and he sat silently, close to Nelly, only managing a wavering smile for Clara.

Although it was early in the day, their hosts made the atmosphere reminiscent of an evening of celebration. Clara told stories of her childhood that facinated the children, her weathered face frowning at some of the revelations of depravation, and wrinkling into laughter at other, more pleasant, memories.

"I was born the youngest of ten chavies, by the side of the road in a bender tent. Like the top of this vardo," she said, pointing behind her at her caravan home, "only without the wheels. We cut branches and bent them over and stuck them into the ground, deep and firm, and covered them with a few pieces of tarpaulin, holding it steady against the wind with turfs and anything else we could find. Warm as a summer's day it was in them benders. Lit by candles we made ourselves from the fat of animals, we'd sit of a winter's night and tell stories, keeping our memories alive for the generations to come. Better'n your books, Oliver. Them stories were real and true."

"How did you find food?" Oliver asked in a whisper.

"There were days when we didn't, young Oliver. We'd scour the hedgerows for something to fill our bellies and there were many days when we had to walk miles for even a drop of water for the babies and for us to make a cup of tea.

"Summertime is good for us travellers, although that be a changin'" a young man added when Clara had fallen silent. "We follow the work all over the country, fruit-picking, labourin' on the hedges and ditches, digging for scrubies – what you call potatoes – and there's the hops for those that can get there in time. No, it's the winter what's hard. Lucky for people like us with a kindly farmer like Leighton to help us, not so fortunate for others.

"How can you get all you need in that small vardo?" Dawn asked, looking into her camera lense as Clara turned to reply.

"What people *need* is very little, what you *want* is another thing altogether. Staying in one place makes you *want* more and more things, but you don't *need* 'em. We only have to remind ourselves that the poor horse has to pull it all and it's easy to abandon what we don't need."

The smoking fire had recovered its humour and was blazing and throwing out a great heat. They moved to sit closer to its cheerful light. Then a young man stood up and disappeared inside a vardo parked behind Clara's. He returned with a fiddle on which he began to play a lively tune. Another man took a mouth organ from his pocket, rubbed it against his coat, and began to accompany the fiddle. To Nelly and George's delight and Oliver's acute embarrassment, the gypsies began to dance, feet tapping almost soundlessly on the cropped, damp grass.

Nelly and George joined in, Nelly's face bright with the excitement of being allowed to enjoy their impromptu celebration. Dawn walked around the dancers snapping, hiding herself under her coat to replace a used film, and snapping again. The young man sang a song about the deprivations of the road and why they couldn't live the life they chose. George sang, too, a lonely song about the sadness of

124

being alone. Nelly guessed he was remembering the years he had travelled the road, homeless and unloved.

With the sound of the fiddle still in their ears, they regretfully left the encampment and headed back down Gypsy Lane and home.

"Got any snaps left, Dawn? Nelly asked.

"A few, d'you think we could go back again tomorrow?"

Nelly walked Dawn and Oliver home, promising to see them in a while at Ethel's. Then she went home to find George taking some baked potatoes out of the oven.

"That cold fresh air has made me glad I put them in. Come on, get out the the rabbit you roasted, there's plenty for tomorrow as well."

Happy to see his appetite returned, Nelly did as he asked.

Ethel's room was already crowded when they arrived there at half past nine. Nelly pushed her way past Phil, Billie, Bert and Johnny, who were playing a game of cribbage at a small table near the kitchen door, and stood in a corner near Johnny's mother and Fay.

"We ain't missed nothin' 'ave we?" she demanded as she tried to take off her coat in the crush. "No interestin' announcements?"

"Who needs announcements in a place like this?" Johnny laughed. "There's nothing kept secret long enough to *be* announced!"

But everyone glanced at Tad and Delina who had come early and talked to Ethel about what they wished to make public knowledge.

"Ten o'clock, Nelly," Netta whispered. "It won't be long."

"Thank 'eavens we wasn't any later."

She told them then of their visit to the gypsy camp and saw with a groan that, unnoticed, Timothy and Evie were in the kitchen. They wouldn't be pleased to hear where she had taken their son on Christmas morning!

It was ten-thirty when Ethel brought out hot pasties and mince pies from the oven, and plates of sandwiches and cakes. Then, with every glass filled, they all stood up and wished Tad and Delina all the best in their future years together.

"But we haven't announced it yet!" Tad laughed.

"You're too slow, boy," Phil said. "The women have been talking about nothing else for days. From pockets and under chairs packages were brought forth and Delina was showered with gifts. The room was like a battlefield, conversation was lively and loud as everyone struggled to reach over and hug Delina and shake Tad's hand. Phil and Johnny began to discuss the best place to live, the women reminisced about weddings and laughter abounded. The food was consumed with opinions, the clatter of plates and cutlery adding to the din.

No one saw how badly Sheila had taken the announcement that Delina, whom she believed had stolen Maurice from her, was to marry. She turned to Bethan, who was spending the Christmas evening with Ethel for the first time, and pretended to make light of the news.

"They'll never marry. Good heavens, it's like a pantomime! One minute she's stealing Maurice from me and pretending he's her great love, the next it's goodbye Maurice, and now it's hello Tad!"

Making the excuse that she had to go back and see to her grandmother, Sheila left before eleven o'clock. Bethan went with her, although disappointed at having to go so soon. This was a side of the villagers she hadn't seen before, stuck away in her fish and chip shop and spending the rest of her time either working outside in the cold yard or hidden in her small bed-sit. She was surprised how friendly Billie Brown had been. He was very different from how she had imagined him, seeing him sailing past on that tractor of his.

Sheila was hurt and jealous of the celebration she had witnessed. "Everyone was pleased for them. They'd bought gifts for them, the stuck up school-teacher and the out of work, ill-tempered little man who sweeps up rubbish in a factory! While I, who was abandoned in such a cruel way, was ignored. Couldn't they see how unkind they were to rub it in how happy Delina was while I, a wife without a husband, was grieving?"

"What about Freddie?" Bethan asked.

"Freddie isn't someone to take seriously! I pass the time with him, try to forget my lost love for a moment or two, while inside I grieve." Sheila was enjoying herself, imagining the scene as portrayed in a novel. The broken-hearted and beautiful young girl, expected to celebrate the happiness of the woman who had ruined her life. But the anger against Delina was real.

The party at Ethel's went on until three in the morning and Nelly was among the last to leave. With Phil, his wife Catrin, and George, she volunteered to stay and clear away the dishes so Ethel wouldn't have to face it in the morning.

"There ain't enough food left to feed a sparrer!" Nelly laughed. "It's the same each year, everyone comes in complaining of being full up from too much turkey and as soon as Ethel waves a plate they all come runnin' like they was starved!"

It was dry when they left. The air was still and a mist hung over the trees as they walked slowly past the edge of the wood. The dogs were sniffing excitedly at hidden trails and on impulse, George said:

"Let's go on a while, past the cottage and behind the houses towards the farm. The dogs will like a stretch."

The ground climbed a little and with only a couple of thin torch beams to guide them they stumbled once or twice as small bushes tripped them. Nelly watched George, looking for a sign of fatigue, but he seemed able to cope with the exercise without effort. Their route took them down again to come out in Gypsy Lane. George began to sing and she joined in. Then she stopped and touched his arm.

Below them the fire between the gypsy caravans glowed and in the misty light they saw the huddle of people still

127

sitting around it, the sound of the fiddle now playing sadder, more melancholy airs, but there was a beauty and a magical feeling to the sight. They didn't go down but turned and retraced their steps towards the cottage.

"Nice to 'ave an 'ome, George. I don't think I'd like to be wandering without a place to call 'ome."

"For the gypsies, home is where they are now, Romanistan, that's what it means. It's their home and their nation.

"Appy Christmas to 'em George, and to us."

CHAPTER TEN

Sheila was very discontented. Freddie was so far away and even though he spent most of his leave with her, there were many days and nights when she had no company and, worse than that, no one to tell her she was beautiful and desirable. Her heart longed for a man's admiration, and her body for fulfillment. It wasn't love she felt for Freddie, that, she thought with a gentle sigh, was reserved for the husband who had abandoned her, but at least he reminded her she was an alluring woman. Alluring . . . yes, she liked that.

Remembering it was a Tuesday, the day on which Bethan didn't open the shop, she decided to call in on her way to work and arrange to go out somewhere, anywhere to get away from the boring four walls of her room.

Bearing in mind the possible visit to a public house, a cafe, or the pictures, she dressed with even greater care than usual. She chose to wear her new winter-white swagger coat with a hood. She had lined the hood with some red taffeta bought at a remnant counter and was pleased with the effect. She considered it dramatic.

Giving her grandmother her breakfast, she explained that she might not be in until late that evening and, gathering up her handbag and the umbrella that matched it, she hurried off down the hill to the main road. The weather was cold, the frost glistened on the ground making puddles into hard, glass-like traps for her high-heeled shoes to slip on. The wind was filled with icy Arctic air and it hurt her forehead as she hurried down towards the bus stop. The new coat wasn't as warm as she had hoped and she almost went back to find another cardigan to add to the jumper she wore, but the prospect of missing Bethan and having yet another boring evening in made her tense herself against the discomfort, hold the hood tighter against her face and hurry on.

In Sheepy Lane she saw Phil-the-post on his rounds heading for his mother's cottage for a second breakfast. Without much hope she asked if there was a letter for her from Australia.

"Only one for Mam, Sheila. Call in on the way home and she'll show it to you for sure."

She shrugged and waved airily to imply that she didn't much care whether she saw it or not and hurried on, across the road and down the lane leading to the back of the fish and chip shop.

Bethan was up and already washing down the yard, which constantly smelt of fish.

"I can't stay a moment," Sheila said, "I have to catch the bus, but are you free to meet me after the shop closes? We could go to the pictures, or just for a cup of coffee?"

"There's nice you look, Sheila. I'll have to find something smart to wear or I'll be in your shadow, won't I?" Bethan smiled. "Yes, I'll meet you outside the shop, shall I?"

It was arranged, and Sheila ran back up the lane and across the road to catch the bus to Llan Gwyn and spend a boring day trying to sell gifts to people still recovering from the spending spree of Christmas.

Bethan went inside and looked through her limited collection of clothes to try and find something suitable to go out with Sheila without being swamped by the girl's elegance. Bethan would love to be elegant but was convinced it was a skill you were born with and couldn't learn.

When Sheila saw her friend waiting for her outside the shop that evening she found it difficult not to laugh. Bethan was wearing a duffelcoat with a small felt hat on her head, half covered by the hood. Her face was flushed with the cold and she clutched a handkerchief in her red and swollen hands

130

like a talisman. Really, what was she doing bothering with this girl? Then she remembered the alternative: to go home and sit listening to the radio with her gran.

She combed her hair and carefully pulled the red-lined hood over it, checked her makeup for the third time and went out to greet Bethan. "Have you decided where to go?" she asked. Silently she thought they ought to go somehere and hide with Bethan looking like she did.

"Pictures," Bethan said at once. "*White Christmas* is on with Bing Crosby. Hurry up, I'm frozen."

"So am I," Sheila said, then added sharply, "but there's no need to look it!"

The queue for the pictures was long and they looked at it in dismay. The other cinemas would be the same.

"A coffee?" Sheila said resignedly.

The cafe was warm and fairly crowded, but Sheila found a seat while Bethan stood hesitantly at the door. The table she chose was facing the door and the two women who were sitting there moved up for them, dragging bags of shopping from under the table with amiable smiles.

"Two coffees, Bethan, please," Sheila said in her high pitched voice, "and a pork roll." She slipped the hood from her head and slowly lowered the coat from her shoulders.

Bethan stood trying to catch the eye of the waitress, then gave their order and sat beside Sheila. She took off her duffelcoat and under it, Sheila saw with surprise, She wore a glittery jumper that flattered her figure surprisingly.

"Amy gave it to me after it had shrunk," she whispered. "I've never dared wear it before."

"It suits you really well," Sheila said kindly, thinking how much better it would look on her.

The shoppers gradually dispersed and the clientele changed to those preparing to go out for the evening. Three boys about nineteen came in, and seeing the two girls sidled over and sat at a table close to them. They were soon bantering and teasing, and before Bethan could think to object, they were invited to join the boys at a nearby pub.

131

"I don't think – they're a bit young, aren't they?" Bethan protested.

"They don't think so, come on."

There was a fire in the bar-room and the girls took off their coats and sat between the three boys, who plied them with drinks. During the conversation they learnt that the boys were in the army and on leave. She gestured for Bethan to follow her to the lavatories and told her:

"No money, long absences. Come on, let's go."

The boys followed them out, pleading for them to stay, promising them a meal later. When this was revealed to be fish and chips, both girls burst into laughter.

It was as they were trying to explain their amusement that Johnny saw them. He ran across the road and pulled Sheila aside.

"Maurice is back!" he said. "Just seen him coming out of the station. I couldn't stop, driving the bus I was, see. But it was him all right."

"When? Are you sure?" Sheila looked at him almost accusingly, convinced that it was either a mistake or a malicious joke.

"I wouldn't make a mistake, not about Maurice. It was him all right, coming out of the station. I'm off home now to tell Ethel. There's excited she'll be."

"There was a letter from him this morning, probably to tell her he was coming after all," Sheila spoke in a daze. She would have to write to Freddie, tell him it was over, that her husband had returned to her. Eyes shining, she said to Bethan, "Sorry, Bethan, but I have to go. My husband will expect me to be there to welcome him. Her heart increased its pumping at the prospect of that reunion. Tonight she would have some real loving, at last.

She ran most of the way up Sheepy Lane, hurrying past Ethel's cottage, convinced that Maurice would be at Gran's, standing there, sturdy and handsome, ready to beg her forgiveness and with love for her shining in his beautiful hazel eyes.

The house was in darkness. Gran had obviously gone to

132

bed. Disappointment hit her like a thin steel blade in her midriff. He wasn't there. Gran would never have gone to bed and left him. She stood at the door, shivering in the bitterly cold night air but hardly aware of the discomfort. What should she do? Was he at his mother's? Surely Ethel Davies wouldn't keep him from her? She took a few steps towards the gate, then returned to the door, undecided whether to go in and wait or run down to the cottage at the end of Sheepy Lane.

It was the coldness that decided her. That first sight of her was important. Standing outside his mother's door, her nose red and eyes smarting against the frostiness of the night, well, it wouldn't show her at her best. She pushed the key into the lock and stepped inside.

It wasn't much warmer in the hall and she hurried through to turn on the electric fire in the living room. Still in her coat, she kicked off her shoes and tucked her feet up inside it as she sat in the armchair and began to make her plans.

He might be here at any minute. She ought to get into something alluring. *Alluring*, she tried out the word again, that was how she wanted him to see her first. She left the fire after a few minutes, afraid to linger any longer, half imagining she could hear his footsteps approaching the house. She took the fire up to her bedroom and plugged it in, and in its thawing warmth, she undressed.

The night dress and matching negligee she had bought for her wedding night were still in the tissue paper where she had replaced them after Maurice had left her. She took them out and shook them from their folds. Shimmering in the yellow firelight they were more beautiful than she had remembered: white satin, insets of delicate lace. The full length figure-hugging night dress was matched by a slightly fuller skirted negligee on which embroidery was added to the lacy splendour. Seed pearls decorated the bodice in a floral pattern that was repeated at the waist. Slowly, ignoring the iciness of the touch, she slipped them on.

The room was cold but she refused to add anything that would detract from the vision she could see in the small mirror on her dressing table. Even though she was alone, she needed to feel glamorous, expecting any moment that knock on her door to announce the arrival of Maurice. The glow from the fire touched the ceiling with gold. She had turned out the over-head light and now she basked in it's radiance, picturing Maurice here beside her, his arms opening, his eyes filled with regret for the wasted months.

When she finally eased herself out of the dream for long enough, she glanced at the clock and saw it was after midnight. The shock brought tears to her eyes. Johnny had been teasing, or mistaken. It hadn't been Maurice he'd seen. If it had been, he would have come straight here to his wife, wouldn't he?

Maurice had caught a bus at about the time Johnny told Sheila he had seen him. He jumped off the bus near Amy's shop with a brief glance towards the flat where his parents-in-law lived and ran across the road. He hid his suitcase in the trees and walked up Sheepy Lane, hoping not to meet anyone he knew. Trilby tilted down to shadow his face, he walked swiftly past his mother's cottage where, even on a cold night like this, the door stood ajar and voices, laughing and talking, came to him on the still air.

Momentary guilt made his feet stumble as he passed out of sight. He wanted to go in and surprise her, but there was something he had to do first.

There were still a few Christmas trees to be seen in the windows of the houses he passed as he walked up through the council houses. Through open curtains he glanced into the lit rooms and saw streamers of coloured paper bedecked with sparkling ornaments and balloons, evidence of the celebration just coming to an end and of some families' reluctance to let it go.

He didn't go to the house where Sheila lived with her gran but to Delina Honeyman's home. It was thoughts of Delina that had prevented him from settling to the new life Australia offered, that and the homesickness that kept him awake at night. He wished he had stayed and faced the old biddies in the village and refused to let Delina go. Why had he been so weak? He wouldn't make that mistake again. It wasn't too late, it couldn't be too late. Delina would still love him. It was that thought that had refused to leave his mind since his voluntary exile.

There was no light showing in her window but he remembered the thickness of the curtains and guessed that behind them the room was occupied. His heart was racing now that he was close to her. He had only to knock on the door and wait and she would open it and see him and . . . and all his misery would be ended.

He raised his hand to lift the knocker but, at that moment, he heard someone approaching, talking and laughing. A couple, just like he and Delina would soon be. He was aware of the slowness of their progress and guessed they were lovers, reluctant to end the blissful solitude of the walk home. He lifted his hand to the knocker and again he hesitated. He would wait until they passed. But they didn't pass. The couple stopped at the gate and in the faint light from the street lamp he tried to recognise them. The gate began to move and he slipped away into the darkness of a corner and watched.

Delina he recognised at once. He smiled at how wrong he had been. Lovers! More likely to be Delina and her brother talking and walking slowly simply because of the hill. But it wasn't her brother. He saw them kiss and then Delina reached out and opened the door and they both went inside. Delina and Tad! How dare he. He'd make the little man pay, oh yes he would.

Maurice stood for a long time, the cold eating into his bones, but Tad didn't come out. He was tired and very hungry but he couldn't leave, not without making certain of what he had seen. Then he would go – but where? He hadn't thought further than seeing Delina, asking her to come back to him and sorting everything out so they could be together.

He didn't move as the door opened two hours later and

he watched as Delina and Tad kissed again, then waited as Tad walked away, short hurried footsteps taking him down the hill to where his daughter was being looked after by Nelly and George.

Only when the footsteps had faded and the door had been closed and bolted did he move. Then he went to his mother's house and asked for food and a bed.

In the house on St Illtyd's Road, high above the small cottage where he finally slept, Sheila sat on her bed, dozing and waiting, hope fading but never quite extinguished.

Ethel Davies rose early. On this morning she made sure her son rose, too.

"Come on, Maurice love, it's time you went to see your Sheila. It would be unfair if she learnt that you were home from someone else."

"Later, Mam. There's something I've got to get sorted first."

"I'd have thought you'd had plenty of time for getting things sorted! Go and see your wife. If you've any kind of life ahead of you you must go and talk things over with her."

"How is Delina?" he asked, dreading his mother's reply.

"Well enough and happy. She was here at Christmas and she and Tad Simmons announced their engagement. We're all pleased for them both." Her dark eyes watched her son, trying to make the words sound casual, knowing they would hurt but knowing too that they had to be said.

"She's going to marry Tad?"

"Why not? He needs someone to look after him and that daughter of his, and they are well suited."

"What about her brothers? She shouldn't be thinking of leaving them now her mother's gone."

"We can't live for other people all our lives, and from what I gather Victor might be giving them a step-mother before very long. Delina has her own life to live."

"She loved me, Mam."

"Love can die and it can be killed. Sheila had more right

136

to your name than Delina. Go now and see Sheila, you'll catch her before she leaves for work."

"I'm going to see Johnny. I'll see Sheila when she get's home."

"Have some breakfast before you – " but he had grabbed a coat and was gone.

Phil-the-post usually called in to his mother's house for a second breakfast. He found Ethel sitting staring into space and no kettle on the boil.

"Mam? You all right, love?" he asked, throwing down his bag and pushing the kettle over the fire. "A bad night, was it?"

"An even worse morning," Ethel said, rousing herself and reaching for the loaf to cut some bread for his toast. "Our Maurice is back."

"But that's great! Where is he? Still in bed? Lazy sod, I'll soon get him out of there, a glass of cold water will do the trick."

"He's gone out. He hasn't been to see Sheila and from the little he's told me, he doesn't much want to."

"Still after that Delina, is he? Well that's soon sorted, tell him she's going to marry Tad."

"He knows." She held the thick slice of bread in front of the fire until it browned, then spread it thickly with butter and handed it to him. "And from the look on his face he isn't greatly pleased."

Phil went on his way after trying to reassure his mother that a few weeks would see the end of Maurice's misery. He told everyone he met and, although there was no letter for Nelly, he went down her path to be greeted by the barking dogs and the chorus of chortling chickens and told her, too.

"When's the party?" she asked, passing him a plate of cakes. "Your mam'll 'ave a party to welcome 'im back like the prodigal son, won't she?"

"Between you and me and the gate-post, Nelly, I'm not sure Maurice is in the mood for parties. I think he expected

137

to come home to Delina and finding out she's promised to Tad, well, it's put him in a bit of a mood, like. Not a word, though, best let him sort it out for himself without everyone knowing."

"I'll only tell as many as you've told, Phil," she laughed.

"That's it then, half the village'll know by dinner time!" he groaned. "Got any more of them cakes?"

"Young Dawn was 'ere last night while Tad took Delina out for 'er birthday. She ate most of 'em, but there'll be some more ready fer tomorrer."

Wednesday was half day for Sheila and she usually stayed in town for a while to do some shopping. Today she wanted to hide. Three people she met asked about Maurice and, unable to admit that as yet she hadn't seen him, she was forced to hurry on and pretend she was shopping for his dinner. Almost without intending to, she bought a joint of beef and some vegetables as if the dinner was a reality. She stepped off the bus with two heavily laden bags, ignored her mother calling her from the doorway of Amy's shop, and hurried home.

She went in hoping against hope that Maurice would be there or would have left a message for her, but there was only Gran sitting in front of the fire reading a library book.

It was only half past three yet there was need for a light as she set about preparing to cook the meal. She did too many vegetables, some foolish faith making her believe that he would come. She resisted the temptation to take off her shoes and put on the slippers she habitually wore at home, and the cardigan she felt the need of was hung over her shoulders, ready to be dropped when Maurice arrived. She touched up her makeup and combed her hair until she was satisfied it was looking its best. The satin night-wear was draped across her bed.

The meat was sending out delicious and tempting aromas, the table was partly set, the rice pudding out to cool, when there was a knock at the door. Sheila froze in the act of

138

carrying a bowl of fruit through to place on the table. She was afraid to answer the door, afraid of another disappointment.

"Door, Sheila," Gran called, unnecessarily.

"I'm going as fast as I can," Sheila hissed, and she dumped the fruit bowl down and hurriedly hid the shapeless cardigan under a cushion.

Taking a moment to calm herself, she walked slowly towards the door. Maurice was raising his hand to rap the knocker again. He stopped, stared at her, and said softly, unsure of his welcome:

"Hello, Sheila, can we talk?"

"I'm just in the middle of getting dinner." She was proud of her calm response.

"I'll wait – if I may?"

"You can join us, there's plenty." She turned and walked away from him towards the kitchen, while he closed the door and removed his coat.

In the kitchen she took another deep breath. He was still as handsome as she had remembered, but so untidy. He hadn't even shaved. Tears of disappointment sprang into her eyes and she looked at the meal in dismay, she didn't think she could eat a thing. She sensed rather than heard him come into the room behind her and without looking around, said:

"Carry the meat in for me, will you?"

"Sheila, I – "

"We'll eat first, Maurice, Gran won't enjoy a cold meal."

Gran was pleased to see him and said so. She didn't ask any questions but chattered between mouthfuls of the delicious meal about mutual friends. Sheila was shaking inside and was thankful that she needed to say little apart from the occasional yes or no.

"Are you staying with your Mam?" Sheila asked, as she abandoned the small amount of food she had put on her plate and stood to fetch the pudding.

"I haven't decided what I'll do," he said. He looked at her

139

and she widened her eyes, trying to look calm and appealing and utterly sensible of his dilemma. "Sheila, I'm sorry for all this."

"Rice pudding or fruit?" she demanded.

They ate the rest of the meal in silence.

Sheila was out of her depth. She didn't know what to say to Maurice or how to behave. He followed her into the kitchen after the solemn meal was thankfully over, congratulated her on her cooking skills, and said she was looking well: small talk, unnatural small talk. She tried to think of amusing things to tell him about what had been happening to her and the people he knew but everything seemed dull and unimportant. He didn't offer any information about what he had been doing and the conversation attempts all ended in failure.

She wanted him, and wondered if there was anything left of the attraction she had once held for him. His face held no clues. He looked tired and suddenly, unable to resist, she said vehemently,

"Pity you couldn't even be bothered to shave before coming to see me."

"I've been walking around half the night and all day, trying to pluck up courage," he said.

"I've never considered myself frightening and certainly not dangerous to a big man like you, Maurice." This was better, a bit of bantering might lead them into some kind of conversation.

"Can I come and see you again tomorrow?"

"If you like. I'll be working all day, mind. But you can meet me after the shop closes."

"Do you have to go in? Can't you ring up and tell them you're sick or something?"

For a moment she was tempted, but she shook her head. Best not be too eager. She didn't want him to think she was here waiting for him without him having to at least do some courting.

"Please, Sheila. I want to talk to you. I've been so miserable."

140

"And what about me? Left here to face them all, having a baby on my own seeing faces turned against me, blaming me – yes me, Maurice – for ruining Delina's wedding."

Her high voice fascinated him, just as it had when she had first attracted him. He hardly heard the words she was saying. He wondered if, after all the mess, there might be a chance of them trying again. She looked at him and saw a slight smile on the stubbly face and hit out at him, a small hand against his muscular chest. He caught hold of her hand and held it.

"Forgive me, Sheila. Stay home tomorrow, tell your boss you aren't well, and we'll talk."

"No, Maurice, I can't let them down."

He reached for his coat and put it on.

"I'll be at Mam's if you change your mind."

Sheila threw the fancy night-clothes off her bed and sat down against the pillows. She wouldn't sleep, there was no chance she'd even close her eyes after such an evening. She wished she had asked him to stay. She was entitled, they were man and wife and she wanted him, needed him in her bed.

Perhaps she would telephone from the box on the corner and tell her boss she was ill. The monthlies, they were always an acceptable excuse for being "unwell", no one asked any questions about that. She reached for her diary to see when she was last "unwell", flipping through the empty pages, days in which nothing had happened worth recording.

Then her face blanched, her blue eyes widened with shock. Her period was due five weeks ago. Surely she wasn't expecting again?

CHAPTER ELEVEN

Hilda didn't enjoy working at Tolly's, the local name for *The Plough*. She had expected to be offered the job of barmaid but being employed as a cleaner made this unacceptable. Even when she went into the bar after her work was finished, dressed in her new clothes and with her hair and nails immaculate, she was still Hilda the cleaner, and although she realised that the work was easy in comparison with the hours spent behind the fish and chip shop, she would have to find something better.

Working in the mornings gave her plenty of time to look for something else and having made up her mind, that was what she did. After going home to change her clothes she went into town day after day, applying for jobs. She decided to be bold and even entered the glass doorway of the gown shop where Sheila had once worked, but without success.

There was an old gramophone at home, the wind-up instrument having escaped her wild sorting and throwing out of most of her furniture, because of the beautiful oak cabinet in which it was housed. One day she wandered into the record shop and stood listening to the faint sounds coming from the cubicle where customers stood to listen to their choices.

On impulse she asked the manager if he had a job for her. He did and she was taken on to begin the following week. Gleefully she went to Tolly's to tell them she would no longer be their cleaner, and went home contented. Her life was falling neatly into place and the problem of how to deal with Griff was still months away. She would work four and a half days at the shop, with Monday off and

Wednesday a half day, and still have time to spare to enjoy herself.

The Saturday morning, early in January, was bleak and the hills had a look of unmelting winter about them as Nelly shepherded the two children up Gypsy Lane to the camp beside the road. They were invited inside the small neat vardo and, to Margaret's delight, were shown how to make some of the flowers the gypsies sold to make a few pennies to eek out their money until the farm work began again in the spring. Her fingers weren't as nimble as Clara's but she soon managed to produce a flower that, if not as good as the others, at least good enough to take home for her mother.

"Why are the gypsies so kind to you, Nelly?" Margaret asked as they walked back down the lane clutching the flowers they had been given. "Mam says they keep to themselves, that means they don't like visitors, doesn't it?"

"Well, it's on account of my Norman Birkett, 'im what died under a London bus. 'E was a gypsy, but for Gawd's sake don't tell my Evie I've let on. She 'ates to think 'er father was anything less than a duke!"

"You mean my real grandfather was a gypsy?" Oliver's eyes glowed with pleasure.

"Yes 'e was an' don't you go lettin' on or Evie'll 'ave me guts fer garters. An' don't tell 'er I said that neither!" Nelly laughed.

"Will you tell me all about him one day?" Oliver asked, still wide-eyed with wonder. Nelly promised that she would.

Amy was inundated with offers to help her with her garden. Although it was too early to do more than some digging, she often went home from the shop to find Billie had cleared a patch ready for planting or Victor had delivered some soil or some shrubs. They would leave notes in her letter box and she began to chuckle as she approached the door each evening, wondering which of

143

them had managed to think of something else to do to please her.

"Billie just won't take no for an answer," she laughed as she told Mavis about the rivalry, one morning. "And Victor is afraid I'll change my mind."

"And will you?"

"No, it's Victor I'll marry if anyone. Not Billie, lovely as he is. Shame, really. If he'd accept what I say, he might look elsewhere. We could have a double wedding, that would be fun, wouldn't it? A double wedding in Hen Carw Parc?"

"Just so long as you didn't end up marrying the wrong one!" snapped Mavis.

"Like your Sheila did?" Amy asked softly. "What's happening with her and that Maurice? Any chance of them trying to make it work?"

"How would I know? Sheila doesn't tell me a thing, never has."

"Where's he staying?"

"With his mother. Ethel says she's tried to make him go back to Sheila, but I doubt that. Her youngest son, her baby, I doubt she'll want him to go."

"You're wrong there, Ethel would want him to be with his wife." Amy spoke more sharply. Whatever Mavis's troubles were with her daughter, it wouldn't help to put blame where it didn't belong. "Have you tried to bring them together?" she asked.

"Sheila won't let me do anything."

"Why not ask them to dinner then go out and leave them to talk? It's talking they must do for sure."

Amy hoped her anxiety didn't show. She had a strong concern for the fate of Sheila and Maurice's marriage. More than she dare admit, she wanted them to come together and live as man and wife. Perhaps then her son Freddie would get over his obsession and find a girl of his own who would love him, not use him, as Sheila was doing.

Sheila's reasons for wanting Maurice to accept her as his wife were even stronger than Amy's. Days passed and still

144

there was no sign of escape from the awful truth. She was expecting another baby. If only she had been strong for a few weeks longer. But Maurice's writing to tell them he wouldn't be home after all had seemed the very end of her hopes. Freddie wanted her so much and his desire had fired her own. What had happened between them had been inevitable, but disasterous. What could she do?

She saw Maurice often. After that first uneasy interview she had begun to call into Ethel's on the way home after work. Sometimes he was there and other times Ethel would explain that she didn't know where he was to be found. On these days she would hurry up the hill hoping he would be waiting for her.

After several disappointments she began to wonder where he went and came up with the thought that it was probably Delina he was spending time with. She put on her best, off-white swagger coat and under it wore a tight skirt with a bright red jumper to match the lining of the hood. Then she walked down to where the Honeyman's lived.

She saw him standing there and walked up to him and asked: "On your way to see me, were you?"

"Oh, hello, Sheila, where are you going? Somewhere nice? you look very smart."

"I thought you said we have to talk? How can we talk if I'm at home and you're standing here like a tom cat on the prowl? She's engaged to marry Tad, Maurice, and in case you've forgotten," she added huskily, "you are married to me."

Her voice revealed no anger or disappointment, her eyes showed a hint of tears as she looked up at him with unhidden love and admiration.

"All right, Sheila, none of this is really your fault. I'll come back and we'll talk.

They talked as they walked to her house, but nothing was decided. He agreed with her comments but made no offer of a solution.

"Give me time," was all he said. "I need time."

How much time he had already had seemed too obvious

145

to point out. How little time she had before the truth about her condition would be impossible to hide was too dreadful to think about.

Nelly complained that since the advent of television there were fewer meetings and social evenings in the village. The enthusiasm of the villagers, gardeners and non-gardeners alike changed all that, for a while anyway.

During February, Bert Roberts and Billie seemed to be involved in some gathering or other every evening.

"It's worse than fire-watching during the war," Brenda Roberts complained one morning when they met in Amy's shop. "No sooner does Bert swallow his meal than he's off to discuss some idea or other with Billie. There's another meeting this evening would you believe? at the usual venue *The Drovers* of course! This time about the number of window boxes and hanging baskets per house. And the meetings never end 'til stop-tap!"

Nelly nodded sympathetically and planned an easy meal for that evening so she could join in the discussion.

"You comin' Amy?" she asked as Brenda left the shop.

"If Margaret will come with me, love. Although I want to leave the planning of my garden to Freddie, if I can persuade Billie and Victor to stop using it as a battle-ground!"

"Still fightin' over you, are they?"

"I'm afraid so. I've told Billie clearly that I won't marry him but he still hopes." She laughed, her earrings twinkling in the artificial light. "Just think of it, talk about bountiful blessings. For years I had no one, no one that was free anyway, now there's Bachelor Billie and Widower Victor."

"'Ang on, Amy, there might be another one on the horizon. Everything goes in threes so they say!"

It was George's idea that they pooled the contributions to the fund. That way no one felt unable to compete. The meeting that evening was to distribute flower seeds and

146

cuttings to those able to protect them from the weeks of frost to come.

"I've got seventeen geranium plants in me back bed-room," Nelly announced. "What I want is some flowers to put with em."

"My Catrina would like some petunias," Phil said.

"To add to what we already have in hand, my wife would like some mesembryanthemums, calceolarias, and some ageratum," Timothy said in his precise manner.

"She would!" was Nelly's hoarsely whispered comment.

The demands and suggestions went on, with Bert trying to write everything down, frustrated as usual by the fact that although he had borrowed a gavel with which to bang on the bar, no one took any notice of him.

Nelly was given drinks by Billie and Victor, both of whom hoped to get her on their side in the fight for Amy. Sheila turned up in the hope of seeing Maurice and was also given a drink, out of sympathy for the way Maurice was behaving. Amy arrived having left Margaret with Delina and Tad brought along a list of materials he had been promised from the factory where he worked.

"There's some material to line the wooden boxes we're making for the window sills," he reported, "and some barrels which we can cut down and fill with plants."

"I'll have a couple of those," the landlord shouted. "The bigger the better. I'll be one of the first houses the judges'll see remember."

Sheila sat sipping the drinks that kept appearing in front of her and watching the door for Maurice to arrive. When he did it was almost nine o'clock and when she half stood to greet him, she felt her head spinning. She rarely drank and sitting here, absorbing the sympathy, she hadn't realised how much alcohol she had also absorbed.

Best not to attempt to talk to Maurice now, she thought. What if she began to stumble over her words. She didn't want him to have any excuse to criticise her or the way she lived. Pushing aside the last two glasses and nodding to Nelly to suggest she might like to finish them, she

147

stood and walked with the infinite care of the unstable to the bar.

"Get me a taxi, will you?" she asked the barman, handing him twopence for the phone.

She went outside to wait having failed to exchange even a glance with Maurice and as the wind was chill she huddled against the wall for shelter.

Light shone on the surface of the car park as the door opened again. A figure came out and stood, lifting his collar high, adjusting the trilby hat on his head. She held her breath. It was Maurice.

Now there was a chance to talk she daren't. She knew she would sound drunk. Hardly daring to breathe she waited until the taxi came from the direction of Llan Gwyn and turned to pull up near the door. Without glancing in the direction of Maurice, she ran to open the door and slid inside. The door on the other side opened as hers closed. Maurice slipped in and gave her address to the driver.

She hesitated to speak, although the cold air and the surprise of Maurice following her out had made her feel less fuddled.

"You don't mind, do you?" he asked as the car sped along the wet road towards the village.

"Going to your mothers, are you?" she said and to her relief her voice sounded normal, high-pitched and, she convinced herself, quite musical.

"No, Sheila, I've put this off long enough. I think we should have that talk, don't you?"

At once her body was swamped with emotions and sensations of loving. In her mind she was already in his arms, felt the warmth of desire flooding through her veins, she remembered surrendering to the passion of his kisses the thoughts coming vividly to her mind and taking her far from the smokey, stale-smelling taxi. She was transported to the trees which were the usual scene of their loving, the warm, sweet-scented summer grass, the cold, crisp winter countryside, magical places as fresh in her memory as if they had happened yesterday not over a year ago. She had to persuade him to come to her bed. She had always been able to persuade him in the past and she didn't think her body was less voluptuous now than it had been then.

He was looking at her, in the reflection of the few streetlights his face was dark and mysterious and she realised she hadn't replied.

"Talk, Maurice? If that's what you want, we'll talk."

Victor walked up Nelly's lane with Amy, Nelly and George. His arm rested lightly on Amy's shoulders. Having to walk up and collect Margaret meant that even if she had wished, Amy had to refuse the lift Billie offered her in his Landrover. Hugging her close, he touched her cheek with a secret kiss unseen by Nelly and George, but the sharp-eared Nelly had guessed from the slightly stumbling footsteps and shouted back,

"Come on there, no snoggin' in the back row like a couple of kids. Can't you wait 'til you get 'ome?"

Margaret and Daniel were quietly reading when they reached Victor's house. Delina, too, was sitting with her head in a book. Of David there was no sign.

"Where's David?" Victor asked as he went in and found Amy a seat near the dying fire.

"Gone to bed," Delina answered.

"I think I bore him, Uncle Victor," Margaret said with a wry smile. "I offered to play ludo or snakes and ladders, but he said they were boring, too."

"Cheeky young pup – "

"It's all right," Margaret smiled. "I said I was happy to read, and he lent me this." She showed him a book about the adventures of "Romany", a man who lived in a caravan and wrote about the countryside. "After I told him about my visit to the gypsies near Mr Leighton's farm. I think he might like to come with Nelly and me one day."

Victor walked Amy and Margaret back to their house, pushing his bike beside him for the ride home. For part of the way, Margaret, still clutching the book David had lent her, sat on the saddle while he pushed her.

149

"If anyone can sort out that unhappy son of mine, perhaps your Margaret can," he whispered to Amy as he kissed her goodnight.

Sheila was nervous when she closed the door and allowed Maurice to relieve her of her coat. The house was cold but she quickly put on the kettle, and added logs to the living room fire to revive it to at least a blaze. She leaned forward into as provocative a pose as possible when she added the logs. Then she stood straight to give a full view of her figure in the tight-fitting jumper. She widened her eyes as she asked if he preferred tea or coffee and wondered if, somewhere deep inside him, there was an echoing response to her desire. His first words gave her little encouragement to hope.

"I came home to start clearing up the mess we made of everything."

"How d'you propose to do that, Maurice?"

"End the farce that was called a marriage, as soon as we can."

She hoped the shock she felt charge through her didn't show. She held the teapot in her hand, intending to take it into the kitchen to fill, and suddenly it was too heavy to hold. Hiding her face, she placed it on the table.

"I'll just go and make the tea," she whispered.

"Damn the tea." He reached out to touch her arm but she pulled gently away.

"Sit down, Maurice. I need a cup even if you don't."

He sat, still wearing his brown overcoat, and with the trilby on his knee. She left him there, seeing in the drooping shoulders the unhappiness he felt. If only she could persuade him to stay. Just one night would do. At least there was a slight chance then of people believing the baby was his, born in wedlock. She took in the tray of tea and stood, her eyes looking at him with such a depth of sadness that he stood up and came towards her. With a few ladylike tears, she clung to him.

"Oh, Maurice, I'm sorry for all this. I was so innocent,

so lacking in knowledge. If I'd been more worldly, less of a child, things needn't have ended the way they did. I loved you enough to say goodbye to you, to have given you up to someone who you loved more than me, but with the baby, I – "

"If Delina had loved me enough, we could have worked something out," he said, moved by her declaration. "I thought she did, and I certainly believed I loved her enough for two of us."

"Is she why you came back, Maurice?" Sheila asked, snuggling a little closer into his arms.

"I thought of her all the time. To say I felt homesick sounds like the confession of a child, but I was. I dreamt night after night of seeing her again, walking down the familiar roads and lanes, have her teach me the names of the beautiful birds and wild flowers that grow in our valley."

Sheila pretended it was herself he had missed, and her lips moved to touch his neck, just the slightest touch but it was enough.

"You don't have to tell me about loneliness, Maurice," she whispered, her breath in his ear.

"Sheila, I must go, this wasn't what I planned, I – "

"Don't leave me again, Maurice, not tonight, please."

"I can't stay. It wouldn't be right."

"But you want to, don't you? And I want you to. Who will know?"

His head turned slowly, he stared down at her; young, desirable and unbelievably willing. After all he had put her through she was able to forgive him and share her love with him. As their lips met and their bodies moved to seek contact, Sheila gave a tiny squeal of triumph.

CHAPTER TWELVE

Amy couldn't decide whether to tell Freddie of Maurice's return or let him discover it for himself. Any mention of Sheila created a barrier between them. She was unable to hide her dislike of the girl and whenever she spoke of her had great difficulty avoiding words of warning like some old gossip. Eventually she put a few words in a letter to him and hoped that the bald statement, "Maurice arrived home last week", would be sufficient to at least prevent him walking in and finding them together.

She wasn't even sure they were together. Seeing them go off home in a taxi didn't mean anything and from what she learned from Phil-the-post – self-appointed purveyor of news – Maurice was still living with his mother.

The response to the letter came swiftly via a telephone call to the shop.

"What's happened, Mam?" he demanded, and Amy knew what he referred to.

"Well, love, all I can tell you is that after Maurice wrote to say he wouldn't be coming after all, something happened to change his mind and he's here. Other than that, I know nothing." She didn't want to volunteer the information that so far as she knew he wasn't living with his wife, although she hoped every day to have news that he was. It would cheer and encourage him to know they were still apart, but she couldn't tell him.

"Where, I mean, where are they?" Freddie asked.

Deliberately misunderstanding, Amy said, "I don't know, love, Sheila will be working I expect."

"Where are they living, Mam?" He began to sound angry,

guessing her reticence, knowing the reason for it. "Are they together, you know what I'm asking."

"I don't know, love," she insisted. "The last time I saw them they were going home together in a taxi. There, does that answer your question. It's the best I can do."

"Find out for me will you, Mam?"

"All right, Freddie love, I'll try," she promised sadly.

When Billie came into the shop a while later she was sitting staring pensively into space and she hardly looked up when he pushed open the door and filled the shop with his substantial size.

"Is something wrong, Amy?" he asked.

"Oh, sorry, Billie, I was day-dreaming."

"Of something sad by the look of you."

"Not really, I was thinking of how trouble-free children are when they're small, yet at the time I remember thinking that it must be the worst time of all, that everything would smooth out once they were over their childhood. But then the problems were mostly solved with a kiss, a cuddle or a dab of ointment. Now, well, everything that happens seems impossible to sort out."

"Freddie."

"Yes, Freddie. And that Sheila Davies. D'you know what's happening there? I wonder if Mary would know. Ordering an extra pint of milk can be a clue to lots of goings on, can't it?"

He chuckled.

"Will you ask her for me?"

"Everything from an unexpected visitor to a children's party, it's all there in the notes left out for Mary. What d'you want to know?"

"If Maurice and Sheila are together or not. I promised Freddie I'd find out and I can't ask them upstairs, can I?" she pointed her finger above her, to where Mavis and Ralph Powell sat watching the window for sight of their daughter returning from work.

"I'll ask. Now, will you come to the farm on Sunday – bring Victor as well, if you must," he added quickly as she raised her fair head to protest. "You and Margaret and Victor, and those boys of his as well if you like, bring an army, but come. Margaret and I have a surprise for you. Oh," he grinned, "and in case you still fear to be compromised or have Victor wild with jealousy, we want Oliver to come as well."

"Billie Brown, you're daft," she laughed.

"That's me," he agreed. "Daft – about you."

"And you'll find out –?"

"I'll find out. See you Sunday?"

"See you Sunday."

Oliver and Margaret often spent Saturday afternoon at the farm, and recently they had been making some boxes for the villagers to place on their window sills and on specially made benches. These would be filled with flowering plants in May, to add to the effort of beautifying their village.

Margaret was not very successful. The nails bent one way then, after being straightened by Billie, would then bend the other way. Her box was finished, but as she only too willingly admitted, it needed a bit of support to keep it upright.

"You are much cleverer at this than me," she told Oliver.

"I've helped Grandad and Uncle Billie lots of times," Oliver said. "It's only practise, like your piano. If you'd helped as often as me, then you'd be able to do it. Probably better than I can, too."

The others who came and went at the farm – Victor, Johnny, Bert, Tad, Phil, and Billie himself – teased Margaret about some of her efforts, but Oliver never did. He'd suffered too much criticism himself to be able to enjoy dealing it out to another, even in fun.

There were several places in the village where work went on making the wooden structures needed for the display, but Billie and Mary's farm had become one of the most popular. Firstly because of the space in the barns he had placed at their disposal, and secondly because of Mary's food. The long walk down through the fields and back again seemed well worth the effort and for her part Mary enjoyed baking platefuls of tarts and cakes and watching them all disappear.

On Sunday, after lunch, Oliver arrived at Amy's house and walked to the farm with Amy and Margaret. Phil was already there. He and his brother Sidney had made containers for Ethel and some for the end of Sheepy Lane. Even houses like Ethel's which were unlikely to catch the judges's eyes, wanted to be a part of the display.

"Look, Mam," Margaret said proudly. In the small utility room, that served as a porchway to the kitchen, was a long trough made of wood and in it were several geraniums that Mary had overwintered in her hall. "I made that and I helped Auntie Mary to fill it with flowers."

"Margaret, you didn't! I bet Billie did it for you."

"All by myself, Mam, except Uncle Billie had to keep straightening the nails."

Amy walked around with Billie and was surprised at the amount of work already achieved. They were laughing at Phil's idea of garlanding the neck of Archie Pierce when Victor arrived. With him were his sons and Delina, Tad and Dawn. Amy saw Margaret's disappointed face and she at once hugged her and reminded her that she was the youngest to have made something, and also the first to display some flowers.

Oliver came to stand beside them as if supporting Margaret and reminding Dawn that she was the latecomer, and Amy chuckled inwardly at the early start to Margaret's romantic perplexities. Amy left them then and went to greet Victor. She noted with relief that there was no unease between Billie and Victor. The crowd was good-natured and the work kept them all occupied.

The weather was cold: there had been a fall of snow on the previous day and remnants of it lay like abandoned sheep-skins against the walls and hedges and in hollows on the hills. The Feburary day was short, with clouds darkening the hills and threatening further falls. The afternoon ended early with a chill gloom. But inside the barn Billie had fixed up lights and the interior was bright and cheerful as the men went on with their tasks. When Mary called to say the third offering of tea and cakes was ready Amy thought it was time to take Margaret and Oliver home, but when she went into the large farm kitchen she saw that Sheila had arrived with Maurice. She was so relieved at seeing them together she gave the girl an unexpectedly warm greeting.

"Sheila, love, how are you? Still enjoying working at the gift shop are you?"

"I'm fine, Mrs Prichard," Sheila said warily.

There was an anxious look in Sheila's fine blue eyes as she looked at Amy. She dreaded Amy mentioning that she and Freddie had been . . . friends: the euphemism came into her mind with practised ease. Lying, even to herself, was necessary to prevent Maurice finding an excuse to leave her again.

They were still living apart, but Maurice had twice called to see her and on both occasions she had ended up in his arms. Precarious as the relationship was, she had hopes that lifted each day and made her heart sing. He was so handsome and his loving so satisfying. They were so good together that it had to be the same for him, it *had* to.

Seeing Delina there was a shock and at once she regretted coming. She knew that Maurice and his ex-fiancée had not yet met, although Maurice still spent some time at the Honeyman's gate, hidden in the shadows, watching her but not speaking. Now, in the enforced intimacy of the small gathering, caught in the oasis of light in the workshop on the dark winter evening, they would have to acknowledge each other.

Her hand crept up to take Maurice's arm but she forced it back down again. Now was not the time to make a move, remind him she was there. It had to be after Maurice had faced his previous love and, hopefully, found the reality less perfect than the memory.

Delina walked towards them as Mary, Margaret and

156

Dawn entered with trays of food. Sheila decided to be bold and not allow the girl to make her lose her nerve.

"Hello, Delina. Hello, Tad. Dawn's busy I see," she said, her high voice making everyone stop and listen. Phil coughed to cover the sudden silence and tried to call Tad over to check on something he had been attempting, hoping to ease the tension of which everyone was suddenly aware. But his attempt to talk only made his cough more apparent and he could only watch as Maurice and Tad faced each other.

"It's like a flaming cowboy film, with the handsome hero and the bulky baddy, meeting with guns slung at the ready!" he whispered to Billie.

Everyone began to busy themselves with the food and there was an air of exaggarated jollity as Phil and the others watched with sideward glances as the two men met and tried at the same time to appear not to be looking at each other. The talk grew louder, and the tea cups rattled. But not for long. Maurice handed the empty cup to Phil and said to Tad:

"I hear you consider yourself engaged then?"

"I don't understand," Tad replied, stepping closer to Delina who stood white-faced and still. "Delina and I announced our intention to marry on Christmas Day at your mother's house, actually. Aren't you going to congratulate us?"

"I don't think so." Maurice turned his back and began to talk to Phil about the plans for their mother's house.

Tad felt rage fill his body, twisting inside him, desperate for release. Delina sensed it and pulled him away.

"Tad, let's find Dawn and the boys and go home," she said firmly. "I don't want there to be any trouble, do you?"

"The man is so damned ignorant. He can't turn his back on you like that!"

"I didn't expect anything else, and you aren't angry for me, you're angry for youself. Come on, please. Look there's Dawn carrying the cups back to the kitchen, it's late enough."

He turned with her and even managed to smile and wave as she called cheerio to everyone. Dawn complained at having to go but pulled her coat around her and admitted that it was getting a bit cold. As they walked away towards the road Tad heard some whispered comment and Maurice's voice swelled to fill the air with derisory laughter. The words "the little chappie" were all he heard and if it hadn't been for Delina's firm grip on his arm he would have turned and smashed his fist into the man's face.

"I'm going to have a bit of fun with that little fella," Maurice said loudly, and although he appeared to be talked around by his brother, Phil, the look on his face was proof that the idea still appealed. If Delina was lost to him then he would make sure the little chappie was humiliated enough to lose her, too. One day he would be free and then he wanted Delina to be free as well.

Nelly was listening to the radio. She and George had enjoyed *Ring For Jeeves* earlier in the afternoon and were now laughing at *Life With The Lyons*. Amy and Margaret and Victor heard their laughter before they had opened the gate and set the dogs barking. They went into the warm, friendly room and sat and listened with them until it ended, with Nelly interspersing a few necessary explanations about what had gone before.

George didn't get up as he usually did to offer the visitors the chair closest to the fire. He smiled at Margaret and offered his knee for her to sit on. His breath was sounding in his chest and she slid to the floor and sat between his feet, afraid her weight would make him feel worse.

"Are you all right?" she asked him in her rather prim way and he hugged her shoulders and nodded.

"Better for seeing you and your mother, young Margaret."

"There seemed a bit of a sparking between Tad and young Maurice," Amy told them when the programme had finished. "Tad seemed ready to take on Maurice. His fists were tight and it was as if they were both just waiting for a wrong word to be spoken to start them off. It was only Delina's calming influence that made him hold back."

"Blimey! We don't want no wars breakin' out 'ere," Nelly said, brown eyes rolling heavenward. "Enough trouble with Bert Roberts trying to organise the flowers I'd 'ave thought!"

"Was it serious?" George asked. "I'd have expected some glaring and a show of disapproval. It will probably blow over."

"Simmering is how I'd describe it," Victor said, pouring the water from the kettle to make a cup of tea. "And simmering, like this kettle, sounds calm and almost peaceful. But the water is bubbling just the same."

"Good heavens, we are getting poetic," Amy laughed.

"I'm afraid that if that particular kettle boils over, my Delina will be scalded, love," Victor said. "Still, let's hope it won't happen, eh? What about a cup of your tea, Nelly. Like one would you?" He reached over to the cupboard where the cups were stored and brought out sufficient for them all.

"Sorry I made light of the rivalry between Maurice and Tad," Amy said as they walked home down the dark lane. "I really didn't think it was that serious, love."

"Mam," Margaret said, taking an arm of each of them, "I didn't like today. Not one bit."

"Why, love?"

"Tad and that show-off Maurice Davies quarrelling frightened me. And George, he isn't well again, is he?"

"All we need now is for Freddie to come home," Amy sighed as she and Nelly began cleaning the storeroom behind the shop. It was Monday and Mavis was serving in the shop. They usually worked on a Sunday morning while the shop was shut, but Nelly had asked to change the day, wanting to spend George's day off with him.

"I don't think it would be a bad idea, Amy," Nelly replied, using her backside to heave a cask of vinegar into place. "P'raps if he saw for 'imself that Sheila an'

Maurice was tryin' again 'e'd be better able to ferget 'er."

"I don't know. The way he feels about her he'd still be her protector, watching out for her in case Maurice didn't look after her properly. Poor Freddie."

When they had finished they went into the shop to find it crowded and Mavis frantically busy serving them all. Nelly sat on a crate of cauliflowers while Amy helped. Evie came in, gave a casual "hello" to her mother and asked for some of the daffodil bulbs that Amy was selling off cheaply.

"They'll be too late, Evie," Nelly told her. "My George put ours in months ago."

"They'll grow and be established for next year," Evie said. "Timothy is becoming quite knowledgable about gardening and he says – "

"Ere, while I think of it, Evie, the gypsies are in the lane with their 'orses. D'you want a barrer load of 'orse sh – "

"Mother! Really!" Evie glared at Nelly and stalked out of the shop.

"'Orse shovellings. What's the matter with er?" Nelly asked of the customers at large. "I was only goin' ter say 'orse shovellings!"

When the shop finally emptied, Nelly announced that she was going for some fish and chips.

"'Ave some fer you an' Margaret why don't yer?" she offered. "Save you goin' all that way 'ome, an' it's perishin' cold out there."

While they were all debating about what they would have, a bus stopped on it's way from Swansea to Llan Gwyn and a khaki clad figure jumped off.

"Freddie!" Amy said, running to greet him, throwing off her apron as she went.

"Extra 'elpin' of fish an' chips then?" Nelly yelled.

With the door blind pulled down and the heater full on, the impromptu picnic was a success. Amy supplied tea and they all sat in the small shop and ate their meal out of the paper in which it arrived. The subject of Sheila was carefully avoided. They all made Freddie laugh with

160

descriptions of Hilda's new life-style, and interested him with explanations of what was being planned for the Best Kept Village Competition.

It was after Nelly had taken her dogs and gone home to prepare a meal for George and Mavis had returned to the flat above the shop that Freddie asked the question that had been burning in his brain.

"What's happening with Sheila and Maurice, Mam?"

"Freddie love, I still don't know."

"Come on, Mam."

"All right. So far as I know Sheila is still with her gran and Maurice is living back at home. They see each other, in fact they turned up at Billie's on Sunday and Maurice and Tad were walking round like two dogs about to spring at each other's throats. There, that's all I know."

"You mean Maurice was still interested in Delina then?"

"He didn't take kindly to the news that Tad and Delina are engaged. But Sheila and Maurice are still married, Freddie, and surely they're likely to try and make a go of their marriage now he's back home?"

"I don't want her hurt again, Mam."

"No, love. But I don't want you involved in a conflict between a man and his wife. If you really care for her – as I'm sure you do," she added quickly, "you'll want what's best for her, and the best would be to make this travesty of a marriage work, wouldn't it?"

"I think I'll go into town and meet her after work. Unless Maurice is there. If he is I'll walk away, right?"

"What ever you think, love. You're a grown man and able to make your own decisions. Just don't get involved in any fights on her behalf."

"I'm not likely to take on Maurice, Mam. He's a mate, even if he is married to Sheila."

Amy watched him go, sturdily built yet young and somehow vulnerable in his uniform. Sheila had been stringing him along for months and now there was a likelihood of a fresh start with Maurice she might be less than pleased to see him. She sighed and opened the door

161

for business. Perhaps she'd find something really nice for their meal tonight, celebrate the fact that at least he would be spending this leave with her and his sister instead of at Sheila's place.

Freddie and Maurice met in town. They were both in the animal foods and garden shop. Maurice was studying the selection of annual seeds and Freddie was looking at the shrubs offered for sale.

"Don't tell me you're going to do some gardening, Maurice," Freddie said.

"Freddie, boy! Where did you spring from? When are we going to do some fishing. Years since we did, or so it seems."

"Won't it be dull catching tiddlers after shark fishing in Aussie land?" Freddie joked. He had been nervous of meeting his friend but Maurice showed no sign of knowing of Freddie's affair with his wife. His handsome face lit up at the sight of his one-time fishing companion and, ignoring their intended purchases, they reminisced about the fun they had had.

Glancing at his watch Freddie realised it was now too late to meet Sheila, she would be on the way to the bus stop.

"Come for a drink?" Maurice asked.

"I can't. I'm still not old enough," Freddie replied.

"Come on, boy, that never stopped you before!" Maurice grabbed his arm and led him to the nearest pub where he ordered them a beer. "Now, before I bore you about my brief visit to Australia, tell me what's been happening in your life."

"Not a lot," Freddie said warily. "I've been planning Mam's garden for this competition the village is entering." He felt in his pocket and on the back of an envelope he drew out the plan for the front garden, with its flower beds and shrubs. "What d'you think?" he asked. Then, as Maurice began to take hold of the envelope, he snatched it back. It was a letter from Sheila. "No, on second thoughts," he said hurriedly, "I don't want to give away my secrets. Get you own plan worked out you lazy so and so!" Laughing, he put the letter back in his pocket and fastened the button with a shaking hand.

They caught the bus back together and when Maurice dropped off at the bottom of Sheepy Lane he called back to remind Freddie of the fishing trip they had mentioned.

"I'll call and see you," Freddie shouted back down the stairs of the bus. "Staying with your mam, are you?"

"That's right, boy. Playing it cagey I am!"

Freddie didn't go straight home but walked along the road towards *The Drovers*, wanting to think and, above all, recover from the tension of talking companionably to Maurice while he remembered making love to his wife. He wished his leave was not as long as a week. Best if he kept away and gave Sheila time to see through Maurice and tell him goodbye. He was sure in his heart that she knew he, Freddie Prichard, offered her the best chance of future happiness. But he was also sure that she needed to get Maurice out of her system.

Maurice went home and sat at the table listening to his mother's quiet chatter, eating the meal she put before him. But his mind was not on the words or the food. He was thinking of Delina. All the time he was away he imagined her waiting for him, still loving him, and learning that she had forgotten him to the extent of becoming engaged to another man had been a severe blow.

To discover that the man was Tad Simmons, someone who had punched the noses of several of the locals and who turned out to be a small, irritable-looking individual had made him want to laugh. Delina must be out of her mind to look at a man like Tad. He had heard of marrying on the re-bound and thought that was the explanation here. He'd show Delina what sort of a man Tad Simmons was, show him up in front of her, make her see clearly what she was settling for. Second best? Not even that.

Throughout the early evening his mother's house filled up with casual visitors. Among them were Phil-the-post and his wife Catrin.

"Well, Maurice, little brother," Phil said to the young man who topped him by six inches. "Tell us, what did you really think of Austalia, you've said so little about it. You couldn't have stayed in the hostel for all the weeks you were there!"

"I didn't go far, I didn't have the money to do any sight-seeing," Maurice replied, settling into a deep armchair and preparing to spend an hour talking. He owed them that much. They had all contributed to the fare for his return.

"Did you bathe?" Catrin asked. "What about this Bondi Beach we hear so much about?"

"*Duw*, not half as good as Rossili! Shark nets, mind, to add a bit of excitement. But it isn't as long as the beach on Gower. There's more sunshine, I have to admit that," he added. "It's all very bright, like a picture postcard of some exotic paradise, palm trees and yucca's, and even the birds wear bright fancy dress. None of your little brown sparrows. Hot sun, scantily-dressed beach-girls but, d'you know, I was home sick almost as soon as I got there. I actually missed the rain pissing down and the hills covered with mist for half the time, and the green grass and," he grinned at them, "and Mam's cooking."

He spoke for a while about his brief sojourn in that far off sunny country but his mind wasn't on what he was saying. He was thankful when Phil stood up and offered Catrin her coat. At nine o'clock he found his own coat and went up the lane to stand and wait once more outside Tad's house for Delina to appear.

By this time he knew her routine. On the evenings Tad attended night-school she walked Dawn home at about eight and would leave Tad's house, alone, at ten. Tonight he would walk home with her and they would talk. He would make her see how foolish she was being, pretending to love that Tad Simmons.

He waited a little way past Tad's house on Hywel Rise and watched as Tad saw her to the door. His fingers curled as he saw them kiss goodnight.

164

"Make the most of that, boyo," he muttered, "it's likely to be the last one you'll get!"

Delina didn't seem surprised to see him. "Hello, Maurice. Waiting for someone, are you?"

"Yes, you, Delina."

"Oh? I didn't think there was anything to say to each other, that was all done with months ago."

"I tried to keep away, knowing about you and Tad, then I realised that for you, as well as me, that was a mistake. Mistakes abound where you and I are concerned, but it isn't too late. At least you can come out of yours easier than I can, and that's a start. Tell him goodbye, Delina. Let you and me start picking up the debris of last year's fiasco and prepare for the future."

She was silent and he glanced at her perfect profile, the lovely blonde hair hidden by a thick woollen scarf. Perhaps the scarf was blocking her ears and she hadn't heard a word of what he had said. Less confidently he began again.

"Delina, it isn't too late for us to regain what we had last year. I still love you and all the time I was in Australia I thought of nothing else but our reunion. It isn't too late but you must tell Tad goodbye and – "

"I heard you, Maurice, I'm just trying to think of how to tell you without hurting your feelings too much. I was mistaken when I thought I loved you. I know that, now, having met Tad. He is my future, not you. I'm sorry."

"You're wrong! You and me, we're – "

"Finished, Maurice. I feel nothing except relief that Sheila's baby prevented me from making a mistake that I'd have regretted all my life." She looked at him then, her expression unseen in the darkness of the winter evening. "Go to Sheila and make a fresh start, Maurice. She's your future, not me."

They had almost reached her house and Maurice took hold of her arm. "You're thinking of Sheila, aren't you? Trying to do what's best for her. But that's crazy, she and I will never make a success of a marriage. It's you I want and I know you want me. Admit it, and let's tell the world, please Delina. I love you. I know you still love me."

"Sorry, there's no chance for us, ever. I'm going to marry Tad and nothing could make me happier." She stepped inside and closed the door firmly, leaving him staring at its lighted glass window, waiting for her to re-appear. Although he waited for more than an hour, she did not.

CHAPTER THIRTEEN

The snow waited around for more and a week later the
Vetch field had to be cleared of six inches of freshly
fallen, white lagging before the Swansea football game
could begin. In the gardens of several houses tall snowmen
appeared, dressed in a variety of scarves and hats raided
from cupboards when parents were otherwise engaged.
Dawn joined Oliver and Margaret in the large garden
behind Nelly's cottage and, assisted by George, made a
magnificent snowman with a pair of George's wellington
boots forming the base and a battered umbrella under
his arm.

Ice formed on his surface, polished by the children's
hands, and gave a sheen that showed in the early evening,
ghostly and alien, giving Bobby and Spotty a fright that
made them bark, walk backwards into the cottage and peer
nervously out through the door.

Delina and Tad came to call for Dawn and stayed to
admire the pale gentleman, and marvel at his sculpted face
and hands.

"We brought your camera, Dawn," Tad said, "in case
you want a photograph.

"Oh yes," Margaret shouted, "come on, Dawn, take
Oliver and me hugging him!"

"No thanks! I can't waste a photograph on that!"
Margaret wondered if "that" meant the snowman or
herself.

Ignoring Dawn's muttered protests, Tad took one of
the three children, Margaret and Oliver laughing, Dawn

showing a pout, the snowman's stony eyes indifferent to the un-spoken quarrel going on around him.

Maurice still lived at the cottage on Sheepy Lane with his mother, although Ethel frequently tried to send him up to the house on St Illtyd's Road with various messages, inviting Sheila for Sunday tea or asking him to take up a cake she had baked, or drop in with a recipe or a knitting pattern. Maurice avoided all her efforts, he could see no future for himself and Sheila as a couple. Sheila was attractive, and sex with her was always exciting, but there was nothing more. Good as it was, you couldn't spend more than a small part of your day lying down naked! They had nothing to talk about and any attempt at a conversation was reduced to Sheila's description of the clothes she wanted or some gossip about her neighbours. She disapproved of most people, he realised, and he began to understand why she seemed to have no friends.

"Why don't you go out with Bethan?" he asked one day as they walked down the snow-edged lane to where she would catch her bus for work. He had been walking in the crisp and clear early morning, across the fields, through the woods to where he could look down on Billie's farm, binoculars around his neck, a small book of bird recognition in his hand.

"She's a bit boring, Maurice," she said, and sighting the book added, "We can walk for hours and she won't see a thing. It's not like that when I go out with you, you make everything interesting, you do, you're so knowledgeable." She looked up at him with her lovely eyes, widening them and showing adoration in their clear blue, shining depths.

"Here's your bus. Lucky you are to be working. I haven't found anything yet," he said, catching hold of her arm and hurrying her towards the bus stop.

"Try to get your old job with the builders," she called from the platform of the maroon bus. "Prue Beynon might be glad to have you back."

She boldly blew a kiss. If only he'd decide to stay then she

168

stood a chance of winning him back. I'll make it clear that I forgive him and will take him back. As if I've left him in any doubt, she thought as she found a seat on her own at the top of the bus where she could day-dream uninterupted.

Perhaps, she decided belatedly, I would have been better to play hard to get when he came back to Hen Carw Parc. But with a strong desire for his loving that was not as easy as it sounded. She was weak, she knew that. She patted her tummy and the reminder of just how weak made her shiver with anxiety. This time it would be different. She would have her baby and go home, to Maurice, who would love them both and never leave them again. If Maurice stayed she wouldn't be weak with anyone else. She wouldn't need anyone else. She imagined telling him about the baby, their baby so far as he or anyone else would know. And in her mind saw him holding her tight, promising never to leave her, weeping with joy. Soon she would tell him and he would realise what she was offering him and accept that their destinies were linked. She sighed deliciously. That sounded so romantic.

Maurice walked back up Sheepy Lane. He didn't go back to his mother's house but walked up to stand and wait outside Delina's house for her to come out.

He knew her movements well, having spent hours watching the comings and goings in her council house. Glancing at his watch he wondered vaguely where she was as the time for her bus approached. Then he saw her hurrying out of her gate, half running, her neat figure with the cap of shining blonde hair swaying with the rhythm of her walk, the heavy bag of books hugged in her arms, unmistakable and heart-breakingly lovely.

He *had* to persuade her to give their romance another chance. He couldn't believe that she was serious about Tad Simmons. From what he'd heard the man was nothing but a bad tempered misery, hitting out when anyone said a word he didn't want to hear. How could a flower like Delina consider sharing a life with a man like that!

"Carry your books, Miss?" he asked, stepping out in front of her.

"Maurice. What are you doing hanging about at this time of the morning?"

"Waiting for you." He took the books from her and matched his pace to hers. "I'll wait for you for ever if necessary."

"Go away, find yourself a job and look after that wife of yours." She spoke quietly, her voice without an edge of anger as she took back the bag of exercise books. But there was a firmness in her expression that dampened his spirits.

So far there had been no sign of a weak spot in the fortification she had built around herself after their wedding plans had fallen apart. But, he promised himself, he would break through, and he might use Tad as the battering ram!

Amy watched as the gypsies gathered across the road. They looked like a flock of exotic birds with layers of clothes topped with richly coloured scarves draped around their hips and over their heads. She guessed they were setting off to sell their flowers and lucky charms to raise some money to help them through the winter. She waved as Clara glanced her way and the old woman came across.

"I want a few things, Amy, and I'd like for you to get them ready for me. I'll call for them later."

"I'll take them up the hill for you if you like," Amy offered. "The errand boy will be coming in after school, if that isn't too late."

"I'll leave the money and you'll send me the change." Clara handed her some coins which, Amy knew from experience, wouldn't be sufficient for what the gypsy needed. "Now, I'd like some flour and some butter and some eggs and a packet of custard powder. I have enough cream of tartar and sugar. Yes, I think that'll be all."

"What are you making, Clara?" Amy asked as she wrote down the woman's order.

"Some loaves of bread."

170

"With custard powder?"

" 'Tis very good, you should try some. Our cooking is wholesome and rich."

"Do me a favour, Clara," Amy whispered. "Here's that Milly Toogood and the Pup, stand in the doorway will you? They won't come in if you're here!"

It was almost time for the children to come out of school for lunch and Clara was still talking to Amy, laughing at the casual way Milly turned and pretended to remember something urgent to take her in the opposite direction.

"I have to close the shop, Clara. Margaret and I have to get home, find some lunch and get back."

"I'll be off. Will you tell Nelly that George will be extra tired tonight?"

"Why, is he ill?" Amy looked alarmed.

"No, 'tisn't that at all. He and that good Mr Leighton are using my dogs to practise for the cricketing."

"This we have to see!" Amy told Margaret when the door closed behind their visitor. "We'll take a meat pie each and some cakes and we'll go and see what's happening."

Maurice decided to talk to Tad, and if the talk led to a quarrel, well so be it. He knew that Tad worked odd hours and when he went to the house at ten o'clock one morning he was surprised to find him out. He walked around to the back door and knocked with growing impatience. The door remained closed and he stood looking down the neat but winter-bare garden.

Tad was obviously making preparations for the spring. The rather weary-looking greenhouse was showing signs of life with seed boxes standing empty and daffodils in troughs against the south wall of the house already spearing their way through the soil. Two daphne shrubs were without their leaves but rich in the sweet-scented magenta flowers. Pots of various sizes were stacked against a wall and, near the back gate, there was a pile of leaves swept up, rotting and, he guessed, ready to add to the compost heap further down the garden. Other rubbish had gathered around its edge and Maurice discarded a cigarette end throwing it casually towards the assortment.

As he watched, a small flame showed, pale and almost invisible in the daylight. Almost without thinking he guided another piece of paper towards it and, without bothering to stamp it out, he left, angry that Tad had failed to arrive thinking, unreasonably, that it showed the man's cowardice. He walked quickly back to his mother's cottage. Tad would keep. The anticipation was good, it made his anger stronger. The little man would get what was coming to him. He'd learn that he couldn't steal Maurice Davies' girl.

Dawn arrived home on her own. Tad had been delayed and she sat on the back step looking down the garden and wondering how soon he would be home to get her meal. She became conscious of the smell of burning before she saw the thin whisps of smoke coming from the side of the house. At first she didn't think much about it. People were always having bonfires to burn unwanted rubbish. Specially now as the preparations for the garden displays intensified.

The movement at the periphery of her vision made her turn her head in time to see a sleepy and very confused hegdehog stagger out from under the leaves of the rubbish pile. She stood and gathered him up in her hands and it was then that she saw the flames gaining strength in the leaves.

She ran back to put the hedgehog in the kitchen, changed her mind and picked him up again. Then stared in horror as the flames began to spread and make the leaves crackle ominously. Still carrying the hedgehog she ran through the house, opened the front door and began to scream. Out through the gate she ran, dancing around wondering where to go for help.

Pete Evans was driving up the hill and saw her about to step out into the road in what appeared to him to be foolish and dangerous behaviour. He slowed the motor-cycle to tell her off and heard her crying that the house was on fire. He abandoned the bike and went through the house with her.

"Have you got a hose?" he demanded.

"Yes, in the shed," she wailed.

"Stand back and if you see anyone, ask them to phone for the fire-brigade," he instructed. Running to the shed he found the hose, connected it to the kitchen tap and had water pouring over the rubbish in moments. Kicking the pile apart, he doused the flames until all that was left was a filthy mess of burned branches and soggy leaves.

Neighbours arrived and tried to calm the frightened girl.

"Put the hedgehog down, love," one of them pleaded. "He'll be all right, disturbed by the fire but he'll be all right."

"He won't!" Dawn insisted. "He'll die. He won't be able to keep warm now he's been woken up and he'll die." It seemed to her that the most important thing to do was nurse the hedgehog and make sure he didn't die.

When Tad arrived, breathless at running up the hill, knowing he was late and worrying about Dawn, the house was still full of people. There were hurried explanations and reassurances that no harm was done. He thanked them all and hugged Dawn.

"What will we do about the hedgehog?" she asked, sobs revived by his return.

"I'll make him a box and a run. He'll be safe if we keep him warm and feed him well until the weather is warm enough to let him go," he promised.

"Thanks, Dad. Can I go and tell Oliver I've got him?"

"Not tonight, love." Tad looked at his daughter, his face frowning and anxious. "Dawn, I have to ask this. Did you start that fire, then get frightened and call for help?"

"No, Dad, I didn't!"

"All right, I believe you. Mind, a few months ago I wouldn't have. It's been better for us both with Delina helping us, hasn't it?"

Phil-the-post spread news of the fire and there was a stream of people calling to see if all was well and to look at the hedgehog.

Pete enjoyed the notoriety of being thought a hero and for a while was content to stay in the noisy household of his friend, Gerry. But the thought of his mother carrying on made him more and more miserable. It was bad enough having everyone know his father was a criminal without people talking about his Ma too.

Tad was uneasy since Maurice had returned although Delina had repeatedly assured him that what there had once been between her and the ex-soldier was over, dead without a trace. When Tad walked up the hill with Dawn one Sunday in late February, his heart began to race when he saw Maurice and Delina walking down to meet him, together. Maurice was holding out a book and he was pointing to something on the page and consulting Delina. That much Tad deduced as they drew closer.

"Tad, Maurice has just seen some redwings," Delina explained as she left Maurice and came to stand beside him. "Look Dawn," she took the book from Maurice and pointed to the thrush-like bird with the patches of red on its sides. "They are winter visitors."

"D'you think I could get a photograph?" Dawn asked.

"I doubt it, you wouldn't get close enough. You'll need a very fine camera if you're going to try wildlife photography."

"Why don't you buy her one if she's that keen," Maurice said, his eyes glinting with the prospect of some fun as he stared at Tad. "Can't you afford to buy one for her? She's keen and I thought any sort of father would want to encourage a hobby like that."

"One day I will," Tad said quietly. "One day she'll have the equipment she needs and deserves."

"One day, some day. It's now she wants it, while she's keen. I'd get her one if she was my daughter, for sure I would." He looked at Delina steadily. "Any child of mine, or woman I loved and cared for, wouldn't go short, I'd see to that."

"Come on, Tad, aren't we going for that walk?" Delina moved away from the other three, sensing trouble in the way Tad's small hands clenched and unclenched. It was a long time since he had hit out at anyone, but the need was very close to the surface. "Come on, Dawn, who knows, we might see a redwing for ourselves."

Maurice didn't move as they walked towards the woods near Nelly's cottage.

"Near Billie Brown's farm they were," he called after them. "Down the bottom of that steep hill. Mind, I wouldn't go if I were you, Tad, the climb back up might be too much for a little chap like you." He laughed as he saw Delina grab Tad's arm as he began to turn back to face him. "Enjoy your afternoon together playing happy families," he muttered to himself, "you won't enjoy many more my quick-tempered friend."

CHAPTER FOURTEEN

Sheila was becoming worried about the forthcoming baby but at the same time, strangely excited. She wanted it. That came as a surprise. Since the death of her baby the previous April she had felt a loss that nothing would fill. But only in her secret inner self. The small ache was something she would never have admitted, even to that secret self. How could she, Sheila Davies, with a life to live and fun to find, be glad she was going to have a child? It was crazy. But crazy or not it was the truth.

Even more crazy was the thought that it was nothing to do with persuading Maurice to stay. Maurice and the need for him to stay with her was a completely separate thing. Whether he stayed or not, she wanted this baby.

She longed to tell someone and thought regretfully of the girls who had worked in the gown salon, who shared every secret with each other. There was no one she could trust with such news. Her thoughts went around the village, trying to think of anyone who would care enough to listen, let alone keep the knowledge to themselves. There was Bethan, but there would be no excitement in allowing her to share the secret. Freddie's mother, Amy who, although having been in the same situation herself, wouldn't offer any comfort. It was Freddie she should be telling, he was the father and would support her whatever she decided. She smiled at the reminder of his unselfish love. But it was Maurice's name she wanted on the birth certificate, both for herself now, and for the baby in the future.

Sighing, she stretched languorously under the bed-covers then began to rise. So far no sickness. That was a blessing.

At least her gran wouldn't suspect. She could tell people when she chose, not have the announcement forced on her. But, she decided, she must talk to Maurice soon. Not about the baby, but to try and persuade him to come back to her in more subtle ways.

The mornings were gradually lightening, the fumbling about in the darkness as she prepared for work no longer a dreary routine. It was still cold though and she was glad to stay in her dressing gown until her regular tasks were finished. Automatically she began preparing breakfast for gran and arranging things ready to cook the meal when she returned.

She stepped out over the step, lifting her umbrella to protect her head from the steadily falling rain, a scarf and the hood of her coat protecting the curls she had spent so much time and discomfort achieving. She was in plenty of time for her bus. It was worth leaving a little early in case she should see Maurice on his early morning wanderings.

On impulse she went the long way around St Hilda's Crescent and down Heol Caradoc. She would pass the Honeyman's house and perhaps meet Maurice, and pretend she had a letter to post if she saw anyone she knew. Her fingers touched the crumpled envelope in her pocket reminding her she ought to write to Freddie. Until Maurice was persuaded back to her, it was wise to keep Freddie tied to her with that invisible string.

"Hello, Maurice," she called brightly when she reached the house and saw him standing looking up at the window of the bedroom. He wore the belt of his brown overcoat tied in a knot, the brim of his trilby slouched forward to protect his face from the rain. "Waiting for Delina are you?" she asked, her head on one side questioningly. "What will Tad Simmons say?" Her voice broke the silence of the early morning and startled him into scowling as he turned to face her.

"What do you want, Sheila?" he demanded in a low whisper.

"What do I want, Maurice? Nothing from you, why?"

177

"Why are you walking this way round. You'll miss your bus." She showed the edge of Freddie's letter, explaining.

"Posting a letter I am. Not a crime, is it? Better excuse than you've got, standing looking up into a girl's bedroom for a sly peep."

He turned again and, leaving the hedge beside which he had been trying to shelter, he walked with her, guiding her away and down the hill.

"Come on, I'll walk you to your bus."

"Thank you, d'you want to come under my umbrella?"

Their closeness was a necessity and Sheila took advantage of it, clutching his arm, pretending it was to make sure he stayed under the protection of the umbrella although, she had to admit, it was rather late for him to worry about keeping dry. He must have been standing beside that hedge for ages.

"D'you fancy coming for a meal tonight?" she asked. "We're having chicken stew and dumplings."

"No, Sheila, it's best not."

"Why? No one need know, if you're ashamed of me. We ought to talk about – things."

"Well, all right, but I won't be able to stay long." His eyes glanced at her smiling face and he added almost nervously, "Meeting Phil for a game of darts I am."

"I'm not bad at darts myself, Maurice," she replied happily.

When she had sailed off on the platform of the bus, with the irate conductor telling her to hurry along inside, Maurice went back up the hill. He was in time to escort an unwilling Delina down for her bus and muttered to himself as he returned to Ethel's house, "I'm like a flaming yo-yo. Up and down that hill twice every morning!"

"Talking to yourself, boy? Bad sign that!" his brother Phil laughed as he placed his bicycle against Ethel's front wall.

Maurice went inside following his brother and found the house full. Even for Ethel that was rather unusual so early in the morning.

"Mam are you starting a morning shift in Sheepy Lane

Cafe now?" Phil asked, then turned and touched Maurice's arm and said, "look at this, boy, look at this. A houseful of Davies'!"

Squeezing in, Maurice saw to his surprise that his three brothers were all present. Sidney was standing with Mr Leighton and George. Teddy, who worked in a factory in Swansea, was sitting on the couch next to Johnny Cartwright.

"Someone's birthday?" Maurice asked.

"No," Phil laughed, "I think I can guess what this is about. Cricket, lovely cricket?"

"We have to think of a way of playing for the village," Sidney explained.

"I live up on the council houses," Johnny added. "But, see, I want to play for the village proper. We were wondering if Bert has made any unbendable rules that makes that impossible?"

"The way Bert writes rules for a game, you'd think he was planning for World War Three! Sorry, but if Bert's got anything to do with it, I think you'll have to play for the council houses, boy," Phil said sadly.

"Mam!" Johnny said firmly. "I'm playing for Mam. She lives next door to you, Phil, if you're playing can't you put me down as a neighbour?" He grinned widely. "Or better still, put Mam down to play, then I can go in as a substitute when she remembers her gammy leg!"

"Worth a try," Phil grinned, "but what about Teddy? He lives in Swansea, how can he play for the village?"

"I'm playing for *our* Mam! Put her name down and I'll come in as a replacement at the last minute!"

With Ethel chuckling as she poured fresh tea and topped up the diminishing plateful of toast the men planned ways of beating the rules and playing for the village proper.

"What about Victor?" Teddy enquired. "He's played a bit, so he tells me. Years ago mind, but at least he'll know which end of the bat to grab hold of. We can't let the council houses have him, now can we?"

"Write down Amy to play and he can play instead of her,"

Johnny laughed. "Damn me, the council houses'll think us a walkover when they see the list of players."

Sidney, Teddy and Phil all had the same thought at the same time. In unison they turned and looked at their youngest brother.

"What about you, boy?" Phil asked with a quizzical look at his young brother. "You playing home or away?"

"If there was a team for Sheepy Lane, I'd be in it," Maurice said sadly.

"Put him down for the village proper, and Maurice," Phil added in a whisper, "don't go back to Sheila until the match is played, there's a good boy."

"Damn me, boys," Johnny laughed, "when Bert Roberts hears of this he'll have a boundary half way up Sheepy Lane and insist on passports!"

The confrontation between Tad and Maurice happened almost by accident. Tad had seen Maurice standing outside Delina's house and the distaste he felt at this intrusion was encouraged into anger by Sheila's remarks to Delina about her encouraging a man who was someone else's husband to watch under her bedroom window like a peeping Tom.

"I think you should tell him to go, unless you like the excitement of having a married man hanging about your house hoping for a glimpse of you," Sheila said as Tad came out of his front door where Delina was waiting for him.

"What d'you mean by that remark?" he demanded. "Delina has tried to tell the man to go away, but other than calling the police and reporting him for being a nuisance, there's nothing she can do!"

"Fancy that," Sheila said, her head on one side. "Fancy you believing that a man like Maurice would stand there without being given some encouragement."

"Come on, Tad, let's go inside." Delina's voice showed her usual calm but Tad's hands were tightly clenched as she led him into the house to wait until Sheila had gone.

When they came out a few moments later to go for the

bus into town Sheila was coming back up the hill. Maurice was with her.

"Told me I was a liar he did and pretended that you had no encouragement from Delina to wait for her each morning and walk with her to the bus regular as clockwork," Sheila taunted.

"What d'you mean, walk with her each morning?" Tad looked at Delina then at Maurice.

"Regular, isn't it, Delina, me carrying your books for you and waving you off on the bus to town."

"It isn't like that, Maurice, and you know it," Delina replied.

"Playing the field and having fun, with my husband," Sheila said. "Isn't she Maurice?"

"You should look after that wife of yours and not go chasing where you aren't wanted," Tad muttered, his chin low, his blue eyes glittering angrily.

Maurice laughed and darted back as if hiding behind the small figure of Sheila.

Delina took Tad's arm and tried to lead him away. She might have succeeded if Tad hadn't heard the softly whispered words from Maurice.

"She's a tart," he breathed, jerking his head towards Delina.

Tad sprang with a speed that should have warned Maurice. He pushed Sheila aside, none too gently. Maurice smiled geefully.

"All right, little fellow, let's be having you then."

"Tad, please," Delina pleaded in vain. Sheila smiled excitedly, two men fighting and, in her vivid imagination, fighting because of her.

Tad forced the anger out of his body. Coldly and calculatingly he faced the more powerful man, six years his junior, fresh out of the army. He was determined to give him a lesson he wouldn't forget.

Maurice lunged at him, his right arm aiming for Tad's face. Coolly Tad stepped aside and felt the breath of the punch as it missed him. Then he dodged the second lunge, this time from the left. He darted inside the man's guard and held Maurice's neck, his small hands locked with alarming strength behind his head. He pulled the larger man to one side. Maurice was too surprised by the move to resist. Tad bent the man to his right kneeing at Maurice's side hard under the ribs, his hands still holding the man's head. The sharp blows were frighteningly hard.

Leaning to the right to evade the bone-jarring blows he was open to a punch on the left. Bending protectively but too late to the left and the right side was unprotected. Tad's jabbing fist found his face and followed with a punch to the side, each time bringing his hands back to Maurice's head.

Tad could have kept it up all day without tiring; left, right, left side, right side, close to his opponent where Maurice's wildly lashing arms couldn't harm him he was in control and Maurice, confused and weakened by the pain he hadn't prepared for and the surprising efficiency of the small man, felt like crying.

He realised in his curtain of pain that Tad's knees had stopping their devastating blows and Tad was jabbing almost playfully at his face, left, right, left, right; pulling on his neck he was bending him each way at will.

It lasted less than two minutes but in that brief time Maurice's body had become sluggish and his movements slow and uncoordinated. He didn't realise it, but he looked like a puppet that had lost some of its strings.

From nearby houses people appeared to stare at the unexpected exhibition. Some of the men growled their disappointment when Tad stood back, his hands at his sides, while Maurice gave a few ineffective swipes towards him, missing by miles. They were remembering how Maurice had left his wife pregnant and felt satisfaction at the beating he received as if it were a deserved punishment.

Tad walked away after Delina who had hurried, almost ran down the path and into his house. He found her sitting, white-faced, in the corner of the room, staring unseeingly down the garden.

"I know I promised I would never strike a blow in anger again," he said, afraid that she would say the words he dreaded. "If it's any consolation, that wasn't anger you saw. I was calmly and coldly telling him in the only language he seems to understand, that you are mine and I'll fight anyway he likes, to keep you. If you'll believe me just once more, it will be the last time. I don't think he'll want any more of that. I didn't hurt him, just shook him up a bit, but his pride was severely damaged. Now, if I can just bathe my knuckles – vinegar and brown paper is best – we'll catch the next bus into town."

Delina went with him and nothing more was ever said between them about the unexpected and brief fight that was the talk of the village for days. Reports travelled from house to house, each telling making it more exciting and longer lasting until the story told of two equally matched men fighting up one hill and down the other, until they were both exhausted, and Tad was able to strike the final lucky blow.

However it was told Tad was the hero of the hour. Even those who felt that, as one of their own, Maurice should have won against the newcomer had to admit that Tad had been the strongest fighter.

Delina and Tad were the only ones who refused to discuss it. Maurice, too, was hesitant to tell anyone who wasn't there what had really happened, content to allow his friends to believe he was badly cheated of a contest he could easily have won and ignoring those who saw it differently.

On the following Monday morning, Maurice was standing outside Delina's house ready to escort her to the bus stop. Delina saw him and rang for a taxi.

In Amy's shop Nelly sat to wait for the customers to be served. When there seemed the likelihood of a lull, she slid off the sack of potatoes on which she had been resting her ample bottom and went through to put the kettle on. She had been looking at the local paper while she waited and now she read a piece out to Amy.

"'Ere, look at this! The nurses at Cefn Coed 'ospital have bin asked if they got any objection to workin' with nurses from Barbados. Fancy 'avin' to ask. People's all the same, ain't they, Amy?"

"I'd have thought it more important to ask them! Fancy leaving all that lovely sunshine and finding yourself here where we seen to live up in the clouds for half the year!"

"Talkin' about 'ospitals, my George ain't well again. I thought once spring was on the way he'd brighten, but that chest of 'is still worries 'im."

"Go and see Clara before she leaves. She knows about healing, doesn't she?"

"Knows about a lot of things, Clara does. Things that'll be lost if the younger ones keep chosin' to go an' live in 'ouses. That granddaughter of 'ers lives in a 'ouse now, and two of 'er sons have found 'omes off the road."

"I can't say I blame them, Nelly, love. I couldn't survive in such cramped conditions."

"Cramped? They got the whole countryside fer 'ome, although less and less of it is free so they tells me. Farmers ain't so glad to see 'em and people turn them away more an' more these days. P'raps you're right, Amy. I'll go an' see if she can 'elp."

"Take this." Amy wrapped a hock cut from a shoulder of bacon and handed it to her. "Make a nice drop of soup, that'll warm him up."

"Thanks, Amy, you're a good friend to me an' George. I'll go and get it in soak straight away."

When she had washed the cups and saucers and returned to the shop, Nellie looked out at the continuing rain and said,

"This ain't good fer George, all this rain. I know 'e's used to it, like Mr Leighton and Billie Brown and – blimey, look at this! Billie on 'is tracker and followin' behind 'avin' 'eard on the bush telegraph, Victor in 'is van! How them two knows what the other is doin' is a mystery to me, but they always arrive at the same time!"

Billie stopped the tractor and jumped down. He came

to the door and smiled, rain running down his face, his waterproof and on to the step.

"Can I come in or will I flood the shop?" he smiled.

"Go on in, man, I'm getting drowned," Victor called from behind him.

The two men entered, Victor carrying some boxes of goods from the wholesalers where he worked.

"I just put the tea cups away. Seems I'd better get 'em out again," Nelly smiled. She went through to the small kitchen and returned with a towel for each of the men. "Dry yer 'eads before yer brains shrink!"

She left them after preparing a tray of tea and collecting the dogs from Amy's yard and went home to start preparing the meal for George.

When she reached her gate she saw that the door was wide open. Now who's called, she wondered, hurrying down to greet her visitor. But it was George who sat in the chair closest to the fire.

"George? What's the matter, you not feeling well?"

To her alarm he could hardly speak. "Stay where you are, I'm goin' back down to ask Amy to phone fer the doctor."

"No need," George whispered. "Rest and – "

"I got to 'urry, Amy'll be closin' fer lunch soon." Leaving the dogs with him, she hurried down the lane and across the road to the shop. It was closed. She went on down the road and across to the end of Sheepy Lane and knocked on the closed back door of her daughter's house. There was no reply. Almost in tears of frustration she turned again and wondered who was the nearest person to help. Mrs French! She set off again and as she passed the shop realised that Victor's van was still outside. Crossing the road yet again she pummelled on the shop door.

"Snogging or not, let me in, Amy," she shouted. With relief she saw the blind raised and Amy's blonde head appear. "It's my George, will you phone the doctor for me, Amy?"

The door opened and Nelly went inside. Victor was

185

leaning against the counter. He looked like a man in shock. "What's the trouble," he asked thickly.

"Chest," was her succintly reply, unaware of his distress. "Somethin' awful it is an' 'as been all winter on and off. Tell 'im to 'urry, will yer?" she said as Amy picked up the phone.

"You go back, love, I'll make sure he comes as fast as possible."

When Nelly re-entered the cottage George was asleep, his breathing troubled. She sat and stared at him while she waited for the doctor and didn't see the dogs help themselves to the bacon knuckle. She wouldn't have cared if she had.

CHAPTER FIFTEEN

When Amy had attended to the phone call she turned to Victor and said with a smile, "Now, love, where were we?"

"You were just explaining why you won't marry me. Amy, I know Imogine's death was a shock and seemed like a warning, telling us that our loving each other was wrong, but time has passed and, well, people forget. Other events happen and make previous disasters fade from importance. Why can't we keep to our decision about us getting married?"

"What about David and Daniel? Have you discussed it with them fully? It's more of a trauma for them than for Margaret. After all, we'll be living in the same house, I'll continue to work here and see her at lunch times, we'll walk home together. Most of her life will continue as usual. It's only the sharing she'll have to accept and you know Margaret, she's a sweet-natured girl and I don't think she'll have any serious problems." She looked at him and smiled wryly. "As for your two, well, I don't know how to handle them. I'd have more success trying to cuddle Dawn's hedgehog!"

"You haven't mentioned Delina, what about her?"

"We've talked around the subject and I think she'd prefer to stay where she is, run the house alone, at least until she and Tad marry. Delina is a very together sort of person, isn't she?"

"Amy, couldn't we have a night together? I know it's difficult with Margaret and my three, but not impossible, surely?"

She went into his arms, her supple body leaving him in no doubt of her sincerity as she whispered, "I want that, too, Victor love, but how can we? If we arranged for someone to mind your sons and my Margaret it would soon be all around the village what we were doing. I've never expected anything else but gossip, with the way I've lived my life I've deserved it. Heaven knows it's no secret that I've had affairs and no husband and no named father for my children but Margaret, and your boys, too, are old enough to be hurt by gossip and I won't risk that. Also, if I can, I want to stay friends with Delina."

"Your house?" he suggested. "If I dressed all in black and came after Margaret was asleep and left before it was light, darting through the lanes and scaring any who was abroad? Or perhaps I could pretend to help Mary-Dairy and slip in carrying a crate of milk!"

"We missed our chance," Amy laughed, "a couple of months ago you could have walked around wearing a red cloak and carrying a lumpy sack!"

"The sack is what I'll be getting, too, if I don't get on with my deliveries."

"A few more minutes," she pleaded, "Margaret's having lunch with Oliver and the shop doesn't open for another ten whole minutes."

When Victor had gone Amy continued to think about their situation. She had moments of doubts, not about their loving each other or of that love lasting, it was the complications of two very different families coming together and making some kind of a whole that kept her from being convinced about their future together. Add to that a helping of resentment from Victor's sons for her coming into their lives and replacing their dead mother and you had a cocktail fraught with the likelihood of unpleasant and long-lasting hangovers!

It was a long time since she had spent more than a few minutes with the boys, she thought guiltily. Perhaps she ought to make more of an effort. But what did you do to befriend boys of eighteen and thirteen? You could hardly go with a new toy or a packet of sweets! She realised she knew nothing about the older age group, even with a son of her own. And what's more she had made no effort so far to learn.

When Merfyn the errand boy came to deliver the orders she had made up, she gave him a note for Delina. It was an invitation for her and Daniel and David to come to tea on Sunday. She smiled, remembering how boring she had considered visiting her parents' friends when she had been their age. Perhaps she'd better invite Tad and Dawn, too. From being just Margaret and me, she realised with alarm, the family was likely to jump to eight people. Nine when Freddie was home, unless that Sheila managed to hang on to him in case Maurice couldn't be persuaded to stay!

At once she began the practical considerations of how she would seat them all. There were only six chairs. The children would have to sit on the stairs. Margaret and Oliver at least, would think that fun. That decided, she brought her mind back to the present and smiled at Milly Toogood who had called for a small cabbage and three carrots, not having had time to go into town where they were cheaper.

When the doctor had examined George he warned Nelly that he might have to go to hospital. He recommended he went to bed and stayed there and promised to call again on the following day.

"Bronchitis 'e said, George." She tried not to show how frightening that sounded. A bad chest without a name seemed less worrying.

"I don't want to go upstairs, Nelly. You'd have to keep trotting up and down tiring yourself out and I'd feel far away from you. D'you think I could just stay here, on the couch? The fire would be a nice sight, too. Better than four walls!"

"Just what I was thinkin' meself. When you ain't sleepin' or restin' you'll be glad to see them who wants to pop in and see yer."

"Thanks Nelly, my dear."

She looked at him, his blue eyes closed and the cheeks showing through the white beard less pink than usual. Lines on his face made her realise with a start that he was no longer a young man. He opened his eyes then and smiled at her before exhaustion made the lids close again, shutting him off from her. Don't die, George, she prayed silently. I'd 'ate to manage without yer.

"Sorry to be so much bother, dear," George murmured. She guessed what he was thinking.

"You worrying about bein' a nuisance, George? If you are you can ferget it. What better than a week or so with you fer company, instead of seein' you off in the mornin's and not clappin' eyes on yer all day!" Adding further reassurance she said softly, "Best thing what ever 'appened to me, George, marryin' you."

The village was a long way from ready for the Best Kept Village competition but the gardens were full of colour. Yellow daffodils had taken the place of yellow crocus and yellow forsythia had replaced the yellow winter-flowering jasmine, golden forerunners of the summer sunshine. The hedgerows were showing the tips of new growth and under their protection violets and primroses bloomed. In every corner boxes into which flowers would be planted were being set in place by Billie, Victor and the others. Arguments abounded as each house insisted on having the same amount of help as the rest.

The competition was to be judged early in June and the cricket match, that other contentious issue, was arranged for the first Saturday in the same month. Nelly predicted that by July no one would be talking to anyone else. She gleefully reported all the arguments and activities to George who, although improving, was unable to return to work.

"I'll make a start on the garden soon, George," she announced one morning as she set off to do her few hours for Mrs French. "I fancy 'aving a go at fixing up one of them baskets Ollie and Billie made for us. Look nice in the apple tree it will."

190

"Please, Nelly, don't try to do it on your own. I'll be able to get out there with you in a few more days." He coughed then and she didn't say any more. She didn't want to worry him. But she looked at the basket and wondered if it was something she could do for herself. It would be a nice surprise for George if she could.

Nelly was becoming worried about money. While George worked they were comfortable, she had been better off than she could ever remember. Now, with the likelihood of him being too ill to work, for a few weeks at least, things were becoming very tight. She wondered if she could find an extra morning, but that seemed doubtful. She considered offering to help Bethan cut up her chips and wash her fish but she shuddered at the thought. No, there had to be a way, there always was.

The weather was a problem. Snow blocked the lane leading from Nelly's cottage to the main road. She daren't tell George and risk him trying to dig them out so she put on her wellingtons and, with the dogs leaping about beside her like demented frogs, she made her way up and down without him knowing her difficulty. The papers reported that the roads between Swansea and Brecon were blocked.

"An' that poor Princess Margaret comin' back from Trinidad to find this!" she sighed to Amy one morning. "I'd go straight back if I was 'er."

"Did you want something, Nelly, love, I'm just about to close."

"Some veg fer soup. Amy, if you 'ear's of anyone wantin' a few hours cleanin' done, will you tell me?"

"Short of money?" Amy asked.

"No, but with George not workin', well, I might be soon and I wants 'im to 'ave good food and no worries."

"I'll let you know," Amy promised.

Nelly decided to do something she hadn't done for a long time; go into town and sell the clothes she had been given by friends and her various employers. Before George came into her life she used to save the occasional coat or dress she was given and, when she had sufficient, she would

191

treat herself and the dogs to a day out. She would fill a suitcase with some of the better clothes, sell them at Mrs Greener's second-hand clothes shop and have a night out on the proceeds. It was after such an evening that she had first met George.

The cupboard in which she stored the expensive clothes was in the back bedroom. For a while this had been George's room but now they shared the same bed in the front room that looked over the garden.

George was asleep when she reached home and leaving the dogs sleeping beside him, she climbed the curved staircase and went to examine her store. There were four dresses, woollen ones unfortunately, Mrs Greener would complain that the season for them had gone. The two coats would be worth a few shillings though. One was grey with a fur collar and the other a soft blue, given to her by Mrs French in the hope she would abandon the ancient and over-sized one she constantly wore.

"Too good to waste wearin'," she muttered as she folded them carefully with lots of tissue as Mrs French had once shown her.

After lunch, when George was comfortable in the armchair near the fire with the radio on and some books, she set off. The load was heavy even divided between two cases, but taking her time and without the dogs to trip her up, she went carefully down the snow-filled lane. At one point she put the cases on their side and kicked them, sending them sliding across the snow like unmanned sledges, before sinking in the soft surface. Her laughter followed them, unnaturally loud in the still air.

The elderly Mrs Greener was full of polite pleasure at seeing her but once she opened the cases, she shook her bright red hair, the old face which it framed wrinkled up in apparent disappointment.

"Nelly, my dear, such beautiful quality as usual, but it's the wrong season. All my clients will be looking for things for summer in a few weeks time."

"D'you want them or not?" Nelly was used to the old

woman's strategy and today had little patience. All she wanted was some extra money to buy food for George to tempt his waning appetite.

"I'll take them from you as we're old friends, Nelly, just wait there and I'll find some money."

Nelly sat in the room behind the shop where clothes racks lined the walls and shuddered. She hated this room where she had sat on so many occasions in the past, waiting for Mrs Greener to return with her payment. The sombre suits and the long dance dresses seemed to retain some ghostly spirit of past owners and she was glad when the red-headed old lady returned with her smile and a handful of money.

"Sorry it isn't more, Nelly, dear."

"So am I!" Nelly said, returning the smile with even less sincerity. "See yer again I expect," she said as Mrs Greener bent her thin body to open the door for her.

"I hope so, dear, such lovely quality you always bring."

With declarations of affection and wails of disappointment that there was never time to chat, they parted, Mrs Greener a grotesque figure with her artificial hair and heavy makeup and Nelly, plump and scruffy in her wide-brimmed hat and her enormous coat fastened with a safety pin.

Maurice seemed to be making no effort to find a job. So far as Ethel knew he hadn't approached Prue Beynon, who owned the building firm her husband had left her. Ethel asked Phil to keep an ear tuned for any likely vacancies but Phil shook his head.

"Mam, I don't think he wants to find work. If he does everyone will expect him to settle down with Sheila."

"And what's wrong with that?"

"That's the problem, everything is wrong with it so far as Maurice is concerned. He doesn't love her, Mam, and I don't think our Maurice will settle for duty so don't even think it. I don't know what he'll do, but I very much doubt if he'll stay."

"Such trouble that girl caused."

"Fair play, Mam, it was Maurice who has to take the most blame!"

"I suppose he was partly to blame, but that girl is trouble, there's no pretending."

Maurice came home that evening having spent part of his afternoon waiting for Delina to come out of school, only to see her walking to a car with someone obviously giving her a lift. Disconsolately he had then wandered through the town and, almost on impulse, called in to the employment exchange to make enquiries about work.

He came out with details of a job as an estimator for a builders' merchants in London. Buying a writing pad and some envelopes, he wrote for further information.

He saw Nelly, carrying her suitcases, one inside the other and called to her.

"Want some help, Nelly?"

"Thanks, Maurice. Goin' to the bus-stop are yer?"

"Wherever you want, I'm not doing anything important," he said.

"Blimey, you sound fed up! An' what's that mark on your face, left from the fight you 'ad with Tad?"

"Yes, took me by surprise, he did."

"Thought that 'im bein' small you'd flatten 'im, did yer?"

"I didn't know he'd done some boxing," he admitted ruefully.

"What you goin' to do with yerself now you've given up on Australia, go back into the army?"

"No, I don't think so. In fact I've just sent off for an interview for a job in London. But not a word to anyone mind, I don't want Mam to know." His face looked troubled and younger, less confident as he added, "Mam has hopes of me settling down with Sheila, see, and between you and me, Nelly, I can't face that. Sorry I am, mind, but there's no future for us. I think even Sheila would see that if she was honest."

"It's 'ard for 'er," Nelly said hesitantly.

"I'll hate to miss the competition, mind, the village is blooming isn't it?"

Coming towards them on her way to the bus stop was Sheila, Nelly looked at her and saw the slight bodily changes already taking place. Startled she said almost unthinkingly:

"Yes, the village and Sheila, everything's blooming, ain't it."

"Maurice, Are you going home?" Sheila asked, her eyes shining with pleasure.

"No, er, I was only helping Nelly with her cases. I'm meeting someone, sorry." Without another word he left them. Nelly wondered if he knew, whether Sheila had told him she was expecting again.

"You all right, Sheila?" she asked softly. She wanted to ask the girl outright but hesitated. Perhaps she was mistaken.

"Of course I am, why shouldn't I be?"

"Only wondered. Does Maurice know yet?"

"Know? Know what?" Sheila's face stiffened and colour suffused her cheeks, but her eyes glared at Nelly, daring her to say more.

"I'd tell 'im soon if I was you, before he decides to buzz off again."

Sheila went upstairs on the bus, refusing to help Nelly get her cumbersome case into the platform. Nelly sat sadly inside. She thought that once again, she had spoken when she shouldn't.

Maurice was feeling more cheerful with hopes of a job away from Hen Carw Parc and the complications of a wife he didn't love. He had planned a day out fishing and the weather was at last turning spring-like. He set out on his bicycle with the bag behind the saddle filled with fishing tackle and a large supply of food, the rods strapped to the cross bar. The only thing he lacked was company. At the bottom of Sheepy Lane he saw Pete Evans and called to him.

"I'm going fishing, fancy coming?"

"I wouldn't mind, Maurice, but I haven't any bait."

"Plenty here for us both. Come on, I'll wait 'til you get your rods."

Half an hour later the two hopefuls set off on Pete's motor-bike for Swansea docks in the hope of catching some mullet. Pete wasn't the company Maurice had hoped for, he spent most of the time complaining about his mother's carryings on with her new boy-friend.

"Can't blame her, boy," Maurice said at least five times, "your dad being arrested like that. It's a wonder she didn't do anything worse." He was glad when it was too dark for them to see and he could suggest they went home.

Pete agreed to take Maurice's fishing tackle back for him and they parted at *The Drovers*. There he found a meeting in progress.

"Not the gardens again," he groaned. A few looked up but after a vague wave returned to the earnest discussions Maurice had interupted. Victor and Billie were arguing about some point of design. They each had paper in front of them bearing a rough sketch of Amy's garden.

"I thought Freddie was deciding how his mam's garden will look," Maurice said, hoping to stir the argument further.

"He is, we're just discussing how to set out the flowers she wants," Victor said before returning his attention to the drawings. An attempt to join in the conversations that were buzzing around him all failed and he drank the beer he had ordered and walked home. The day which had begun with such optimism had collapsed into dull, boring nothingness.

The thought of Sheila came uninvited into his mind and the prospect of an evening with her seemed preferable to spending the next few hours with his friends. They were all either too boring to contemplate or lost to him with a wife or a career. He had been away too long. What people said about it being impossible to go back to a place once you have left seemed regrettably true. London beckoned, his youthful optimism giving him dreams of a full and adventurous life once he had shaken off the dust of Hen Carw Parc. But until then, he might as well see Sheila.

Delina had made it clear she wanted nothing to do with him, although he hadn't finished with Tad Simmons yet. He would be dealt with before he left. In the meantime, there was Sheila. He increased his pace and began to walk back through the village heading for the council houses.

Sheila had called in to see Bethan. With Maurice still showing no signs of coming back to her she was becoming anxious about the baby. Soon people besides Nelly would guess and already she knew she was giving clues in the way she automatically pulled her coat around her when she was out. And the way she tied her apron less tightly when she was home. She tried pretending she wasn't expecting, allowing her coat to swing as she usually did to show off her generous figure to everyone who passed. If only she *could* pretend and stop trying to hide the barely perceptible swelling of her tummy.

It was a time when Bethan was preparing to open the shop for the evening customers, but she stopped and made a cup of tea when she saw her visitor.

"I only called to say hello, Bethan. I'm sorry I haven't been to see you lately, I'm so busy, what with Gran and everything. There's Mam and Dad to keep an eye on too," she went on in her musical voice, her eyes rolling in exasperation. "They worry so much I have to make sure they're all right. Then there's Maurice." She lowered her head sorrowfully. "I have to see him now and again. He pesters me to go back to him, but I can't. You understand how I fear being hurt again, don't you?"

Bethan nodded wisely but wondered how Sheila could turn him away. "I wouldn't be as strong as you, Sheila," she admitted. "He's so handsome and after all he is your husband."

"We'll go out next Tuedsay evening, shall we? Perhaps to the pictures, we haven't had a real chat for ages."

"Lovely. Then come back here and we'll have supper before you go home. I'll wait on you for a change. You deserve a treat, all that you have to do for others."

Sheila walked out through the shop, warm and steamy with the first batch of chip about to go into the hot fat. She waved goodbye and ran across the road, knowing she ought to go and see her parents but afraid to, imagining Mavis taking one look at her and knowing about the baby.

She was passing the lych gate of the church when a shadow stretched and came out towards her.

"Maurice!" she screamed. "Oh, how you frightened me." She pressed a hand to her chest and leant against the fence as if too weak to stand and Maurice took her arm, full of remorse.

"Sorry, Sheila, I thought you saw me. I waved as you came out of the fish and chip shop. I was on my way to see you."

"Where have you been? You smell of fish! She leaned towards him and breathed deeply. "And of the sea."

"I went fishing with young Pete Evans. God what a misery-guts he is, all he did was moan."

They walked together up the lane, past his mother's house, Sheila, confused by the darkness as they left the main road behind them, needed the support of Maurice's arm. It was fate, she decided. Fate had guided him to her tonight so she could tell him.

Gran had eaten the casserole she had prepared before work that morning and the dish had been returned to the oven. There wasn't much but it would do, she decided. Putting it on to two plates she sat with Maurice in the chilly kitchen, an electric fire shedding more light than warmth. She hoped Gran would go to bed early so she and Maurice could sit in comfort and talk.

Gran wasn't tired and although Sheila hinted as blatantly as she could, the old woman refused to budge from the fire and go to her cold bedroom. Sheila tried to wait patiently but she found it more and more impossible to contain herself. He had to know and from the way he was behaving tonight, he'd be pleased. She was excited, hugging the prospect of her announcement to her and the mood made her excellent and amusing company. She made Maurice relax and her brightness was contagious. He, too, was light-hearted, having spent a dull day that had suddenly become more exciting. He told her some of his adventures in Australia and during the journey there and basked in the admiration of this not unattractive wife of his.

"I'm glad we've had this chance to talk, Maurice, there's something I want to tell you." She couldn't wait a moment longer.

He looked at her recognising in her voice a hint of a changed mood. "Tell me something?" he asked. It must be about the divorce. How should he treat the subject; kindly and with regret? or matter of fact, cold and business-like? "That sounds ominous, Sheila," he said cautiously.

"I'm afraid it's news that will alter our lives once again, Maurice."

Suddenly he knew. He looked at the faint blush on her cheeks, the way her eyes were staring down at her fingers on which she twisted her wedding ring in a nervous yet telling gesture. She was expecting again! He stood up and left the table.

"Sorry, Sheila, I've just realised the time. Mam will be wondering, I was only calling in for a pint and there's me keeping you talking all this time."

"But Maurice, don't you want to hear – "

"Thanks for the meal, it was great." Grabbing his overcoat he hurried from the house, blowing a kiss and slamming the door after him, shutting himself off once again from her.

Sheila stared at the door, her heart racing. He had known. He must have known. If that was so, then his attitude was horrifyingly clear, he didn't want anything to do with her, ever again.

"Maurice gone, has he?" Gran called.

"Definately," Sheila sobbed.

CHAPTER SIXTEEN

After the rush of Saturday shoppers had petered out around half past three, Amy asked Mavis to manage on her own and went home. There was plenty to do if tomorrow were to be a success and although she couldn't really decide what she meant by "success", she wanted to make sure that at least the food was satisfactory.

Calling for Margaret who was staying with Evie and Timothy meant, as she guessed, that she would have Oliver as well.

"All right, he can come back with us, but can you come and fetch him, Evie, I won't have time once I start cooking." Reluctantly, Evie agreed.

The children were soon involved with her preparations and as pasties and cakes began to appear on the table of the kitchen their excitement grew.

"It'll be a real party, Mam," Margaret said, her brown eyes shining with pleasure. "Can I wear my best dress?"

"Of course you can, love."

"And Mam – "

Amy guessed the next question and said, "And of course Oliver can come, too, if his mother agrees."

Amy was nervous about the next day. Having invited Victor's family she began to have doubts at the wisdom of it. Perhaps she and David would have been better to spend an afternoon together without all the rest. He was the one she would find the most difficult to befriend. She admitted to herself that the rest had been invited to ease the situation, make it less likely that she and Victor's sons would have a conversation of any length.

Delina would support her, she guessed, but the girl was very cool and rather aloof, unless falling in love with Tad had opened her out. Aloof and cool would describe Daniel too. She pushed aside the cake she had iced and shivered. The more she thought about belonging to Victor's family the less attractive it sounded.

Oliver was the first to arrive on Sunday afternoon, his parents taking the opportunity to visit friends without him. He and Margaret sat in the front room where the piano was heard from time to time, sometimes with Margaret's skilled hands and at others with Oliver trying to pick out a familiar tune. With everything done Amy sat and listened to their laughter, envying them the freedom of being only ten years old.

Victor arrived looking rather self-conscious, with Daniel and David immaculately dressed and shoes shining. Behind him were Delina, Tad and Dawn. Thankfully, Amy darted into the kitchen to busy herself with the food wondering how she would get through the next few hours.

The table was set and chairs had been borrowed with Billie's help, so somehow nine people could cram around the table. After a laughter filled effort, Margaret and Oliver announced they were going to sit on the stairs and Dawn, though uninvited, followed, dragging David with her. Amy found herself with only Daniel and Delina to deal with, yet she wished the others would return. It was David she needed to get to know.

In fact the conversation flowed with ease. Delina and Tad began to discuss their plans and Amy realised that for them, too, this might have been a bit of an ordeal. The trouble, she analysed as she poured lemonade for the children, was that the Honeymans had always kept themselves separate from the rest of the neighbours. Their mother had created a wedge that the boys were finding difficult to remove.

So you won't be marrying until the year after next?" Amy nervously tried to add to the conversation. "Is it necessary to wait that long?"

"I want to be able to support Delina," Tad said quietly.

201

"Pity."

"What d'you mean?" Tad frowned.

"Pity for anyone putting pride before happiness is what I mean. Heaven knows there isn't much and it so transcient, we ought to grab it."

"I won't have Delina working to support me and Dawn. It might be different without Dawn."

"What would, Dad?" Dawn called from the door as she and Oliver entered to replenish their plates.

"Nothing for you to worry about, Dawn," Tad replied.

Amy said at once, "It is to do with her. Who else if not your daughter?"

"We are discussing how soon your father and I can be married," explained Delina. "He knows that I will have to work and look after you, or wait for about two or three years. It isn't that we want to wait, I'd love to have you for a daughter, but it's a question of money."

"I could do a paper round after school?" Dawn didn't wait to hear more, there was a far more interesting conversation going on on the stairs. The others began to laugh as her bright face smiled at them, made the suggestion and disappeared, eating and talking at the same time.

Tad tip-toed to the door and beckoned Delina to join him. The children were laughing at David's graphic story of the fight between himself and Maurice. Uncomfortably, Tad tip-toed back.

"Now what about you and Dad?" Delina asked softly. "Daniel and I would like you to know that we'll support you and help with David." Formally spoken, the smile on Delina's face softened the words and Amy felt close to tears.

"You really don't mind, you and Daniel?"

"I'll be going to university next year and I'll only need a place to come during the holidays." Daniel spoke rarely, but Amy guessed the blue eyes, so like Delina's, were taking in everything, and behind that smooth fair forehead his mind was calculating what was best for himself. She decided that, difficult as he was, she preferred David.

"We have a lot more to think about," Victor said, reaching out and taking Amy's hand. "Where will we live? Is there room for us here?"

"I think David has already chosen which bedroom he will have," Daniel surprised them by saying. "I heard them whispering about it when I went past a while ago. He wants the room Margaret now has. The other is too small for him to share with Freddie when he comes home on leave."

"I think we'd better clear the table and call the children in." Amy said firmly. "This discussion must include them."

"When will you get married, Mam?" Margaret asked when they were all together again.

Amy looked at Victor then at his family. Victor smiled and said, "Before the competition. After it there'll be a problem getting all our friends to come." Imitating known voices he went on, "'I'm not coming if *she*'s coming'. 'You can count me out if *he'll* be there'."

"We aren't that bad," Amy laughed, "and anyway if that happens we'll have two parties so no one misses out."

"Come on, then, let's name a date."

With a feeling of being forced, Amy looked at the faces raised expectantly: her daughter smiling; David frowning and Daniel looking as if it were nothing to do with him. Then she saw Delina and the girl's face was radiant, smiling encouragement. When she hesitated Delina released her hand from Tad's and blew her a kiss. Amy turned to the calendar hanging beside the fireplace and said,

"The eighteenth of June." She leaned over and kissed Victor on the cheek and repeated, "Your father and I will be married on June the eighteenth and my lovely Margaret will be our bridesmaid."

The party changed then as the wedding was discussed and suggestions made for their honeymoon, and at first no one heard the knock at the door.

Sheila had tried many times to talk to Maurice. She almost convinced herself at times that she had been wrong, he hadn't guessed what she was going to say. She went each

203

evening to the house on Sheepy Lane and waited with Ethel for Maurice to appear, but he stayed away from the house until long after she had given up and gone home, even on Tuesday when she had called after going to the pictures with Bethan.

She began to feel frightened. It was all right having a baby if everything in your life was perfect; if, like Fay, there was a loving husband on the scene to share the joy of it. But for her, nothing in life was right.

She thought she might have to turn to Freddie again, tell him the truth and allow him to help her as he had before. Then she changed her mind. She wanted everyone to believe the baby was Maurice's and that meant Freddie, too. At least that way the baby would have a name.

Mansel Davies, that sounded nice, or Grant Davies, or even Humphrey after Humphrey Bogart, one of her favourite film stars, all tough and masculine. Diana might be suitable for a girl, she thought, thinking of Diana Dors and imagining her child growing up with such sex-appeal. Or what about Muriel? No, they'd call her Moo. She thought of her own name, Sheila. Now if she had been given a name with more charisma, like Isadora, Guinevere or Petronella, who knows what she might have achieved?

She dragged her anxious mind back to the realities and sighed. If only there was someone she could talk to. Bethan wouldn't understand even if she did have a son and no visible father. She had better tell her mother-in-law if she hadn't already guessed. Really, the old women around here were like witches, calling in day after day, and, wanting so desperately to talk to Maurice, she had given Ethel enough of a clue anyway. At least knowing the baby was her grandchild Ethel would support her and try to make Maurice do the same.

Rain was falling steadily and with the intent of continuing all evening. Sheila hesitated, almost turning back from her intended visit to Ethel, but something made her determined to face up to the situation and let her secret out into the open. Covering her fair hair with a scarf and sheltering beneath an umbrella, she bent over and hurried down the road to Sheepy Lane.

The leaves on the trees bordering the lane were hardly unfurled and the street lights were not yet hidden by the growth of early summer. The Lane's wet surface shone in the pools of light and the rain pattered an accompaniment to her running steps. The light flowed out from the cottage door as she picked her way across the grass to the gate. She called and Ethel invited her in. When she closed her umbrella, took off her scarf, complained about the weather and walked into the warm living room, it was to see Maurice standing beside his mother.

"Mam says you want to see me, Sheila," he said.

Something in his expression made her heart leap with anxiety. There was a coldness about his eyes. She forced herself to stay calm and decided that she would boldly state the facts and count on support from Ethel.

"I've been trying to talk to you for days, Maurice," she said, allowing an edge of sharpness in her voice. "There's trouble and I need your advice."

"My advice?" His voice was still cold and held a warning. "Why should you need my advice? You and I are separated Sheila and waiting for a divorce."

"The trouble is, Maurice, I am expecting again. Are you going to leave me to face it alone? Again?"

Ethel remained silent although her eyes were sad. Maurice asked, "When, Sheila? When is the baby expected?"

"Nine months from when you and I first spent the night together," she said boldly, staring at him, conscious of his slight surprise and pleased she had thought so quickly.

"I don't think so. I think this time you are trying to use me. Who is the father? It isn't me, I'm certain of that. I've been very careful for one thing and for another I've counted the weeks. Freddie Prichard, is it? Have you found him a consolation for your empty bed?"

"Maurice! How can you say such things!" Sheila tried in vain to bluster and protest but Maurice was adamant. Ethel said nothing at all, but Sheila felt sympathy emanating from the solemn-faced woman. When there was no more to say she picked up her coat and went out into the night.

"See her home, boy, at least see her home," she heard Ethel plead, and in case he was persuaded Sheila ran, still half into her coat, into the trees. She saw Maurice stand in the lighted doorway for a moment and she held in the breath that was choking her with the desire to cry and scream. He went back inside and she dressed, threw her umbrella into the hedge and, in the still pouring rain, walked through the village towards *The Drovers*.

At Amy's house she turned up the drive and knocked on the door. Amy would have to listen to her. She'd tell her everything, there was a pain in her that needed exorcism and talking it out to anyone who would listen was the only way.

It was Victor who left the group and opened the door. Sheila heard the laughter and lively chatter from inside and at once made her excuses.

"Oh, you have visitors. I only called for a chat with Mrs Prichard. Tell her I'll see her again, will you?" She ran back to the road without waiting for Victor's reply.

As she reached the road she almost bumped into the figure of Nelly, her over-sized coat flopping in the night breeze.

"Sheila?" Nelly grabbed the girl's arm as she tried to hurry on. "'Ere, you bin cryin?"

Unable to control her misery any longer Sheila began to sob. "It's all gone wrong," she wailed. "Let me go, I want to be on my own."

"You're comin' back with me. Look, I bin to buy a small brandy fer George's night-cap. Much better 'e is but a drop of brandy at night will do 'im good." Nelly chattered without giving Sheila a chance to say anything and she kept a grip on the girl's arm so she couldn't run off. From the state of her, she wasn't safe to be on her own. Desperate she looked and to Nelly that meant she needed a chat and a good cup of tea.

Wearily, Sheila submitted to Nelly's determination and went into the cosy room where George sat on the couch drawn up to the fire, wrapped in a blanket. He rose when they came in, looking pleased to see them.

"Sheila, you are welcome, but what a state you're in, haven't you got an umbrella?"

"It went inside out," she lied, "and I threw it into the hedge."

Nelly fetched a towel for her to dry her hair and then made the tea from water that had been simmering on the side of the fire. A lump of soot slid from the side of the chimney and Nelly hooked it out of the teapot without any concern.

"We'll 'ave to 'ave this chimney swept again, George, that's the second time today a bit of soot's fallen."

For some reason Sheila found this casual appproach to cleanliness amusing and she began to laugh. "You don't worry about anything, do you, Nelly?" she spluttered as she tried to hide her laughter in her handkerchief.

"I don't suppose I've ever 'ad as much to worry about as some, like you." She poured the teas and put her head on one side like a curious bird. "It's about the baby I suppose?"

"Nelly, love," George protested.

"Yes, I'm going to have a baby and I've tried telling Maurice it's his so at least the baby will have a legal name and – ". Tears held precariously by the almost hysterical laughter, fell again. "And he says he knows it isn't his and – Oh, Nelly, I'm in trouble and on my own again."

"No you ain't. You don't ever try to make people like you, Sheila, and the way you keep poor Freddie 'anging on makes some of us mad with yer, but you ain't on yer own. Are you goin' to tell me 'oo the real father is?" She crossed her fingers, knowing the likelihood was it was Freddie, but hoping she was wrong.

"It's Freddie," Sheila said in a low murmur. "Believe me, Nelly. I don't want it to be him but it is. I realised just as Maurice came back and I thought, I hoped – "

"Who knows, apart from Maurice and Ethel?"

"You guessed didn't you? I suppose others have, too."

"I think that Maurice owes you something fer the way he treated you last year. Perhaps if I had a chat with Ethel and made her see the fairness of a little 'elp now, he might be persuaded to at least let everyone think the baby is his." She looked at George, wondering if he would guess that her protective attitude was more for Amy and Freddie than the unfortunate girl sitting here hoping for some miraculous solution to her troubles.

"I think you should say as little as possible to anyone until Maurice and Ethel have had a chance to think about it, Sheila," George said. "Least said, soonest mended, is good philosophy."

"'Ow d'you feel about the baby, Sheila? Want it do yer?"

"I do. I find myself thinking about it, wondering if it will be a daughter or a son, and feeling protective and determined he or she will have every care."

Nelly exchanged a look with George and they smiled. This wasn't the usual fanciful talk of Sheila Davies, this was a young woman already enfolded in the aura of motherhood.

Sheila, relaxed by the warmth and the concern shown by the two people she usually ignored, went home with Nelly and the dogs for escort feeling less unhappy and in full agreement for Nelly to talk to Ethel.

"Come to Ethel's after work tomorrow, I'll be there," Nelly promised.

Inside the dark house, with her gran in bed and no one else to greet her, tears returned. This time they were hardened into anger against Maurice, then Ethel and finally, as sleep overtook her, against Delina, the real cause of it all. Delina who with her ladylike ways, had stolen Maurice from her and begun the disasters then casually found herself another love, leaving Maurice and herself with the mess of her disloyalty.

*   *   *

208

"It's all secrets! Wherever I go I'm told to clear off there's secrets to discuss," Phil-the-post complained to Nelly the following morning. "I went to Mam's last night and found her and Maurice sitting there like two victims of a bomb blast, and although I begged them to tell me what was wrong all they'd say was, 'nothing, Phil'. Nothing Phil my foot!" He looked hopefully towards the teapot and asked, "Want another cup of tea, George?" As Nelly re-filled their cups he went on, "What with all the secret garden plans, with greenhouses being painted to keep seed labels hidden from spying eyes and plants being nurtured behind barricades, I haven't a chance. Do you know, that Frank Taylor in St Hilda's Crescent cut a hole in his fence so he could see what his neighbour was growing? And another bloke waters his cuttings with fertiliser, at night? *Boys Own Paper* could get some good plots from what's going on here in Hen Carw Parc lately and no mistake!"

"There's always plenty goin' on 'ere, Phil," Nelly said. "What about the cricket match, are the teams chosen yet?"

"Our Maurice is talking about going to London to work. Pity mind, he'd be a useful bat. Still, I suppose he and that Sheila have to accept they can't live together. Fancy a divorce in the family, never thought I'd see the day." If he noticed that Nelly and George weren't adding to his chatter he didn't mention it, putting their silence down to the fact that George was still unwell and finding it hard to get the breath to talk.

"I'll 'ave to go an' talk to Ethel, George," Nelly said when Phil had taken another cake and gone on his rounds. "I promised Sheila, and although she ain't my favourite person I'll 'ave to keep me word."

"Go straight after finishing work," George said. "I'll get dinner in the oven, meat left over from yesterday will make a nice casserole.

"What's your Maurice doin' about Sheila?" Nelly came straight to the point when she went to see Ethel later that day. "I knows about the baby so you can talk straight with me."

"What a mess it all is, Nelly," Ethel sighed. "They were arranging for a divorce and now, well, how can they apply on the grounds of breakdown of marriage with her expecting! Maurice was advised to sue for adultery but I begged him not to. There are enough lives ruined already without bringing Freddie into it. He's only a boy and doesn't deserve to become entangled in all this."

"If it is his baby, then he is tangled good and proper, ain't 'e?"

"You don't really think it's his, do you?"

"You don't think it isn't?" Nelly countered.

"I think *I'll* emigrate to Australia and stay there until all this is settled," Ethel smiled. "Pity Maurice didn't stay there, poor boy."

"I think Sheila deserves some of yer pity," Nelly said, her eyes watching Ethel as she poked the fire and added more coal. "She ain't no saint, but I think Maurice owes her somethin' fer what 'e did to 'er last year, marryin' 'er then leavin' 'er to face the baby and the death of it all alone, don't you?"

"You're right I'm sure, Nelly, but Maurice is my son and I can't help putting him first."

"I found Sheila walking along in the pourin' rain last night. 'Owlin' 'er eyes out. I was frightened at the state of 'er, Ethel, afraid she might do somethin' to 'erself. She was soaked and didn't care. 'Air all scraggling, no umbrella, only a soggy scarf on. Frightened and with no one to 'elp 'er. Gas ovens ain't only the solution fer the simple-minded, they're a temptation fer the despairin'. She's only young, Ethel. Talk to your Maurice why don't yer?"

Nelly went home and sat waiting for six o'clock when she had arranged to go back to Ethel's and meet Sheila there. The rain continued to fall and Nelly's coat was put in front of the fire to steam and spread a stale, damp smell through the room.

At six o'clock she and Ethel sat waiting for Sheila to

arrive. They said little and the room was silent apart from the slow ticking of the wall clock and the gentle restlessness of the simmering kettle. At seven-thirty they faced the fact that she wasn't coming.

In town, Sheila had turned back as she was about to step on to her bus. She was unable to face the inquisition of Ethel and Nelly, unwilling to bargain for some begrudging help for herself and her baby. She would survive, with or without Ethel's support she'd make a life for herself and this baby. Delina would see how much stronger she was. Delina wouldn't see her begging for crumbs. Paying her money, she went into the cinema and sat enthralled through *Creature from the Black Lagoon*.

Johnny wanted to buy something for his new baby. He knew that with her usual efficiency Fay would have bought all they needed, but he wanted to give the baby a present from himself, something he had chosen and bought.

Occasionally on the way through town between work and home he would stop and look self-consciously in shop windows displaying baby clothes, but he lacked the nerve to go inside. There were usually young women inside looking at the garments the assistants placed on the counter for them to see, smiling and holding up each small item, discussing the merits with the assistants and finally choosing and seeing it placed in a bag to be carried home.

Several times he told himself he was a fool, lacking the confidence to buy for his own child, and even managed to get as far as the door, but he couldn't go inside. One shop was just changing its window display and in the centre of the window was a beautiful pram-suit. Too large he guessed from his study of the contents of several shops and the age and measurements marked on them. But when winter came the baby would be sitting up and then . . . He wanted it. Of all the garments he had hesitated over this was the best. He marched to the door, looked through the glass window, and backed away. Three young women were inside being

211

attended to by assistants. He couldn't go in there, not with all those women.

He turned, desperately looking for a solution to his problem and saw Sheila walking towards him. She would help. He'd ask her to go in and buy it for him.

"Sheila, will you do me a favour? It won't take a minute."

Not answering, Sheila looked at him and the way he was gesturing towards the baby clothes in the window.

"Go in and buy a pram-suit, will you? I can't go in there but it'll be easy for you to go in, you being – ". Being a woman he was about to say but to his surprise and alarm Sheila shrieked at him.

"Mind your own business, Johnny Cartwright! Find someone else as a butt for your schoolboy humour!"

"Sheila, I only wanted you to – " he saw to his alarm that she was crying and for a few moments he followed her but she slipped away from him. Worried about how he had upset her, he went home.

At his mother's house he called and went in. Netta was ironing, her rosy face bright with the heat, her white hair a glorious frame. His wife, Fay, was sitting near the fire.

"Fay, love, there's a nice surprise. Been working local have you?"

"No, I haven't been to work today."

"Not ill are you?" Johnny asked anxiously and Fay and Netta both smiled.

"No, I've just stopped work."

"*Yn wir*? Honestly? *Duw*, that's good news, isn't it, Mam?"

"Only until July. I've been promised I'll have my job back. Someone who has retired is going back to look after my customers for me for a few months, just to give me time to get my strength back and find someone really suitable to look after the baby."

"Oh, I see. I thought – "

"Johnny, I only stopped work this morning and already

212

I'm bored and thinking about how soon I can get back! I'd never settle for domesticity."

"No, my lovely. You know best." He smiled and hugged her. "My clever wife who'll be the best mother Hen Carw Parc has ever seen. Lucky baby he'll be."

Netta put the ironing away and brought in a tray of tea. She said nothing when the subject of Fay's career was mentioned. She hoped that something would happen to change Fay's mind but was wise enough not to show her dismay when so far it had not.

"Mam," Johnny asked flopping into an armchair, "what's up with Sheila?"

"Unhappy about Maurice not wanting her. Being abandoned twice is enough to make anyone unhappy. Why?"

"I saw her in town and asked her to go in and buy something for me and she acted as if I'd insulted her." He explained about the pram-suit for his baby and Netta frowned.

"Sounds as if you hit a nerve. Perhaps she's expecting again. Funny, Phil next door hasn't said anything and he's always first to spread the news."

"If you like the pram-suit, I'll go and buy it for you, Johnny," Fay smiled.

"No, no. It's something I want to do. But it's funny about Sheila, isn't it?"

"I'll go and see Ethel, she'll know although she might not want to say," Netta said. "Perhaps Amy will know. No, best I don't ask her in case she thinks of Freddie. Oh dear, I suppose we'd better wait for Phil-the-post to tell us."

So, gradually, the news of Sheila's new baby was spread around the village with a variety of reactions. Maurice was embarrassed but warned by Ethel not to deny or accept responsibility. Sheila was brazen, holding herself so people could see that her usually slim figure was gradually swelling. But nothing was spoken about the situation between Sheila and Maurice.

People who knew them both, reacted with amusement or disgust. Few supported her and among those who did were Nelly and Bethan. Bethan and she recommenced their Tuesday evenings out and dressed up for the occasional walk on Sunday afternoons, laughing and flirting when the opportunity presented itself. The few brave enough to ask outright what Sheila intended to do were told firmly and not too politely to mind their business. Around her curiosity simmered.

CHAPTER SEVENTEEN

Having made the decision to marry Victor, Amy began to prepare for the wedding. She knew that however she tried to make it a small, private affair in deference to the still recent death of Imogine, the village would not allow the event to pass without a real celebration.

"What a year this'll be, Amy," Nelly said as she scrubbed the floor of the storeroom one Sunday morning. "Cricket matches that threaten to start a war, Best Kept Village and all the little jealousies that's brought to the surface, and your weddin'. Lovely it'll be, we'll all find some really smart clothes fer that day, Amy."

"You mean you won't turn up in George's wellingtons?" Amy laughed.

"I wouldn't let you down, not on yer weddin' day," Nelly said solemnly. Then with a grin added, "Not unless it's rainin' o' course!"

"Of course," Amy smiled.

"You 'avin' the church, all? Pity the new one ain't finished. You being married to your Victor would start it off in style."

"Victor and I have already seen the Reverend Barclay Bevan and he's agreed to marry us and let us have the hall. I don't think I'll get caterers in, though, I want to do it myself with some help from friends, of course. That way it'll be a real village wedding."

"You inviting that poor Billie Brown?" was Nelly's next question.

"Of course. I want all my friends there."

"Blimey, I 'opes them two rivals don't start a punch up!

215

Which reminds me, have you 'eared anything more about the argument between Maurice and Tad? Fancy 'im bein' a fighter, although I should have guessed the way he punched my George's nose for 'im once."

"Delina and Tad seem very happy now and as for Maurice, he seems to be keeping his head well down. Because of Sheila's condition probably. What Ethel must think about the way he's behaving to that poor girl I can't imagine!" She superstituously crossed her fingers as she spoke.

"So things is lookin' up all round?"

"Yes, at least they were, look who's coming."

Sheila walked towards the shop door which stood open to dry the floor Nelly had just washed.

"We're closed, Sheila, sorry," Amy said.

"I only wanted a word, Mrs Prichard," Sheila glared at Nelly. "In private."

Amy's heart sank. A discussion about the pregnancy was something she hoped they wouldn't have, now it seemed it was about to happen. Well, nothing was ever gained by putting off the inevitable.

"Go and put the kettle on will you, Nelly love?" She gestured to Sheila to come inside. "I can't be long, mind, I have to get back and cook for Margaret and Oliver."

"On their own, are they?"

"Only for an hour or two," Amy said sharply. Surely this girl wasn't telling her how to look after Margaret now?

"You know I'm expecting?" Sheila touched her stomach with a proud hand.

"I've heard. What are you going to do? Is Maurice going to stay this time? I think he should, he owes you that much and more for the way he treated you last year." Amy spoke fast as if to drown out the words she dreaded to hear. "I think everyone in the village thinks he was wrong to go like he did, best he settles down now and faces his responsibility."

"It's not Maurice's baby and he knows it. I tried to pretend it was his but he knew it wasn't. Freddie is the father. I've told Maurice and his mother but so far I haven't told Freddie or anyone else, except my friend, Bethan. What d'you think I should do now, Mrs Prichard?"

"What d'you want me to say, Sheila? You know I don't want Freddie tied to a married woman who doesn't love him. You still want Maurice, don't you?"

"I want some support for me and my baby, Mrs Prichard. What d'you think I should do?" she repeated, her blue eyes widening, her face showing childlike anxiety. "I haven't anyone to talk things over with, only Bethan, and she thinks you should help. Unless I tell Freddie, of course. Glad to help he'd be, don't you think, Mrs Prichard?"

Was it her imagination or did Sheila emphasise the Mrs? Amy was no more a married woman than Sheila was a virgin. They were silent for a while, each sizing up the other. Through a crack in the door Nelly watched and listened.

"What do *you* think I should do?" Amy asked in a low voice.

"That's up to you, but if we don't want Freddie involved, then at least you could help me with some money. There'll be a lot to buy if this baby isn't going to suffer. I don't want him to suffer the embarrassment of not having enough clothes or a decent pram."

"You're asking me for money?"

"Well, yes, Mrs Prichard. And help when the baby comes, you know how useless Mam and Dad will be. For Freddie's sake really, isn't it?"

"Go now, we'll talk later." Amy opened the door to its widest and watched as Sheila walked down the road and turned down the lane to the back of the fish and chip shop. She was going to relate the interview, word for word, point by point, with Bethan.

"Tell 'im, Amy!" Nelly came into the shop as Amy was closing the door behind her visitor. "You can't carry the burden of that fer one single day. Write to Freddie an' tell 'im what she's sayin'."

"I've been in her situation, Nelly, without anyone to help.

I can't wish it on her. Not liking her just makes it that much harder, but I have to help her."

"All right, but you still have to tell Freddie."

"You're right, of course, but it will ruin his chances of a happy life. I want so much for him and Margaret to be happy." More briskly, she added, "And Victor and I will have to shelve our plans to marry. I can see me having to look after the baby while Sheila works just like I looked after Prue's baby while she was ill. Someone will have to help and I can't see those two upstairs being willing to, can you?"

Sadly, Nelly agreed. "When will things start going right for you, Amy?"

"Not until I'm too old to care!"

Amy saw very little of her sister, Prue. Since recovering from the depressive illness that had hit her after the birth of her daughter, Sian, almost a year ago, she had been looked after by a woman employed to help in the house and share responsibility for the baby. It had worked out well, but some animosity, as yet unexplained, separated her from Amy. She rarely came into the shop, preferring to go into town and get what she needed. Twice she had walked out of Amy's house when Freddie appeared.

"It's as if most of her resentment is aimed at Freddie, but I can't imagine why," she told Victor when Prue had again walked past them without speaking. They were in town for a rare visit to the cinema with Delina and Tad and Daniel looking after the children.

"Didn't Freddie work for her?" Victor asked.

"Yes, until he left to join the army."

"Perhaps she is angry with him for leaving her after her husband died? Illness can turn disappointment into a grudge."

"Perhaps. I don't understand why she's been so odd. Since she moved back to her own home with Florrie Gwyn to look after her she's hardly set foot in my house, and all

218

those months while she was in hospital I cared for little Sian as if she were my own."

"Now you might have a baby to mind once again."

"So it seems. Funny, that gypsy friend of Nelly's told me I'd have a baby in my arms. I'd better go and see if she can see another. Nice to know where I stand," she laughed.

"Whatever happens, we stand together, Amy love, remember that."

"Victor, if I have to help bring up Sheila's baby, I can't marry you. We've been over this time and again and well, I can't do it to the boys. They'll resent me enough without inflicting a crying baby on them. Different house, different family and attitudes *and* a squealing child? We couldn't do it, Victor. It wouldn't be fair."

"Don't cancel anything yet, promise me that. Who knows what Sheila will do? Who knows what your Freddie will do? And there's Maurice. He might decide to accept the baby and stay. There is an ironic justice in that. So many 'if's' there's got to be a slight chance for us among them?"

"All right, we'll give it to the end of April and decide then."

They went to join the queue for the cinema but changed their minds as they approached the head of the queue where the uniformed man was gradually allowing a few people at a time to cross the foyer and buy their tickets.

"Come on, Amy, let's go to a pub and talk instead."

Near Nelly's gate in the lane there was a tap. Before Evie and Mrs Norwood Bennet-Hughes had arranged for the new bathroom to be installed in the cottage Nelly and George had used it, carrying all their water down the cinder path into the house. Now it was only used by Farmer Leighton to fill the old bath in the field where he kept his old plough-horses.

Coming up the lane one day, after cleaning for Mrs Williams, Nellie heard voices and when she turned the corner saw a crowd of young people around the tap, filling bottles and drinking from them, laughing, chattering.

219

Among them were Bobby and Spotty enjoying cuddles and the occasional tid-bit, and George.

It was the first time since his recent bout of illness that he had felt strong enough to walk up the path to the gate and she hurried to make sure he was all right.

"'Ello, you some of them ramblers?" she called, seeing from the trousers and waterproof coats and thick boots that they were out on a walk.

"Nelly, love, these people are a bit lost. They've come from the old brick-works at Cymer and are heading for Leighton's place."

Nelly didn't reply immediately, she was counting heads. "If you don't mind a few cups without 'andles we can offer you a cup of tea before you carry on, eh?" she offered. "Then me an' the dogs'll see you on your way." Her words were greeted with an enthusiastic chorus of thank you's.

The dogs, sniffing around the gathered legs, had already made friends and the lively party made their way down the path to sit on their macs on the grass. There were eight of them aged from about twelve to sixteen, three girls, one of whom went into the house after easing off her muddy boots to help Nelly with the tea.

"I'm Doreen," she said, "the leader for today."

Nelly looked at the girl's pleasant smiling face that was covered in freckles and saw a friend. Her brown hair with reddish tints was freed from a woollen bobble hat and fell about her shoulders in untidy curls. Hazel eyes shone with good humour and health. Nelly warmed to her.

"Glad to meet you, Doreen. I'm Nelly, everyone calls me that and I don't see why you should be no exception. My 'usband is George."

"He hasn't been well, has he?" Doreen whispered.

"No 'e ain't and I don't think 'e should be standin' out there on that damp grass with 'is slippers on."

"Right, Doreen said firmly, 'I'll go and persuade him he's needed in here.'"

She went out and returned almost immediately, chattering to George, coaxing him to sit near the fire.

"Now, George, so I can help and not be a nuisance, you tell me where everything is kept. The cups for a start."

"Down in that cupboard but they'll need a wash," he said. "We don't use that many very often."

"Consider it done," Doreen said, bending and dragging out a box containing some assorted china. She wiped each cup and saucer and placed them on the table, chatting away as she did so. "This is very kind of you both. We're a bit tired and some of the younger ones will be better for a breather like this. Better than a sit down at the side of a field and a slurp of cold water!"

"How far have you come?" George asked, accepting the first cup of tea handed to him by their bright and friendly visitor.

"My George used to walk a lot, miles he'd cover in a day, wouldn't you George?" Nelly said, noting with pleasure the way the girl was looking after him.

"We've come seven miles and we have another two to get to where we're being picked up," Doreen explained. "But tell me, George, what was the longest you've done in a day."

"About twenty-five," George replied and soon the two of them were engrossed in discussions about the various journeys they had undertaken.

Nelly was beaming. The house and garden filled with young people and with this natural and delightful girl making sure George was made to feel someone special. Her heart went out to Doreen and she wished they could all stay longer.

When several pots of tea had been consumed and the tin of cakes had been emptied, Nelly and the dogs walked with the group across the lane and up the hill behind the houses where Mrs French and Prue Beynon lived and over to where they were in sight of Leighton's farm. Doreen found their place on her map and Nelly pointed out the gypsy's camp far below them. Then she stood with the dogs and waved at the walkers until they were out of sight. She sighed happily and went home. What a surprise. That'll be something to tell Phil when he called in the morning and wondered why there was no cake

A few days later Phil called and surprised them by saying: "There's a letter for you Nelly and George, from Cardiff, and it isn't a bill!" Phil poured himself a cup of tea while Nelly opened the envelope, a frown of curiosity on her face.

"It's from that Doreen," she said. "Look, George, thanking us fer our hospitality. What d'you think of that then?"

"See the address, Nelly," George said, pointing at the top of the letter. "They were from a children's home in Cardiff."

"All them kids not 'avin' an 'ome. George, if we were twenty years younger we could take the lot of 'em!"

The gypsies were on the verge of leaving. Nelly had seen, from the top of the hill, that the horses were back from their winter stay in one of Leighton's fields, tethered close to the vardo. And the piles of wood, gathered for the cooking fires had diminished, the remainder scattered among the hedgerow. Clara and her family were about to set off on their summer wanderings.

She went up to see them for the last time before going to work. There was joy in every season, each change bringing new delights for Nelly. But this year the departing of Clara, besides announcing the approach of summer, left her feeling anxious.

"It's George," she told Clara. "I know the doctor says 'e'll be all right now the worst of winter is be'ind us, but I felt 'appier knowin' you were 'ere to give some 'elp.

"You have some tonic, Nelly, my friend, and with your love and care he'll come nicely."

"You really think he'll be all right again soon?" Nelly stared into the wise, dark eyes of the gypsy, begging for hope and reassurance.

"Later rather than sooner, but you never fear, he'll come well, in time."

There was a warning rather than comfort in the words. Nelly feared she was being prepared for worse to come.

"I'd 'ate to lose him. Me an' 'im , we're so 'appy."

"Nelly, my friend, you will always be happy. There's some that never are, always wanting and wanting, missing what's under their noses. You're a clever one, clever and wise, accepting what you've got and valuing it."

"I value George, Clara. And will for a long time yet, I 'opes."

"I'll see you both next year," Clara said, hugging her friend, hoping she was right.

"Have you heard from Freddie yet, Sheila?" Bethan asked. "You did write, didn't you?"

"No, I thought I'd best leave it to his mam. I want him to feel unpressured by me. If he wants to help, well, I haven't pleaded, have I?"

"Aren't you scared, being on your own in all this?"

"Were you?"

"Yes, and I had similar problems to you. My mother and father practically disowned me, then insisted on bringing up Arthur and leaving me to act the grieving widow."

"I won't let my mother and father bring up my child I'd hate to think of her going through what I suffered!"

"It is a disgrace in their eyes, you can't blame them for worrying."

"All right, they might be embarrassed by what's happening now, but what was their excuse for treating me the way they did before all this?"

"Perhaps you were a bit too soon after *their* wedding," Bethan suggested with a laugh. "It's been known, you know. We aren't the only generation to have emotions we can't control, even if they'd like us to think we are! Half the village are too scared to celebrate their wedding anniversaries for fear of someone counting the months". Bethan added.

"Now there's a thought for first thing in the morning."

* * *

223

Freddie waited impatiently for his leave. He couldn't write to Sheila, not with the chance that she would show his letter to Maurice. His mother didn't seem too sure about whether they were together or not and until he could see Sheila and talk to her, he thought it wiser to do nothing.

He was confused and anxious. What should he do? He couldn't marry Sheila and for the first time there was the tiniest doubt about whether he wanted to. Marrying her had been his dream for so long. She was small and helpless and seemed to attract trouble. She made him feel strong and he wanted to look after her. She hadn't anyone to care for her and he wanted to make up to her for all the unhappiness she had faced alone. But she wasn't free, she had a husband. How would Maurice would feel? He'll probably want to kill me! He realised he was afraid to face his friend.

For a moment he wanted to cancel his leave, or perhaps he would go home with one of his friends, he was always being invited. Best if he waited, said and did nothing, waited until things had calmed down, given Maurice a chance to make his decision. Yes, that was best, him turning up to add his four penn'orth would only add to the confusion.

He left camp on a Friday towards the end of March. His decision made he went straight home, leaving the railway station and hurrying through the town to the bus stop; then running up the steps of the bus, head down, ostrich-like, in the hope he wouldn't see anyone he knew. He went past his mother's shop, looking down from the bus to see the windows advertising Easter Eggs and announcing that orders were being taken for simnel cakes.

Getting off the bus at the stop before *The Drovers*, he shouldered his kit-bag and hurried up the drive into his house as if a thousand eyes followed his every step.

CHAPTER EIGHTEEN

Evie had found herself a job. With too little to do in the neat and orderly house with only an orderly husband and an organised son, she found time hanging heavily on her.

"I've decided to return to work," she told Oliver one morning when he sat eating breakfast. "Your father will be here to take you to school in the mornings and I will be home before you finish in the afternoons."

"Oh," Oliver said, swallowing the last of his toast.

"Only 'oh', Oliver?" Evie smiled.

"I thought you might say I have to go to Gran's, er, Grandmother's every day," he admitted. "Lots of the boys in school have to go to their grans until their mother's finish work."

"We aren't like that, Oliver. Your father and I will make arrangements for you between ourselves."

"If Father has something important, then I'll have to go to Gran's, won't I?"

"If Amy or one of your other friends can't help, well, yes, maybe."

"Good. George, I mean Grandfather, isn't well enough to work and he'll be glad of my company."

"I'm sure he will," Evie said, tight-lipped.

"So am I," Oliver said guilelessly. "Quite sure, he's always saying so."

"I don't think it will often be necessary, Oliver."

"Where will you be working?"

"In an office in Llan Gwyn. I – I'll have to try to pass my driving test again soon, then I won't be out of the house so long."

"Will I have to sit while you take lessons?" Memories of long, boring hours sitting in the back of the car while his mother practised three point turns and hill-starts came back to him with clarity. "Perhaps," he said hopefully, "you'd con-cen-trate better if I stayed with Gran or Margaret?" He smiled, pleased with himself for remembering that long word that Gran had explained. His mother seemed not to notice.

"We'll see, Oliver. Now hurry boy, you are such a dawdler. Your father will be down in a moment expecting you to be ready to leave."

Margaret crossed over the road and went into the shop-cum-post-office after school had finished and looked quizzically at her mother.

"Freddie home yet, Mam?"

"I haven't seen him, Margaret love. Perhaps he's gone straight to the house.

"Can I go home now and see?"

"No, in case he hasn't, I don't want you there on your own. Mavis will be down in a minute and we can leave together." Mavis arrived a few moments later and they hurried away.

With Margaret skipping beside her mother, they walked along the main road to their house. It was not yet dark and seeing no light on in the house didn't surprise them. Opening the door Amy called: "Freddie?" she shrieked with delight when he appeared in the kitchen doorway.

"Saw you coming and I put the kettle on, Mam," he said over the rich red hair of his sister's head as he hugged her. "Finished early, did you?"

"We weren't sure what time you'd be here. We don't want to waste a moment of your leave," Amy said as she hung up her coat and went for her welcoming hug. "Glad to see you, Freddie."

"Sorry about all this, Mam," he began, but he stopped when Amy shook her head and frowned and instead asked Margaret about her recent exam.

Margaret had seen the warning flash from her mother's eyes and her heart sank. So there was a secret and she wasn't to be included.

"Oh, it was all right," she said off-handedly. "Mam, shall I make the tea while you and Freddie get your boring talk over and done with?" She half closed the kitchen door, rattled a few cups and crouched to listen behind the door.

"Is it true, what Sheila says?" Amy asked in a low voice. "I need to know all the facts, Freddie, so I can decide what's best to do."

"I don't know, Mam. With Sheila you never know, but it's possible, mind." He looked away from her a blush creeping up his cheeks. "Maurice has been home, hasn't he?"

Amy thought, as she looked at his reddening face, that he looked young and unprepared for this situation. Too young surely for this to be happening? He was still a boy.

"It is possible?" Her tongue refused to form the necessary words. "You and she have – ?" She stared at him, his blue eyes behind the rimless glasses again sliding away from her gaze down to the floor where he followed the pattern in the carpet with his foot. "Freddie, answer me."

"Yes, Mam, it's possible."

"Why?" Exasperated she sighed and looked at him. "Why Sheila of all people. You knew she was married and to your friend, too."

"Sorry, Mam."

The kettle was boiling its head off and Margaret still knelt and listened uncomprehendingly behind the door. The sound of the rattling kettle lid reached Amy's ears and she stood up in time to catch Margaret just rising from her knees.

"Margaret, love, when it's time to involve you in something I'll tell you. Until then don't listen to things that don't concern you and which you won't understand."

Margaret was shocked. It wasn't often her mother scolded her and this seemed so unreasonable. It must be something dreadful.

227

"Freddie's my brother and if he's in trouble I ought to know." She ran to her room and closed the door firmly. She waited but Amy didn't go up and explain as Margaret expected.

The light outside her window faded, turning the glass into mirrors. The sun, disappeared long since, sent its last glow across her ceiling as she lay on her bed and listened to the murmur of talk from below. She was hungry and cold but she wasn't going down until Mam came to fetch her. Childishly she switched on her light, picked up a book and began to read. She would look quite unconcerned when her mother eventually remembered her. In her gymslip pocket, stuck with a few hairs and oddments of fluff, she found a sweet and, after licking it to remove most of the surplus, she began to suck it noisily.

When Amy went up after preparing their meal, she found a scowling Margaret still reading and refusing to come down.

"I'll give you and Freddie some peace so you can decide what to tell me," she said in a prim tone. "I know I'm not old enough to understand."

"Margaret, love. This is something that's private to Freddie. When it's sorted, then we can discuss it, not before. All right? Now, come down and see what Freddie brought home for you. A whole packet of Devon cream toffees. And dinner is ready on the table. Poached haddock, your favourite."

The thought of food made Margaret put her book aside after only token hesitation and follow her mother down to the warm fire and appetizing food and Freddie.

On her way to the farm on Saturday morning, Dawn stopped, changed her route and went to see the Honeymans instead. She noticed that many of the gardens already had borders filled with small plants and saw several polyanthus and pansies showing colour amid the spring display of daffodils and grape hyacinths. Others had cleared the ground and

228

neatly dug it ready for the displays of annuals planned for the competition.

She sighed. Their front had only some scruffy grass and a few straggly remnants of last autumn's blooms. Some of the neighbours had promised them some flowers but Dawn began to resent the organisation behind the majority of houses and felt an impulse to destroy their efforts in an attempt to bring them down to the level of her and her father. It wasn't fair.

She cheered as she approached the house where Delina lived. Theirs wasn't that good. The hedge hadn't been regularly cut and it showed gaps where the boys had pushed their way through. The grass, hidden from the sun by the over-tall privet was poor and the flowerbeds weren't neatly edged as in most of the other gardens. Mr Honeyman was too busy looking after Amy Prichard's garden, or so she had heard people say. She thought she would tell Delina what a mess her garden looked.

No one answered her knock for a while and she began to wonder what she would call Mr Honeyman if he were to become her father's father-in-law. Grandfather-in-law? That sounded funny. She had written down all the relationships with her father's help the previous evening and now, as she knocked at the back door and waited for someone to open it, she suddenly remembered that if Delina married her father besides Delina becoming her step-mother, David and Daniel would be her uncles. She had been told but until now hadn't given it a second thought.

David opened the door and Dawn smiled at him and said:

"Hello, Uncle David, is Uncle Daniel in?"

"What game are you playing now, Dawn Simmons?" David asked grumpily.

"No game, David, you really will be my uncle when your sister marries my dad."

David frowned at her as if about to argue then his face opened into a smile.

"Really? I'll be an uncle? How odd."

229

"Can I come in, Uncle David?"

"You can't stay, I'm going into town with Dad."

"Pity, I thought you might like to come to the farm with me. We've got a secret."

"Boring."

"Not this one. It's something we're practicing in secret. Only Uncle Billie and Auntie Mary knows."

"You and Margaret and Oliver I suppose."

"Yes, and I'll have to ask them before I can tell you."

"Boring." But he put on his coat and called to his father that he would only be a little while and followed Dawn through the garden and out into the fields.

Throughout the village several hundred fushia plants were flourishing. Cuttings taken the previous year and nurtured in a variety of places by many of the villagers were all ready to be moved to their alloted place in the displays which were already set up and waiting to be filled. Coleus seeds grew on a dozen windowsills and each trayful was listed as to its eventual home.

Geraniums and pelargoniums, those most reliable and beautiful flowers, numbered hundreds as cuttings were strongly developing in their pots to be transplanted into their summer homes once the worst danger of frosts had gone. Then there were the annuals growing in living rooms, kitchens, bathrooms; germinating in airing cupboards and being potted on in out-houses cold-frames and barns. The largest collection was in the barn belonging to Billie and Mary Brown.

When Dawn arrived at the farm she usually went to help in the barn where she would find Margaret and Oliver already watering or transplanting under the guidance of either Billie or Mary. Today, Dawn went to the small room beside the kitchen and sat to wait for the others. In a corner of the slate-floored room were a collection of home-made instruments.

With Billie's help, Oliver had made a tea-chest and a broom handle into a single string bass instrument. It was played by placing one foot on the box and plucking the string, changing the note by moving the broom handle backwards or forwards to tighten or loosen the tautness of the string. Billie had cut holes in the front of the box for the sound to come out.

Beside it was an old wash-board belonging to Mary, who had recently bought a new washing machine. In a wooden box there were two mouth-organs and a kazoo. A half finished maraca was drying on the windowsill.

David, looked at the Skiffle band with interest. "This isn't any good. What you want is a guitar," he said disparagingly.

"We know that," Dawn said impatiently. "Why does everyone have to tell us what we already know? What they don't tell us is how we can get one. I expect Margaret could play it if we could get hold of one."

"I can play, a few chords anyway," David said. "Mam taught me, a long time ago so we could sing carols together." His face clouded at the reminder that his mother was no longer there. "I expect I've forgotten."

"I bet you haven't! Go and get it, David. Please, Uncle David," Dawn said with a smile. "Go on, the others'll be here soon and they'd be ever so pleased."

An hour later David had managed to avoid the intended visit to town and was sitting with Margaret, Oliver and Dawn trying to remember how to tune the six strings of his guitar. After a frustrating hour, they all trouped off to see if Mrs French could help them.

Amy left early to open the shop and left Freddie poring over seed lists and drawings of how he hoped the garden would look. He had no desire to go out and she knew he was afraid of how he would be received should he bump into either Sheila or Maurice. It was Maurice he feared most. At least Sheila wasn't likely to attack him in rage.

Seeing Mavis waiting for her to open the shop door she took a deep breath. Whatever happened, Mavis would soon learn that Freddie was responsible for her Sheila's condition. Once Maurice told everyone that he and Sheila were still separated every eye in the village would turn accusingly on Freddie. She didn't know what to do and wondered if she should go and talk to Ethel. It was all right Sheila flaunting her condition for all to see, but another to expect Maurice to remain silent. One day soon, she thought with a frisson of panic, he would just leave again and they would have to sort out the problem of Sheila without him.

"Mavis," she said on impulse, "I think we should have a little talk."

"About Freddie? I thought you'd never face up to it, Amy," Mavis surprised her by saying.

"You know! I mean, you suspect?"

"I know that Sheila was expecting before Maurice came back. That Freddie is responsible follows from that."

"But you haven't said a word!"

"Best you came to me. It's been hard, mind, for me to keep quiet, but I knew that once Freddie was told and you and he had a chance to talk, that you'd do the right thing."

"What *is* the right thing? Your Sheila is married to Maurice. How can Freddie 'do the right thing'? Mavis, I wish you and your daughter had never come here. She's been nothing but trouble for you and her father, and for me and my son!"

"But she is going to have a baby and it will be your grandchild."

Mavis ended the brief conversation by snapping up the door blind and letting in their first customer.

"I'll go and see Ethel after the shop closes," Amy said between serving stamps to Netta Cartwright and some chocolate to Arthur Toogood.

"Go now. I'll manage here," Mavis said, tight-lipped. "Sooner better than later in a case like this with that Maurice Davies likely to dart off any minute!"

*   *   *

Ethel's kitchen was upside down. Nelly's fat hips were sticking out from under the table, waggling enthusiastically as she scrubbed the linoleum. The table held four chairs and numerous ornaments and the rag mats which usually covered most of the floor were rolled up near the door.

"Oh, I see you're busy. I'll call back, Ethel." Amy knelt down and asked Nelly why she wasn't at Mrs French's.

"Them kids called and as I'd done upstairs first she asked me to leave the downstairs and do it later." Nelly's red face appeared as she flopped the floor cloth into the bucket of water she had near her.

"Margaret and Oliver? I thought they were at the farm with Billie?"

"And Dawn, and David Honeyman."

"Oh? What are they doing, d'you know?"

"I know but I ain't allowed to say nothin'." Nelly mimed cutting her throat and made a horrible noise as she said, "Cut me throat an' 'opes to die."

"Nelly, they aren't bothering Mrs French, are they?"

"Botherin' 'er? No, o' course not. She's enjoyin' 'erself. And they ain't up to anything you'd disapprove of so forget it until they tell you themselves. Okay?"

"Okay," Amy laughed. "I'll still leave what I wanted to see you about and come back later, Ethel," she said to the woman sitting quietly beside the fire, polishing brass ornaments.

"I expect it's about Freddie," Ethel said. "I heard he was home."

"How did you –? No, don't answer that. There isn't much goes on here that isn't broadcast by your Phil and swifter than the BBC news!"

"Don't mind me," Nelly puffed. "I got to wait fer this to dry before polishin' it again. Get some cups out, shall I?" She stood up and abandoned the coarse apron she was wearing and dried her red hands on her skirt. She went into the kitchen and Ethel gave a sad smile.

"What are we going to do, Amy?"

"We'll have no say in any of it. What Maurice does is the

main thing. Then Sheila comes next. Freddie is hanging in mid-air waiting for them to make up their minds."

"I can't talk to Maurice. He's my son but I can't talk to him."

"Freddie and I can talk but it doesn't get us anywhere. Sheila is married to your Maurice and whatever we say, that can't be altered in five minutes. D'you think if Freddie and I tried to discuss it with Maurice we'd get somewhere approaching a solution?"

"Freddie will face him, will he?"

In spite of the seriousness of their discussion, Amy smiled.

"'Course he will Maurice ain't likely to kill 'im is 'e?" came from the kitchen, where Nelly was unable to resist listening.

"I don't think anything will be decided until they meet, the three of them: Sheila, Maurice and young Freddie. Sheila has to face up to the two of them."

They decided to ask all three protagonists to meet them at Ethel's house the following morning, Sunday, when Sheila was free and the other two had no pressing plans.

"I'll go up an' put a note through Sheila's door if you like," Nelly offered.

"Where's Maurice?" Amy asked "We'll have to tell him as soon as we can.'"

"I don't know," said Ethel. "Fishing maybe. He wanders around from early morning until late at night but he doesn't tell me where he's been."

Freddie had put aside his garden planning and put on a coat. He couldn't spend the whole of his leave in the house. Sheila was at work. Perhaps he would go in and meet her, try to have a word with her. He left a note for his mother and walked towards the bus stop. He glanced at his watch. There was fifteen minutes to wait, so he walked on to wait outside *The Drovers*. As the public house came into sight he saw Maurice.

Maurice was watching him and there was no point in turning away. Apprehensively he waited while Maurice walked towards him.

"What have you been doing messing about with my wife, Freddie Prichard." Maurice's voice was low and threatening.

"I want to care for Sheila, Maurice, and – "

"I care for my wife, it's my job, not yours you snivelling apology for a man."

"You weren't doing a very good job of caring for her. She would have had that baby of yours all alone last year if I hadn't been there. And she had to face the death of it alone. Where were you? Caring d'you call that? Funny way of looking after your girl, that is."

Freddy felt the tension rising and threatening to choke him as Maurice took another step towards him. He knew this would end with blows but he was determined to have his say while he could still talk clearly.

"Someone had to befriend her after you ran like a coward just about as far as anyone *could* run." He thought his voice was higher and was afraid he sounded like a frightened girl. It added to his defiance and he almost shouted, "Coward you are, Maurice Davies, running from a woman after ruining her life. I'd have looked after her proper."

When Maurice ran it was as if he had flown towards him. Suddenly Freddie was facing a heavy and fit opponent whose eyes were wild and twice their normal size and whose hands seemed like battering rams. He bent in a semi-protective stance and waited for the pain. He was no fighter and all he could do was try and dodge the blows and hope that Maurice would change his mind about injuring him.

"What'll this prove?" he shouted as he danced first one way and then the other. "This won't make what you did any better."

"I'll make you wish you'd left my wife alone," Maurice growled.

The first fist to hit Freddie caught him against the chin and he was shocked by a sensation of numbness that was

235

quickly followed by an excruciating agony that engulfed him. He wanted to curl up and recover but Maurice took advantage of the boy's confusion and hit him again and again, to the chest and the face: the pain came in waves and Freddie staggered around unable to stop Maurice from showering him with ferocious jabs and punches.

Then it stopped and he tried to open his eyes to see why he had been reprieved from death. His eyes felt stickly and swollen and unwilling to open but when they did it was to see a furious Tad holding Maurice in a vice-like grip, his arms behind his back, bent against one of the man's knees.

"Freddie is almost a part of my family," Tad was grunting. "If you have any disagreements with *any* of my family, you come to me. Right?"

"Right." Maurice was afraid of the man's strength, imagining his arms being dislocated. When Tad slowly released him, he stood up and brushed imaginary dust from his clothes and said, "What should I do? He's got my wife in the family way."

"Where were you when all this happened?" If Tad was surprised by the announcement his voice gave no sign of it. "On your way back from Australia was it? And what were you doing there? Running away from your wife, was it? Go home, boy, and grow up. Ask your wife to forgive you. You've behaved far worse than she has."

In the doorway of *The Drovers* several heads were peering around doors. The wild-eyed one sticking out the furthest belonging to Phil who was being restrained from going and assisting his brother. He was shouting:

"Leave him, Tad, he's bigger than you, mind!" Which brought forth a chorus of laughter from those holding him back.

When Tad had stepped away from Maurice, he and Freddie looked at each other, Freddie through eyes that were red and already beginning to swell. Tad looked from one to the other, decided he could trust Maurice not to re-start the fight and said:

"Take him home, Maurice, and clean him up before Amy sees him. I don't think you've done any real harm. Luckily for you."

Maurice walked over to Freddie and nodded his head towards the boy's house.

"Sorry, mate. That's no way to settle things. Come on, you'd better get that face of yours sorted before your Mam sees it or my face'll get a battering from her."

The doors of the pub opened and the small audience spilled out into the carpark. Discussions went on for a long time but Tad didn't take part. He was smiling, imagining telling Delina how he had stopped the violence without becoming involved himself. He had stepped in to help one of his future family, had acted calmly and properly to prevent Freddie being hurt without losing his temper. Delina would be pleased. His step was almost jaunty as he set off to find her.

The intended meeting between Sheila, Maurice, Freddie, Amy and Ethel didn't take place. Maurice was told of it, but he and Freddie went fishing instead.

CHAPTER NINETEEN

News that Freddie was responsible for Sheila's condition spread quickly and Amy was at the receiving end of comments ranging from the amused to the outraged. Of the latter, the most outspoken was her sister Prue.

"What's this I hear about your son," she demanded coming into the shop one day with her one-year old, Sian, in her arms. "Like mother like son! I don't know how you can stand there, serving people as if nothing is wrong, Amy! Your own past is bad enough, but for you to pretend all is well with a married woman bearing Freddie's child, well, it's enough to make me want to leave the village because I'm your sister."

Amy took a deep breath for her intended retort but when she saw her sister's face she let her breath out and instead asked, "Prue? What's the matter?" Her sister's thin face was white and her eyes were wide and full of . . . Amy couldn't decide whether they showed anger or confusion. "Freddie has been taken in by a pretty face and a gorgeous figure. He isn't the first and he won't be the last. You hardly speak to him these days so what are you getting all upset for?" She glared at her sister then and added defiantly, "It isn't as if you aren't used to dramas where me and mine are concerned. This is another one. I don't suppose this will be the last, either!"

Prue was fidgeting, her long fingered hands twisting one inside the other, her shoulders hunched, her jaw stiff. Sian was standing near her, looking around the shop and touching things that interested her. Prue was clearly very upset and unable to relax. Amy wondered why and was

238

concerned. Since her sister had been seriously depressed last year, she was always afraid of seeing the symptoms returning. But how could anything Freddie did be the cause of a relapse?

"Where's Florrie today?" she asked.

"She's gone into town for some shopping. Sian needs a few more things for her birthday party next month. I'm making the cake tomorrow and I'll want some decorations."

"I sell those, Prue! Have a look in that box and take anything you want. Candles, as well. Just help yourself. I can't let my little niece lack anything for her first birthday cake."

"She isn't your niece!" Prue snapped, and before a surprised Amy could ask what she meant, she picked up the little girl and hurried out.

When Mavis came to take over at lunch-time Amy went across to see if Florrie was home. Sian was sleeping in her pushchair near the back door, her little form covered cosily with a beautiful blanket. She peeped at her then called through the kitchen:

"Florrie, are you there?"

"No," Prue said, coming into the room and looking her normal self. "What is it? She won't be long, I expect her back on the next bus. Stay for a cup of tea if you like."

Amy was confused. Her sister seemed just as she always was, curt and unwelcoming but not fraught as she had been a few hours earlier. Perhaps it had been nothing more than a mild temper. If someone had upset her, and that was easily done, Prue always let everyone know how she felt.

"Thank you. Yes, that would be nice. I can't stay long, mind. I have to get back to – " About to say "Freddie" Amy stopped. Whatever had upset her sister earlier might be revived if his name was mentioned. She sighed as she watched Prue taking out the cups and saucers and setting a tray neatly and with almost painful precision. It seemed as if it was "walking on egg-shells" time again.

She had seen little of her sister since Prue had come out of hospital and Florrie had moved in to look after her. She had presumed that all was well, that Prue had returned to her previous good health and ill-tempered ways, but perhaps she had been wrong. Perhaps the illness hadn't left her and Florrie had simply been covering up.

She drank the tea and ate a biscuit and talked casually about anything that came into her mind, anything that is except Freddie and Sheila. Watching her sister she was reassured. Prue seemed a different person from the angry woman who had entered the shop a few hours before. Her thin hands dealt with the tea without any sign of stress, her face was less angular as she smiled easily at some of Amy's remarks about her customers and people they knew, her eyes were calm and not darting about in anguish. Anguish? Amy chided herself, what could Prue be anguished about where Freddie was concerned? Convinced she had over-reacted, she wondered if she could leave before Florrie came and she had to invent some reason to talk to the woman.

The gate chinked as it closed and both women looked expectantly at the door. Florrie entered and smiled at their visitor.

"Come to see our little Sian, have you? I'd better wake her, Prue, or she'll never settle tonight." She went and picked the sleepy little girl out of the pushchair.

"I called to ask you both what you'd like me to buy for Sian's birthday," Amy said. "I wanted you both here so you could make sure it's something no one else is buying. Now I thought of clothes with a small toy as well. On her birthday she must have something to enjoy. What d'you suggest?"

If Prue was surprised at the curious excuse she didn't show it and the three women played with Sian, admiring her progress and discussed clothes and toys for about ten minutes, then Amy stood up to leave.

"Come to the party, won't you?" Prue said as Amy closed the gate behind her.

240

"Thank you, I will. If I can arrange it with Mavis."

"But don't bring that son of yours anywhere near my daughter, d'you understand?"

Startled, Amy looked at her sister and saw that the tension was back. Worried and wondering what to do about it, Amy collected her bicycle from the shop and hurried home.

Maurice had gone away again. Sheila went to Ethel's to try and see him but Ethel told her he had gone for a job in London.

"He left an address this time, though, Sheila," Ethel explained, handing her a piece of paper. "But I doubt if it will do us any good. London seems as far away to me as Australia did."

"What's he going to do, Mrs Davies?" Sheila asked, her pert face less confident than usual. "I want this baby you know. Yes, it's surprising but I really want it. I won't give it up, even if Maurice doesn't stay. But it will have his name, me being married legally to him."

Ethel didn't reply, her dark eyes were sad and she stared into the red glow of the fire as if seeing all her hopes for her son burning in the heart of it.

"You must do what you think best, Sheila, and I'll support you in any way I can, you know that. Look upon this as your home and on me as your mother-in-law, because that's what I am, no matter what happens. I'm your mother-in-law."

"Thank you, Mrs Davies."

"I think you should write to Maurice and ask him to tell you what he plans to do. You must know soon, so you – so we can make plans." She smiled then and touched Sheila on the shoulder. "Fun it'll be, to look forward to a new baby. It's always a source of joy, a little one coming into the world for us to love and enjoy."

"I wish Mam and Dad thought so," Sheila said bitterly.

"They will. All babies come with the art of attracting love."

241

Sheila wrote a letter with Ethel's assistance and posted it that day, but a week passed and there was no response. She called daily to the cottage on Sheepy Lane but Ethel had heard nothing either. They commiserated with each other at the lack of news, becoming more relaxed and easy together. To her surprise, Sheila began to look forward to the brief visits between work and going home to cook for her gran, more and more. Phil was often there and occasionally Sidney, too. Their wives each made a knitted garment for the expected baby. Sheila was developing a sense of belonging.

Freddie had returned to camp with nothing decided about Sheila and their baby. Seeing Maurice and knowing how he had cheated on his friend had been a numbing experience. He felt dread of the future and wished he, like Maurice, could run from it.

Instead of the strength he had expected to show, he had avoided any discussion and instead spent the time working in the garden or fishing. What had happened to his determination to persuade Maurice he should divorce Sheila? Why hadn't he tried to convince Maurice that Sheila's future was best in his, Freddie's, hands: that Maurice should go away and leave them to make the best of the situation until the divorce came through and they could marry? When he had seen Sheila and Maurice he knew he no longer loved Sheila and feared the future if it meant being tied to her. He already had one child he couldn't acknowledge. That was a secret never to be told. This was an open secret and he would never be able to forget it, not in a village like Hen Carw Parc. The future seemed a tangle from which he would never be able to extricate himself.

Cards on the table time he decided and, taking up a pen, he tried to put all his thoughts and fears down on paper, first to his mother and then, with less honesty, to Maurice and Sheila.

*   *   *

242

Amy received the letter while Victor was with her and they read it together, lying on her bed, a tray of tea beside them. She had the morning off from the shop and they were stealing an hour together in the house before he went on with his deliveries. The van was parked in the drive, as it was when ever they could arrange to meet and enjoy being alone.

"Freddie has accepted there's no future for him with Sheila. Thank goodness for that at least. But that doesn't set me free. Sheila will still expect me to help her with Freddie's baby whether or not Maurice stays. What chaos I seem to attract. There's never a time when things are calm and stable. D'you think there ever will be? Think of Nelly, look at how her life suddenly came together and she settled into a happy, contented relationship with George, a tramp she met on a pub crawl! I ask you, who would believe it? Then there's me. I can't ever see my life sorting itself out like hers."

"Not even with me?"

"I can't see us ever being given the chance."

"Now seems a good time to try. So many changes, what's one more? It seems you were right," Victor said slowly, touching her cheek with his lips. "You and I, my love, will have a baby to look after." He raised a hand in front of her and counted on his fingers. "Besides David and Daniel and Delina and Margaret and Freddie to make a home for we might have Freddie's and Sheila's baby." He waggled his fingers but he was smiling. "But, love, we'll be together. Let's marry and sort out all the problems afterwards?"

"The date is still fixed," she said. "But Victor, it's so much to sort out. Two families *and* a baby to mind?"

"David seems happier and Delina might be staying in the house. Daniel will be at university next October." He was lowering the raised fingers, one by one, as he spoke. "Margaret and Freddie aren't problems. There's only the baby and you. And I think I can manage you all right. Please, Amy, let's marry as we planned. Sometimes the only way is to face the difficulties head on and defy the

243

fates. Let's do it, let's marry in June, give the village a good party and start our life together. We'll snatch happiness and make it work for all of us. Please, Amy."

"Victor, I can't – "

"Please, Amy love."

"– Can't think of a reason not to."

"Go and order your dress tomorrow and I'll order the cake before you can change your mind. Amy, love, I promise I'll do everything to make sure you never regret marrying me. I love you more every day and – " the rest of his declaration was lost in their kiss.

CHAPTER TWENTY

Oliver and Margaret were pleased to include David Honeyman in their secret plans to organise a skiffle group. Margaret had played the melody on a mouth organ, but the guitar was much better and, after some practise, David played quite well. He remained rather surly and unfriendly but gradually his enthusiasm for what they were doing was easing him into a happier mood. He looked forward to showing his family his ability.

"I spoke to the headmaster," Margaret told them one morning as they prepared to rehearse, "but Mr Chartridge says our music isn't suitable for the school. So, where are we going to play for people to hear us?"

"After all this practise we haven't anywhere to play?" moaned Dawn. "I think Mr Chartridge is a pig! He lets you play piano, doesn't he?"

"He says skiffle is for fun and not for things like the end of term concert. What are we going to do?"

"What about playing here, in Uncle Billie's barn?"

"Better still," Oliver said, his eyes bright with the thought of it, "what about playing in the castle ruins?"

The ruined old castle stood not far from Nelly's cottage, in the woods high above the village. From the tallest part of the walls all you could see of the village was the church spire. In 1953 the community had celebrated the Coronation there with a party and games that included the people of Hen Carw Parc and many of the villages around. It was there, too, that the end of the Second World War had been celebrated. What fun it would be to have an out of doors concert there.

"We'd have to do it properly," Margaret said solemnly, "and I think Mrs French is the one to talk to first. She would sell tickets and we'd have to give the money to the school or the church."

"The church," the others chorused, still angry with their headmaster.

It was difficult for them to carry their box-bass to Mrs French's house and they didn't think they could ask her to come to Uncle Billie's barn, so Mary-Dairy took them and their instruments in her milk van.

Mary had telephoned first and Mrs French came out to meet them as the van drew up at her gate. She helped them inside and listened with great interest while they gave her an impromptu concert. She was interested in talking to David, who showed an ability to pick out a melody as well as produce pleasing chords. When they left, the instruments being left for the kind-hearted Mary to collect later, Mrs French had ideas buzzing in her head. Another concert at the castle. That was something that always brought a response from children and adults. There was some magical excitement in performing in a building that had seen so much history, so many changes in music and dress.

"Yes," she promised the children as they waved goodbye. "I think it's an excellent idea and we'll meet soon to discuss your ideas. *Your* ideas," she assured them. "I'll help, but this is your concert and will remain so."

Amy was waiting for Margaret when she returned home. She had something important to discuss with her.

"Margaret, love, I want to talk to you."

"I've only been down the farm, Mam, and Auntie Mary brought us home."

"It's all right, I wasn't worried about where you were, I know you and Oliver and Dawn go to the farm every Saturday."

"David as well. He came with Dawn one day and now he likes us and comes often."

246

"That's good. It's partly about David I want to talk to you. You see, love, I've been undecided about whether Uncle Victor and I should marry and, well, we're going ahead with the plans for June. Now, are you happy about having Uncle Victor for a father and Daniel and David for brothers? You'll have a sister, too. Delina will be your new sister."

"Can I have a blue dress, Mam?"

"We'll go in on Monday to choose it. And ribbons for your hair and some flowers."

"And Uncle Victor will come here and live with us?" she frowned. "Where will we all sleep?"

"Uncle Victor will share my bedroom and David will have Freddie's room. They'll share when Freddie's home on leave. We'll buy an extra bed. Daniel and Delina will stay in their house until Delina marries Dawn's father. There, is that your questions answered?"

"Uncle Victor will sleep in your bed, with you? Will there be room for me sometimes?"

"Always, love. Two people who marry always want to sleep in the same bed, but there'll be room for you when you come for a cuddle, I promise."

"Will we have a party?"

"The best ever. But I haven't decided yet where we'll hold it, there are so many people who Uncle Victor and I'll want to be there. The church hall is hardly big enough for half the village!"

"I think I'll talk to Mrs French. She's good at arranging things." Margaret hugged her mother. "Mam, can I go and see her now?"

"If you wish, love, but telephone first in case she's busy."

Johnny Cartwright jumped off the bus at the end of Sheepy Lane and ran up the hill to St David's Close. Fay's car was outside and he sighed with relief. She had intended to go shopping that day and he was afraid that with the baby due she might have become ill. He was

247

puffing and gasping for breath as he opened the door and called her.

She didn't run to meet him and he called again looking into room after room until he had searched the house and not found her. With a shaking hand he rang the hospital. Yes, his wife had been brought in. She was all right and so far the baby hadn't been born.

Johnny took a bottle of milk and drank some of it. He cut a slice of bread and a piece of cheese. There was no time to make tea, the carelessly prepared snack would stave off his hunger.

He drove back the way he had come and, after a brief call to put his mother in the picture, went to the hospital in Llan Gwyn. Like fathers for generations he walked up and down, asked every nurse he saw if there was news, and waited for his baby to announce its arrival. He smiled, remembering how Fay had scolded him for rushing and said:

"Johnny, I left a note propped up against the teapot. I was sure you'd see that first." Teapot: all he had thought of when he reached home was his lovely Fay having to suffer the pains of child-birth.

Johnny hurried up to George and Nelly's cottage with news that was too exciting to whisper. From the gate he ran down the cinder path, calling:

"I'm a dadda, I'm a dadda. My lovely Fay has a little boy and he's beautiful. Gregory Lewis Cartwright he's called and isn't that a wonderful name?"

Nelly and George laughed with him and shared in his delight.

"A son, Johnny, what a lovely start to a family," Nelly said, hugging the excited young man. "'Ow ever many you 'ave they'll 'ave a big brother to look out fer 'em, eh, George?"

"I envy you, Johnny, a beautiful wife and now a son. I wish you well in the years ahead." George too hugged the proud father.

"Thank you both. Well, I got to go, spread the word,

248

like. I think I'll put a bit in the paper, so everyone will know, what'd you think, Nelly?"

"I reckon you could shout it an' everyone'll know, Johnny," Nelly laughed. "Shout it from yer bus as you drives along. But yes, a notice in the paper would start young Gregory Lewis' baby book off a treat. An' get young Dawn to take a picture of 'im why don't yer?"

"I expect there'll be a real fancy christening fer that baby, George," Nelly laughed when Johnny had gone. "We'll need our best clothes on fer that.

"I don't think posh christenings are for the likes of me, Nelly," George said. "Now Amy's wedding, I reckon that will be more fun somehow."

"Yes, that'll be a good laugh that will Amy will make sure of that."

Mrs French called to see Amy in the shop just before she closed for lunch on Monday.

"Pull the blind down would you, Monica, or I'll never get home. Thank goodness I have the bicycle, it saves a few minutes. What can I get you?"

"I want to talk about your wedding," Mrs French smiled. "I have an idea for your party. Do you mind my offering some help?"

"I think we'd better walk as we talk or I won't get home at all." Amy closed the shop, collected her bicycle and met Mrs French on the road. "Now, what idea have you come up with?"

"It's your Margaret, really. But before I tell you will you promise not to mention our conversation until I've spoken to her again?"

Curious and intrigued, Amy listened.

"The children have organised themselves into a small band playing home-made instruments and a guitar which, incidentally, is played rather well by young David Honeyman. Now they want to perform to an audience and I thought, why not for your wedding? I know this might be different from what you and Victor planned, but I know how highly thought of you are and can guess at the many people who'll want to come and share your day with you. So what about the castle grounds? Make it an afternoon wedding then an evening of celebration, like we did for the Coronation?"

"Monica, you've taken my breath away!" Amy's eyes glowed as she imagined the scene. Her long diamante earrings jangled and glittered as she shook her blonde head as if unable to believe such a thing. "We couldn't, could we?"

"Why not?"

"I'll have to ask Victor, of course, but I admit the idea appeals to me. Now, you talk to Margaret and the others and I'll talk to Victor. I'll come and see you tomorrow morning and we'll see what has been decided, right?" Laughing almost breathlessly at the very idea of such an unusual wedding, Amy raced home on her bicycle. Throwing it against the wall she burst through the door and rang the wholesalers where Victor worked to ask if they could send an urgent supply of dried fruit. It would have to be a very large cake to feed the whole village

Griff Evans came out of prison to find no one waiting for him. He caught the bus from Swansea to Hen Carw Parc, passing *The Drovers* and seeing a few of his former workmates standing chatting outside in the warm sunshine. He had no idea of his reception from them or from his wife and son. Hilda hadn't visited or written and it was only from Pete he had any news of her.

The boy had been hesitant in what he'd said and Griff had a mental image of Hilda, still with her over-large teeth and with curlers in her scraggy hair, who had perhaps bought a new coat. Surely nothing else would change?

These long months while he had been in prison she was entitled to feel anger towards him, but surely when she saw him it would all be forgiven? It had been Pete who had exchanged information that dealt with his release, not Hilda, but he put that down to the fact that as Hilda was uneasy filling in forms and writing letters she had gladly accepted Pete's willingness to deal with it for her. Silly old fool that she was, she was still his wife and would remember her duty and welcome him back with relief that her loneliness was over.

For better or for worse, wasn't that what the preacher said? Well it might have been worse but only for a few months, not enough, surely, to have to beg forgiveness? He didn't fancy doing that. Pity she found out about him and Bethan though, that was always a hard thing for a woman to accept, he realised that. They would have to be more careful in future. He turned into the lane behind the row of cottages, not wanting to pass Bethan's fish and chip shop. He'd deal with one thing at a time. First he had to face Hilda.

Hilda had been warned of the approximate time of Griff's arrival. Pete had been in contact with the prison authorities and had been told of his release date and time. Hilda sat in her newly furnished room and waited. The key for the replaced locks was in her hand. She tapped it occasionally as she waited.

She wore a new red and grey woollen dress with a gathered skirt and a shaped bodice. Her hair was freshly set in a becoming style, the expensive cut framing her carefully madeup face where only the slightest hint of agitation showed. She knew she looked smart. Her nylon stockings flattered her slim legs, now free from the marks of sitting too close to the fire after freezing in the cold water preparing chips and fish for Bethan. Her red lips curled in a smile as she imagined Griff's face on seeing her for the first time for months.

The back gate stuck and she heard the scrape of it as Griff pushed it open. She stiffened slightly but relaxed again. This was her scene and she'd enjoy it.

Griff went to the back door and looked inside. It looked different. The sink was the same but the cupboards were new and such a bright red. He didn't know if he appproved of that. Too gaudy, altogether. Hilda didn't have much idea but he'd soon get that put right. The door to the living room was ajar and he called but there was no reply. Bolder now he was on home ground he pushed open the door and saw

251

a strange woman sitting in a strange chair beside a grate he didn't recognise. Damn it all! He'd walked into the wrong house. Then the woman spoke.

"Hello, Griff, so you've called to see me have you?"

"Hilda? Bloody'ell, what you done to yourself? And what's all this?" He dropped his suitcase and waved his arms to encompass the room with its new wallpaper, carpet and furniture. "If you planned to surprise me then you have, I don't know that I approve, mind, I think you've gone a bit too far."

"It's no business of yours, Griff. This is for me, no one else. You can go and share Bethan's little room behind the fish and chip shop, more in your line that is. I have to ask you to leave now, I have an appointment.""

"Leave? What you talking about woman. I live here."

"No more you don't. The rent book has always been in my name and I've been to check to make sure. This is mine, Griff, you'll have to shift for yourself. Close the door behind you, will you."

"I'm not moving from this room, this is my home and you can stop fooling about, right?"

"I'm not fooling, Griff." She stood up and pushed her way past him to where he had dropped his suitcase. She picked it up and threw it out into the grden.

"That's enough, Hilda. Go and fetch that back in." He was alarmed. This wasn't how he had imagined his homecoming. "Go on, fetch that case back in here."

"You can go out after it and as the locks have been changed, you can stay out, for good."

"Hilda." He tried a different approach, his voice softened and he began to plead. "Stop this fooling, I'm your husband and I've come home to you after five miserable months."

"I haven't found them miserable at all, Griff. In fact they've been marvellous. The only thing is they made me realise what I'd been missing being married to a poisonous toad like you. Now go."

"You going to make me?" He started to walk towards her and she called.

"Tommy?"

From the front room the large bulk of Tommy Thomas, a recently acquired friend, materialised. "Hello there, Griff, boy. Your wife thought you might be a bit difficult. Asked me to come just in case of trouble, but there isn't going to be any, is there?"

Bluff, arguments and pleading were to no avail. Hilda returned to her chair and Griff was escorted out through the neat red kitchen by Tommy Thomas who stood and watched the man walk off with some sympathy, but not enough to try and persuade Hilda to reconsider. Then he went back to where he had parked his car near the school. He didn't get in but walked back across the road and went into the fish shop.

"Are you Bethan?" he asked the surprised woman behind the counter.

"Yes, what d'you want?" Her eyes looked frightened and her helplessness appealed to him. The words he had intended to use to hurt her on Hilda's behalf were swallowed. Instead, he said:

"I just thought you'd like to know that Griff is back home and Hilda has chucked him out good and proper. I'd lock your doors if I were you, love. You don't want any more bother with the likes of him." He took a piece of paper from the pile on the counter and wrote his telephone number down. "Ring me if you have any problems, I know how to deal with Griff and his like."

"Thank you – er Mr, er – "

"Tommy Thomas they call me, just call me Tommy," he smiled.

Amy and Victor discussed the idea for their wedding with their children. Then, having agreed to leave much of the planning in Mrs French's hands, they went to tell some of their friends. They went first to see Nelly and George.

"Nelly, what's the largest cake we can make in an ordinary kitchen? I want the largest wedding cake ever seen."

Nelly looked thoughtful for a while then said, "Out instead of up. How about that?"

"Lovely, but what are you talking about?"

"Well I don't see that we could go up more than, say, five tiers. But if we was to go out, then it can be as big as the table."

"How?" Victor asked. "Don't cakes have to be cooked in a tin? And where's the oven as big as a table?"

George began to chuckle, the chuckle ending in a cough as was usual these days, but his eyes were twinkling as he spluttered, "I think Nelly might be thinking of more than one oven, eh, Nelly?"

"Yer right, George. I reckon that if about twenty of us all cooked a cake in our biggest baking tins, then iced them all together, it would cover a table. 'Ow would that do yer, Amy?"

"Nelly, you're brilliant! But George, how did you know what Nelly was thinking?" Victor asked.

"I often do know what she has in her mind. Living together and sharing things, it has that effect sometimes."

"Only in very special cases, George," Amy said. "You two are the perfect pair. I only hope Victor and I become as close a partnership."

"When d'you want me to start on the cake, Amy. If it's fer June we ought to get it done this week."

Maurice did not stay long in London. The job failed to materialise and he returned to Hen Carw Parc and spent a lot of time searching for work. In between he went fishing. He continued to avoid Sheila, needing time alone to consider both what he wanted to do and what he ought to do. There seemed to be no common ground for the two.

He didn't love Sheila and no matter how he tried to be compassionate it seemed ironic that a baby he had fathered had ruined his chances of marrying Delina and now a baby fathered by Freddie was expected to mend his marriage to Sheila. There was no anger in him towards Freddie and he found that strange. He assumed it was his lack of love for his wife that was responsible for the lack of jealously.

Coming back from Llan Gwyn early one evening, having spent the afternoon at the cinema, he was caught in a confrontation with Sheila that he couldn't avoid. He had jumped on the bus and run upstairs without looking at the rest of the people waiting. As the bus began to move off he heard someone climbing the metal stairs and turned to see if it was anyone he knew. It was Sheila.

"Maurice, now you wouldn't be so ungentlemanly as to run away and jump off a moving bus rather than talk to me, would you."

"Sheila, hello. No, I won't run away, but I don't know what we can find to say to each other."

"I have only one thing to say, Maurice and that's this." She stopped while the conductor came and took their fares and gave them tickets. When he had returned to the platform she went on, "I've been to see a solicitor and I've told him to go ahead with our divorce. I don't want to be married to you and I want us to be divorced just as soon as it can be arranged. I don't want you to name Freddie, mind. Just keep this between us. If you have anything to say you can write to my solicitor, here's his name and address." She took a card from her handbag then stood up. "I think I'll go and sit downstairs. I don't like the atmosphere up here."

Maurice stared at the empty seat beside him and then at the card. He was confused. All the time they had known each other Sheila had been chasing him, displaying her love for him, pestering him. And now this.

On the lower deck, ignoring the attempts of other passengers to talk to her, Sheila sat, pale-faced, wondering if her final shot would have the desired effect of bringing Maurice back to her, or would she lose him for ever.

CHAPTER TWENTY-ONE

Bert Roberts was in trouble with his cricket team. Several of his strongest hopes had faded into disappointments. One of them was George. During early practice Nelly's husband had shown himself to be both a very useful bat and a reliable bowler. His being ill had robbed the team of what Bert had hoped would be its number two player. He planned to be number one.

The practice sessions in the field behind Evie and Timothy's were unsatisfactory affairs for Bert, troubled as they were by a chorus of jeers from supporters of the council houses team who had discovered their secret. All the usual jokes were repeated plus some new ones; the favourite chant with some of the younger children was, "Bert's Wearing A Skirt", when he tied his pullover in the approved manner around his waist.

"I can sympathise now with some of them keen gardeners who feed their plants at night," Bert snapped to PC Harris after the ball had been stolen for the seventh time that evening. PC Harris who, in spite of living in the council houses, used his official capacity to play for the village he served sighed and once more went up to the top of the field to plead for the ball's return.

"I wonder if Griff will play for us?" Bert suggested when Constable Harris came back with the ball and prepared to bowl. "He isn't so fat and useless as he was, him being forced to eat less and take some exercise like. Give him a try, shall we?"

"I think he might play, but not for us. Hilda threw him out and he's got lodgings up in St Non's road."

"Play for the council houses you mean?"

"I expect so."

"Traitor! I hope he slips and cracks his fat head."

"Now, Bert, this is only a game."

"A game? A game? Who told you that yarn? This, boy, is war!"

Maurice appeared at the edge of the crowd and Bert irritably waved him over.

"Come on, boy, thought you'd never get here. Go and stand by the wicket and see how you fare against Constable Harris."

"Sorry, Bert, but I'm playing for the council houses. Me being married to Sheila and that being my official address."

"What?" Bert exploded.

"I said I'm playing for the council house, me being – "

"I heard what you said. I just didn't believe my ears!"

"Are you deaf, ref?" the kids shouted.

The session lasted until Bert officiously shouted that light had stopped play and they all dispersed, most to chuckle over Bert's organisation, Bert to pore over the lists of players trying to make a team out of them. He had eleven players including old Archie Pierce who insisted he was a deadly fielder, and old farmer Leighton who had played once or twice in his youth. He wished he had chosen the date for the cricket match during the week he and Brenda were visiting his sister in Bristol.

At the edge of the crowd watching the practice, Griff Evans stood some distance from the rest. The children were in awe him being a criminal who had been in prison, and the adults, most of them victims of his various thieving activities, were unwilling to respond to any of his attempts at renewed friendship. His son, Pete, was the only one near him.

"Coming for a pint, Dad?" Pete invited, as they walked home.

"You aren't old enough."

"That's right, I'm not. You coming then?"

They walked up past Nelly's cottage towards Sheepy Lane then, when Pete thought his father had chickened out and was about to say so, Griff turned right at the bottom and they strolled passed the church and the school. Tad was on his way up the lane with Dawn holding his hand when he saw them and called:

"Griff? Can you spare a minute? I'd like a chat."

Griff and his son stopped and waited for Tad to reach them.

"What is it?" Griff tried not to smile in pleasure at the prospect of talking to someone. Since his release from prison few had exchanged more than a begrudging word.

"It's about the cricket. You living up at the council houses I wondered, we wondered, if you'd play for us? That is unless the village have already asked you?"

"No no, they haven't asked. Yes, I'd love to play, I'll need a bit of practice, mind, won't I Pete? Haven't played since he was a lad."

"We'll give you all the practice you need."

"I'll play for you as well if you like," Pete offered. "I've put my name down for the village team but, well I'd like to play on the same team as Dad."

"Bert won't like it if you've agreed to play for the village," – Tad said hesitantly.

"I live up on the council houses, too, and with Dad playing like – "

"Great!" Tad grinned. "Who'll tell Bert, you or me?"

"I will!" Pete chuckled, throwing an arm around his father's shoulders. "I love a bit of a laugh. Go and do it now shall we Dad? He's bound to be propping up the bar." Thanking Tad they turned and headed for *The Drovers*.

As they walked past the cottages they saw Archie Pierce struggling to lift a trough containing French marigolds and pansies and some trails of ivy. Griff didn't want to see him. He had burgled the poor old chap's house before he was caught by the police and now felt remorseful and ashamed. But he made himself stop and ask:

"Want any help, Archie? That looks too heavy for you."

"Bugger off you thieving sod." Little Archie, given the strength of outrage, lifted the trough and staggered indoors with it. The door closed with a bang that startled Griff almost as much as the words.

"What's he doing?" Griff asked to cover his embarrassment.

"He was given that flower display and he takes it in every night and puts it out every morning," Pete grinned.

"I'm shamed at the sight of him. How could I have robbed him, a workmate and an old man? I shouldn't have done it, Pete. I must have been out of my mind."

"You can make it up to him one day."

"I wish I knew how," Griff said sadly. "It all seemed such fun at the time. Starting with a bit of poaching, well, no one calls that stealing, do they? Then picking up a few pounds here and there from bets held back from the boys. I sort of got an obsession to save money and after a while I didn't care how I got it. People like Archie Pierce seemed easy victims. It was a bit of a laugh really because it was so easy. I used to listen to him telling us of how nervous he was about going out after dark and I thought it was a joke. Can you believe it, Pete?"

"Can't you pay the money back?"

"No, son, your Mam's spent it."

Some were less than pleased to have Griff on their team but when they saw him play and realised that he was a better than average bowler, they gradually withdrew their objections.

With several village members finding excuses to play for the opposing team and council house tenants insisting their loyalties were with the village proper, there was hardly a family who didn't spend their time arguing. Johnny insisted he was playing for his mother and not the place where he and Fay and Gregory Lewis lived. Mary-Dairy was threatened that if her brother Billie didn't play for the council houses where she earned her money, she would lose half her milk round.

"The sooner this match is played and forgotten the better," Phil said to Nelly and George one morning after being told of Griff and Pete's defection. "I hope you'll be playing for us, George?"

Trying to explain how much he'd like to, George only spluttered into a bout of coughing.

"Me mind's made up, George!" Nelly said firmly, lifing her painful leg from the supporting stool. "I'm going to try and get a message to Clara. She's the only one to get you right."

"How?" Phil asked, helping himself to more tea. "You don't know where she's parked herself. You can hardly send a letter. Good as the post office is, there's no address that'll find a small vardo in some unknown field somewhere in England or Wales, now is there?"

"No, but I saw some gypsies in Llan Gwyn a week ago. With luck they'll still be about here somewhere."

"I'll ask around, someone might know where they're living, and what about asking Johnny? He sees plenty from that bus of his. Will any gypsies do?"

"They'll pass a message and that's all I want. She'll come when she knows I needs 'er," Nelly said confidently. "You, George, are goin' to play in that cricket match and show 'em 'ow it should be done!"

"Yes, Nelly," he chuckled, his face brighter than usual, the coughing having taken its toll.

There was another visitor to the cottage. Victor left his van on the main road and ran up to find them both dosing in front of the fire.

"Pair of hooligans," he laughed as the dogs barked a welcome, their tails wagging in unison like the pendulum of some strange clock. "Got a licence for them, have you?"

"Yeh, the same as Amy's got a licence to park her vegetables on the pavement. Tell the world why don't yer," Nelly retorted."

"Sorry for waking you, I can't stay a minute or Constable Harris'll have my guts for garters. Parked across the end of the lane I am."

Nelly roused herself and reached to push the kettle over the fire.

"Move it and stay fer a cuppa why don't yer?" she asked sleepily.

"I can't, though I'd like to. I've been on an errand for Amy. She asked me to go into the office in town and find out what benefits you two are entitled to, you not being able to work."

"Benefits? We ain't paid no stamps so we can't claim nothing. Ain't that right, George?" Pulling himself slowly out of his slumbers George nodded agreement.

"Wrong, mate. There's some National Assistance, probably three pounds three shilling for the pair of you. It went up by ten shillings in February. What about that then? You have to go down and see them and sign some forms. Okay? Got to dash. Amy will have the details, she'll write them down for you. Great about the wedding isn't it? What a day that'll be. Got to get well for that, George. You and Billie Brown are down for a duet, right?" Leaving two bewildered and bemused people behind, Victor ran back down the lane and began to drive away just as the wobbling wheel of PC Harris' bicycle appeared at the corner.

PC Harris was also on his way to see Nelly and George. He parked his bicycle against the gate and walked down to be greeted by the excited dogs. They escorted him to the door, ran back to pee against his bicycle, then down again to continue with their rowdy welcome.

George rose to make the essential pot of tea and the constable settled in the armchair George had vacated.

"Look, I don't want to embarrass you two at all, but, well I know things haven't been too good for you lately and I wondered if you'd consider taking a lodger. Someone who would pay a bit of money and not be too much of a burden."

"A lodger? We've often joked about that, haven't we George? But I don't know. This place ain't no palace and we'd 'ave to keep tidyin' up and cookin' proper meals and all that. No, I don't think we could cope with a stranger."

"I agree with Nelly," George said, putting a cup of tea where the constable could reach it. "As you see, Nelly is recovering from a fall she had a while ago and I, well, I've had this cough that won't shift and we find it enough just to look after ourselves."

"Tell us 'oo it is, though," Nelly added. "P'raps we'll 'ear of a place that's more suitable."

"It's someone you know. Only slightly, mind, but she's sure you'll remember her."

"She? Funny that, I always thinks of lodgers being blokes. A woman, is she? I don't think I fancy puttin' temptation in George's way, not with Clara likely to come and make him fightin' fit again!" Her loud laughter rang out and George joined in.

"If your friend Clara has some medicine that can make me want to chase girls again she ought to bottle it and make herself a fortune."

"Her name is Doreen."

"Doreen? That nice girl who called when they were all out on a walk? I remember 'er. Smashin' girl she was, remember, George?"

"She'll be leaving the Children's Home soon and will need a place to live until she can find somewhere of her own. A room of her own would be all right for later, but for a while it would be better if she had someone to keep an eye on her, help her to adjust to being away from the safety and security of the home."

"Poor child," George said. "Imagine being suddenly on your own at that young age."

"Think about it will you? She will probably be found a room in Cardiff if you can't help, but she specifically asked to be found a place in Hen Carw Parc. There's a job for her at the fish and chip shop apparently helping Bethan, but only if she finds some suitable digs. The people at the Home try to make sure she will be safe and given a good start."

"Can't they find something better than the fish and chip shop?" George asked.

"She asked for something around here and there doesn't seem to be anything else."

"'Ow long? 'Ow long before she 'as to decide?"

"A couple of weeks. I'll come and talk to you again or you can talk to the Reverend Barclay Bevan. It was he the Home got in touch with. He mentioned it to me and I offered to come and see you."

"Have another cup of tea why don't yer?" Nelly's dark, intelligent eyes were shining and she saw when she looked at George that once more their thoughts were running on similar lines.

Maurice had been shocked by Sheila's decision to go ahead with their divorce. He had expected her to use his mother as an ally and try to persuade him to go back to her. The irritation that caused had turned to disappointment. His pride was hurt and there was something else he couldn't put into words. The fact that she was expecting another man's child seemed irrelevant to both her and his mother. Yet he was beginning to wish that things were different. The jobs he had tried for in London and several other places far from Hen Carw Parc had not been offered to him. Others, nearer home, he had refused. But time was passing and soon he would have the reputation of sponging off his widowed mother and not wanting to work.

He saw Sheila regularly, almost unconsciously managing to catch the same bus home after spending the afternoon in Llan Gwyn. She nodded with casual politeness but didn't sit near him unless the bus was crowded enough to make it impossible not to. From choice, if he were downstairs, then she would go up. If she climbed the stairs and saw him she would cause chaos on the narrow, curving stairs and insist on going back down, proclaiming to any objectors that she was "expecting" and needed to find a seat near the platform or she'd be sick. That usually quietened the objectors he noticed with a smile.

He began to admire the way she was dealing with her situation; the haughty manner, the attitude that it was the rest of the world that was wrong, not she: the way she out-stared anyone rude enough to make remarks within her hearing. Her looks, too, were enough to make him watch her with increasing pleasure.

Motherhood was giving her young skin a delightful bloom and her eyes an extra glow. She was very lovely and deep within him was a guilt like a leaden weight at the way he had used then abandoned her. She would have fought for him if the roles of her and Delina had been reversed, he was certain of that. The thought gave him an inexplicable warm feeling.

Sheila was aware of Maurice's change of attitude but was wise enough to do nothing. When they alighted from the bus at the same time she would only nod and walk on, her high-heels giving a sway to her walk that she knew men liked. But when, on two occasions he asked her to come in and have a cup of tea with Ethel, she shook her head and peremptorily refused.

She hurried up Sheepy Lane: the evenings drawing out as springtime expanded everything around her, but she was not aware of the burgeoning hedges and fields or the increasing bird-song; she was conscious only of Maurice standing near his mother's cottage watching her walk away from him. She was breathless when she turned into Hywel Rise and was lost to his sight.

That evening she was engrossed in making a cake. Of all people *she* was helping to make Amy and Victor's wedding cake. She was tempted to add black pepper and chilli powder instead of spices, but she didn't. The recipe planned by Amy and Mrs French filled the large flat baking tin to the required depth and she smoothed the top of the rich mixture level with pride. She'd show them how well she could cook *and* she'd show all the old biddies in the village that she could bring up a baby without constant moaning about the lack of a man, too. Whether Maurice changed his mind or not, her baby would be as well cared for as any child could be.

When she wrapped the cooked cake and set off with it the

264

following evening to give it to Amy she saw Fay walking up the hill with her new baby. With a shared interest, Sheila stopped her and admired the tiny bundle with only a small face visible under woollen blankes and woollen hat.

"Pity for him, you going back to work. I'll be staying home to look after my baby when he comes," Sheila couldn't resist saying.

"He'll be well cared for," Fay said. "Johnny and I will make sure of that"

"Of course you will. But, poor dab, but it won't be the same will it, little Gregory Lewis not having his mam when he cries? I've made a piece of Amy's wedding cake," she said as Fay began to climb the hill again pushing the Silver Cross pram.

"I've just delivered mine," Fay said, not telling the irritating girl that it was Johnny who had done most of it.

Going first to show Bethan her cake and let her smell the delicious aroma, she walked on through the village and saw Prue Beynon and Florrie out with baby Sian. Keen on babies since her decision to welcome her own she waited for the double-decker bus from Swansea to pass then ran across the road and bent over the pushchair.

"There's lovely, a one year old now, isn't she?" she smiled, tickling the little girl under her plump chin.

Prue's thin, hard face softened as she watched her daughter smile at Sheila. Then, glancing up, she saw Freddie. He had alighted from the Swansea bus and was coming their way. In panic she began to push Sheila away. She had to stop him looking at her baby.

"Steady, Mrs Beynon, you nearly had me over, I'm expecting remember." Sheila caught hold of the pushchair to support herself while she recovered and by then it was too late, Freddie was upon them.

"Freddie!" Sheila hugged him and, given the opportunity, Prue began to push past him. Sheila grabbed the handle of the pushchair and said,

"Look, Freddie, your little niece. Isn't she lovely? I wonder if I'll have a little girl or whether it will be a boy.

Welcome whatever, eh, Mrs Beynon?" She stopped when she saw Prue's face. It was almost blue with temper. Prue raised her handbag and aimed it at Freddie. Time and again she tried to hit him, growling in the back of her throat and muttering.

"She isn't your niece! Get away from her, I don't want her to look at you, ever!"

Army saw them and ran out, narrowly missing being hit by a car and held her sister's arm.

"Prue. Calm yourself. Whatever is it? It's only Freddie, why are you hitting him? What's he done?"

"He isn't Sian's father. He isn't. I'll deny it in any court in the land! He's nothing to do with her. I must keep him away." Almost demented, Prue's long, thin hands gripped the push chair and her words became a low wail. Slowly, murmuring softly and soothingly, Florrie started to walk her home. Amy was shaking.

"Funny thing for her to say, isn't it?" Sheila said quietly to Florrie Gwyn. "Wasn't her husband the baby's father then?" Florrie ignored her, concentrating on soothing the distressed Prue.

Amy stared after them with a troubled look in her blue eyes. "Whatever brought that on? What could she be thinking of, talking about you being Sian's father?" Almost unaware of Sheila's presence she said, "She's terribly ill again. Why didn't Florrie tell me? Freddie, what can we do?"

"Nothing, Mam. Just wait until she gets over it again. Florrie's a nurse, she'll look after her." It was then that Sheila said, sweetly:

"Enough to start a rumour in this place, something like that, isn't it Mrs Prichard? Nosy lot round here."

With work on the gardens and now the castle grounds to tidy up ready for Amy and Victor's wedding party, everyone was busy. But not too busy to call regularly to see Nelly and George and keep them up to date with what was happening. The stream of visitors rivalled that

266

of Ethel's cottage. The only one who hadn't visited them was Evie.

"Me own daughter and she's never called to see 'ow we are." Nelly brushed up the last crumbs of the ruined attempt at her portion of the wedding cake and threw them out for the chickens. "Lucky she didn't come this morning, eh, George, and seen that burnt cake!" She was moving easier now that the bruising from her fall had begun to fade and when Phil came that Wednesday morning she was taking the second and successful cake from her oven and preparing to return to her normal work for Mrs French.

When Evie called that afternoon having finished her hours in the office in Llan Gwyn, Nelly guessed it was because of Phil's reminder.

"You needn't come just because Phil says you should be ashamed of yerself," Nelly said as soon as Evie had stepped inside the door. "Me an' George will manage without your 'elp. Plenty of friends we've got."

George came in from the garden where he had been reinforcing the ties on the hanging basket Nelly had put in the apple tree.

"I think that basket will have to come down and be repacked, Nelly, love," he said after greeting Evie. "The birds have taken most of the moss for nest-building."

"Cheeky little devils," Nelly smiled. Then, turning to her daughter again she said:

"An' where's young Ollie? We don't see 'im these days, told 'im what a bad influence we are, have yer?"

"Oliver is busy planning something with Margaret and that Dawn Simmons girl, but I'm not allowed to know what. That's the reason I've come, Mother." She pushed the empty cake tin aside and, after using her hand to brush pointedly at the crumbs on the wooden table, fussily placed her handbag on it and went on. "I thought you might know what they're doing. Timothy says I mustn't interfere, but you know how unjudgemental children are."

"Unjudgemental? Blimey, Evie, you're gettin' worse. What job 'ave you got fer Gawd's sake?"

"It simply means – "

"I know what it means! You're afraid young Ollie will be involved in something 'e's too stupid to see is wrong. Well you needn't worry: considerin' who 'is mother is he's got a lot of common sense."

"Come on, ladies," George said. "Sit down and talk quietly. You both love the boy and want what's best for him."

"What's this to do with you?" Evie said clutching her bag and preparing to leave.

"Goodbye, Evie," Nelly growled, her head stuck forward in a threatening posture. "Call again why don't yer."

"I knew it was useless to ask for your help."

"You ain't got nothin' to worry about, Evie. Just don't try and find out. Them kids is plannin' a real nice surprise. Don't spoil it."

"Well, if you can assure me there's nothing for me to be concerned about – "

"There ain't."

"Well, goodbye, Mother, George. I'll take your word that Oliver isn't doing anything silly."

Nelly stood and watched her daughter walk up the path, as different from her mother as it was possible to be. "Why is it we can't never meet for five minutes without quarrelling?"

"What *are* Margaret, Dawn, David and Oliver doing, Nelly?" George asked.

"Gawd knows," Nelly shrugged. "But I know it won't be anythin' bad and she should know that, too!"

Victor saw a difference in his youngest son. He still did whatever homework he was given but now he hurried through it and went out to join Margaret, Dawn and Oliver either at Mrs French's house or at Billie's farm.

"Will you come into town this Saturday, David?" he asked one morning. "Delina says you need new shoes and a shirt for the wedding."

"Dad, must I? We've something planned for Saturday."

268

"What about meeting your sister after school and doing it then?"

"Thanks, Dad."

"You're happy about it all, are you? I mean me marrying and you having to accept an enlarged family?"

"Margaret's all right I suppose," he said grudgingly.

"What about Amy?"

"So long as she doesn't try to boss me around."

"I think she'll be too busy for that, son," Victor smiled.

When Victor went down to see Amy later David collected his guitar and went with him. He and Margaret ensconced themselves in the front room and the piano and guitar were each played by both expert and amateur hands.

"They seem to be getting along better these days," he whispered to Amy.

"They've found they have something in common, music," Amy replied. "I don't know what they're planning but they all seem to be enjoying it. Saturday morning Mrs French is going down to Billie's barn with them, but she won't tell me exactly what they're doing."

"Saturday morning? I can get the morning off, what about you?"

"Freddie will be gone back then. He won't be home again until our wedding." She looked at him, a smiling promise in her blue eyes, she fluffed out her hair, curved her body towards him provocatively and said, "Your place or mine?"

CHAPTER TWENTY-TWO

Doreen came to live with Nelly and George a few days later. A telephone call to and from Barclay Bevan speeded the arrangements and Doreen arrived on the train at Swansea early on Saturday morning to be met by PC Harris. He brought the girl to Hen Carw Parc on the bus and by the time they reached the village they were friends.

Nelly was rosy-faced, having spent hours beside the oven range cooking and baking cakes. George was sitting in his usual chair sharing in Nelly's excitement.

"I hope she doesn't change her mind once she sees us again, Nelly my dear," George said as he saw the pile of food mounting. "I think we'll have enough for Amy's wedding without anyone else helping if she does."

"'Ere they come so we'll soon find out." Nelly pushed back her hair and slipped off the apron she had been wearing, throwing it out of sight under the table. The dogs heard the gate, too, and were up the path to greet the visitors, barking their welcome and drowning out Nelly's shouts of, "Come on in an' find a seat why don't yer."

As before Doreen seemed to make herself at home straight away and before Nelly could pour the teas, she had reached for the teapot and done it for her.

"Thank you for agreeing to try me as your lodger," she said, sharing her smile between Nelly and George. "I know it's a cheek, me asking if I could stay, but if you agree, only for a little while, I'll be careful not to be a nuisance. It would be lovely to stay here with you two if you'll have me. I love the village and I can't explain it but this cottage seems like the home I've never known."

"*Swn Y Plant* it's called," Nelly said. "Sound of Children, ain't that nice?"

"I'll leave you to talk if you don't mind," Constable Harris put in. "There are things I must see to."

"We walked up Sheepy Lane," Doreen told them when the constable had gone. "What's going on in the field at the bottom, behind the house where Constable Harris says your daughter lives, Nelly?"

"Cricket practice. That lot are playin' a match next week."

"Have they picked their team? I'm no mean batsman myself!"

"You play?"

"I certainly do. My bowling isn't so hot but I've scored a few winning sixes for our team back at the Home."

"Let's walk down and watch them, shall we? There's a nice steak an' kidney puddin' simmerin'. We'll 'ave that for our dinner with a few vegetables."

"Smashing!"

"Then I'll 'ave to go an' do me work fer Mrs French. Late today but she didn't mind, not when I told 'er you was comin'."

"I'll walk down with you, Nelly my dear. If I feel too out of puff I'll take my time coming back."

"If you're sure, George."

Bert's voice could be heard complaining before they came in sight of the players. The dejected team were sprawled around the pitch listening to Bert's interpretation of the rules and from the faces of the intended team, his popularity was at an all time low.

"Has there been an argument?" Doreen grinned, her young, fresh face showing impish delight. "It's just like at the Home: all chiefs and no indians."

"If they was indians they'd 'ave stuck an arrow through Bert's gullet ages ago," Nelly retorted.

The disagreement was one that had been repeated at almost every practice, Bert's insistence that he should go in to bat first. He stood at the crease facing an empty wicket

271

at the other end of the pitch, he banged the bat on to the ground repeatedly as if that action alone could make one of the others take his alloted place and prepare to bowl. Doreen looked at Nelly.

"Shall I break the deadlock?" she asked.

"Go on," George urged. "If someone doesn't do something the council houses will win without anyone seeing the ball."

"Hi, I'm Doreen, I'm hoping to come and live here for a while. D'you think I could join in the practice?"

"You're a girl," said Bert.

"Never!"

She took the bat from his tight grip and looked around.

"Anyone willing to bowl for a girl?" she asked.

Johnny stood and picked up the ball from where Victor had thrown it in despair and prepared for his run-up. The "team" raised themselves and took an interest as Doreen prepared to defend the wicket. She hit the ball such a swipe that the team ducked and the ball sailed over their heads to disappear into the hedge.

"Was that a fluke, girl, or can you do it again?" Phil asked in awe.

"Try me," Doreen grinned.

The practice was taken out of Bert's hands and one after another the men tried to get Doreen out. Archie Pierce sidled into place behind the wicket and when he tried to catch the ball he fell over backwards and was just picking himself up when the next ball was bowled. It was Tad, there to assess the opposition, who finally succeeded in toppling the bails, but even he had to admit that she was one of his finest opponents.

"When is she moving in, Nelly?" Phil asked. "Damn me, she'll have to be a resident in time for the match, won't she Bert?"

"Resident or not, I'm not having a girl on my team!" Collecting his bat, the wickets and the balls, Bert marched home. Practice was over. Doreen, not the light, had stopped play.

*   *   *

272

It was Doreen who helped Nelly trim the piece of wedding cake to the correct size. She seemed to be a girl who could do practically everything. She learnt from everyone she met, exchanged ideas, and added to what others told her in a way that made Nelly and George marvel.

She climbed the apple tree and fixed the hanging baskets, using layers of netting wide apart as a means of preventing the birds from stealing the moss and fixing a metal contraption to hold the last two-feet six-inches of the hose-pipe rigid to enable Nelly to water them without climbing on to dangerous stools and ladders.

"I've never seen no one like 'er fer thinking things out, Amy," Nelly boasted on the following Friday, the morning before the cricket match was to be played. "It's like 'avin' an inventer in the 'ouse."

"Tell her to invent a way of getting all the twenty pieces of my wedding cake together," Amy pleaded. "I don't think the idea is going to work after all."

"Why not? Pity if it doesn't, Amy, all the village are expecting to go and see it on display." Twenty minutes later, Nelly having gone home and explained the dilemma, Doreen came into the shop, the dogs with her, and said hesitantly.

"Mrs Prichard, did you really want suggestions about putting the wedding cake together? I'll help if you like."

"I like," Amy said with relief. "Mrs French and I have tried but it doesn't stay together."

"It will, I promise."

The wedding cake was to be displayed in the church hall on trestle tables, before being sliced and carried up to the castle grounds on the day of the wedding. Doreen went to discuss the preparations with Mrs French with some trepidation. She had only just arrived in the village and didn't want to earn the reputation of being a busy-body, even if she was one as she confided to Nelly.

But Mrs French welcomed her and they went together to the church hall where the last of the cakes had arrived,

273

all wrapped in grease-proof paper and white tea-towels. They measured each one and cautiously cut the sides so they would lock together. Some slanting up and some slanting down until they fitted together like a giant jigsaw.

With the help of Netta, Fay and others they covered the whole lot with twenty five pounds of marzipan. The cake measured three-feet four-inches by six-feet three-inches and was spread over four trestle tables. It took them from eight-thirty until twelve o'clock, then they went home to prepare to watch the cricket match. In their absence the local baker was coming to plan how he would ice it. When he saw it he almost ran away. Then he decided it was an excellent opportunity to give some practice to his apprentice.

The day was fine but with a threat of rain in the air. Grey clouds hovered over the hills threatening to obliterate the watery sun as Bert stood, wet finger raised like a blessing, feeling the wind direction and ordering the crowd to keep back and stay orderly or he'd have the constable escort them from the field. The council houses won the toss and went in first.

Tad made a surprising fifteen runs before being caught out by his future father-in-law, Victor. Daniel Honeyman set up a partnership with young David and between them they made another twelve. By the time Mark Rees had made ten and Gerry Williams a surprising eighteen, Bert was looking worried. In a small match like this, six was good scoring. Where did these people get their practice? He'd had his spies out and hadn't heard a word about a ball being bowled.

Griff missed an easy catch and the cheering seemed to be excessive until Bert realised that the crowded were remembering his robberies and were expressing satisfaction at the man's embarrassment.

Sheila sat huddled up against the damp chill under a Welsh blanket. Beside her was Bethan. The two girls watched the cricket for a while but then their enthusiasm faded and they began to talk.

"Have you and Maurice made any progress towards a reunion?" Bethan asked.

"No, and I'm not sure I want one now. Somehow I've settled for bringing up my baby on my own. It isn't Maurice's and everyone knows it so what's there to pretend about. He doesn't love me and I doubt if he'd stay loyal. There'd be rows and there'd always be the same end to arguments, him not being the father of the baby. No, I don't know how I'll manage and sometimes that frightens me, but somehow I will."

"Mind your mother doesn't take over like mine did," Bethan warned sadly.

"Can you see me allowing that to happen?" Sheila's high voice carried and Nelly heard her add, "My mother has been nothing but trouble to me."

Nelly chuckled. She imagined that her daughter, Evie would say the same about her.

Nelly and Doreen were watching the game but George hadn't come. The walk back up the steep field on the previous Saturday had tired him and he had needed a day or two to recover. Nelly knew little about cricket but, as she watched, Doreen explained the procedures and shared each mistake with her. But Nelly's attention strayed and she looked around the crowd, noting many things.

Maurice was still avoiding Sheila but he was constantly looking in her direction. There was something going on she suspected and although Sheila wasn't her favourite person, she hoped he wouldn't mess up the girl's life again.

A crowd had congregated beside Ethel who sat in a chair brought by Phil and Catrin. She was finding it increasingly difficult to walk with her arthritic hips and sitting on the ground would have been impossible, yet she hadn't wanted to miss the match. Hilda Evans sat near her, pointedly ignoring Griff. Milly Toogood and the Pup were not far away. Arthur Toogood, Nelly observed, was with

275

his grandmother not his mother, and Bethan seemed not to be worried.

She looked around the field for Oliver and found him with Dawn, Margaret and David, who was hovering, having been warned that he would bat next. Prue Beynon sat awkwardly on the ground with Florrie and baby Sian. Nelly walked towards them to ask about the little girl's progress but as she reached them Sian suddenly left Florrie's arms and crawled across the pitch. Margaret ran and picked her up and, to Nelly's alarm, Prue snatched her from the girl's arms and began to shout at Margaret in fury.

"Don't touch my daughter. She's nothing to do with you or that disgusting brother of yours. Go away and don't dare even look at her again!"

"But Auntie Prue, she might have been hurt by the ball. I was only – " Margaret began to sob, the shock of the abuse so unexpected and unfair.

"Don't touch her, d'you hear me?" Prue gestured to Florrie who had run up to calm Prue down. "Come on, Florrie, we're going home. I don't want to breathe the same air as Amy and her illegitimate children!"

Margaret had heard that word before and remembered its intent to hurt. She pushed past Nelly and ran to the shop where her mother was serving Emlyn and Gwen Parry.

"Oh, Mam, Auntie Prue called me that name and told me never to look at Sian again. What have I done to her?"

"Nothing, Margaret, love, it's what I've done she can't forgive."

Ignoring the startled looks of the customers, Margaret insisted, "No Mam, it's me and . . . oh, Mam, she called Freddie disgusting."

"Out of her mind again is she, poor dab?" Gwen said in a low sympathetic voice. "Sorry I am. If there's anything we can do, just ask."

"Thank you, now if you have all you need – "

Dismissed by Amy's sharp tone, Gwen and Emlyn left, a little dismayed not to have the full story and disappointed, too, not to finish their complaint about Bert Roberts not asking Emlyn to join the cricket team.

Griff didn't know where to sit. He had Pete for company for a while until he was called to field, then he looked around at the heads turned away from him and wondered if things would ever return to normal. Hilda was sitting near Ethel. He walked over to them and asked how they were but the response was brief and there was no encouragement to try and build a conversation on the simple enquiry. Hilda didn't speak to him. Like the rest, her head was turned, her gaze set at some dot in the far distance.

He walked around the pitch, watching the play, wishing the nightmare would end. Perhaps he would move away, start again where people didn't treat him as if he had some dread disease.

Hilda watched him and there was sympathy in her heart. They had been married for twenty years, it was hard to pretend she bore no responsibility for his happiness any longer. He seemed such a sad, drooping figure, a stranger and nothing like the man of just a few short months ago when he had been a popular friend of everyone. What he had done was cruel but how many punishments should he be given? And how long should his sentence last?

Another chair was carried into the field and placed near Ethel's. This one was for Grandad Owen who, although past ninety, was quite interested in all that went on and had been determined not to miss the first cricket match to be played in the village for many years. He spent the next hour laughing as old Archie Pierce crouched expectantly behind the batsman and continued to miss the ball and fall backwards in his efforts to take a wicket. Grandad Owen's daughter-in-law, Megan, and her two daughters danced attendance on him handing him sweets, biscuits and an occasional drink of hot tea from the flask they had brought with them. He smiled a toothless smile at Ethel and Hilda but spoke to no one.

Delina took Dawn over to meet him and to take a

surrepticious photograph. He offered them one of his sweets but didn't say much. His bright eyes seemed unable to leave the players who were now arguing as Rod Taylor, the council houses captain, tried to set out his fielders to meet the bowling of Johnny Cartwright who was being encouraged by Phil and Victor, to "smash 'em".

Most of the crowd had brought sandwiches and these had begun to disappear long before the break between innings. When Bert's fielders had succeeded in getting the tenth man out, this by a spectacular catch by Nelly's son-in-law Timothy, most of the food had already been consumed. Even with swearing, pleading and stamping up and down, Bert was unable to prevent the two teams from disappearing towards the bus stop to go to *The Drovers*.

Two hours later they trooped back and Bert looked at the glowering sky with dismay. Two and a half hours to better the score of eighty-nine. What a disaster this would be. He was so agitated that, after insisting on his right to bat first, he was out to a catch by Gerry Williams at cover without scoring. The chorus of "Quack, Quack, Quack" didn't help his self esteem.

Victor did better achieving seven runs, partnered by Johnny Cartwright who went on to make seventeen. Sidney hit a low shot which had the effect of waking up a bored Daniel at square leg in time to duck but not attempt a catch, and managed one run.

Phil was tenth man and with an hour to play and twenty runs to get, he decided that it was best to produce an injury.

"Sorry, Bert, but I've put my thumb out. You'll have to ask Doreen to go in instead of me."

"Phil Davies you're a pain in the neck! All you have to do is go in and stay in. No one expects you to manage the twenty runs we need to win, just hold us to a draw, right?" Bert glared at him but Phil smiled, raised his injured hand and sighed.

"Can't be done, boy. Best to ask Doreen."

"I can't send a girl in."

"Then give her Grandad Owen's cap and call her Harry," Johnny suggested, "only let's get on, shall we?"

Grandad Owen gladly lent his cap and allowed his head to be covered by a blanket. Doreen hid her hair under the flat cap and walked to defend the wicket. There were mutters of curiosity but those who recognised her said nothing and those who didn't began to complain that an outsider, a mystery marvel, a secret celebrity, had been infiltrated into the team.

"Now no clever stuff," Bert hissed. "No trying for runs, or you'll be out and we'll lose. Just stay in there, right?"

For a while she did as he asked, sending the ball gently along the pitch and not attempting to run. Impatiently she saw two easy hits and rolled them to the edge of the field, past two disbelieving fielders and scored eight. Instead of being pleased, Bert was in such a state that for a moment Doreen was afraid he would eat his cap. Johnny was facing her and occasionally he would shout for her to run but an echoing shout from Bert made her shake her head sadly and gesture for him to stay at his crease.

Over followed over in boring defensive play and when the time was almost up, Johnny faced the bowling of Tad and he sent a ball running through the cut grass to the boundary for another four. Doreen faced the batting for the next over and with a grin at Johnny, she hit the ball with all her strength and saw it sail across the boundary for a six. The village had won!

There was laughter as Doreen shook her hair free of Grandad Owen's flat cap. As the crowd dispersed arguments over the validity of Doreen playing went on, but most agreed the game and been fun and should be repeated. Archie Pierce walked off more stiffly than old man Owen and swore he'd never be able to sit comfortable again.

Most went home having arranged to meet later at *The Drovers* for the post mortem. Nelly and Doreen went over to the shop to see why Margaret hadn't returned.

"They've gone home. Margaret being upset," Mavis Powell told them. "Something wrong with Amy's sister again I gather, got it in for young Margaret from all accounts. Called Freddie all sorts of things, too. Something there we haven't been told for sure."

"Yes, well, I expect you'll soon find out." Nelly glared at her, head forward like a huge bear defending its young, then walked out. "I think I'll go and see if Amy's all right before I goes 'ome, Doreen. Go an' stay with George and tell 'im all about the match, will yer?"

She walked quickly through the village, poking a tongue out childishly as she passed Nosy-Bugger Prue Beynon's house and muttering dark threats if she dared to upset Margaret or Amy again.

She found Amy and Margaret sitting in front of the fire. The light hadn't been switched on and they were cuddled together on the couch. There was an open box of chocolates beside them.

"Come in, Nelly, love," Amy called.

"'Oo's bin upsettin' you, Margaret?" Nelly demanded.

"It was Auntie Prue. But Mam's explained about her illness and how she doesn't really mean half of what she says. Mam thinks she'll have forgotten all about it by now."

"Why d'you think she's so angry with us?" Amy asked when Margaret went upstairs to change into her new skirt with the stiff petticoats that held it out like a frou-frou, to show Nelly.

"'Ow do I know," Nelly shrugged. "But it looks like she's ill again, Amy. Picking on those you love isn't that unusual."

"She shouted that Freddie wasn't Sian's father. What a daft thing to even think! And she won't stay in the same room as him. What can be the explanation for that?"

Nelly shrugged again. "Freddie worked for 'er didn't 'e? 'Elped in that garden of 'ers. Per'aps he did something to annoy 'er and 'er muddled mind got it all mixed up and wrong."

"Harry wasn't Sian's father you know. She told me herself that her husband wasn't the baby's father. I remember how pleased I was, knowing that she and Harry, well, that it was me who he loved and not my sister even if she was his wife. Wicked that was, being glad. But I hated the thought of him sharing a bed with her. It was me he loved, Nelly."

"So who was the father, then?"

It was Amy's turn to shrug. "She didn't tell me that. Only that it wasn't Harry."

"But who could it have been?"

"I've racked my brains but I can't imagine. But whatever delusions she's suffering, it could hardly be my Freddie." Amy smiled. "He was only a boy at the time."

Walking home Nelly met several of the cricketers on their way to *The Drovers*. To her surprise Hilda was walking with Griff, not arm in arm but with civil looks on both their faces.

"Nelly, come and join us," Phil called.

"Go and fetch George and we'll have a sing-song," Billie invited.

"No, I don't think I can cope with more excitement today." Nelly bared her crooked teeth in a laugh. "Ere, you two friends again, are yer?" she added as Hilda, Pete and Griff passed her.

"We have things to discuss, Nelly," Hilda said primly, her lip-sticked mouth pursed into a bow. Then she turned back and gave Nelly a broad wink.

Nelly walked up the lane and, aware of how long she had left George, increased her speed when she reached the top. The two ungainly dogs got stuck in the door as they both tried to push their way through at the same time to run and greet her. She accepted their exuberant welcome and went towards the now wide open door. Her smile widened as she heard laughter coming from the cottage. What a treat to have Doreen there. The lively and affectionate girl would do George and herself a power of good. She crossed her fingers and hoped she would stay for ever.

But it wasn't only Doreen and George who were laughing at the reports of the cricket match. The dark-clad figure of

281

her gypsy friend, Clara, sat on a chair close to the table and beside her were some bottles of herbal medicines for George.

"I find your George much improved," the wrinkled face smiled. "Much down to your new lodger I don't doubt."

"And lots of loving care," George smiled. "Now, Nelly my dear, tell me more about the match. I wish I'd have done what Doreen suggested and sat in the wheel-barrow for you to transport me down to the field in style. It was something I shouldn't have missed by Doreen's account."

"Always take the opportunity for laughter," Clara said. "Medicine that is, even if you can't pour it from a bottle."

Nelly looked at George, his pink mouth widely smiling amid the white beard, blue eyes bright and creased with contentment. As the stories and opinions flowed she had to agree: George was improving, he would get well again. She saw that in the look on Clara's face. The sad and doubtful frown had gone and hope showed in its place. She gave a rare exhibition of her feelings and gave him a hug. He would get well again. She just knew it.

"Push the kettle over why don't yer and we'll all 'ave a nice cup of tea and some of Doreen's cake."

CHAPTER TWENTY-THREE

Phil called on the Monday following the match with lots of news. He rubbed his nose in a gesture familiar to Nelly and George which told them he was about to impart a confidence.

"I heard that Griff and Hilda went home together last night," he said, adding sugar to the tea Nelly had poured. "Didn't go in, mind, but he saw her home, just like they're courting. Funny that, courting your own wife. Damn me, after all these years I wouldn't know where to start."

"Good luck to him," George said. "He's paid for his mistakes and Hilda is punishing again it seems to me."

"He was liked well enough, before he turned criminal that is. He was always thought of as a bit of a lad, mind, but with a chuckle as if he was the bit of a devil that others would like to be," Phil said. "Now everyone treats him like a leper. But if you think of it, that is a part of his punishment."

"People'll ferget," Nelly said. "Although I doubt that Archie Pierce will! Curses 'im up in heaps, 'e does."

"He's been offered his job back up at the forestry. Rod Taylor handed him a letter after the cricket match. That's hopeful. They'll watch him, mind! Young Pete shows he's forgiven his wayward Dad so there's only Hilda and I suspect she's enjoying her freedom too much at present."

"Can't blame 'er fer 'aving a fling, can yer? All them hours cutting up spuds and 'im spending money on Bethan Toogood. It's a wonder she didn't murder 'im!"

"Oh dear," George looked at Phil then hid his face

behind his hand. "I'd better be careful, I don't like the look in Nelly's eyes, do you, Phil?"

"You an' me's different, George. We're free and we stay together because we want to."

"How's your lodger settling in?" Phil wanted to know.

"She's a smashin' kid, Phil. A joy to 'ave around."

"So helpful and she treats us as if we were her favourite aunt and uncle," George smiled. "Funny thing, she seems to know the cottage. She described the landing and bedrooms before she went up the stairs.

"An' clean. She'd bath every day if she could. But we can't afford to light two fires every day, can we George? She 'as to make do with a good wash and a bath once a week, like we do."

"Working with that Bethan then?"

"Not yet," George told him. "We told her not to rush into anything, we hope she'll find something better before long."

"Johnny says there's a vacancy for a farm hand at Billie's place. Fancy that, would she? Helping Mary with the herd and on the round? Sometimes working with Billie?"

Nelly's dark eyes lit up. "She might, Phil, she just might."

Johnny always ran up Sheepy Lane when he finished his shift on the buses. It was wonderful to know that Fay would be there with baby Gregory Lewis, waiting for him, impatient to tell him about their day. He imagined what it would be like when Gregory didn't need his mother to translate for him and would run to meet him while Fay watched and laughed at his tottering, rolling walk. Then he stopped himself. Now was to enjoy, it was madness to waste the perfect now, dreaming of what was to come.

The house was silent when he entered and at once his spirits fell. He had become used to having Fay there when he came in. Monday, he mused, where could she be? He knew his mam went to the church hall to the Sewing Bee where the ladies made articles to sell at the bi-annual fairs

284

the church held. But that wasn't Fay's idea of a pleasant afternoon.

He looked around the house; nothing out of place and each room sweet-smelling and shining. Outside the clothes line was filled with small garments and white napkins, dazzling his eyes with their brightness. Perfect he thought, but nothing without Fay and the baby. He made himself a cup of tea and sat nervously waiting for them to return.

His anxiety escalated when she finally arrived home. He heard the car stop and ran out, trying to hold back his agitation. The baby was in his carry-cot on the back seat, held secure with cushions. He kissed Fay and saw from her expression that she had something on her mind. He smiled, hoping it didn't waver as much as he felt it did, then went to lift the baby out of the car. Whistling cheerfully, he went inside.

"I didn't know how long you'd be, lovely, so I didn't start cooking anything."

"Can we go out for a meal tonight, Johnny?"

He stared at her in surprise. Since she had temporarily given up her work they had been careful not to spend money unnecessarily. But he could see this was something she wanted to do.

"Ask Mam to baby-sit then, shall we?"

He dressed with extra care putting on a navy suit and a white shirt. His dark straight hair he slicked down and he carefully trimmed his moustache. He had to do her justice, she was so beautiful.

They went to a restaurant in Llan Gwyn where scampi was on the menu and they tasted it for the first time. Johnny didn't savour a thing. He kept a conversation going, talking about some of the episodes of his day driving the bus, but it sounded to him like a monologue, long and boring, as Fay did little other than smile and nod or shake her blonde head. He was so proud of her: she had a natural elegance that made heads turn and waiters give them that little extra care and attention.

He wanted her to tell him what was on her mind, although

his lack of confidence where she was concerned made him dread to hear. Perhaps she was leaving him? Women did. What if she left and took Gregory Lewis with her? What would he do without them?

They finished their meal and walked to the car. The evening was rather chilly after a day of rain and he put an arm around her, holding her close to him. He helped her into the car and sat in beside her. He couldn't stand it any longer.

"Fay, my lovely, what is it you've been trying to tell me ever since you came home this afternoon?"

"Am I that obvious, Johnny?"

"Full of surprises you are, never obvious, never boring like me. Now, what is it that's been creasing your beautiful forehead these past hours. Tell me and we'll work it out, together."

"I went to see my boss today and took Gregory Lewis to show him off."

"I see." This was Johnny's second most dreaded situation. Fay was going back to work. He knew it had to come but every day he hoped for another week and another. "Tell me, lovely, when are you going back to work? It's your decision and we'll sort it out between Mam and whoever you choose to look after little Gregory. It won't be for long each day, what with Mam helping and me working shifts, and – "

"Johnny, I don't want to leave him."

"Of course you don't, marvellous Mam that you are. But it's what you want, so we'll make it as painless as we can."

"I mean I *can't* let someone else mind him. I want *us* to be the ones to watch him grow and be thrilled with every new thing. D'you think we could manage if I stayed home, just for a year or two?"

Johnny shook so much he half expected the car to fall to pieces. "Manage my lovely? Of course we can manage. Is that what's been worrying you? I'll work all the over-time I can scrounge and we won't want for a thing."

286

He wondered afterwards how he had managed to drive home without putting the car through a hedge. He was so happy that the car seemed to drive itself and all he had to do was float along beside Fay and imagine a future with the three of them always together, a home filled with her presence and their combined love.

They went home and told Netta, who smiled and said, "It's no surprise to me, Johnny. I knew that when Fay saw her first-born she'd find it hard to hand him over for someone else to enjoy."

"Impossible, Mam, impossible," he beamed.

When Amy saw Prue passing the shop she ran out to enquire after her health. Not wanting to show how worried she was about her sister, she pretended a different reason for running down the road after her and Florrie and baby Sian.

"Thank you for making the cake for me, Prue," she called but when her sister stopped and turned, her smile faded. There was hatred in the icy blue eyes. Prue's face was ashen and she looked as if she hadn't slept for several nights. "Are you all right, love?" she asked with a glance at Florrie. Prue took a small step towards her and Amy backed away as if preparing for flight. What had happened to make her sister ill again?

"Go away, Amy. Keep away and keep that son of yours away, too."

"But what's the matter, Prue? Why are you so angry with Freddie?"

"He's nothing to do with this," Prue almost screamed the words.

"Exactly. So why are you angry with him. God 'elp, Prue, you haven't seen him for more than five minutes since Sian was born."

"Don't mention my daughter in the same breath as that wicked son of yours."

"Wicked? Oh, I see," Amy said, thinking she at last understood. "So it's about him and Sheila Powell, is it?

Well, I'm not proud of that either, but what's it got to do with you? Or baby Sian?"

"He's just like you. Having babies and them left without a father."

"Freddie will face up to his responsibilities," Amy said with rising anger. "He'll do whatever Sheila and he decide, not what you or anyone else think. How could you possibly understand." She hurried back to the shop and Prue almost ran in the opposite direction.

"What's up with her?" Mavis asked. "Still on about your Freddie and my Sheila, is she? Can't say I blame her. It isn't nice to have a disgrace in the family."

"Shut up! Or better still, go home," Amy snapped. She had to stay on at the shop all day instead of having the afternoon off.

Amy was furious with herself for snapping at Mavis, and with her sister for making her so angry in the first place. She walked up and down in the shop like a trapped animal, thinking of all that she should be doing. Her wedding was only weeks away and there was so much to sort out. She had planned to make a poster for the shop window and the church hall inviting everyone to come to the party after the marriage service. No point in trying to send out formal invitations, there were too many and she'd be sure to forget someone and cause even more trouble in the village.

The shop wasn't busy and she ignored the shelves that needed tidying, hoping that once Mavis had calmed down she would be able to persuade her to come back to work and deal with them. Taking a piece of sugar paper she began to plan the poster. *ALL WELCOME*, it began, then in small letters underneath she added, *except my dear sister Prue!* She crossed it out, ashamed of the childish gesture, and began again.

The phone rang. It was Freddie.

"Hello, Freddie, love, don't say you aren't coming home for the wedding."

"It's all right, just that I'll be home a bit earlier that's all, so if there's anything to do up at the castle, well, leave some of it for me, okay? Mam, how's Sheila?"

"I saw her walking up the lane last night with Maurice, but I don't think they're together again if that's what you want to know. I'll go and see Ethel if you like and ask her what's new."

"Will you, Mam? Thanks."

"Has she written to you lately?"

"No, that's the trouble. I don't know what she plans to do, about the baby I mean."

"I'll go and see her after I close the shop."

"I tried home first, I thought this was a day when Mavis took over after lunch?"

"I told her to shut up or go home and she did both," Amy said ruefully.

"You'd better be nice to her, Mam. How will you manage to have a honeymoon if she doesn't mind the shop?"

"Oh, Freddie! I hadn't thought of that. I'll make a cup of tea, call her down and grovel. Now this minute."

Margaret was with Mrs French and after phoning and asking if she could stay a while longer, Amy went to see Ethel. Maurice was there and he stood to leave when she came into the room.

"Ethel, have you a minute? No, don't go, Maurice, I'd like to talk to you, too, if you don't mind. It's for my Freddie really. He rang an hour or so back and asked if you and Sheila have come to any decision?"

"No, we haven't," Maurice said rudely. "And if I see your Freddie around here I'm probably punch him in the face for his nerve."

Amy sat down suddenly, as if her knees had failed her, and stared at Ethel. "D'you know, Ethel, I think my wedding plans are driving me out of my mind. First Prue shows a tendancy to return to her depression and blames me, *and* she tells me I have a wicked son for no reason at all. Now Maurice, who spent Freddie's last leave with him as if they were the greatest of friends, says he wants to punch him. Can you tell me what's going on?"

"It's only what Prue says in her confused state. But she's very convincing, mind, even if she is a bit tense."

"What had Prue been saying?" Amy demanded. "Tell me so I know what's being passed around the village gossips. If I don't know I can't very well put everyone straight, can I?"

"She says Sheila isn't the only one in the village to have a child fathered by Freddie."

"Nonsense!"

"She says her own child was the result of him seducing her while he was working on her garden, just before Harry died."

Bile rose in Amy's throat. Shock travelled through her like worms under the skin.

"My sister says she was seduced by my son? Her nephew?"

"It's only in her confused mind, like I said, Amy. We all understand," Ethel said sadly. "Poor dab, she doesn't know what she's saying."

"A boy, that's all he is. A boy."

Amy's first instinct was to cancel the wedding. She'd go now and tell Victor it was off. It wasn't true, of course it wasn't true; but people would believe it. Few could resist a bit of really juicy gossip and this was a story to whet even the most jaded of palates. How could she face them all while this tittle-tattle went the rounds? She'd be a laughing stock and so would Freddie. And what about Margaret? How would her lovely, happy daughter be affected by such wicked talk? She hurried to Victor's house, shivering, sickness threatening to overwhelm her.

Victor was pleased to see her but with Dawn, Tad, Delina and the boys there, it was impossible to talk.

"Come on, Amy, we'll go to your house, we can have a few private moments there. Margaret won't be back until you ring to say you're home, will she?"

Amy didn't say anything until they were inside the house and the door was pushed to. Then she repeated what she

290

had been told and added the details of Prue's behaviour. And then she remembered how uneasy Freddie had been with his aunt and how upset he had been when he had heard of his aunt's pregnancy. By the time she had finished talking to Victor she had convinced herself the rumours were true.

"It all fits now, Victor. But what am I going to do? Freddie won't come home ever again once this becomes general knowledge and with Ethel knowing and then the mother of Phil-the-post, how can it *not* become headline news?"

"Don't go so fast, love. Calm down. You've convinced yourself of Freddie's guilt without giving him a hearing. Now that's not like you, is it?"

The phone ran and she stood up to answer it.

"That'll be Margaret to ask if she can come home I expect." But it was Freddie. Unprepared, unable to stop herself from asking the one question she shouldn't have asked, she demanded:

"Freddie, are you the father of baby Sian?"

"What? Who have you been talking to, Mam?"

"Are you? Tell me the truth, Freddie. I can face anything so long as I'm told the truth."

"I'm sorry, Mam, I don't know how it happened, she – " Amy slammed down the phone and when it rang a few moments later, she took it off the hook and left it hanging.

"Oh, Victor. What can we do?"

He held her tightly, talked soothingly and calmed her down, but as despair eased, passion grew and he led her up the stairs and they lay on the bed together, seeking escape from the disasters of the day in love.

Margaret smiled at Mrs French.

"There's no answer, Mrs French. Mam must have put it down after that phone call and not put it on the hook properly. It's all right, though, she's home. The phone being engaged wouldn't happen if she wasn't home."

Margaret walked down the drive turning twice to wave to Mrs French and when she touched the front door she didn't need to knock, it was open. The radio wasn't playing but her mother's coat and Victor's jacket were on the chair. In the kitchen were the unwashed cups and saucers from a tray of tea.

She frowned, wondering where her mother could be, half tempted to run out and catch up with Mrs French. Since, they had been burgled, she had been uneasy in the house on her own. Then she heard voices and knew they were upstairs. Quietly, intending to shout and surprise them, she tip-toed up. The bedroom door was ajar and through the crack she saw them in bed. Giving a wail that ended in a scream, she ran from the house and disappeared through the hedge and into the field beyond.

Amy sat up and ran down the stairs to reach for the phone.

"Please don't let that be Margaret," she prayed. "Please don't let it be her." The phone rang and rang without a reply then, a slightly breathless Mrs French picked it up.

"Monica? Amy here. Is Margaret on her way home yet? Sorry I was delayed."

"She left a while ago. Isn't she there?"

"I – I think so. In fact I think she's hiding, intending to surprise me. Thanks for looking after her, I'll explain what happened tomorrow." Without waiting for any more she pushed Victor aside and reached for her coat. "Where will she have gone?"

"Olivers. Nelly's. Back to Mrs French?" Victor's mind was racing as fast as hers. "You go and try Nelly and I'll go to see if she's at Olivers. Another call to Mrs French first." Babbling like two idiots they made their plans and ran off, leaving the door open and a note in case she returned on her own. Amy felt she was on a non-stop ride to hell. What would happen next? Hugging her coat around her and holding back sobs, she ran up the lane to Nelly's cottage.

Nelly and George were in the garden. Doreen was

putting the finishing touches to a flower bed at the edge of the lawn.

"Don't know 'ow long that'll last with me chickens rampagin' like a herd of buffalos," Nelly laughed, "but it's nice, ain't it? Doreen and George did it."

"Have you seen Margaret, Nelly?" Amy said, gasping for breath having run up the steep lane."

"She's inside with Ollie, they're supposed to be fetchin' us all a drink of lemonade, stay an' 'ave one why don't yer?"

Amy ran down the path and into the cottage and saw Margaret, her beautiful Margaret, sobbing in a corner. The dogs were on her lap trying to lick the tears away.

"Margaret, love, let me try to explain."

"How could you, Mam!"

"I'm sorry you came home just then, but when two people love one another and – " she stumbled, trying desperately to find the right words. It was almost a relief when Margaret interrupted her.

"To go and get married without me being your brides-maid."

"What?" Once again Amy thought her wits had left her. "What did you say, my darling?"

"You and Uncle Victor were in bed together and you told me that's something people do after they're married. You had a wedding without me being your bridesmaid."

"My love, we aren't married. Uncle Victor and I were just lying down talking."

Oh, the beautiful, beautiful innocence of children. Amy took her daughter in her arms and didn't know whether to laugh or cry, and did both.

"Going to the wedding, Maurice?" Sheila asked when she and her husband stepped off the bus one evening after travelling separately from Llan Gwyn. "Anyone can go. No invitation list, mind, just everyone who wants to can be there. More like a Royal command than an invitation if you ask me. *And* we've all been asked to

293

help with the food. Who do they think they are, these people?"

"Very popular, Amy Prichard is and Victor, too. I don't think anyone wants to be left out," Maurice defended. "Mam's having a taxi, she doesn't want to miss it bad hip or no bad hip. Though how we'll get her to the castle grounds I don't know."

"Going with her are you?"

"All the Davies', yes. Sidney and Rita and their two, Teddy and his family and Phil and Catrin of course. We'll carry Mam if necessary."

"I'll probably go with Bethan to keep her company. I won't stay, though, I'm not keen on a lot of foolish nonsense and that's what it'll be for sure."

"You can come with us if you like, Sheila. Mam would like that."

Sheila shrugged and tried to look indifferent. "You can call for me if you like."

"There's more thievery going on in this village than when Griff was at his worst," PC Harris complained to Phil. "If I've had one complaint about window boxes being robbed and plants vanishing, then I've had fifty. I thought this was a village versus village competition. Yet the houses are vying with each other as if it were house versus house! The Taylors aren't speaking to those either side of them, the Jenkins are insisting that their neighbours' pond attracts vermin that eat their asters. Fred Mathias' rabbits got out and nibbled next door's nasturtiums, and Fred woke up the next morning and found that someone had sprayed his phlox and Canterbury bells with weed-killer. It's unbelievable. Now this!"

"This" was a once fine display of coleus, the leaves in every hue from pale cream through yellow, green, pink and orange to deepest crimson. Freddie had been growing them on the windowsill in the shed for a display on an arrangement of shelves outside *The Drovers*. Someone had flattened them and daubed them with red paint.

"Who would have done it?" Amy asked miserably. "Surely no one hates me or Freddie that much? Anyway, it wasn't even for me. Freddie raised them to display outside the pub. What reason could any one have for spoiling them?"

"Some don't need a reason," PC Harris said sadly. Then he saw Freddie's bicycle.

"Looks as if Freddie is the target, not you, Mrs Prichard. His friends are a bit old for childish pranks, aren't they?" He frowned. The tyres were punctured, the frame and handlebars covered in the still sticky wet paint. "Done recently by the look of it. I'll see what I can find out but I don't think that will help those poor coleus."

Amy remembered seeing Florrie on a step-ladder painting the door of Prue's garage. It was red like the rest of the woodwork on the house. Fearing that her sister might be responsible she said:

"No, Constable Harris. Don't bother to make any enquiries. I don't want to know who did it. Freddie will be home a little while before the competition and we'll buy some plants to replace these."

"I'm off to look at the damage to Tad Simmons' garden now. Dug up it was and all the flowers given by neighbours torn up. I just don't know what this place is coming to, Mrs Prichard. I really don't. Well, if I happen on any information I'll call and see you."

He went off slowly, wavering on his bicycle until he reached the road, then he made good speed in the hope of sorting out Tad's complaint and getting back in time to hear the news.

He lifted his leg up and off his bicycle and as he walked up Sheepy Lane pondered on the cantankerous gardeners of Hen Carw Parc.

Maurice felt waves of anger towards Freddie every time he thought of him. They had been friends and last year, when Sheila was expecting, he had been amused at Freddie being thought responsible. He had teased him later, called him the boy wonder, and all the time he had been playing games. Perhaps he *had* been giving Nosy-Bugger Prue Beynon more than a bit of help in the garden. An old woman like that, too. The boy deserved a hammering.

Why had Sheila chosen to seek sympathy and comfort with Freddie? Then the thought occurred to him that perhaps it hadn't been Freddie. If he fancied his auntie for heaven's sake, would he be interested in someone as different as Sheila?

He smiled. She had been a victim of a brief affair and got out of her depth. The smile widened, he knew only too well that she was a victim of her own strong desires. Perhaps blaming Freddie was the simplest thing to do after last years' fiasco? His chance to ask her came on the following day when he walked down Sheepy Lane from his mother's house and met her at the bus.

"Sheila, about this baby you're expecting. It isn't Freddie's is it? Come on, you can tell me the truth. There's a young man somewhere who doesn't know where a brief moment of passion has landed you, isn't there? Remember, I know you and your . . . unbridled passion."

What did he want her to say? Sheila was confused. The expression on his face suggested that if it were someone other than Freddie Prichard he might be better pleased. She widened her eyes, looked up at him and said nothing. Unbridled passion, she liked the sound of that and from the way his hazel eyes were shining, so did Maurice.

"I don't want you to tell me who he was. I'd want to kill him if I knew. Just tell me it wasn't Freddie."

Sheila still hesitated. He walked beside her, looking down at her in an almost protective way. He was smiling and there was no undercurrent of anger that she could detect. He didn't care who it was, as long as it wasn't Freddie.

"Why would you want to kill him? What is it to you, Maurice Davies?"

"I don't blame you, Sheila, I know what it's like to be lonely. But you wouldn't have to resort to finding that sort of comfort from a little twirp like Freddie Prichard."

"It's been very difficult for me," she said in a whisper, flashing him a look, pleading a little sympathy.

"I know and I'm not proud of what I did. I was obsessed by Delina and you were part of the reason I lost her. I had to get away from you all. I'm sorry. I was less than a man, leaving you to face everything alone."

She wanted to lean just that fraction of an inch to allow them to touch, but she daren't. Intuitively she knew that a wrong move and this would be her very last chance gone.

"Come out with me tonight and we'll talk about how we can best make amends. You can forget the nonsense about involving Freddie. I'll look after you."

"You'd take on someone else's baby?" She stopped and stared at him, her eyes wide with hope.

"I'll meet you at half-past seven and we'll talk. Right?"

He left her at the bus stop and went back up St Hilda's Crescent into Hywel Rise. When he passed Tad's house he jumped over the low wall and flattened the remainder of the plants left standing. The curtain twitched and he saw the face, not Tad's, but that of Constable Harris. He stood transfixed until the door opened and the angry voice of the law demanded:

"Come here, Maurice Davies. I think there's a bit of explaining you can do."

"All right, I confess! I'm a secret garden-hater. Where are the cuffs," he held his wrists out obligingly as the outraged constable came up the path followed by Tad.

CHAPTER TWENTY-FOUR

The gardens in Hen Carw Parc were lovely. Everywhere Nelly looked there were flowers of every imaginable hue. The displays began outside *The Drovers* with troughs and boxes of geraniums and their trailing accompaniments. Along the verges right through the village borders of colour swept the eyes forward. The flowers didn't end at the main road, but branched off into every turning. Even the lane leading up to Nelly's cottage had flowers growing in the banks and, apart from the area where Leighton's old horses chewed them, they made a rich display.

The flowers seemed endless. Besides the road edges, each house had designed their own riot of colour. Amy's shop blazed orange and gold with annuals that had been encouraged to bloom a little early. Marigolds, Amy's favourite, glowed like jewels amid the sacks of vegetables outside the shop window. That she was blocking the pavement more than usual seemed irrelevant to the patrolling policeman who decided that pride in the village must take precedent over the law for a little while – at least until the village had been judged.

In spite of or perhaps, Nelly told George, *because* of the arguments and rivalry between the enthusiastic gardeners, every person who could walk had spent hours preparing for the day of the judges examination. They hadn't been told exacty when this would take place, only that it would be sometime in June.

Nelly's pond was showing the beginnings of life; heavily speckled with small frogs that hopped around the already flourishing waterweed and bog-loving irises and primulas supplied by Billie, rose tall and added a look of maturity to the new structure.

But although enthusiasm continued to grow as proud owners trimmed and nurtured their flower beds and containers and argued over which were the best kept gardens, the spirit of the village swelled and prepared to celebrate that other great event, Amy and Victor's wedding.

The Reverend Barclay Bevan generously agreed to marry Amy and Victor in church. "After all," he explained to Nelly, who had helped to persuade him, "as you point out, Victor is a widower and Amy is, in the eyes of the law if not the church, a spinster of this parish. If we ignore the fact that she has two illegitimate children there'll be no difficulty." His round face looked troubled all the same. He had agreed, but in his heart he was already regretting the decision.

"She's got more right than several of them pillars of society that go down on their knees every Sunday, an' well you know it." Nelly began to add further protests but Barclay Bevan hurried on his cassock swishing her further arguments away like irritating flies.

Clara was with Nelly and about to leave and catch up with her family. She had decided to take the bus into Swansea and then travel by train. It was generous, kind-hearted Amy who had given her the fare and some food for her journey. She had been sleeping in one of Farmer Leighton's barns, refusing Nelly's invitation to stay at the cottage, insisting that houses were creepy places to sleep in.

"I slept in a house once," she had explained to Nelly and George, "but that I'll never do again. My littlest chavy woke in the morning crying and asking who was the man who kept coming and sitting on her bed. Now there was no one in that house but her and me. Don't tell me houses aren't haunted, for I know full well that they are. Barns are warmed and sweetened by the breath of animals and 'tis only their spirits that roam across the straw and hay and watch you while you sleep. And my ancestors who guard us, of course. But they can't guard us when we're enclosed in bricks and cement. No, you'll never get me in a house of a night."

Now she was leaving. George smiled and hugged the small, wiry, dark-skinned woman.

"I wish you weren't leaving, Clara," he said.

"You don't need me no longer and there's others who do." She stood on the platform of the bus and waved until Nelly and George were lost to her view around a bend in the road.

Nelly wasn't working that day. Amy's wedding was an excuse for most of the village to abandon their usual tasks and the celebrations began early. Phil was smiling stupidly when he arrived with the post more than two hours later than usual.

"'Ere, Phil, I thought you was to be best man?"

"Don't worry, Nelly, I'll be there as sober as – what is it you're supposed to be as sober as?"

"You'd better have some black coffee or you'll be turning up at the wrong church," George laughed, spooning coffee powder into a cup.

"All right, and one of Nelly's cakes to soak up the whisky I had at Victor's house."

"And that's not all you've had."

"It's all I remember having," Phil replied seriously. He thanked them profusely, walked up the path, came back for his sack of letters, smiled even more stupidly, then mounted his bicycle. He was singing as he rode down the lane. At the bottom he turned into the main road, wavered, and fell off.

Freddie was making tea for his mother who, in her ankle length wedding dress of pale blue, with skirt upon skirt of lace-trimmed fullness, looked lovely. Her hair had been fluffed out into its usual fullness but the hair-dresser had added small glinting threads that were woven through her hair falling from the small hat and veil which matched the dress. Her shoes were silver. She had on a necklace of pearls interspersed with silver beads and there were similar

300

decorations on the hat. At great expense she had had gloves made from the same material as the dress.

"You don't think I've over-done it, do you?" she asked her son as she looked in a mirror.

"Mam, you look fantastic."

"Doesn't that mean unbelievable?"

"You look lovely. Victor will be bowled over when you walk into that church."

"And all the old biddies will accuse me of being dressed too young."

"Only those who are jealous, Mam," he smiled. "And they'll be plenty jealous of me, too, with my Mam and my beautiful sister."

Margaret came down the stairs in the long, slightly darker blue dress she had chosen and stood beside her mother.

"Mam, Freddie and I want to say we love you and we're thrilled to be joining Uncle Victor's family and having brothers and another sister. We bought you this." She handed Amy a small gift-wrapped parcel.

Inside was a pair of earrings, each tiny golden dropper was in the shape of a rose.

"We hope it'll be roses all the way, Mam," Freddie said as they both kissed her.

The walk down the aisle was completely unrehearsed, but to the villagers attending Amy and Victor's wedding it was a touching and beautiful scene. All the members of the two families were waiting for the bride outside the ancient grey-stone building. Delina and Tad walked behind Amy and Margaret, holding Dawn's hands. David and Daniel behind them formal but smiling in their new suits and shiny shoes and flattened down hair. Amy was kissed by them all before they formed the impromptu procession and walked behind her and Margaret into the church.

As she entered the church, over-flowing with friends there to wish her well and share her day, she felt the warmth of the surrounding love flow over her. She went slowly down the aisle, smiling at all the familiar faces. Billie

301

was there and he blew her a kiss. Gasps of delight followed her progress. The procession followed her and remained behind as she met Victor at the altar.

It was all Victor could do to restrain from hugging them all there and then. He smiled at his bride to be and her entourage like a man in shock, his throat choked with emotion. The moment was so dream-like, the sight so wonderful, that he trembled with the joy of it. Phil touched his shoulder for reassurance.

Amy was so touched. First Margaret and Freddie's surprise gift and now this, her new family showing their support and love. The wonderful gesture was unexpected, emotion made swallowing difficult. Her beautiful blue eyes were shimmering with unshed tears and she was afraid that if anything else as wonderful happened they would spill over and she would ruin it all by crying.

The hymns were sung with enthusiasm, everyone joining in, and with the church filled right out to the porch and to the steps beyond, it sounded as perfect as the finest rehearsed choir, the core of it being just that.

In spite of his early celebrations Phil stood up to the ordeal of acting as Victor's best man and managed to produce the ring without any last minute panics. The touching service went without a hitch of any kind and the congregation was moved by the way the couple turned and looked into each other's eyes to give their vows.

When Amy and Victor as Mr and Mrs Honeyman stepped outside into warm sunshine, the roar of cheering was almost frightening. Victor was startled out of a dream. Since turning and seeing his bride entering the church, glowing and utterly beautiful, surrounded by his family, he had been responding like an automaton to what was happening around him. In the first photograph Dawn took as Amy entered the church, he looked as if he were sleep-walking.

Amy threw her bouquet of white rose-buds with their ornamental silver ribbons and it was caught by a startled Delina, who looked at Tad shyly and, to everyone's delight,

302

blushed profusely. The moment was captured perfectly by Dawn's camera.

Many people were using cameras but it was Dawn who, in her new pale green, flower-print dress, seemed the most determined. She even pushed people out of the way and ordered them to, "Be still, this is a colour film and I can't waste it!" to get the shot she wanted. There were no complaints. The happy mood seemed set to last through the whole of the day and the sun shone, determined to light up every corner.

Nelly was in several photographs, her wide-brimmed hat decorated with flowers from her garden starting off straight but, due to the crush, tilting drunkenly before the last click of a shutter. George tried to straighten it but gave up. His own trilby was also awry, giving his bearded face a saucy air.

The wedding breakfast was to be a family affair and Amy and Victor with their combined family were cheered off to drive to a restaurant in Llan Gwyn to enjoy a few hours of comparative peace before the party in the castle grounds. No one said much, everyone sated in the excitement of the happy morning. When the cars brought the united families back to the village they found flags had been hung across the drive and around the front door of their house. Nelly and George had come to tidy up the chaos of their preparation and were waiting with a huge bunch of flowers to welcome them home, but they didn't stay.

"We'll see yer all later," Nellie called and, taking George's arm, hurried off down the lane.

Left alone, the combined families of Amy and Victor just hugged each other and even David, who had seemed determined to remain as difficult as possible, succumbed to the happiness of the day. They changed their clothes, Amy and Victor almost shyly sharing their bedroom, aware of the children below. Then, in more casual wear, prepared to leave for the castle grounds.

*   *   *

From the lane behind Nelly's cottage there was only a rough track leading to the ruined castle, but the chauffeur managed to drive them almost to the walls, the Austin bumping its way along the deeply rutted surface without complaint. Johnny followed with David, Daniel and Freddie and Margaret.

"We should have borrowed Billie's tractor," Victor said.

Amy shared the laugh but she remembered with sadness and a touch of guilt that it was in Billie's arms she'd once thought to find the happiness she longed for. It wasn't to be. Her heart had told her it was Victor she loved and now it was Victor who held her future in his hands.

Within the ruined castle walls lights shone out over the scene. Some of the trees were floodlit and these, with the black countryside beyond, was a spectacular backdrop to the setting for the wedding party. Dancers were already adding colour and movement. Oliver was proudly helping his father, Timothy Chartridge, who had arranged to be there with a collection of records and his old wind-up gramophone.

Dance music met Amy and Victor as they alighted from the cars. Dawn was there with her camera. The dancers abandoned the grassy dance-floor and swarmed towards them, dragging them to start the next dance. Timothy put on a slow waltz and the evening was underway.

From the edge of the roped off dance area, Hilda and Griff watched. They had walked up separately but, once there, Griff had attached himself to her although little was said. He wanted to talk to her but didn't know how to begin. Looking at her face, so different and so attractive with the carefully applied makeup and the new clothes, he felt like a gauche and pimply youth.

"Come on, Mam, I know how you like to dance," Pete called. He offered his hands to his mother and Hilda went to join the throng. A few moments later, while they danced, a hand touched Pete's shoulder and Griff said.

"Is this an excuse me? I'd like to dance with my wife."

304

Pete grinned and left them as they tentatively touched; the minimum possible contact to enable them to dance.

"Hilda, can we start again? I won't rush you, I promise that, but I'm lost without you to support me. I don't know how to start again alone. I depend on you."

"Depend on me? How's that for a laugh then! What about Bethan? You gave *her* much more of yourself than you ever gave me."

"Flattery I suppose. She's young and you and I were, you know, sort of flat, dull, used to each other and –". He looked at her for help.

"You robbed me, Griff Evans, Robbed me of my youth long before time. Short of money, never going out apart from working in that girl's back yard. Because of you I was lacking in any self-esteem, wearing old cast-offs, being pitied by everyone who knew me, especially those who knew about you and Bethan. I was worse off than Dirty Nelly – I mean Nelly Luke."

"It just happened, gradually, our losing interest in each other. I was unaware of it happening and I think you were, too."

The record ended, the dancers stood waiting for another to begin and Hilda and Griff stood like two protagonists without any fire in their arguments. They both wanted to go home and pretend the last year hadn't happened, but neither could suggest it.

The music began again, a quick-step, and they went into each other's arms, still stiff and afraid, but with no wish to change partners.

Maurice and Sheila were dancing together but already Maurice was regretting his attempt at a reunion with his wife. He knew that once again he had been too easily persuaded by his mother and his brothers into accepting the bed he had made and was expected to lie on. If the bed's uncomfortable, I get up and make it, he thought wryly.

"Sheila, I'm fond of you, you know that," he began, wondering if there was a convenient hole he could jump into. "Very fond but – "

305

"I know, Maurice, you don't love me," Sheila finished for him brightly. "I don't mind, fond is enough for the moment. I'll have to make you change your mind about loving me, won't I? By being a perfect wife. When the baby's born it will be different, a little family and with a home of your own. I know that's what you want, Maurice, and I really don't mind about the other. Love is only an addling of the brain anyway, isn't it? It's friendship and caring that count. I know you'll care for me and that's enough for now."

Maurice didn't reply, it was all hopeless. The bars were closing around him. He could hear the clanging of doors reverberating through his head. And he was unable to prevent them making him a prisoner. The sentence was life.

Ethel sat in a chair carried up for her by Phil-the-post and Sidney and Teddy. It was good to have all her sons around her. She watched her youngest son in nervous attendance on his wife. She guessed from Sheila's fading smile which was followed by a strained expression and from Maurice's attitude that something was about to happen.

Excusing himself from Sheila, Maurice went to talk to his mother and brothers. He explained his dilemma and, after a few attempts to persuade him, they agreed to look after Sheila for him. He stood and watched her for a while, then as the dancers began a lively rock 'n' roll number, he walked through the woods and headed for the bus stop.

Phil-the-post was unsteady on his feet but he managed to take Sheila's arm and guide her to where Ethel waited to begin an explanation and offer her sympathy and regrets. To their surprise, Sheila seemed almost relieved.

"I'm over Maurice now, really I am," she said, after Ethel told her Maurice was gone. "I just want to be free of him. I'd never have a moments peace wondering who he was with and when he'd decide to up and leave me again. No, Mrs Davies, we'll be all right me and my baby, you'll see."

When Amy and Victor thought their surprises of the day were over the Reverend Barclay Bevan added another. He climbed up on to a temporary stage errected by Billie and Johnny with help from Oliver and George and called for silence.

"The entertainment for this evening is supplied by your capable selves," he began. "This village has the happy knack of creating enjoyment and good fun out of nothing more than the goodwill that surrounds us all. There is one small exception tonight. May I introduce to you Hen Carw Parc's own skiffle group, the Farm House Four!"

Amy and Victor were pushed to the front of the crowd and they saw Margaret, Oliver, David and Dawn climb up and their instruments handed to them, the tea-chest bass lifted by Billie.

They began with a brief melody written by Margaret and David, then they began to play "Rock Around The Clock" and the dancers tapped their feet, wanting to dance but knowing this was music for them to listen to and enjoy.

Evie frowned as they were introduced and even more when she saw the collection of instruments, Oliver's being an old wash-board. But as the crowd showed their approval she relaxed and accepted the admiring glances as people turned to her and smiled their admiration. After all, it couldn't be too terrible if Barclay Bevan had introduced it.

When the children had finished and jumped down, she went to find her son and said, loudly:

"Oliver, I'm proud of you. That was very clever."

"Well done, young man," his father echoed. "That was a treat for us all." Oliver felt his insides swelling painfully, overwhelmingly. His father's smile and the way his mother hugged him was like the return of a long lost treasured possession.

Nelly was drunk. The wedding and its party was a double celebration: seeing George almost recovered made the day perfect and she accepted every drink she was offered with enthusiasm. Doreen offered to walk her home, fussing about her like an anxious hen. Freddie saw Doreen with an arm around Nelly at eleven o'clock, pleading with her to go home and sleep.

"Want any help?" he asked. His uniform abandoned, he wore casual grey trousers and a sports jacket that, since his months in the army, had grown too tight. "I'm Freddie," he explained. "Freddie Prichard."

"I know who you are," Doreen smiled. "If you can persuade Nelly to go home before she falls down we might get her there without having to carry her."

"Where's George?" Freddie looked around.

"Asleep on three chairs in the castle kitchen being looked after by Netta and Fay." She laughed and shook her curly head. "What a pair they are. I love them as if I've known them all my life."

"Come on, Nelly. Time to go."

Gradually they supported her under the arms and half carried, half dragged her until they were near the kitchen. Huge quantities of food had been consumed but there was still a lot left. The remainder was packed in boxes and bags and placed on shelves to be disposed of the following day. Brenda Roberts, Bert's patient wife, and the ladies who had helped serve had abandoned their posts and had gone to join in the fun.

George was snoring gently. They put Nelly to lie on three more chairs close to him. Instinctively, Nelly's hand reached out and found George's searching for hers and, hands held tightly, they both slept.

"Fancy a dance?" Freddie asked. Smiling, Doreen followed him to join the rest.

No one knew quite how the argument began. Some said it was an unguarded word from Emlyn and Gwen Parry about the way Hilda Evans had carried on while her poor husband was in prison. Others insisted that it was Bert Roberts tripping over Archie Pierce who had laid down for a rest, and Johnny seeing them and thinking Archie was being attacked.

It was long past midnight yet few had left to go home.

308

The drink was lasting out, the dancing continuing, although fewer were actually dancing as more and more people found their feet unwilling to behave. There were several present who liked the thought of going home but who weren't too sure in which direction their homes lay.

Above the music the argument grew and soon involved the majority of those revellers still fully awake. Those who began as by-standers were pushed unintentionally by others, took offence and pushed back and the field, lit by flood lighting was awash with fallen bodies and fighting groups. No one knew why they were fighting, but the occasion demanded it. Only the women moved to escape the rolling, shouting figures and even they stayed close enough to watch and shout encouragement.

Bert, among the first to be hit, was soon standing holding a handkerchief to his nose and trying to act as referee. His wife was trying to drag him away, calling him names she'd never dare to use when he was sober. The opportunity was too good for Milly Toogood to miss and, amid the confusion, she ran up and clouted Griff around the side of his head.

"That's for ruining my Bethan," she shouted. She ducked through the crowd and followed, as always, by Sybil Tremain, scuttled home.

Griff turned and seeing Milly's husband Tommy standing there thought him responsible and hit him on the ear with an open hand. Tommy didn't retaliate but shouted after Milly and threatened to do the same to her if she didn't clear off home this instant.

Archie Pierce, crawling away out of trouble managed to trip up seven people, leaving behind him a trail of angry bemused men looking for someone to blame. They hit out at any who were near. It was a war with as many sides as there were participants.

The survivers swooped into the kitchen and, grabbing the left over food for weapons, began pelting each other with it, sometimes pausing to take a bite out of a sandwich before throwing it.

Nelly and George, snoring peacefully on the chairs, were roused from their sleep sat up stiffly and reached for the floor with their feet. They wondered vaguely where they were, half remembered and tried to open their eyes wide enough to check. The floor wasn't level. The light was swinging and making shadows dance. The room was full of stangers fighing to get at the food. Nelly decided it was all a dream and went back to sleep. George did try to get up but decided it wasn't worth the effort and did the same.

The fight moved across the fields, men falling as they tripped over unseen obstacles and being trodden on by those who followed. Some of the women had grabbed boxes of food and were on their way home with their spoils but the men snatched the food, which made excellent weapons, when they reached the top of the council estate, and soon the missiles were flying between one group and another.

Down through the village the fight continued, more slowly now as exhaustion overcame them all and sense began to seep back and make them wonder why they were fighting. Milly Toogood opened her window to demand silence and forgot about the geraniums on the sill. The pot fell and knocked Bert on the side of his head. It seemed to have little effect but he walked home on rubbery legs with Brenda accusing him of carelessness in getting in the way of the flying flowers.

Rain began to fall, softly and steadily, and this cooled heads and added to the gradual ending of the battle. Food, abandoned by the laughing merry crowd continued to be thrown whenever a target offered itself, wrappings and boxes were left where they lay and soggy paper bags slid across the road and the pavements like forlorn flags.

Doreen and Freddie went to find Nelly and George after the sandwich and fruit-cake warriors had trailed off towards the village and the rain had persuaded the last of the crowd it was time to leave. They helped them home, propped them both up on the couch and covered them with blankets.

"I'll come and see them tomorrow, shall I? Make sure they're all right?" Freddie said.

Doreen smiled her generous smile. "That would be nice."

It was four o'clock before the last light was extinguished in the village. That was in Bert Roberts' house, where an angry Brenda was roughly bathing Bert's bruises and telling him he was responsible for all the trouble. No one woke early the following morning, which was unfortunate.

The village and the council estate were a mess, with rainsoaked food and patterns of cast-aside paper spread across the roads and gardens, wrapped around gate posts by an impish wind, trailing like ribbons from fences and trees. Pots of geraniums, upended by the wilder participants of the previous nights' battle, lay on the pavements abandoned and forlorn.

At ten o'clock a car drove around the silent streets. Several local dignitaries sat looking out at the chaos. The mayor, one of the judges in the Best Kept Village Competition looked at Mrs Norwood Bennet-Hughes and frowned.

"Are you sure this village has entered? It looks as if no one has made any effort at all."

"I don't understand it, they've all worked so hard."

The car sailed serenely on.

It was several days later that the vicar called in to Amy's shop to put a notice on her window saying that the judging had taken place. The shop was full: George had called in after going up to see Farmer Leighton about working part-time, Netta was waiting for the bread to arrive. Most had really come to see the new assistant.

Amy was training a new helper since Mavis announced she would no longer work for her. The boy, young Merfyn, Gerry Williams' young brother was slow but willing and he took all Amy's impatient instructions without complaint.

"We didn't win, then," Milly Toogood said. "Not surprising really. This village hasn't got the right attitude for things like that."

311

"Who cares, eh, George?" Nelly said. "We 'ad the fun of preparin'."

"And the fun of losing!" Merfyn piped up. "*Duw*! What a night that was." His voice hadn't broken and he sounded like a girl, to his amusement and every one else's.

"Don't have so much to say for yourself, young Merfyn, or I'll tell your mother how cheeky you are," Milly Toogood said sharply. "Fun of losing indeed. What an attitude."

"'E's right though," Nelly chuckled. "We ain't had so much fun in ages, 'ave we, George?"

"Everything is fun where you are, Nelly," George chuckled. "Coming home, my dear?"

The dogs had been tied outside as the shop was full and they jumped up to greet them and knocked a bag of onions all over the pavement. Nelly looked around and decided that someone with younger knees could cope. She knocked on the window and waved to young Merfyn, gesturing for him to come out and see to them.

Chuckling she took George's arm as they crossed over the road.

"D'you think Amy an' Victor'll be 'appy, George?" she asked as they turned up the lane where Farmer Leighton's retired horses watched them over the hedge.

"If they can be as happy as we are, Nelly, what more could any one ask?"

"You're right, George, and that's a fact."

Compared with many, Nelly had nothing, but as she expected little from life, every small joy was a bonus. They released the dogs from their leads and walked on to the cottage where a casserole was simmering in the fire oven and a freshly baked loaf stood cooling on the windowsill.